PRAISE FOR
Christopher Moore

Fluke

"Moore is endlessly inventive. . . . This cetacean picaresque is no fluke—it is a sure winner." —*Publishers Weekly* (starred review)

Lamb

"An instant classic. . . . Terrific, funny, and poignant."
—*Rocky Mountain News*

The Lust Lizard of Melancholy Cove

"Reads like author Christopher Moore laughed his head off while writing it, quite possibly taking hits of nitrous oxide between sentences." —*Miami Herald*

Island of the Sequined Love Nun

"Humor that seamlessly blends lunacy with larceny . . . habit-forming zaniness. . . . The careers of the writers with even a quarter as much wit and joie de vivre as Moore are always worth following." —*USA Today*

Bloodsucking Fiends

"Goofy grotesqueries . . . wonderful . . . delicious . . . bloody funny . . . like a hip and youthful 'Abbott and Costello Meet the Lugosis.'" —*San Francisco Chronicle*

Coyote Blue

"Brilliant. . . . Moore's raucous, lewd, hip novel is part love story and part spiritual search." —*Santa Barbara Independent*

Practical Demonkeeping

"Christopher Moore is a very sick man, in the very best sense of the word." —Carl Hiaasen

Charlee Rodgers

About the Author

CHRISTOPHER MOORE is the author of seven novels, including this one. He began writing at age six and became the oldest known child prodigy when, in his early thirties, he published his first novel. His turn-ons are the ocean, playing the toad lotto, and talking animals on TV. His turn-offs are salmonella, traffic, and rude people. Chris enjoys cheese crackers, acid jazz, and otter scrubbing. He lives in an inaccessible island fortress in the Pacific. You can e-mail him at BSFiends@aol.com. Visit the official Christopher Moore website at www.chrismoore.com.

ISLAND
OF THE SEQUINED
LOVE NUN

ISLAND OF THE SEQUINED LOVE NUN

CHRISTOPHER MOORE

HARPER PERENNIAL

NEW YORK • LONDON • TORONTO • SYDNEY

A hardcover edition of this book was originally published in 1997 by Avon Books.

ISLAND OF THE SEQUINED LOVE NUN. Copyright © 1997 by Christopher Moore. All rights reserved. Printed in the United States of America. No part of this book may be used or reproduced in any manner whatsoever without written permission except in the case of brief quotations embodied in critical articles and reviews. For information address HarperCollins Publishers Inc., 10 East 53rd Street, New York, NY 10022.

HarperCollins books may be purchased for educational, business, or sales promotional use. For information please write: Special Markets Department, HarperCollins Publishers Inc., 10 East 53rd Street, New York, NY 10022.

First Avon Trade Paperback edition published 2000.
Reprinted in Perennial 2003.
Reissued in Perennial 2004.

Designed by Kellan Peck
Map by Lynn Rathbun

Library of Congress Cataloging-in-Publication Data

Moore, Christopher.
    Island of the sequined love nun/Christopher Moore.
       p.   cm.
    I. Title.
PS3563.059417   1997   96-54696
813'.54—dc21   CIP

ISBN 0-380-81654-7 (pbk.)
ISBN 0-06-073544-9 (reissue)

08 RRD 20 19 18

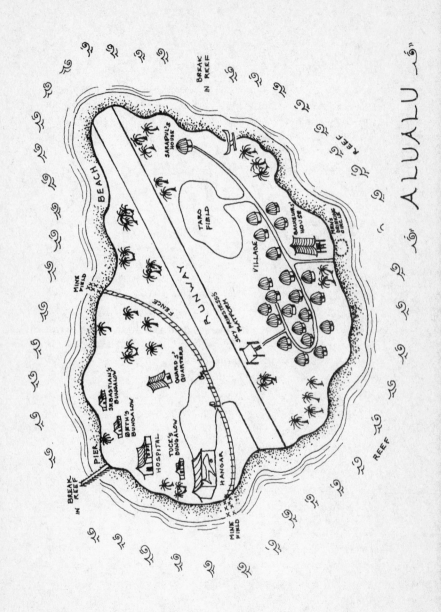

PART ONE

The Phoenix

The Cannibal Tree

Tucker Case awoke to find himself hanging from a breadfruit tree by a coconut fiber rope. He was suspended facedown about six feet above the sand in some sort of harness, his hands and feet tied together in front of him. He lifted his head and strained to look around. He could see a white sand beach fringed with coconut palms, a coconut husk fire, a palm frond hut, a path of white coral gravel that led into a jungle. Completing the panorama was the grinning brown face of an ancient native.

The native reached up with a clawlike hand and pinched Tucker's cheek.

Tucker screamed.

"Yum," the native said.

"Who are you?" Tucker asked. "Where am I? Where's the navigator?"

The native just grinned. His eyes were yellow, his hair a wild tangle of curl and bird feathers, and his teeth were black and had been filed to points. He looked like a potbellied skeleton upholstered in distressed leather. Puckered pink scars decorated his skin; a series of small scars on his chest described the shape of a shark. His only clothing was a loincloth woven from some sort of plant fiber. Tucked in the waist cord was a vicious-looking bush knife. The native patted Tucker's cheek with an ashy callused palm, then turned and walked away, leaving him hanging.

"Wait!" Tucker shouted. "Let me down. I have money. I can pay you."

The native ambled down the path without looking back. Tucker struggled against the harness, but only managed to put himself into a slow spin. As he turned, he caught sight of the navigator, hanging unconscious a few feet away.

"Hey, you alive?"

The navigator didn't stir, but Tucker could see that he was breathing. "Hey, Kimi, wake up!" Still no reaction.

He strained against the rope around his wrists, but the bonds only seemed to tighten. After a few minutes, he gave up, exhausted. He rested and looked around for something to give this bizarre scene some meaning. Why had the native hung them in a tree?

He caught movement in his peripheral vision and turned to see a large brown crab struggling at the end of a string tied to a nearby branch. There was his answer: They were hung in the tree, like the crab, to keep them fresh until they were ready to be eaten.

Tucker shuddered, imagining the native's black teeth closing on his shin. He tried to focus on a way to escape before the native returned, but his mind kept diving into a sea of regrets and second guesses, looking for the exact place where the world had turned on him and put him in the cannibal tree.

Like most of the big missteps he had taken in his life, it had started in a bar.

The Seattle Airport Holiday Inn lounge was all hunter green, brass rails, and oak veneer. Remove the bar and it looked like Macy's men's department. It was one in the morning and the bartender, a stout, middle-aged Hispanic woman, was polishing glasses and waiting for her last three customers to leave so she could go home. At the end of a bar a young woman in a short skirt and too much makeup sat alone. Tucker Case sat next to a businessman several stools down.

"Lemmings," the businessman said.

"Lemmings?" asked Tucker.

They were drunk. The businessman was heavy, in his late fifties, and wore a charcoal gray suit. Broken veins glowed on his nose and cheeks.

"Most people are lemmings," the businessman continued. "That's why they fail. They behave like suicidal rodents."

"But you're a higher level of rodent?" Tucker Case said with a smart-ass grin. He was thirty, just under six foot, with neatly trimmed blond hair and blue eyes. He wore navy slacks, sneakers, and a white shirt with blue-and-gold epaulets. His captain's hat sat on the bar next to a gin and tonic. He was more interested in the girl at the end of the bar than in the businessman's conversation, but he didn't know how to move without being obvious.

"No, but I've kept my lemming behavior limited to my personal relationships. Three wives." The businessman waved a swizzle stick under Tucker's nose. "Success in America doesn't require any special talent or any kind of extra effort. You just have to be consistent and not fuck up. That's how most people fail. They can't stand the pressure of getting what they want, so when they see that they are getting close, they engineer some sort of fuckup to undermine their success."

The lemming litany was making Tucker uncomfortable. He'd been on a roll for the last four years, going from bartending to flying corporate jets. He said, "Maybe some people just don't know what they want. Maybe they only look like lemmings."

"Everyone knows what they want. You know what you want, don't you?"

"Sure, I know," Tucker said. What he wanted right now was to get out of this conversation and get to know the girl at the end of the bar before closing time. She'd been staring at him for five minutes.

"What?" The businessman wanted an answer. He waited.

"I just want to keep doing what I'm doing. I'm happy."

The businessman shook his head. "I'm sorry, son, but I don't buy it. You're going over the cliff with the rest of the lemmings."

"You should be a motivational speaker," Tuck said, his attention drawn by the girl, who was getting up, putting money on the bar, picking up her cigarettes, and putting them into her purse.

She said, "I know what I want."

The businessman turned and gave his best avuncular-horndog smile. "And what's that, sweetheart?"

She walked up to Tucker and pressed her breasts against his shoulder. She had brown hair that fell in curls to her shoulders, blue eyes, and a nose that was a tad crooked, but not horribly so. Up close she didn't even look old enough to drink. Heavy makeup had aged her at a distance. Looking the businessman in the eye, as if she didn't notice Tucker at all, she said, "I want to join the mile-high club, and I want to join it tonight. Can you help me?"

The businessman looked at Tucker's captain's hat on the bar, then back at the girl. Slowly, defeated, he shook his head.

She pressed harder against Tucker's shoulder. "How about you?"

Tucker grinned at the businessman and shrugged by way of

apology. "I just want to keep doing what I'm doing."

The girl put on his captain's hat and pulled him off of the barstool. He dug into his pocket for money as she dragged him toward the exit.

The businessman raised a hand. "No, I've got the drinks, son. You just remember what I said."

"Thanks," Tuck said.

Outside in the lobby the girl said, "My name's Meadow." She kept her eyes forward as she walked, taking curt marching steps as if she was leading him on an antiterrorist mission instead of seducing him.

"Pretty name," Tucker said. "I'm Tucker Case. People call me Tuck."

She still didn't look up. "Do you have a plane, Tuck?"

"I've got access to one." He smiled. This was great. Great!

"Good. You get me into the mile-high club tonight and I won't charge you. I've always wanted to do it in a plane."

Tucker stopped. "You're a . . . I mean, you do this for . . ."

She stopped and turned to look him in the eye for the first time. "You're kind of a geek, aren't you?"

"Thank you. I find you incredibly attractive too." Actually, he did.

"No, you're attractive. I mean, you *look* fine. But I thought a pilot would have a little more on the ball."

"Is this part of that mistress-humiliation-handcuff stuff?"

"No, that's extra. I'm just making conversation."

"Oh, I see." He was beginning to have second thoughts. He had to fly to Houston in the morning, and he really should get some sleep. Still, this would make a great story to tell the guys back at the hangar—if he left out the part about him being a suicidal rodent and her being a prostitute. But he could tell the story without really doing it, couldn't he?

He said, "I probably shouldn't fly. I'm a little drunk."

"Then you won't mind if I go back to the bar and grab your friend? I might as well make some money."

"It could be dangerous."

"That's the point, isn't it?" She smiled.

"No, I mean really dangerous."

"I have condoms."

Tucker shrugged. "I'll get a cab."

Ten minutes later they were heading across the wet tarmac toward a group of corporate jets.

"It's pink!"

"Yeah, so?"

"You fly a pink jet?"

As Tuck opened the hatch and lowered the steps, he had the sinking feeling that maybe the businessman at the bar had been right.

~~~~~~

2

I Thought This Was a Nonsmoking Flight

Most jets (especially those unburdened by the weight of passengers or fuel) have a glide rate that is quite acceptable for landing without power. But Tucker has made an error in judgment caused by seven gin and tonics and the distraction of Meadow straddling him in the pilot seat. He thinks, perhaps, that he should have said something when the fuel light first went on, but Meadow had already climbed into the saddle and he didn't want to seem inattentive. Now the glide path is too steep, the runway a little too far. He uses a little body English in pulling back on the steering yoke, which Meadow takes for enthusiasm.

Tucker brings the pink Gulfstream jet into SeaTac a little low, tearing off the rear landing gear on a radar antenna a second before impact with the runway, which sends Meadow over the steering yoke to bounce off the windscreen and land unconscious across the instrument panel. The jet's wings flap once—a dying flamingo trying to free itself from a tar pit—and rip off in a shriek of sparks, flame, and black smoke, then spin back into the air before beating themselves to pieces on the runway.

Tucker, strapped into the pilot's seat, lets loose a prolonged scream that pushes the sound of tearing metal out of his head.

The wingless Gulfstream slides down the runway like hell's own bobsled, leaving a wake of greasy smoke and aluminum confetti. Firemen and paramedics scramble into their vehicles and pull out onto the runway in pursuit of it. In a moment of analytical detachment, one of the firemen turns to a companion and says, "There's not enough fire. He must have been flying on fumes."

Tucker sees the end of the runway coming up, an array of antennae, some spiffy blue lights, a chain-link fence, and a grassy open field where what's left of the Gulfstream will fragment into pink shrapnel. He realizes that he's looking at his own death and screams the words "Oh, fuck!", meeting the FAA's official requirement for last words to be retrieved from the charred black box.

Suddenly, as if someone has hit a cosmic pause button, the cockpit goes quiet. Movement stops. A man's voice says, "Is this how you want to go?"

Tucker turns toward the voice. A dark man in a gray flight suit sits in the copilot's seat, waiting for an answer. Tuck can't seem to see his face, even though they are facing each other. "Well?"

"No," Tucker answers.

"It'll cost you," the pilot says. Then he's gone. The copilot's seat is empty and the roar of tortured metal fills the cabin.

Before Tucker can form the words "What the hell?" in his mind, the wingless jet crashes through the antenna, the spiffy blue lights, the chain-link fence, and into the field, soggy from thirty consecutive days of Seattle rain. The mud caresses the fuselage, dampens the sparks and flames, clings and cloys and slows the jet to a steaming stop. Tuck hears metal crackle as it settles, sirens, the friendly chime of the FASTEN SEAT BELTS sign turning off.

Welcome to Seattle–Tacoma International Airport. The local time is 2:00 A.M., the outside temperature is 63 degrees, there is a semiconscious hooker gurgling at your feet.

The cabin fills with black smoke from fried wires and vaporized hydraulic fluid. One breath burns down his windpipe like drain cleaner, telling Tucker that a second breath may kill him. He unfastens the harness and reaches into the dark for Meadow, connecting with her lace camisole, which comes away in shreds in his hands. He stands, bends over, wraps an arm around her waist, and picks her up. She's light, maybe a hundred pounds, but Tucker has forgotten to pull up his pants and Jockey shorts, which cuff his ankles. He teeters and falls backward onto the control console between the pilot seats. Jutting from the console is the flap actuator lever, a foot-long strip of steel topped by a plastic arrowheadlike tip. The tip catches Tuck in the rear of the scrotum. His and Meadow's combined weight drive him down on the lever, which tears though his scrotum, runs up inside the length of his penis, and emerges in a spray of blood.

There are no words for the pain. No breath, no thought. Just deafening white and red noise. Tucker feels himself passing out and welcomes it. He drops Meadow, but she is conscious enough to hold on to his neck, and as she falls she pulls him off the lever, which reams its way back through him again.

Without realizing it, he is standing, breathing. His lungs are on fire. He has to get out. He throws an arm around Meadow and drags her three feet to the hatch. He releases the hatch and it swings down, half open. It's designed to function as a stairway to the ground, designed for a plane that is standing on landing gear. Gloved hands reach into the opening and start pulling at it. "We're going to get you out of there," a fireman says.

The hatch comes open with a shriek. Tuck sees blue and red flashing lights illuminating raindrops against a black sky, making it appear as if it is raining fire. He takes a single breath of fresh air, says, "I've torn off my dick," and falls forward.

3

And You Lost Your Frequent Flyer Miles

As with most things in his life, Tucker Case was wrong about the extent of his injuries. As they wheeled him though the emergency room, he continued to chant, "I've torn off my dick!, I've torn off my dick!" into his oxygen mask until a masked physician appeared at his side.

"Mr. Case, you have not torn off your penis. You've damaged some major blood vessels and some of the erectal tissue. And you've also severed the tendon that runs from the tip of the penis to the base of the brain." The doctor, a woman, pulled down her mask long enough to show Tucker a grin. "You should be fine. We're taking you into surgery now."

"What about the girl?"

"She's got a mild concussion and some bruises, but she'll be okay. She'll probably go home in a few hours."

"That's good. Doc, will I be able to? I mean, will I ever . . . ?"

"Be still, Mr. Case. I want you to count backward from one hundred."

"Is there a reason for that—for the counting?"

"You can say the Pledge of Allegiance if you want."

"But I can't stand up."

"Just count, smart-ass."

When Tucker came to, through the fog of anesthesia he saw a picture of himself superimposed over a burning pink jet. Looking down on the scene was the horrified face of the matriarch of pyramid makeup sales, Mary Jean Dobbins—Mary Jean to the world. Then the picture was gone, replaced by a rugged male face and perfect smile.

"Tuck, you're famous. You made the *Enquirer*." The voice of Jake Skye, Tuck's only male friend and premier jet mechanic for Mary Jean. "You crashed just in time to make the latest edition."

"My dick?" Tuck said, struggling to sit up. There was what appeared to be a plaster ostrich egg sitting on his lap. A tube ran out the middle of it.

Jake Skye, tall, dark, and unkempt—half Apache, half truck stop waitress—said, "That's going to smart. But the doc says you'll play the violin again." Jake sat in a chair next to Tuck's bed and opened the tabloid.

"Look at this. Oprah's skinny again. Carrots, grapefruit, and amphetamines."

"Tucker Case moaned. "What about the girl? What was her name?"

"Meadow Malackovitch," Jake said, looking at the paper. "Wow, Oprah's fucking Elvis. You got to give that woman credit. She stays busy. By the way, they're going to move you to Houston. Mary Jean wants you where she can keep an eye on you."

"The girl, Jake?"

Jake looked up from the paper. "You don't want to know."

"They said she was going to be okay. Is she dead?"

"Worse. Pissed off. And speaking of pissed off, there's some FAA guys outside who are waiting to talk to you, but the doctor wouldn't let them in. And I'm supposed to call Mary Jean as soon as you're coherent. I'd advise against that—becoming coherent, I mean. And then there's a whole bunch of reporters. The nurses are keeping them all out."

"How'd you get in?"

"I'm your only living relative."

"My mother will be pleased to hear that."

"Brother, your mother doesn't even want to claim you. You totally fucked the dog on this one."

"I'm fired, then?"

"Count on it. In fact, I'd say you'd be lucky to get a license to operate a riding lawnmower."

"I don't know how to do anything but fly. One bad landing?"

"No, Tuck, a bad landing is when the overheads pop open and dump people's gym bags. You crashed. If it makes you feel any better, with the Gulfstream gone I'm not going to have any work for at least six months. They may not even get another jet."

"Is the FAA filing charges?"

Jake Skye looked at his paper to avoid Tuck's eyes. "Look, man, do you want me to lie to you? I came up here because I thought you'd rather hear it from me. You were drinking. You wrecked a million dollars' worth of SeaTac's equipment in addition to the plane. You're lucky you're not dead."

"Jake, look at me."

Jake dropped the paper to his lap and sighed. "What?"

"Am I going to jail?"

"I've got to go, man." Jake stood. "You heal up." He turned to leave the room.

"Jake!"

Jake Skye stopped and looked over his shoulder. Tucker could see the disappointment in his friend's eyes.

"What were you thinking?" Jake said.

"She talked me into it. I knew it wasn't a good idea, but she was persistent."

Jake came to the side of the bed and leaned in close. "Tucker, what's it take for you to get it? Listen close now, buddy, because this is your last lesson, okay? I'm out of a job because of you. You've got to make your own decisions. You can't let someone else always tell you what to do. You have to take some responsibility."

"I can't believe I'm hearing this from you. You're the one who got me into this business."

"Exactly. You're thirty years old, man. You have to start thinking for yourself. And with your head, not your dick."

Tucker looked at the bandages in his lap. "I'm sorry. It all got out of hand. It was like flying on autopilot. I didn't mean to . . ."

"Time to take the controls, buddy."

"Jake, something weird happened during the crash. I'm not sure if it was a hallucination or what. There was someone else in the cockpit."

"You mean besides the whore?"

"Yeah, just for a second, there was a guy in the copilot seat. He talked to me. Then he disappeared."

Jake sighed. "There's no insanity plea for crashing a plane, Tuck. You lost a lot of blood."

"This was before I got hurt. While the plane was still skidding."

"Here." Jake tucked a silver flask under Tuck's pillow and punched him in the shoulder. "I'll call you, man." He turned and walked away.

Tuck called after him, "What if it was an angel or something?"

"Then you're in the *Enquirer* next week too," Jake said from the door. "Get some sleep."

4

Pinnacle of the Pink Pyramid

A low buzz of anticipation ran through the halls of the hospital. Reporters checked the batteries in their microrecorders and cell phones. Orderlies and nurses lingered in the hallways in hope of getting a glimpse of the celebrity. The FAA men straightened their ties and shot their cuffs. One receptionist in administration, who was only two distributorships away from earning her own pink Oldsmobile, ducked into an examining room and sucked lungfuls of oxygen to chase the dizziness that comes from meeting one's Messiah. Mary Jean was coming.

Mary Jean Dobbins did not travel with an entourage, bodyguards, or any other of the decorative leeches commonly attached to the power-wielding rich.

"God is my bodyguard," Mary Jean would say.

She carried a .38-caliber gold-plated Lady Smith automatic in her bag: the Clara Barton Commemorative Model, presented to her by the Daughters of the Confederacy at their annual "Let's Lynch Leroy" pecan pie bake-off, held every Martin Luther King Jr. Day. (She didn't agree with their politics, but the belles could sure sell some makeup. If the South did not rise again, it wouldn't be for lack of foundation.)

Today, as Mary Jean came through the doors of the main lobby, she was flanked by a tall predatory woman in a black business suit—a severe contrast to Mary Jean's soft pastel blue ensemble with matching bag and pumps. "Strength and femininity are not exclusive, ladies." She was sixty-five; matronly but elegant. Her makeup was perfect, but not overdone. She wore a sapphire-and-diamond pin whose value approximated the gross national product of Zaire.

She greeted every orderly and nurse with a smile, asked after their families, thanked them for their compassionate work, flirted when appropriate, and tossed compliments over her shoulder as she passed, without ever missing a step. She left a wake of acutely charmed fans, even among the cynical and stubborn.

Outside Tucker's room the predatory woman—a lawyer—broke formation and confronted the maggotry of reporters, allowing Mary Jean to slip past.

She poked her head inside. "You awake, slugger?"

Tuck was startled by her voice, yanked out of his redundant reverie of unemployment, imprisonment, and impotence. He wanted to pull the sheets over his head and quietly die.

"Mary Jean."

The makeup magnate moved to his bedside and took his hand, all compassion and caring. "How are you feeling?"

Tucker looked away from her. "I'm okay."

"Do you need anything? I'll have it here in a Texas jiffy."

"I'm fine," Tucker said. She always made him feel like he'd just struck out in his first Little League game and she was consoling him with milk and cookies. The fact that he'd once tried to seduce her doubled the humiliation. "Jake told me that you're having me moved to Houston. Thank you."

"I have to keep an eye on you, don't I?" She patted his hand. "You sure you're feeling well enough for a talk?"

Tucker nodded. He wasn't buying the outpouring of warm fuzzies she was selling. He'd seen her doing business on the plane.

"That's good, honey," Mary Jean said, rising and looking around the room for the first time. "I'll have some flowers sent up. A touch of color will brighten things up, won't it? Something fragrant too. The constant smell of disinfectant must be disturbing."

"A little," Tuck said.

She wheeled on her heel and looked at him. Her smile went hard. Tuck saw wrinkles around her mouth for the first time. "Probably reminds you of what a total fuckup you are, doesn't it?"

Tucker gulped. She'd faked him out of his shoes. "I'm sorry, Mary Jean. I'm . . ."

She raised a hand and he shut up. "You know I don't like to use profanity or firearms, so please don't push me, Tucker. A lady controls her anger."

"Firearms?"

Mary Jean pulled the Lady Smith automatic out of her purse and leveled it at Tucker's bandaged crotch. Strangely, he noticed that Mary Jean had chipped a nail drawing the gun and for that, he realized, she really might kill him.

"You didn't listen to me when I told you to stop drinking. You didn't listen when I told you to stay away from my representatives. You didn't listen when I told you that if you were going to amount to anything, you had to give your life to God. You'd better damn well listen now." She racked the slide on the automatic. "Are you listening?"

Tuck nodded. He didn't breathe, but he nodded.

"Good. I have run this company for forty years without a hint of scandal until now. I woke up yesterday to see my face next to yours on all the morning news shows. Today it's on the cover of every newspaper and tabloid in the country. A bad picture, Tucker. My suit was out of season. And every article uses the words 'penis' and 'prostitute' over and over. I can't have that. I've worked too hard for that."

She reached out and tugged on his catheter. Pain shot though his body and he reached for the ringer for the nurse.

"Don't even think about it, pretty boy. I just wanted to make sure I had your attention."

"The gun pretty much did it, Mary Jean," Tucker groaned. Fuck it, he was a dead man anyway.

"Don't you speak to me. Just listen. This is going to disappear. *You* are going to disappear. You're getting out of here tomorrow and then you're going to a cabin I have up in the Rockies. You won't go home, you won't speak to any reporters, you won't say doodly squat. My lawyers will handle the legal aspects and keep you out of jail, but you will never surface again. When this blows over, you can go on with your pathetic life. But with a new name. And if you ever set foot in the state of Texas or come within a hundred yards of anyone involved in my company, I will personally shoot you dead. Do you understand?"

"Can I still fly?"

Mary Jean laughed and lowered the gun. "Sweetie, to a Texas way a thinkin' the only way you coulda screwed up worse is if you'd throwed a kid down a well after fessing up to being on the grassy knoll stompin' yellow roses in between shootin' the President. You ain't gonna fly, drive, walk, crawl, or spit if I have anything to say about it." She put the gun in her purse and went into the tiny bathroom to check her makeup. A quick primping and she headed for the door. "I'll send up some flowers. Y'all heal up now, honey."

She wasn't going to kill him after all. Maybe he could win her back. "Mary Jean, I think I had a spiritual experience."

"I don't want to hear about any of your degenerate activities."

"No, a real spiritual experience. Like a—what do you call it?— an epiphany?"

"Son, you don't know it, but you're as close to seeing the Lord as you've ever been in your life. Now you hush before I send you to perdition."

She put on her best beatific smile and left the room radiating the power of positive thinking.

Tucker pulled the covers over his head and reached for the flask Jake had left. Perdition, huh? She made it sound bad. Must be in Oklahoma.

5

Our Lady of the Fishnet Stockings

The High Priestess of the Shark People ate Chee-tos and watched afternoon talk shows over the satellite feed. She sat in a wicker emperor's chair. A red patent leather pump dangled from one toe. Red lipstick, red nails, a big red bow in her hair. But for a pair of silk seamed stockings, she was naked.

On the screen: Meadow Malackovitch, in a neck brace, sobbed on her lawyer's shoulder—a snapshot of the pilot who had traumatized her was inset in the upper-right-hand corner. The host, a failed weatherman who now made seven figures mining trailer parks for atrocities, was reading the dubious résumé of Tucker Case. Shots of the pink jet, before and after. Stock footage of Mary Jean on an airfield tarmac, followed by Case in a leather jacket.

The High Priestess touched herself lightly, leaving a faint orange stripe of Chee-to spoor on her pubes (she was a natural blonde), then keyed the intercom that connected her to the Sorcerer.

"What?" came the man's voice, weary but awake. It was 2:00 A.M. The Sorcerer had been working all night.

"I think we've found our pilot," she said.

6

Who's Flying This Life?

At the last minute Mary Jean changed her mind about sending Tucker Case to her cabin in the mountains. "Put him in a motel room outside of town and don't let him out until I say so."

In two weeks Tucker had seen only the nurse who came in to change his bandages and the guard. Actually, the guard was a tackle, second-string defense from SMU, six-foot-six, two hundred and seventy pounds of earnest Christian naïveté named Dusty Lemon.

Tucker was lying on the bed watching television. Dusty sat hunched over the wood-grain Formica table reading Scripture.

Tucker said, "Dusty, why don't you go get us a six-pack and a pizza?"

Dusty didn't look up. Tuck could see the shine of his scalp through his crew cut. A thick Texas drawl: "No, sir. I don't drink and Mrs. Jean said that you wasn't to have no alcohol."

"It's not Mrs. Jean, you doofus. It's Mrs. Dobbins." After two weeks, Dusty was beginning to get on Tuck's nerves.

"Just the same," Dusty said. "I can call for a pizza for you, but no beer."

Tuck detected a blush though the crew cut. "Dusty?"

"Yes sir." The tackle looked up from his Bible, waited.

"Get a real name."

"Yes, sir," Dusty said, a giant grin bisecting his moon face, "Tuck."

Tucker wanted to leap off the bed and cuff Dusty with his Bible, but he was a long way from being able to leap anywhere. Instead, he looked at the ceiling for a second (it was highway safety orange, like the walls, the doors, the tile in the bathroom), then propped himself up on one elbow and considered Dusty's Bible. "The red type. That the hot parts?"

"The words of Jesus," Dusty said, not looking up.

"Really?"

Dusty nodded, looked up. "Would you like me to read to you? When my grandma was in the hospital, she liked me to read Scriptures to her."

Tucker fell back with an exasperated sigh. He didn't understand religion. It was like heroin or golf: He knew a lot of people did it, but he didn't understand why. His father watched sports every Sunday, and his mother had worked in real estate. He grew up thinking that church was something that simply interfered with games and weekend open houses. His first exposure to religion, other than the skin mag layouts of the women who had brought down television evangelists, had been his job with Mary Jean. For her it just seemed like good business. Sometimes he would stand in the back of the auditorium and listen to her talk to a thousand women about having God on their sales team, and they would cheer and "Hallelujah!" and he would feel as if he'd been left out of something—something beyond the apparent goofiness of it all. Maybe Dusty had something on him besides a hundred pounds.

"Dusty, why don't you go out tonight? You haven't been out in two weeks. I *have* to be here, but you—you must have a whole line of babes crying to get you back, huh? Big football player like you, huh?"

Dusty blushed again, going deep red from the collar of his practice jersey to the top of his head. He folded his hands and looked at them in his lap. "Well, I'm sorta waitin' for the right girl to come along. A lot of the girls that go after us football players, you know, they're kinda loose."

Tuck raised an eyebrow. "And?"

Dusty squirmed, his chair creaked under the strain. "Well, you know, it's kinda . . ."

And suddenly, amid the stammering, Tucker got it. The kid was a virgin. He raised his hand to quiet the boy. "Never mind, Dusty." The big tackle slumped in his chair, exhausted and embarrassed.

Tuck considered it. He, who understood so much the importance of a healthy sex life, who knew what women needed and how to give it to them, might never be able to do it again, and Dusty Lemon, who probably could produce a woody that women could chin themselves on, wasn't using it at all. He pondered it. He worked it over from several angles and came very close to having a religious experience, for who but a vicious and vengeful God would allow such injustice in the world? He thought about it. Poor Tucker. Poor Dusty. Poor, poor Tucker.

He felt a lump forming in his throat. He wanted to say something that would make the kid feel better. "How old are you, Dusty?"

"I'll be twenty-two next March, sir?"

"Well, that's not so bad. I mean, you might be a late bloomer, you know. Or gay maybe," Tuck said cheerfully.

Dusty started to contract into the fetal position. "Sir, I'd rather not talk about it, if you don't mind," he whimpered. There was a knock on the door and he uncurled, alert and ready to move. He looked to Tucker for instructions.

"Well, answer it."

Dusty lumbered to the door and pulled it open a crack. "Yes?"

"I'm here to see Tucker Case. It's okay, I work for Mary Jean." Tuck recognized Jake Skye's voice.

"Just a second." Dusty turned and looked to Tucker, confused.

"Who knows we're here, Dusty?"

"Just us and Mrs. Jean."

"Then why don't you let him in?"

"Yes, sir." He opened the door and Jake Skye strode through carrying a grocery bag and a pizza box.

"Greetings." He threw the pizza on the bed. "Pepperoni and mushroom." He glanced at Dusty and paused, taking a moment to look the tackle up and down. "How'd you get this job? Eat your family?"

"No, sir," Dusty said.

Jake patted the tackle's mammoth shoulder. "Good to be careful, I guess. Momma always said, 'Beware of geeks bearing gifts.' Who are you?"

"Jake Skye," Tuck said, "meet Dusty Lemon. Dusty, Jake Skye, Mary Jean's jet mechanic. Be nice to Dusty, Jake, He's a virgin."

Dusty shot a vicious glare at Tuck and extended a boxing glove size mitt. Jake shook his hand. "Virgin, huh?"

Jake dropped his hand. "Not including farm animals, though, right?"

Dusty winced and moved to close the door. "You-all can't stay long. Mr. Case isn't supposed to see no one."

Jake put the grocery bag down on the table, pulled out a four-inch-thick bundle of mail, and tossed it on the bed next to Tucker. "Your fan mail."

Tucker picked it up. "It's all been opened."

"I was bored," Jake said, opening the pizza box and extracting a slice. "A lot of death threats, a few marriage proposals, a couple really interesting ones had both. Oh, and an airline ticket to someplace I've never heard of with a check for expenses."

"From Mary Jean?"

"Nope. Some missionary doctor in the Pacific. He wants you to fly for him. Medical supplies or something. Came FedEx yesterday. Almost took the job myself, seeing as I still have my pilot's license and you don't, but then, I can get a job here."

Tucker shuffled through the stack of mail until he found the check and the airline ticket. He unfolded the attached letter.

Jake held the pizza box out to the bodyguard. "Dopey, you want some pizza?"

"Dusty," Dusty corrected.

"Whatever." To Tuck: "He wants you to leave ASAP."

"He can't go anywhere," said Dusty.

Jake retracted the box. "I can see that, Dingy. He's still wired for sound." Jake gestured toward the catheter that snaked out of Tucker's pajama bottoms. "How long before you can travel?"

Tucker was studying the letter. It certainly seemed legitimate. The doctor was on a remote island north of New Guinea, and he needed someone to fly jet loads of medical supplies to the natives. He specifically mentioned that "he was not concerned" about Tucker's lack of a pilot's license. The "need was dire" and the need was for an experienced jet pilot who could fly a Lear 45.

"Well," Jake said, "when can you roll?"

"Doctor says not for a week or so," Tucker said. "I don't get it. This guy is offering more money than I make for Mary Jean. Why me?"

Jake pulled a Lone Star from the grocery bag and twisted off the cap. Tuck zeroed in on the beer. Dusty snatched it out of Jake's hand.

"The question is," Jake said, glaring at Dusty, "what the fuck is a missionary doctor in Bongo Bongo land doing with a Lear 45?"

"God's work?" Dusty said innocently.

Jake snatched back his beer. "Oh blow me, Huey."

"Dusty," Dusty corrected.

Tucker said, "I'm not sure this is a good idea. Maybe I should stay here and see how things pan out with the FAA. This guy wants me right away. I need more time."

"Like more time will make a difference. Damn, Tucker, you don't have to sink eyeball deep in shit to know it's a good idea to pull yourself out. Sometimes you have to make a decision."

Tucker looked at the letter again. "But I . . ."

Before Tucker could finish his protest, Jake brought the Lone Star in a screaming arc across Dusty Lemon's temple. The bodyguard fell like a dead tree and did a dead-cat bounce on the orange carpet.

"Jesus!" Tucker said. "What the fuck was that?"

"A decision," Jake said. He looked up from the fallen tackle and took a pull on the foaming Lone Star. "Sometimes this high-tech world calls for low-tech solutions. Let's go."

7

Travel Tips

"I can't believe you hit him," Tucker said. He was in the passenger seat of Jake Skye's camouflaged Land Rover. It was much more car than was required for the Houston expressway, but Jake was into equipment overkill. Everything he owned was Kevlar, Gor-Tex, Polarfleece, titanium alloy, graphite-polymer composite, or of "expedition quality." He liked machines, understood how they worked, and could fix them if they didn't. Sometimes he spoke in an incomprehensible alphabet soup of SRAM, DRAM, FORTRAN, LORAN, SIMMS, SAMS, and ROM. Tuck, on the other hand, knew most of the words to "Mommas, Don't Let Your Babies Grow Up to Be Cowboys" and could restore burned toast to new by scraping off the black stuff.

Of the two, Jake was the cool one. Tucker had always found being cool a little elusive. As Jake put it, "You've got the look, but you can't walk the walk or talk the talk. Tucker, you are a hopeless geek trapped in a cool guy's body, but out of the goodness of my heart, I will take you on as my student." They'd been friends for four years. Jake had taught Tuck to fly.

"He'll be fine. He's a jock," Jake shouted over the buffeting wind. He hadn't bought a top for the Land Rover, opting instead for the Outback package with the "patented rhinoceros poking platform."

"He was just a kid. He was reading the Bible."

"He would have ripped my arms off if I'd let him."

Tuck nodded. That was probably true. "Where are we going?"

"The airport. Everything you need is in that pack in the back."

Tucker looked into the back of the Rover. There was a large backpack. "Why?"

"Because if I don't get you out of the country right now, you're going to jail."

"Mary Jean said she had that handled. Said her lawyers were on it."

"Right, and I go around smacking kids with beer bottles for recreation. The hooker filed a civil suit this morning. Twenty million. Mary Jean has to throw you to the wolves to save her own ass. She has to let the court prove that you fucked up all on your own. I grabbed your passport and some clothes when I got your mail."

"Jake, I can't just take off like this. I'm supposed to see a doctor tomorrow."

"For what?"

Tuck pointed to the lump of bandages in his lap. "What do you think? He's supposed to take this damn tube out of me."

"We'll do it in the bathroom at the airport. There's some antibiotics in the first-aid kit in the pack. I confirmed you for a flight to Honolulu that leaves in an hour. From there you go to Guam, then to someplace called Truk. That's where this doctor is supposed to meet you. I've got it all written down. There was an e-mail address at the bottom of the letter. I sent him a message to expect you tomorrow."

"But my car, my apartment, my stuff."

"Your apartment is a pit and I put your stuff worth keeping in a ministorage. I've got the pink slip for your Camaro. Sign it over to me. I'll sell it and send you the money."

"You were pretty fucking sure I'd want to do this."

"What choice do you have?"

Jake parked the Land Rover in short-term parking, shouldered the pack, and led Tucker into the international terminal. They checked the pack and found a rest room near Tucker's departure gate.

"I can do this myself," Tucker said.

Jake Skye was peering over the door into the stall where Tucker was preparing to remove his bandages and, finally, the catheter. A line of businessmen washed their hands at a line of lavatories while trying not to notice what was going on behind them in the stall.

"Just yank it," Jake Skye said.

"Give me a minute. I think they tied a knot inside it."

"Don't be a wuss, Tucker. Yank it."

The businessmen at the sinks exchanged raised eyebrows and one by one broke for the rest room door.

Jake said, "I'm going to give you to five, then I'm coming over the stall and yanking it for you. One, two . . ."

A rodeo cowboy at the urinals hitched up his Wranglers, pulled his hat down, and made a bowlegged beeline for the door to get on a plane to someplace where this sort of thing didn't happen.

"Five!"

Security guards rushed through the terminal toward the screaming. Someone was being murdered in the men's room and they were responsible. They burst into the rest room with guns drawn. Jake Skye was coiling up some tubing by the sinks. There was whimpering coming from one of the stalls. "Everything's fine, officers," Jake said. "My friend's a little upset. He just found out that his mother died."

"My mother's not dead!" Tucker said from the stall.

"He's in denial," Jake whispered to the guards. "Here, you better takes this." He handed the tubing to one of the guards. "We don't want him hanging himself in grief."

Ten minutes later, after condolences from the security staff, they sat in the departure lounge drinking gin and tonics, waiting for Tuck's boarding call. Around them, a score of men and women in suits fired out phone calls on cell phones while twenty more performed an impromptu dog pile at the bar, trying to occupy the minuscule smoking area. Jake Skye was cataloging the contents of the pack he'd given to Tuck. Tucker wasn't listening. He was overwhelmed with the speed with which his life had gone to shit, and he was desperately trying to sort it out. Jake's voice was lost like kazoo sounds in a wind tunnel.

Jake droned, "The stove will run on anything: diesel, jet fuel, gasoline, even vodka. There's a mask, fins, and snorkel, and a couple of waterproof flashlights."

The job with Mary Jean had been perfect. A different city every few days, nice hotels, an expense account, and literally thousands of earnest Mary Jean ladies to indulge him. And they did, one or two at each convention. Inspired by Mary Jean's speeches on self-determination, motivation, and how they too could be a winner, they sought Tucker out to have their one adventurous affair with a jet pilot. And because no matter how many times it happened, he was always somewhat surprised by their advances, Tucker played a part.

He behaved like a man torn from the cover of ۱ novel: the charming rogue, the passionate pira\ morning, take his ship to sea for God, Queen course, usually, sometime before morning, the wo\ that under the smooth, gin-painted exterior was a his shorts to check their wearability. But for a mome\ for him, he had been cool. Sleazy, but cool.

When the sleaze got to him, he needed only to suck a few hits of oxygen from the cabin cylinder to chase the hangover, then pull the pink jet into the sky to convince himself he was a professional, competent and in control. At altitude he turned it all over to the autopilot.

But now he couldn't seduce anyone or allow himself to be seduced, and he wasn't sure he could fly. The crash had juiced him of his confidence. It wasn't the impact or even the injuries. It was that last moment, when the guy, or the angel, or whatever it was appeared in the copilot's seat.

"You ever think about God?" Tucker asked Jake.

Jake Skye's face went dead with incomprehension. "You're going to need to know about this stuff if you get into trouble. Kinda like checking the fuel gauges—if you know what I mean."

Tucker winced. "Look, I heard every word you said. This seemed important all of a sudden, you know?"

"Well, in that case, Tuck, yes, I do think about God sometimes. When I'm with a really hot babe, and we're going at it like sweaty monkeys, I think about it then. I think about a big old pissed-off Sistine Chapel finger-pointin' motherfucker. And you know what? It works. You don't come when you're thinking about shit like that. You should try it sometime. Oh, sorry."

"Never mind," Tucker said.

"You can't let that kid with the Bible get to you. He's too young to have given up on religion ... doesn't have enough sin under his belt. Guys like us, best bet is that it's all bullshit and we go directly to worm food. Try not to think about it."

"Right," Tucker said, totally unsatisfied. If you had a question about any piece of gadgetry on the planet, Jake Skye was your man. But spiritually, he was a hamster. Which, actually, was one of the things Tucker used to like about him. He tried not to think about it and changed the subject.

"So what do I need to know about flying a Lear 45?"

Jake seemed relieved to be back into the realm of technology. "I

. seen one yet, but they say it flies just like Mary Jean's old
ir 25, only faster and a longer range. Better avionics. Read the
manuals when you get there."

"What about navigation equipment?" Tucker's navigation was
weak. Since he'd gotten his jet license, he'd depended completely on
automatic systems."

"You'll be fine. You don't buy a four-million-dollar plane and
cheap out on the navigation and radios. This doctor's got an e-mail
address, which means he's got a computer. You'll be able to access
charts and weather, and file flight plans with that. Check the facilities
at your destinations, so you'll know what to expect. Some of these
Third World airstrips just have a native with a candle for night land-
ings. And check your fuel availability. They'll sell you sewer water
instead of jet fuel if you don't check. You ever deal with Third World
airport cops?"

Tucker shrugged. Jake knew damn well he hadn't. He'd gotten
his hours flying copilot in the Mary Jean jet, and they'd never taken
that outside of the continental United States except for one trip to
Hawaii.

"Well," Jake continued, "the catchword is 'bribe, bribe, and
bribe.' Offer the highest amount you can at the lowest level of authority. Always have a thick roll of American dollars with you, and
don't bring it to the table if you're not willing to lose it. Keep something stashed in your shoe if they tap you out."

"You think this doctor is going to have me hauling drugs?"

"Good chance of it, don't you think? Besides, it doesn't matter.
These people are brutal. Half the time the government guys have
the same last name, so if you move up the ladder, you're just talking
to the uncle of the last one that hit you. He has to charge you more
out of pride."

Tucker cradled his head in his hands and stared into his gin and
tonic. "I'm fucked."

Jake patted him on the arm, then drew back at the intimacy of
the act. "They're calling your flight. You'll be fine."

They rose and Jake threw some cash on the table. At the gate
Tucker turned to his friend. "Man, I don't know what to say."

Jake extended his hand. "No sweat, man. You'd have done it for
me."

"I really hate flying in the back. Check on that kid from the
motel, okay."

"I'm on it. Look, everything you need is in the pack. Don't leave it behind."

"Right," Tucker said. "Well . . ." He turned and walked down the ramp to the plane.

Jake Skye watched him go, then turned, walked to a pay phone, dialed some numbers, and waited. "Yeah, it's Jake. He's on his way. Yeah, gone for good. When can I pick up my check?"

8

The Humiliation of the
Pilot As a Passenger

 Once on the plane, Tucker unfolded the letter from the mysterious doctor and read it again.

Dear Mr. Case:

I have become aware of your recent difficulties and I believe I have a proposition that will be of great benefit to us both. My wife and I are missionaries on Alualu, a rather remote atoll at the northwestern tip of the Micronesian crescent. Since we are out of the normal shipping lanes and we are the sole medical provider for the people of the island, we maintain our own aircraft for the transport of medical supplies. We have recently procured a Lear 45 for this purpose, but our former pilot has been called to the mainland on personal business for an indefinite time.

In short, Mr. Case, given your experience flying small jets and our unique requirements, we feel that this would be a perfect opportunity for us both. We are not concerned with the status of your license, only that you can perform in the pilot's seat and fulfill a need that can only be described as dire.

If you are willing to honor a long-term contract, we will provide you with room and board on the island, pay you $2,000 a week, as well as a generous bonus upon completion of the contract. As a gesture of our sincerity, I am enclosing an open airline ticket and a cashier's check for $3,000 for traveling expenses. Contact us by e-mail with your arrival time in Truk and my wife will meet you there to discuss the conditions of your employment and pro-

*vide transportation to Alualu. You'll find a room reserved for you
at the Paradise Inn.*

> Sincerely,
> Sebastian Curtis, M.D.
> Sebcurt@Wldnet.COM.JAP

Why me? Tuck wondered. He'd crashed a jet, lost his job and
probably his sex life, was charged with multiple crimes, then a letter
and a check arrived from nowhere to bail him out, but only if he
was willing to abandon everything and move to a Pacific island. It
could turn out to be a good job, but if it had been his decision, he'd
still be lingering over it in a motel room with Dusty Lemon. It was
as if some combination of ironic luck and Jake Skye had been sent
along to make the decision for him. Not so strange, he thought. The
same combination had put him in the pilot's seat in the first place.

Tuck had grown up in Elsinore, California, northeast of San Diego, the only son of the owner of the Denmark Silverware Corporation. He had an unremarkable childhood, was a mediocre athlete,
and spent most of his adolescence surfing in San Diego and chasing
girls, one of whom he finally caught.

Zoophilia Gold was the daughter of his father's lawyer, a lovely
girl made shy by a cruel first name. Tuck and Zoo enjoyed a brief
romance, which was put on hold when Tuck's father sent him off to
college in Texas so he could learn to make decisions and someday
take over the family business. His motivation excised by the job
guarantee, Tuck made passing grades until his college career was cut
short by an emergency call from his mother. "Come home. Your
father's dead."

Tuck made the drive in two days, stopping only for gas, to use
the bathroom, and to call Zoophilia, who informed him that his
mother had married his father's brother and his uncle had taken over
Denmark Silverware. Tuck screeched into Elsinore in a blind rage
and ran over Zoophilia's father as he was leaving Tuck's mother's
house.

The death was declared an accident, but during the investigation
a policeman informed Tuck that although he had no proof, he sus-
pected that the riding accident that killed Tuck's father might not
have been an accident, especially since Tuck's father had been allergic to horses. Tuck was sure that his uncle had set the whole thing

up, but he couldn't bring himself to confront his mother or her new husband.

In the meantime, Zoophilia, stricken with grief over her father's death, overdosed on Prozac and drowned in her hot tub, and her brother, who had been away at college also, returned promising to kill Tucker or at least sue him into oblivion for the deaths of his father and sister. While trying to come to a decision on a course of action, Tucker met a brace of Texas brunettes in a Pacific Beach bar who insisted he ride back with them to the Lone Star state.

Disinherited, depressed, and clueless, Tucker took the ride as far as a small suburban airport outside of Houston, where the girls asked him if he'd ever been nude skydiving. At that point, not really caring if he lived or died, he crawled into the back of a Beechcraft with them.

They left him scraped, bruised, and stranded on the tarmac in a jockstrap and a parachute harness, shivering with adrenaline. Jake Skye found him wandering around the hangars wearing the parachute canopy as a toga. It had been a tough year.

"Let me guess," Jake said. "Margie and Randy Sue?"

"Yeah," Tucker said. "How'd you know?"

"They do it all the time. Daddies with money—Rosencrantz and Guildenstern Petroleum. Hope you didn't cut up that canopy. You can get a grand for it used."

"They're gone, then?"

"An hour ago. Said something about going to London. Where are your clothes?"

"In their car."

"Come with me."

Jake gave Tucker a job washing airplanes, then taught him to fly a Cessna 172 and enrolled him in flight school. Tucker got his twin-engine hours in six months, helping Jake ferry Texas businessmen around the state in a leased Beech Duke. Jake turned the flying over to Tuck as soon as he passed his 135 commercial certification.

"I can fly anything," Jake said, "but unless it's helicopters, I'd rather wrench. Only steady gig in choppers is flying oil rigs in the Gulf. Had too many friends tip off into the drink. You fly, I'll do the maintenance, we split the cash."

Another six months and Jake was offered a job by the Mary Jean Cosmetics Corporation. Jake took the job on the condition that Tucker could copilot until he had his Lear hours (he described Tuck as a "little lost lamb" and the makeup magnate relented). Mary Jean did her own flying, but once Tucker was qualified, she turned the controls over to him full-time. "Some members of the board have pointed out that my time would be better spent taking care of business instead of flying. Besides, it's not ladylike. How'd you like a job?"

Luck. The training he'd received would have cost hundreds of thousands of dollars, and he'd gotten most of it for free. He had become a new person, and it had all started with a bizarre streak of bad luck followed by an opportunity and Jake Skye's intervention. Maybe it would work out for the better this time too. At least this time no one had been killed.

9

Cult of the Autopilot:
A History Lesson

The pilot said, "The local time is 9:00 A.M. The temperature is 90 degrees. Thank you for flying Continental and enjoy your stay in Truk." Then he laughed menacingly.

Tuck stepped out of the plane and felt the palpable weight of the air in his lungs. It smelled green, fecund, as if vegetation was growing, dying, rotting, and giving off a gas too thick to breathe. He followed a line of passengers to the terminal, a long, low, cinderblock building—nothing more really than a tin roof on pillars—teeming with brown people; short, stoutly built people, men in jeans or old dress slacks and T-shirts, women in long floral cotton dresses with puff shoulders, their hair held in buns atop their heads by tortoiseshell combs.

Tuck waited, sweating, at one end of the terminal while young men shoved the baggage through a curtain onto a plywood ramp. Natives retrieved their baggage, mainly coolers wrapped with packing tape, and walked by the customs officer's counter without pausing. He looked for a tourist, to see how they were treated, but there were none. The customs officer glared at him. Tucker hoped there was nothing illegal in his pack. The airport here looked like a weigh station for a death camp; he didn't want to see the jail. He fingered the roll of bills in his pocket, thinking, *Bribe.*

The pack came sliding through the curtain. Tucker moved through the pall of islanders and pulled the pack onto his shoulders, then walked to the customs counter and plopped it down in front of the officer.

"Passport," the officer said. He was fat and wore a brass button uniform with dime store flip-flops on his feet.

Tuck handed him his passport.

"How long will you be staying?"

"Not long. I'm not sure. A day maybe."

"No flights for three days." The officer stamped the passport and handed it back to Tucker. "There's a ten-dollar departure fee."

"That's it?" Tucker was amazed. No inspection, no bribe. Luck again.

"Take your bag."

"Right." Tucker scooped up the pack and headed for an exit sign, hand-painted on plywood. He walked out of the airport and was blinded by the sun.

"Hey, you dive?" A man's voice.

Tuck squinted and a thin, leathery islander in a Bruins hockey jersey stood in front of him. He had six teeth, two of them gold. "No," Tucker said.

"Why you come if you no dive?"

"I'm here on business." Tucker dropped his pack and tried to breathe. He was soaked with sweat. Ten seconds in this sun and he wanted to dive into the shade like a roach under a stove.

"Where you stay?"

This guy looked criminal, just an eye patch short of a pirate. Tucker didn't want to tell him anything.

"How do I get to the Paradise Inn?"

The pirate called to a teenager who was sitting in the shade watching a score of beat-up Japanese cars with blackened windows jockeying for position in the dirt street.

"Rindi! Paradise."

The younger man, dressed like a Compton rapper—oversized shorts, football jersey, baseball cap reversed over a blue bandanna—came over and grabbed Tucker's pack. Tuck kept one hand on an arm strap and fought the kid for control.

"You go with him," the pirate said. "He take you Paradise."

"Come on, Holmes," the kid said. "My car air-conditioned.

Tucker let go of the pack and the kid whisked it away through the jostle of cars to an old Honda Civic with a cellophane back window and bailing wire holding the passenger door shut. Tuck follow him, stepping quickly between the cars, each one lurching forward as if to hit him as he passed. He looked for the driver's expressions, but the windshields were all blacked out with plastic film.

The kid threw Tuck's pack in the hatchback, then unwired the door and held it open. Tucker climbed in, feeling, once again, completely at the mercy of Lady Luck. Now I get to see the place where they rob and kill the white guys, he thought.

As they drove, Tuck looked out on the lagoon. Even through the tinted window the blue of the lagoon shone as if illuminated from below. Island women in scuba masks waded shoulder deep; their floral dresses flowing around them made them look like multicolored jellyfish. Each carried a short steel spear slung from a piece of surgical tubing. Large plastic buckets floated on the surface in which the women were depositing their catch.

"What are they hunting?" Tuck asked the driver.

"Octopus, urchin, small fish. Mostly octopus. Hey, where you from in United States?"

"I grew up in California."

The kid lit up. "California! You have Crips there, right?"

"Yeah, there's gangs."

"I'm a Crip," the kid said, pointing to his blue bandanna with pride. "Me and my homies find any Bloods here, we gonna pop a nine on 'em."

Tucker was amazed. On the side of the road a beautiful little girl in a flowered dress was drinking from a green coconut. Here in the car there was a gang war going on. He said, "Where are the Bloods?"

Rindi shook his head sadly. "Nobody want to be Bloods. Only Crips on Truk. But if we see one, we gonna bust a cap on 'em." He pulled back a towel on the seat to reveal a beat-up Daisy air pistol.

Tuck made a mental note not to wear a red bandanna and accidentally fill the Blood shortage. He had no desire to be killed or wounded over a glorified game of cowboys and Indians.

"How far to the hotel?"

"This it," Rindi said, wrenching the Honda across the road into a dusty parking lot.

The Paradise Inn was a two-story, crumbling stucco building with a crown of rusting rebar beckoning skyward for a third floor that would never be built. Tuck let the boy, Rindi, carry his pack to an upstairs room: mint green cinder block over brown linoleum, a beat-up metal desk, smoke-stained floral curtains, a twin bed with a torn 1950s bedspread, the smell of mildew and insecticide. Rindi put the pack in the doorless closet and cranked the little window air conditioner to high.

"Too late for shower. Water come on again four to six."

Tuck glanced into the bathroom. Mistake. An exotic-looking orange thing was growing on the shower curtain. He said, "Where can I get a beer?"

Rindi grinned. "We have lounge. Budweiser, 'king of beers.' MTV on satellite." He cocked his wrists and performed a gangsta rap move that looked as if he'd contracted a rhythmic cerebral palsy. "Yo, G, we chill with the phattest jams? Snoop, Ice, Public Enemy."

"Oh, good," Tuck said. "We can do a drive-by later. How do I get to the lounge?"

"Down steps, outside, go right." He paused, looking concerned. "We have to shoot out driver's side. Other window not go down."

"We'll manage." Tuck flipped the kid a dollar and left the room, proud to be an American.

An unconscious island man marked the entrance to the lounge. Tuck stepped over him and pushed his way through the black glass door into a cool, dark, smoke-hazed room lit by a silent television tuned to nothing and a flickering neon BUDWEISER sign. A shadow stood behind the bar; two more sat in front of it. Tuck could see eyes in the dark—maybe people sitting at tables, maybe nocturnal vermin.

A voice: "A fellow American here to buy a beer for his countryman."

The voice had come from one of the shadows at the bar. Tuck squinted into the dark and saw a large white man, about fifty, in a sweat-stained dress shirt. He was smiling, a jowly yellow smile under drink-dulled eyes. Tuck smiled back. Anyone that didn't speak broken English was, at this point, his friend.

"What are you drinkin', pardner?" Tuck always went Texan when he was being friendly.

"What you drink here." He held up two fingers to the bartender, then held his hand out to shake. "Jefferson Pardee, editor in chief of the *Truk Star*."

"Tucker Case." Tuck sat down on the stool next to the big man. The bartender placed two sweating Budweiser cans in front of them and waited.

"Run a tab," Pardee said. Then to Tuck: "I assume you're a diver?"

"Why would you assume that?"

"It's the only reason Americans come here, other than Peace Corps or Navy CAT team members. And if you don't mind my saying, you don't look idealistic enough to be Peace Corps or stupid enough to be Navy."

"I'm a pilot." It felt good saying it. He'd always liked saying it. He didn't realize how terrified he'd been that he'd never be able to say it again. "I'm supposed to meet someone from another island about a job."

"Not a missionary air outfit, I hope."

"It's for a missionary doctor. Why?"

"Son, those people do a great job, but you can only get so much out of those old planes they fly. Fifty-year-old Beech 18s and DC3s. Sooner or later you're going into the drink. But I suppose if you're flying for God . . ."

"I'll be flying a new Learjet."

Pardee almost dropped his beer. "Bullshit."

Tuck was tempted to pull out the letter and slam it on the bar, but thought better of it. "That's what they said."

Pardee put a big hairy forearm on the bar and leaned into Tuck. He smelled like a hangover. "What island and what church?"

"Alualu," Tuck said. "A Dr. Curtis."

Pardee nodded and sat back on his stool. "No-man's Island."

"What's that mean?"

"It doesn't belong to anyone. Do you know anything about Micronesia?"

"Just that you have gangs but no regular indoor plumbing."

"Well, depending on how you look at it, Truk can be a hellhole. That's what happens when you give Coke cans to a coconut culture. But it's not all that way. There are two thousand islands in the Micronesian crescent, running almost all the way from Hawaii to New Guinea. Magellan landed here first, on his first voyage around the world. The Spanish claimed them, then the Germans, then the Japanese. We took them from the Japanese during the war. There are seventy sunken Japanese ships in Truk's lagoon alone. That's why the divers come."

"So what's this have to do with where I'm going?"

"I'm getting to that. Until fifteen years ago, Micronesia was a U.S. protectorate, except for Alualu. Because it's at the westernmost tip of the crescent, we left it out of the surrender agreement with the Japanese. It kind of got lost in the shuffle. So Alualu was never an American territory, and when the Federated States of Micronesia declared independence, they didn't include Alualu."

"So what's that mean?" Tuck was getting impatient. This was the longest lecture he'd endured since flight school.

"In short, no mother government, no foreign aid, no nothing.

Alualu belongs to whoever lives on it. It's off the shipping lanes, and it's a raised atoll, only one small island, not a group of islands around a lagoon, so there's not enough copra to make it worth the trip for the collector boats. Since the war, when there was an airstrip there, no one goes there."

"Maybe that's why they need the jet?"

"Son, I came here in '66 with the Peace Corps and I've never left. I've seen a lot of missionaries throw a lot of money at a lot of problems, but I've never seen a church that was willing to spring for a Learjet."

Tuck wanted to beat his head on the bar just to feel his tiny brain rattle. Of course it was too good to be true. He'd known that instinctively. He should have known that as soon as he'd seen the money they were offering him—him, Tucker Case, the biggest fuckup in the world.

Tuck drained his beer and signaled for two more. "So what do you know about this Curtis?"

"I've heard of him. There's not much news out here and he made some about twenty years back. He went batshit at the airport in Yap after he couldn't get anyone to evacuate a sick kid off the island. Frankly, I'm surprised he's still out there. I heard the church pulled out on him. Cargo cults give Christians the willies."

Tuck knew he was being lured in. He'd met guys like Pardee in airport hotel bars all over the U.S.: lonely businessmen, usually salesmen, who would talk to anyone about anything just for the company. They learned how to make you ask questions that required long windy answers. He'd felt sympathetic toward them ever since he'd played Willie Loman in Miss Patterson's third-grade class production of *Death of a Salesman*. Pardee just needed to talk.

"What's a cargo cult?" Tuck asked.

Pardee smiled. "They've been in the islands since the Spanish landed in the 1500s and traded steel tools and beads to the natives for food and water. They're still around."

Pardee took a long pull on his beer, set it down, and resumed. "These islands were all populated by people from somewhere else. The stories of the heroic ancestors coming across the sea in canoes are part of their religions. The ancestors brought everything they need from across the sea. All of a sudden, guys show up with new cool stuff. Instant ancestors, instant gods from across the sea, bearing gifts. They incorporated the newcomers into their religions. Sometimes it might be fifty years before another ship showed up, but every time they used a machete, they thought about the return of the gods bearing cargo."

"So there are still people waiting for the Spanish to return with steel tools."

Pardee laughed. "No. Except for missionaries, these islands didn't get much attention from the modern world until World War II. All of a sudden, Allied forces are coming in and building airstrips and bribing the islanders with things so they would resist the Japanese. Manna from the heavens. American flyers brought in all sorts of good stuff. Then the war ended and the good stuff stopped coming.

"Years later anthropologists and missionaries are finding little altars built to airplanes. The islanders are still waiting for the ships from the sky to return and save them. Myths get built around single pilots who are supposed to bring great armies to the islands to chase out the French, or the British, or whatever imperial government holds the island. The British outlawed the cargo cults on some Melanesian islands and jailed the leaders. Bad idea, of course. They were instant martyrs. The missionaries railed against the new religions, trying to use reason to kill faith, so some islanders started claiming their pilots were Jesus. Drove the missionaries nuts. Natives putting little propellers on their crucifixes, drawing pictures of Christ in a flight helmet. Bottom line is the cargo cults are still around, and I hear that one of the strongest is on Alualu."

"Are the natives dangerous?" Tuck asked.

"Not because of their religion, no."

"What's that mean?"

"These people are warriors, Mr. Case. They forget that most of the time, but sometimes when they're drinking, a thousand years of warrior tradition can rear its head, even on the more modernized islands like Truk. And there are people in these islands who still remember the taste of human flesh—if you get my meaning. Tastes like Spam, I hear. The natives love Spam."

"Spam? You're kidding."

"Nope. That's what Spam stands for: Shaped Protein Approximating Man."

Tucker smiled, realizing he'd been had. Pardee let loose an explosive laugh and slapped Tuck on the shoulder. "Look, my friend, I've got to get to the office. A paper to put out, you know. But watch yourself. And don't be surprised if your Learjet is actually a beat-up Cessna."

"Thanks," Tucker said, shaking the big man's hand.

"You going to be around for few days?" Pardee asked.

"I'm not sure."

"Well, just a word of advice"—Pardee lowered his voice and leaned into Tucker conspiratorially—"don't go out at night by yourself. Nothing you're going to see is worth your life."

"I can take care of myself, but thanks."

"Just so," Pardee said. He turned and lumbered out of the bar.

Tuck paid the bartender and headed out into the heat and to his room, where he stripped naked and lay on the tattered bedspread, letting the air conditioner blow over him with a welcome chill. Maybe this won't be so bad, he thought. He was going to end up on an island where God was a pilot. What a great way to get babes!

Then he looked down at his withered member, stitched and scarred as if it had been patched from the Frankenstein monster. A wave of anxiety passed through him, bringing sweat to his skin even in the electric chill. He realized that he had really never done anything in his adult life that had not—even at some subconscious level—been part of a strategy to impress women. He would have never worked so hard to become a pilot if it hadn't been for Jake's insistence that "Chicks dig pilots." Why fly? Why get out of bed in the morning? Why do anything?

He rolled over to bury his face in the pillow and pinned a live cockroach to the spread with his cheek.

10

Coconut Telegraph

Jefferson Pardee dialed the island communications center and asked them to connect him to a friend of his in the governor's office on Yap. While he waited for the connection, he looked down from his office above the Food Store on the Truk public market: women selling bananas, coconuts, and banana leaf bundles of taro out of plywood sheds; children with bandannas on their faces against the rising street dust; drunk men languishing red-eyed in the shade. Across the street lay a stand of coconut palms and the vibrant blue-green water of the lagoon dotted with outboards and floating pieces of Styrofoam coolers. Another day in paradise, Pardee thought.

Pardee had been out here for thirty years now. He'd come fresh out of Northwestern School of Journalism full of passion to save the world, to help those less fortunate than himself, and to avoid the draft. After his two years in the Peace Corps were up—his main achievement was teaching the islanders to boil water—he'd stayed. First he worked for the budding island governments, helping to write the charters, the constitutions, and the requests for aid from the United States. That work finished, he found himself afraid to go home. He'd gone to fat on breadfruit and beer and become accustomed to dollar whores, fifty-cent taxis, and a two-hour workday. The idea of returning to the States, where he would have to live up to his potential or face being called a failure, terrified him. He wrote and received a grant to start the *Truk Star*. It was the last significant thing that he'd done for twenty-five years. Covering the news in Truk was akin to taking a penguin census in the Mojave Desert. Still, deep inside, he hoped that something would happen so that he could flex his atrophied journalistic muscles. Something he could get passionate about. Why couldn't the United States nuke a nearby island? The French did it in Polynesia all the time. But no, the United States nukes one little atoll in Micronesia (Bikini) and they go away, saying, "Well, I guess that ought to do for twenty-five thousand years or so." Wimps.

Then again, maybe there was something going on out on Alualu. Something clandestine and dirty. Jefferson Pardee had lost his ambition, but he still had hope.

"Go ahead," the operator said.

"Ignatho, how you doing, man?"

Ignatho Malongo, governor's assistant for outer island affairs, was not in the mood to chat. It was lunchtime and he was out of cigarettes and betel nut and no one had come to relieve him on the radio so he could leave. His office was in a bright blue corrugated steel shed tucked behind the offices of the governor. It housed a military-style steel desk, a shortwave radio, a new IBM computer, and a wastebasket full of tractor-feed paper stained with red betel nut spit under a sign that emphatically declared NO SPITTING. He was round, brown, and wore only a loincloth, a Casio watch, and a Bic pen on a string around his neck. He was sweating into a puddle that darkened the concrete floor around his desk.

"Pardee, what do you need?"

"I was wondering if you've heard anything going on out on Alualu?"

"Just the same. Occasionally the doctor radios for supplies to be sent out on the *Micro Trader*. They're not officially in Yap state, so they don't go through my office. Why?"

"You hear any rumors, maybe from the *Micro Trader* crew?"

"Like what? The Shark People don't have contact with anyone since I can remember. Just that Dr. Curtis."

Pardee didn't want to be in the business of starting rumors. More than once he'd had to track down a story to find out that it had started with a drunken lie he'd told in a bar that had circulated through the islands, changed enough to sound credible, and landed back on his desk. Still, Malongo wasn't giving anything today. "I hear they have a new aircraft out there. A Learjet."

Malongo laughed. "Where did you hear that?"

"I've heard it twice now. A couple of months ago from a guy who said he was going out there to fly it for them and just now from another pilot on his way."

"Maybe they're starting a new airline. Be serious, Jeff. Are you that desperate for a story? I've got some grants you can write if you need the work."

Pardee was a little embarrassed. Still, he had no doubt that Tucker Case had been contacted by Dr. Curtis. Something was up. He said, "Well, maybe you can ask the guys on the *Trader* to keep an eye out. Ask around and call me if you hear anything."

Suddenly Pardee had a flash of motivational inspiration. "If someone's buying jet airplanes, there might be some untapped government money out there that you guys don't know about." He could almost hear Malongo snap to attention.

Malongo was thinking air conditioner, laser printer, a new chair. "Look, I'll ask out at the airport. If someone's flying a jet off of Alualu, then they have to use the radio, right?"

"I suppose," Pardee said.

"I'll call you." Malongo hung up.

Pardee sighed. "And once again," he said to himself, "we lead with the 'Pig Thief Still at Large' story."

A half hour later the phone rang. The phone never rang. Pardee picked it up and could tell by the clicking that he was being connected off-island. Ignatho Malongo came on the line. He sounded like he was in a better mood. Pardee guessed that he was in a state of foreign aid arousal.

"Jeff, the *Trader* is in the harbor. Some of the crew was having lunch at the marina and I asked them about your Learjet." Malongo was smoking a Benson & Hedges and chewing a big cud of betel nut. He was in a better mood now.

"And?"

"No one's seen it, but they did see some Japanese on the island the last time they were there."

"Japanese? Tourists?"

"They were carrying machine guns."

"No shit."

"Do you think this means there's some military money coming our way?" Malongo was thinking air-conditioning, a case of Spam, a ticket to Hawaii to go shopping.

Pardee scratched his two-day growth of beard. "Probably the crew off of a tuna boat. They've been threatening to shoot some of the islanders off Ulithi if they keep stealing their net floats. I'll check with the Australian Navy, see if they know about a Japanese boat fishing those waters. Meantime, I owe you a bag of betel nut."

Malongo laughed. "You owe me about ten bags by now. How you going to pay if you never leave that shithole of an island?"

"You'll see me soon enough." Pardee hung up.

~~~~~~

11

Paging the Goddess

The Shark men had been beating drums and marching with bamboo rifles since dawn, while the Shark women prepared the feast for the appearance of the High Priestess.

In her bed chamber the High Priestess was doing her nails. The Sorcerer entered through a beaded curtain, moved up behind her, and cupped her naked breasts. Without looking up, she said, "You know, I used to get a pretty good buzz doing this in my studio apartment. Close the windows and let the fumes build up. Want a whiff?" She held the polish bottle out behind her.

He shook his head. He was in his mid-fifties, tall, thin, with short gray hair and ice blue eyes. He wore a green lab coat over Bermuda shorts. "Missionary Air just radioed. Their Beech is broken. They're waiting for a part from the States and won't have it fixed for a month. Our pilot's stuck on Truk."

The High Priestess fired a glare over her shoulder and he could feel himself going to slime, changing, melting into the lowest form of sea slug. She could do that to him. Her breasts felt like chilled river rocks in his hands. He stepped away.

"It's all right," he said. "I've sent him a message to fly to Yap. He can catch the *Micro Trader* there tomorrow and he'll be here two days later."

She was not impressed. "Don't you think it might be a good idea for me to meet this one before he gets here? It took long enough to find him."

The Sorcerer had backed all the way to the beaded curtain. "You were the one that didn't want any more military types."

"Because it worked so well last time. It's bad enough I have to be surrounded by ninjas. I don't like it."

The Sorcerer couldn't believe anyone could walk that slowly and still express so much; it was positively symphonic. He said, "They're not ninjas. They're just guards. This will all be over soon and you can live in a palace in France if you want."

He held his arms out to receive her embrace. She turned on a red spiked heel and quickstepped back to the vanity. "We'll talk about this later. I have to go on in an hour."

Feeling stupid, he dropped his arms and backed through the beaded curtain. In the distance the Shark People began the chant to call forth the Priestess of the Sky.

12

Friendly Advice

Tuck was sweating through a slow-motion dream rerun of the crash. The end of the runway was coming up too quickly. Meadow Malackovitch was bouncing off of various consoles in the cockpit. Someone in the copilot seat was screaming at him, calling him a "fuckin' mook." He turned to see who it was and was awakened by a knock on the door.

"Mr. Case. Message for you."

"Just a second." Tucker scrambled in the darkness until he found his khakis on the floor, shook them to evict any insect visitors, then pulled them on and stumbled to the door. Rindi, the driver-rapper, stood outside holding a slip of paper.

"This just come for you from the telecom center." He reached past Tuck and clicked the light switch. A bare bulb went on over the desk.

Tuck took the note, dug in his pants pocket for a tip, and came up with a dollar, but Rindi had already shuffled off.

The note, on waxy fax paper, was covered with greasy fingerprints. Tuck guessed it had probably passed through a dozen hands before getting to him. He unfolded it and read.

To: Tucker Case c/o Paradise Hotel
From: Dr. Sebastian Curtis
Mr. Case,

I deeply regret that my wife will not be able to meet you on Truk as planned. We have reserved a seat for you on tomorrow's Air Micronesia flight to Yap, where we have arranged transport aboard *the supply ship,* Micro Trader, *to Alualu. Your plane will arrive at 11:00 A.M. and the* Micro Trader *is scheduled to sail at noon, so it will be necessary for you to take a taxi to the dock as soon as you clear customs.*

I apologize for the inconvenience and would ask that you refrain from discussing the purpose of your visit with the crew of the Micro Trader—*or with anyone else, for that matter. It would be unfortunate if this research reached the FAA before it had been thoroughly investigated. Rumors travel quickly in these islands.*

I look forward to discussing the intricacies of the particular strain of staphylococci with you.

> *Sincerely,*
> *Sebastian Curtis, M.D.*

Staphylococci? Germs? He wants to discuss germs? Tuck couldn't have been more confused if the message had been in Eskimo. He folded it and looked again at the fingerprints.

That was it. He knew that other people would be reading the note. The germ thing was just a red herring to confuse nosy natives. The bit about the FAA obviously referred to Tuck's revoked pilot's license. In a way, it was a threat. Maybe he ought to find out a little more about this doctor before he went running out to this remote island. Maybe the reporter, Pardee, knew something.

Tuck dressed quickly and went down to the desk, where Rindi was listening to a transistor radio with a speaker that sounded like it had been fashioned from wax paper. Someone was singing a Garth Brooks song in nasal Trukese accompanied by an accordion.

"It sounds like someone's hurting animals." Tuck grinned.

Rindi did not smile. "You going out?" Rindi was eager to get into Tuck's room and go through his luggage.

"I need to find that reporter, Jefferson Pardee."

Rindi looked as if he was going to spit. He said, "He at Yumi Bar all the time. That way." He pointed up the road toward town. "You need ride?"

"How far is it?"

"Maybe a mile. How long you be gone?" Rindi wanted to take his time, make sure he didn't miss any of Tuck's valuables.

"I'm not sure. Do you lock the door at midnight or something?"

"No, I come get you if you drunk."

"I'll be fine. I'll be checking out in the morning. Can I get an eight o'clock wake-up call?"

"No. No phone in room."

"How about a wake-up knock?"

"No problem."

"Thanks." Tucker went out the front door and was nearly thrown back by the thickness of the air. The temperature had dropped to the mid-80s, but it felt as if it had gotten more humid. Everything dripped. The air carried the scent of rotting flowers.

Tuck set off down the road and was soaked with sweat by the time he reached a rusted metal Quonset hut with a hand-painted sign that read YUMI BAR. The dirt parking lot was filled with Japanese beaters parked freestyle. A skeletal dog with open running sores, a crossbreed of dingo and sewer rat, cowered in the half-light coming through the door and looked at him as if pleading to be run over. Tuck's stomach lurched. He made a wide path around the dog, who looked down and resumed concentration on its suffering.

"Hey, kid, you're not going in there, are you?"

Tuck looked up. There was a cigarette glowing in the dark at the corner of the building. Tuck could just make out the form of a man standing there. He wore some kind of uniform—Tuck could see the silhouette of a captain's hat. Anywhere else Tuck might have ignored a voice in the dark, but the accent was American, and out here he was drawn to the familiarity of it. He'd heard it before.

He said, "I thought I'd get a beer. I'm looking for an American named Pardee."

The guy in the dark blew out a long stream of cigarette smoke. "He's in there. But you don't want to go in there right now. Wait a few minutes."

Tuck was about to ask why when two men came crashing through the door and landed in the dirt at his feet. They were islanders, both screaming incomprehensibly as they punched and gouged at one another. The one on the top held a bush knife, a short machete, which he drew back and slammed into the other man's head, severing an ear. Blood sprayed on the dust.

A stream of shouting natives spilled out of the bar, waving beer bottles and kicking at the fighters. Earless leaped to his feet and backed off to get a running attack at Bush Knife, who was rising to his feet. Earless hit him with a flying tackle as Bush Knife hacked at his ribs. A pickup truck full of policemen pulled into the parking lot and the crowd scattered into the dark and back into the bar, leaving the fighters rolling in the dirt. Six policemen stood over the fighters, slamming them with riot batons until they both lay still. The police threw the fighters into the bed of their truck, climbed in after them, and drove off.

Tuck stood stunned. He'd never seen violence that sudden and raw in his life. Ten more seconds and he would have been in the middle of it instead of backpedaling across the parking lot.

"Should be okay to go in now," said the voice from the dark.

Tuck looked up, but he couldn't even see the cigarette glowing now. "Thanks," he said. "You sure it's okay?"

"Watch your ass, kid," said the voice, and this time it seemed to come from above him. Tucker spun around, nearly wrenching his neck, but he couldn't see anyone. He shook off the confusion and headed into the bar.

The skeletal dog crawled from under a truck, seized the severed ear from the dust, and slunk into the shadows. "Good dog," said the voice out of the dark. The dog growled, ready to protect its prize. A young man, perhaps twenty-four, dark and sharp-featured, dressed in a gray flight suit, stepped out of the shadows and bent to the dog, who lowered its head in submission. The young man reached out as if to pet the dog, then grabbed its head and quickly snapped its neck. "Now, that's better, ain't it, ya little mook?"

The bar was as dingy inside as it was out. Yellow bug bulbs gave off just enough light to navigate around drunken islanders and a beat-up pool table. An old Wurlitzer bounced American country western songs off the metal walls. A khaki-wrapped hulk, Jefferson Pardee, sweated over a Budweiser at the bar. Tucker slid in next to him.

Pardee looked up with red-rimmed eyes. "You just missed all the excitement."

"No, I saw it. I was outside."

Pardee signaled for two more beers. "I thought I told you not to go out at night."

"I'm leaving for Yap in the morning and I need to ask you some questions."

Pardee grinned like a child given a surprise favor. "I'm at your service, Mr. Tucker."

Tuck weighed his need for information against the ignominy of telling Pardee about the crash. He pulled the crumpled fax paper from his pants pocket and set it on the bar before the reporter.

Pardee lit a cigarette as he read. He finished reading and handed the fax back to Tucker. "It's not unusual to have changes in travel plans out here. But what's this about bacteria? I thought you were a pilot."

Tucker took Pardee though the crash and the mysterious invitation from the doctor, including Jake's theories about drug smuggling. "I think the bacteria stuff was just to throw off anyone who got hold of the fax."

"You're right there. But it's not drugs. There aren't any drugs produced in these islands except kava and betel nut, and nobody wants those except the islanders. Oh, they grow a little pot here and there, but it's consumed here by the gangsta wanna-bes."

"Gangsta wanna-bes?" Tuck asked.

"A few of the islanders have satellite TV. The people who look like them on TV are gangsta rappers. The old rundown buildings they see in the hood look like the buildings here. Except here they're new and rundown. It's a Coke and a smile and baby formula their babies can't digest. It's packaged junk food shipped here without expiration dates."

"What in the hell are you talking about, Pardee?"

"They buy into the advertising bullshit that Americans have become immune to. It's like the entire Micronesian crescent is one big cargo cult. They buy the worst of American culture."

"Are you saying I'm the worst America has to offer?"

Pardee patted his shoulder and leaned in close. Tuck could smell the sour beer sweat coming off the big man. "No, that's not what I'm saying. I don't know what's going on out on Alualu, but I'm sure it's no big deal. Evil tends to grow in proportion to the profit potential, and there's just nothing out there that's worth a shit. Go to your island, kid. And get in touch with me when you figure out what's going on. In the meantime, I'll do some checking."

Tuck shook the reporter's hand. "I will." He threw some money on the bar and started to leave. Pardee called to him as he reached the door.

"One more thing. I checked around. I heard that there's some armed men on Alualu. And there was another pilot that came through here a few months ago. Nobody's seen him. Be careful, Tucker."

"And you weren't going to tell me that?"

"I had to be sure that you weren't part of it."

13

~~~~~~

Out of the Frying Pan

Tuck's first thought of the new morning was *I've got to catch a plane.* His second was, *My dick's broke.*

It happens that way. One has a "private" irritation—hemorrhoids, menstrual cramps, swollen prostate, yeast infection, venereal disease, bladder infection—and no matter how hard the mind tries to escape the gravity of the affliction, it is inexorably pulled back into a doomed orbit of circular thought. Anything that distracts from the irritation is an irritation. Life is an irritation.

Inside Tuck's head sounded like this: *I have to catch a plane. I'm pissing fire. I need a shower. Check the stitches. No water. It looks infected. Probably leprosy. I hate this place. I'm sure it's infected. When does the water come on? It's going to turn black and fall off. Whoever heard of a place with satellite TV but no running water? I'll never fly again. I'm thirty years old and I have no job. And no dick. And who in the hell was that guy in the parking lot last night? I smell like rancid goat meat. Probably the infection. Gangrene. I can't believe there's no running water. I'm going to die. Die, die, die.*

Not a pleasant place to be: inside Tuck's head.

Outside Tuck's head the shower came on; brown, tepid water ran down his body in gutless streams; pipes shuddered and trumpeted as if trying to extrude a vibrating moose. The soap, a brown minibar made from local copra, lathered like slate and smelled of hibiscus flowers and suffering dog.

Tuck dried himself on a translucent swath of balding terry cloth and slipped into his clothes, three days saturated with tropical travel funk. He shouldered his pack, noticing that the zippered pockets had been tampered with and not giving a good goddamn, then trudged down to the front desk.

Rindi was sleeping on the desk. Tuck woke him, made sure that the room had been paid by the doctor as promised, then stood in the tropical sun and waited as Rindi brought the car around.

It seemed like a very long ride to the airport. Rindi ran over a chicken, then got out and fought an old woman who claimed the chicken, each tugging on a leg, testing the tensile strength of poultry to its limit before Rindi busted a kung fu move that secured his dinner and left the old woman sitting in the dust with a sacred chicken foot in her hand. (The old woman was from the island of Tonoas, where magic chickens were once called up by a sorcerer to level a mountain for a temple, the Hall of the Magic Chickens.)

At the airport Tuck gave Rindi a dollar for the cab ride, which was twice the going rate, and waved off the bloody handshake the aspiring gangsta offered. "Keep the peace, home boy," Tuck said.

14

Espionage and Intrigue

Yap was cleaner than Truk and hotter, if that was possible. Here the beat-up taxis actually had radio antennas to identify them. The roads were paved as well. The airport, another tin roof over concrete pylons, was filled with natives: men in loincloths and topless women in hand-woven wraparound skirts. Tuck caught a cab at the airport and told the driver to take him to the dock.

The driver spat out the window and said, "The ship gone."

"It can't be gone." What had moments ago been a pleasant drunk from four airline martinis turned instantly to a headache. "Maybe it was another ship that left."

The driver smiled. His teeth were black, his lips bright red. "Ship gone. You want to go to town?"

"How much?" Tuck asked, as if he had a choice.

"Fourteen dollar."

"Fourteen dollars? It's only fifty cents on Truk!"

"Okay, fifty cents," the driver said.

"That's your counteroffer?" Tuck asked. He was thinking about what Pardee had said about these islanders absorbing the worst of American culture. This was his chance to help, if only in a small way. "That's the most helpless bargaining I've ever heard. How do you ever expect your country to get out of the Third World with that weak shit?"

"Sorry," the driver said. "One dollar."

"Seventy-five cents," Tuck said.

"You find another taxi," the driver said, digging in his fiscal heels.

"That's better," said Tuck. "A dollar it is. And there's another one in it for you if you don't run over any chickens."

The driver put the car in gear and started off. They passed though several miles of jungle before breaking into a brightly lit, surprisingly modern-looking town with concrete streets. Occasionally, they passed a tin house with stone wheels leaning against the walls. The stones ranged from the size of a small tire to seven feet in diameter and were covered with varying degrees of green moss. "What are those millstone-looking things?" Tuck asked the driver.

"*Fei*," the driver said. "Stone money. Very valuable."

"No shit, money?" Tuck looked at a piece of *fei* standing in a yard as they passed. It was five feet tall and nearly two feet thick. "What do your pay phones look like?" Tuck asked with a grin.

The driver didn't find it funny. He let Tucker out at the dock, which was suspiciously shipless.

Tuck saw a bearded, red-faced white man sitting in the shade of a forklift, smoking a cigarette.

"G'day," the man said. He was about thirty. In good shape. "*Impela my tribe?*"

"Huh?" Tuck said.

"American, then?"

Tuck nodded. "You Australian?"

"Royal Navy," the man said. He pulled a hat from behind him and tapped on it. "Join me?" He motioned for Tuck to sit next to him on the concrete.

Tuck dragged his pack into the shade, dropped it, and extended his hand to the Australian. "Tucker Case."

The Australian took his hand and nearly crushed it. "Commander Brion Frick. Have a seat, mate. Looks like you been on the piss for a fortnight, if you don't mind my saying."

He handed Tucker a business card. It bore the seal of the Royal Australian Navy, Frick's name and rank, and the designation NAVAL INTELLIGENCE. Tuck looked again at the scruffy Australian, then back at the card.

"Naval Intelligence, huh? What do you do?"

"I'm a spy, mate. You know, secret stuff. Very hush-hush."

Tuck wondered just how secret a spy could be who had his status printed on a business card.

"Espionage, huh?"

"Well, right now we're watching the Yapese Navy don't make a move."

"Yap has a navy?"

"Only one patrol boat, and she's broken right now. Yapese put gas in the diesel engine. But you can't be too careful, lest the little buggers get it in their mind to launch a surprise attack. That's her over there." He nodded down the wharf. Tuck spotted a rusted boat designed like a Chinese junk with the word YAP stenciled on the side in flaking orange Rust-Oleum. A half-dozen Yapese, thin brown men with high cheekbones and potbellies, were lounging on the deck in loincloths, drinking beer.

Tuck said, "I guess an attack *would* be a surprise."

"Ain't as easy a job as it looks. Yapese can lull you into a false sense of security. They might sit there without moving for two, three weeks, then just when you start to relax, *wham*, they make their move."

"Right," Tucker said. The only damage the patrol boat looked capable of inflicting was a case of tetanus for the crew.

A mile past the Yapese Navy waves crashed on the reef, just a line of white against the turquoise sea. Cottony clouds rose out of the sea into shining columns. Tuck scanned the horizon for a ship.

"Is the *Micro Trader* in yet?"

"Been in and gone," Frick said. "She'll be back around in six weeks or so."

"Dammit," Tuck said. "I can't fucking believe it. I need to get to Alualu."

"Why'd you want to go out there?"

"I'm a pilot. I'm supposed to be flying for a missionary out there."

"Boys and I were out there in the patrol boat last week. God-forsaken place."

Tuck lit up at the mention of the patrol boat. Maybe he could catch a ride. "You have a patrol boat?"

"Seventy-footer. Some of the boys are out with it now, tuna fishin' with the CIA. Don't mention it, though. Secret, you know."

"What's the CIA doing down here?"

Frick raised a blond eyebrow. "Keepin' an eye on the Yapese Navy."

"I thought you were doing that."

"Well, I am, ain't I? And when they come back, it's my turn to go fishin'. Lovely, us bein' allies and all. Cuts the work in half. Want to suck some piss?"

"Pardon?" Tuck wasn't ready for any kind of bizarre native customs.

"Drink some beers, mate. If you keep an eye on the Yappies, I'll run down to the store and grab some beers."

"Sounds good." Tuck was ready to take the edge off his headache. Besides, there was still a chance for a ride out to the island.

Frick put his hat on Tuck's head. "Right then. By the power invested in me by the Australian Royal Navy, et cetera, et cetera, I hearby deputize you as official intelligence officer until I get back. Do you swear?"

"Swear what?"

"Just swear."

"Sure."

"There it is." Frick started walking off.

"What do I do if they make a move?"

"How the bloody hell should I know?"

Tuck watched the Yapese Navy for an hour before they all stood up and left the boat. He was pretty sure that this did not constitute a defense emergency, but just in case he decided to walk up the street to see what had happened to Frick. The pack felt even heavier now, and he guessed that it was the responsibility for Australian people that weighed him down. (A woman had once offered Tucker a goldfish in a bowl, and Tuck had graciously declined it on the basis that it was too much responsibility and would probably die anyway. He felt the same way about the Australians.)

The concrete streets of Colonia were bleached white and stained with three-foot red strips of betel nut spit on either side and lined with thick jungle vegetation. Off the streets Tuck could see tin hovels, children playing in the mud, women passing the hottest part of the day combing lice from each other's hair in the shade of a tin-roofed porch. The women wore wraparound skirts, black with brightly colored stripes, and went topless. All but the youngest of them were enormously fat by Western standards, and Tuck felt his idealized picture of the beautiful island girls fade to a lice-infested, rotund reality. Still, there was something in their gentle grooming and in the quiet concentration of the children that made him feel sad and a little lonely. If only he could run into a woman he could talk to. A Western woman—she wouldn't have to know he was a eunuch.

He broke out of the jungle into the open street of Colonia's main "business district." On one side was a marina with a restaurant and bar (or so the sign said), on the other a two-story, stucco minimall of shops and snack bars. Around it, in the shade of the modern portico, stood perhaps a hundred Yapese, mostly women, some young men in bright blue loincloths, all shirtless. The islanders all had bright red lips and teeth from chewing betel nut. Even the little children were chewing the narcotic cud and spitting periodically into the street. Tuck walked in among them, hoping to find someone to ask about Frick's whereabouts, but none made eye contact. The women and girls turned their backs to him. The men just looked away or pretended to pay attention to sprinkling powdered coral on to a split green betel nut before beginning a chew.

He went into a surprisingly modern grocery store and was relieved to see that the prices were in American dollars, the signs in English. He picked up a quart of bottled water and took it to the checkout counter, where a woman in a lavalava and a blue polyester smock rang up his purchase and held out her hand for the money.

"Do you know where I can find Commander Brion Frick?" Tuck asked her.

She took his money, turned to the cash drawer, and turned back to him with his change without uttering a word. Tuck repeated his question and the woman turned away from him. Finally he left, thinking, She must not speak English.

He ran into Frick coming out of the store. The spy had a six-pack tucked under his arm.

"I was looking for you," Tuck said. "The Yapese Navy took off."

"You could have asked inside. They knew where I was."

"I did. The woman wouldn't talk to me."

"Not allowed to," Frick said. "It's bad manners to make eye contact. Yapese women aren't allowed to talk to a man unless he's a relative. If a woman and a man are seen speaking in public, they're considered married on the spot. Shame too. Ever seen so many bare titties in all your life? Tough grabbin' a snog if you can't talk to them."

Tucker didn't want to talk about it. "You were supposed to come back to the wharf."

Frick looked affronted. "I was on my way. Didn't think you'd desert your post. I hope you're a better pilot than you are a spy. Letting them sneak off like that."

"Look, Frick, I need to get to Alualu right away. Can you take me in your patrol boat?"

"Love to, mate, but we've got a mission as soon as the boys get back from fishin'. We've got to tow the Yapese patrol boat down to Darwin for repairs. Won't be back for a fortnight at least."

"Doesn't it make more sense to leave it broken? I mean, in the interest of watching them?"

The spy raised an eyebrow. "What threat are they with a broken boat?"

"Exactly," Tuck said.

"You obviously don't know a wit about maintaining job security. Missionary Air might take you out, but I hear their plane is down for a while. Fishing boats are all Chinese. Buggers wouldn't piss on you if you were on fire. You might charter a dingy, but I doubt that you'll find anyone willing to take you across four hundred kilometers of open sea in an outboard. There's fellows do it off Perth, but the West Coast is full of loonies anyway. Get yourself a room and wait. We'll take you out when we get back."

"I don't know if I can wait that long." Tuck stood up. "Where should I go to charter a boat?"

Frick pointed to a large Mobil oil tank at the edge of the harbor. "Try heading down to the fueling station. Should be able to find someone down there who needs the gas money."

"Thanks, Frick, I appreciate it." Tucker shook the spy's hand.

"No worries, mate. You watch yourself out there. I hear that doctor's a bedbug."

"Good to know." He waved over his shoulder as he walked down to the edge of the harbor. A group of women chewing betel nut in the shade of a hibiscus tree turned away from him as he passed.

He walked along the bank and looked into the cloudy green water at the harbor's edge. Tiny multicolored fish darted in and out of the shallows, feeding on some kind of shrimp. Brown mud skippers, their eyes atop their heads like a frog's, walked on their pectoral fins across a small mudflat that had formed around the roots of a mangrove tree. Tucker stopped and watched them. They were fish, yet they spent most of their time on land. It was as if they had evolved to a certain point, then just couldn't make a decision to leave the water, grow into mammals, and finally invent personal stereos. For sixty million years they had been hanging out on the mudflats, looking at each other with periscope eyes and goofy froggy grins and saying: "What do you want do?" "I don't know. What do *you* want to do?" "I don't know. Want to go up on the land or stay in the water?" "I don't know. Let's hang out on the mudflat a little longer."

Tuck completely understood. Although if he had been a mud

skipper, after a couple of million years of dragging himself around the mudflat, he would have lost his patience and yelled, "Hey, can I get some feet over here!", thus moving evolution along.

He was enjoying the superiority of the Monday morning quarterback (And in a world created in six days, what day but Monday could it be?), feeling a little smarter, a little more worldly than the mud skippers, when it occurred to him that he had no idea how to proceed. He could find the telecom center, if there was one, and contact the doctor, but then what would he do? Sit for two weeks on Yap until the Australians returned? Maybe they were wrong. Maybe there was a privately owned plane on the island. What about a dingy? How bad could it be. The sea looked calm enough. That's it, take to the sea.

Or perhaps he should just stay on Yap and find a sympathetic woman to take his mind off the problem. It had always worked before, not to positive results, but it had worked, dammit. Women made him feel better. He ached for a Mary Jean Cosmetics consultant. A cool, thin, married woman, armored in pantyhose and a bulletproof bouffant. A sweet, shocked, backsliding Born Again on a one-time sin quest to remind her of why redemption was so so good. Mud skipper thinking.

He was reeling with the heat and the lack of possibilities when he saw her, up ahead, walking by the water's edge, her back to him: a thin blonde in a flowered dress with a swing to her walk like a welcome home parade.

15

The Navigator

Out on the edge of the world, with no place to stay, no way to move on, no job, no life, no friends; hurt, confused, hot, thirsty, and irritated, Tuck was desperate. Desperate for just the momentary satisfaction that might come from attracting an attractive woman. No matter that he couldn't do anything about the attraction.

What was she doing out here? Who cares? What a walk!

He quickened his pace, his legs and shoulders protesting against the weight of his pack, and approached within a couple of steps of the blonde.

"Excuse me," he called.

She turned. Tuck stopped and backed up a step. Something is wrong here. Very, very wrong.

"Oh, baby," she said, hand to her chest as if trying to catch her breath. "You scare little Kimi. Why you sneakin' up like that?"

Tuck was dumbfounded. She wasn't a natural blonde. Her skin was dark and she had the high cheekbones and angular features of a Filipino. Long false eyelashes, bright red lipstick, but lines in the face that were a little too harsh, a jawline that was a little too square. The dress was tight around the chest and there was nothing there but muscle. She wore a huge black medallion at her throat that looked as if it was made of animal fur. She needed a shave.

"I'm sorry," Tuck said. "I thought you were something—er, someone else."

Then the medallion turned its head and looked at him. Tuck let out an involuntary scream and jumped back. The medallion was wearing tiny rhinestone sunglasses. It squeaked at Tucker. It was the biggest bat he had ever seen, hanging there upside down with its wings folded.

"That's a bat!"

."Fruit bat, baby. Don't be scared. This Roberto. He no like the light. He like you, though." Roberto squeaked again. He had the face of a fox or perhaps a small dog—a shaven Pomeranian with wings. "I'm Kimi. What you name, baby?" Kimi extended his hand limply to shake or perhaps for a kiss.

Tuck took two fingers, keeping his eye on the bat. "Tucker Case. Nice to meet you, Kimi." He was horrified. Thirty seconds ago he'd been having lustful thoughts about a guy! A guy wearing a fruit bat!

"You look like you need a date. Kimi love you good long time, twenny bucks. Whatever you need, Kimi can do."

"No, thanks. I don't need a date. What I need is a boat."

"Kimi can get boat. You like it in boat? Kimi take you round the world in a boat?" He giggled and patted Roberto's little upside-down head. "That funny, huh?"

Tucker forced a smile. "No, I need a boat and someone who can pilot it out to an island."

"You need a boat, Kimi can get boat. Kimi can pilot too."

"Thanks anyway, but I really . . ."

Roberto shrieked. Tuck jumped back. Kimi said, "Roberto say he want to go on boat with you. How far is island?"

Tucker couldn't believe he was having this conversation. He hadn't really decided he would go by boat. "It's called Alualu. It's about two hundred and fifty miles north of here."

"No problem," Kimi said without hesitation. "My father was great navigator. He teach me everything. I take you to island and maybe we have party too. You have money?"

Tuck nodded.

"You wait over there in shade. We be right back." Kimi turned and wiggled away. Tucker tried not to watch him walk. He was feeling sick to his stomach. He walked to a grove of palm trees that grew along the harbor and sat down to wait.

Kimi piloted the eighteen-foot fiberglass skiff out of a shantytown built over the water, across the harbor, to a dock in front of the marina restaurant. Roberto had unfolded his wings and was crawling spiderlike over Kimi's head and back, looking for a comfortable spot to get out of the light.

Tucker walked to the dock and looked at the boat, then out past the harbor, where waves were crashing on the reef, then back at the little boat. He wasn't sure what he had expected, but he was sure this wasn't it. Something bigger, maybe a cabin cruiser, with twin diesels and a big wheelhouse with some radar stuff spinning on the top—a modest but well-stocked wet bar, perhaps.

"I got you boat!" Kimi said. "You give me money now, I go get gas and look at map."

Tucker didn't budge. The engine was a forty-horse Yamaha outboard. A rubber tube ran from the motor to a gas tank that took up nearly all the space between the two seats. Tuck guessed it would hold at least a hundred gallons of fuel, maybe more. "Are you sure this thing has the range to make it out there?"

"No problem. Give me money for gas. Five hundred dollar."

"You're insane!"

"Gas very expensive here."

"You're insane and your bat's glasses are crooked."

"I have to pay man for boat. The rest is for pilot. You buy water, flashlight, and two mango, two papaya for Roberto, and two box Pop Tarts for Kimi. Strawberry. "

Tucker felt he was being hustled. "For five hundred dollars you can get your own mangoes and Pop Tarts."

"Okay, bye-bye." Kimi said. "Say bye-bye to cheap sweaty American, Roberto." Kimi moved Roberto onto his shoulders and pulled the cord to start the engine.

Tuck imagined himself stuck on Yap for another two weeks. "No, wait!" He unclipped the flap of his pack and dug inside.

Kimi killed the outboard, turned, and grinned. There was lipstick on his teeth. "Money, please."

Tuck handed down a stack of bills. He didn't like it, but he didn't have a choice. Actually, not having a choice made it a little easier. "Are we going to leave right away?"

"We go through reef before dark so we no smash up and drown. After that it better to go in dark. Go by stars."

Smash up? "Shouldn't we call for weather?"

Kimi laughed. "You smell storm? See storm in sky?"

Tuck looked around. Except for a few mushroom-shaped clouds beyond the reef, it was clear. He smelled only tropical flowers on the breeze and something skunky rising up from his armpits. "No."

"Meet me here in half hour." Kimi started the motor and putted off across the harbor toward a big tank with the Mobil logo stenciled on the side.

Tuck walked to the store and bought the supplies, then found the telecom center a few doors down and sent a handwritten fax to the doctor on Alualu to let him know that his new pilot was on the way.

He was waiting at the dock when Kimi returned in the skiff, his wig tied down with a red chiffon scarf. Roberto wore a smaller scarf with holes cut for his ears. Strangely, the scarf, in conjunction with the sunglasses, made Roberto look a little like Diana Ross. They say there is a finite number of faces in the world . . .

Tucker threw the heavy pack into the front of the boat, then climbed in and sat down in front of the enormous gas tank. Kimi threw the transmission lever on the motor, twisted the hand grip, and piloted the skiff out into the harbor toward the reef.

Kimi steered the boat out of the deep green of the harbor to the turquoise water of the channel. Tuck could see the reef, tan and red coral, just a few feet below the surface at the edge of the channel. He spotted small fish darting around great heads of brain coral. They were more like streaks of color than animals, and as one disappeared another appeared in the line of sight. A few long, slender trumpet fish, looking as if they had been forged from silver, swam adjacent to the boat, then turned and cruised into the reef.

They passed the edge of the reef and into the open sea with only a slight bump into the first few swells. Kimi cranked up the motor and the skiff lifted and rode across the tops of the waves, bucking and dropping a gentle six inches, thumping out a drumbeat as counterpoint to the whining outboard. Tucker relaxed and leaned back as Kimi skirted the reef, traveling toward the setting sun until he cleared the island and could make the turn north to Alualu.

For the first time since the crash, Tucker felt good, felt as if he was on his way to something better. He'd made a decision and acted on it and in eighteen hours he would be ready to start his new job. He'd be a pilot again, making good money, flying a great aircraft. And with some healing, he'd be a man again too.

A quarter mile from Yap, Kimi made a gradual turn that put the sun at their left shoulders. Tuck watched the sun bubble into the ocean. Columns of vertical cumulus clouds turned to cones of pink cotton candy, then as the sun became a red wafer on the horizon, they turned candy-apple red, with purple rays reaching out of them like searchlights. The water was neon over wet asphalt, blood-spattered gunmetal—colors from the cover of a detective novel where heroes drink hard and beauty is always treacherous.

Tucker searched the sky for cumulus clouds that looked like they might have aspirations to become thunderheads. How in the hell were you supposed to see weather from sea level?

Just then a swell lifted the front of the boat and slammed it down. Tuck felt his tailbone bark on the edge of the seat and was just bracing himself when another swell bucked him to the floor of the boat and a sudden gust of wind soaked him with spray.

16

And Now, the Weather Report

The High Priestess sat on the lanai watching the sunset, taking sips from a glass of chilled vodka between bites of a banana. The intercom beeped inside the house and she cocked an ear to the open window.

"Beth, can you come down to my office? This is important." The Sorcerer was in a panic.

He's always in a panic, she thought. She put her vodka down on the bamboo table and tossed the banana out into the sand. She padded across the teak deck, through the french doors to the intercom, and laid an elegant finger on the talk button.

"I'm on my way," she said.

She started toward the back door of the house—a two-room bungalow fashioned from bamboo, teak, and thatch—and caught sight of herself in the full-length mirror. "Shit." She was naked, of course, and she'd have to cut across the compound to get to the Sorcerer's office. Life had become a lot more complicated since they had hired the guards.

She stormed into the bedroom and grabbed an oversized 49ers jersey with the sleeves cut off out of her closet, then stepped into some sandals and headed out the back door. She wasn't really dressed, but it might keep the Sorcerer off her back and the ninjas off her front.

The compound consisted of half a dozen buildings spread over a three-acre clearing covered with white coral gravel and concrete and surrounded by a twelve-foot chain-link fence topped with razor wire. At the front of the compound was a pier and a small beach that led to the only channel through the reef. At the back a new

Learjet sat on a concrete pad, just inside the fence. Outside of the fence, the concrete runway bisected the island. Past the runway lay the jungles, the taro patches, the villages, and the beaches of the Shark People.

The office was a low concrete building with steel doors and a roof covered in solar electric panels that shone red in the setting sunlight. She nodded to the guard by the door, who didn't move until she passed, then tried to get a glimpse in the side of her jersey. She slammed the door behind her.

"What's up? You almost done with the satellite dish? My shows are coming on."

He turned from a computer screen, a piece of fax paper crumpled in his hand. "We've hired an idiot."

"Do you want to be specific or should I assume that one of the ninjas has distinguished himself above the others?"

"The pilot, Beth. He missed the *Micro Trader* on Yap."

"Shit!"

"It's worse." He held out the fax to her. "It's from him. He's chartered a small boat. He says he'll be here tomorrow."

She looked over the fax, confused. "That's sooner than he was going to get here. What's the problem?"

"This." The Sorcerer pushed back in his chair and pointed to the computer screen. The image looked like a blender full of green and black paint.

"It looks like a blender full of green paint," she said. "What is it?"

"That, my dear, is Marie."

"Sebastian, you've been out here too long. I know you like abstract art and all . . ."

"It's a satellite picture of typhoon Marie. And she's a big one." He pointed to a dot to one side of the screen. "That's Alualu."

"So it's going to miss us."

"We'll catch the edge of it. We'll have to put the jet in the hangar, tie everything down, but it shouldn't be too bad. The problem is that the eye will pass right over where our pilot is going to be. I can't believe he went to sea without checking the weather."

She shrugged. "So we have to get a new pilot. Tucker Case, meet Marie." She smiled and her eyes shone like desolate stars. Too bad, she thought. The pilot would have been fun.

17

Foul-Weather Friend

Tuck was amazed by what the human body could achieve when pressed to its limits: lift tractors, trek a hundred miles through the tundra after being partially eviscerated by a Kodiak bear, live for months on grubs and water sucked from soak holes, and in this particular case, vomit for two hours straight after having ingested nothing but alcohol and airline peanuts for two days. The stuff coming out of him was pure bile, burning acrid and sour, and with the bull rider pitching of the boat, half of it always ended up down the front of him. And between heaves there was no respite, just constant motion and soaking spray. His stomach muscles twisted into knots.

It started with the swells rising, first a few feet, then to ten. Kimi piloted the boat up the face of each as if climbing a hill; they were dashed by the whitecap, then a sled ride down into a trough where they were faced with the next black wall of water. Roberto climbed down into Kimi's dress and clung there like a furry tumor. The navigator cried out each time the spray washed over him as Roberto's wing claws dug into his ribs.

"Tie down you pack. Tie you belt to the boat," Kimi shouted.

Tuck found a coil of nylon rope and a folding knife in his pack and tied himself and the pack to the front seat. He noticed that the space under the seat was filled with dense Styrofoam. The boat was, theoretically, unsinkable. Good, someone would find their beaten, shark-eaten bodies. He threw a length of rope to Kimi, who secured it around his own waist.

The wind came up as if someone had spooled up a jet engine, going from ten to sixty knots in an instant, dumping gallons of water into the boat with each wave, drowning out the sound of the out-board.

Kimi screamed an order to Tuck, but it was lost in the wind. Tuck caught one word: "Bail!"

Riding down the face of a wave, he took the time to look around the boat for a container, but found only the gallon of drinking water. He took the folding knife from his pocket and slashed the top off of the jug. He dumped the fresh water, then, with his feet braced against the inside of the bow and his spine against the seat, he began bailing between his legs, taking a full gallon with each scoop, throwing it with the wind. He bailed as if in a "run for your life" sprint and he was winded and aching after only a minute, but he couldn't seem to get ahead of the storm. The boat was riding lower in the water.

He ventured a glance back to Kimi and saw the navigator had found a coffee can and was braced between the seat and the gas tank, bailing with one hand while steering with the other. His scarf and fallen around his neck and was trailing the blonde wig behind him in the wind. The motor was cranked full-out, and Kimi was trying to keep the boat steered into the waves. If one caught them from the side, they would roll and continue to roll until the storm consumed them.

Tuck slowed his pace and tried to fall into some kind of sustainable rhythm. It began to rain, the drops coming in almost horizontal, and as they topped the next wave Tuck realized that half of the sky had disappeared. They were only at the edge of the storm. The navigator was screaming at him. The sea, the sky, the boat faded to black. One second he was squinting saltwater out of his eyes and staring at an obsidian wall ahead of the bow, then everything went black. Total sensory overload, total sensory deprivation. He looked around for the stars, the moon, a highlight or shadow somewhere, but there was nothing but wind and wet and cold and ache. He shivered and nearly curled into the fetal position in the bow to wait for death. The navigator's screaming gave him a bearing.

"We need light!"

Tuck braced himself, then dug into the saturated pack until he came out with two waterproof flashlights. *Bless you, Jake Skye.*

He hit the sealed switches.

Light. Enough to see that Kimi was steering them parallel to an ominous wall of water. They would be swamped. The navigator slammed the outboard to one side and gunned it. The little boat whipped around just in time to meet the oncoming wave, ride up and over it. Tucker clung to the boat like a newborn monkey to its mother.

Tuck lashed the lights to the anchor pulley at the bow, one pointed forward, one into the boat, then he resumed bailing.

A monster wave rose up thirty feet and slammed down over them. When Tuck blinked the salt out of his eyes, he saw that the boat was all but a foot full of water. Another wave like that would swamp the motor. Without the motor to steer, they were lost. Bailing wasn't enough.

We're going to die, he thought.

Then the noise of the storm was gone.

"No, you're not," came the voice, "you fuckin' mook." The roar of the wind and the screams of the navigator were gone. There was only the voice. "There's a tarpaulin in your pack. Lash it over the boat so you don't take on any more water. Then move to the stern and bail."

Now there was a picture in Tuck's mind of what he was to do. There were eyelets on the outside of the gunwales to accommodate the line around the edges of the tarp. He needed only to hook the line around the boat and tie it off back by Kimi, leaving just enough of the boat open for the navigator to steer and him to bail water.

"You got it, ace?"

Tuck could see it and he knew he could do it. "Thanks," he said. Forget questioning where the voice was coming from. He nodded. The storm roared back over him.

Five minutes later the boat was covered and began to rise in the water as Tuck sat next to the navigator and bailed.

"You steer!" Kimi screamed.

Tucker took the tiller as the navigator let go and tried to rub his hand out of a cramped claw.

Tuck took the boat up the face of a monster wave and the skiff went airborne. With no resistance on the propeller, the motor shrieked and Tuck dumped the throttle to keep it from blowing up. The bow tilted skyward and Kimi grabbed the gunwale just in time to avoid being dumped off the stern. They landed hard and the motor nearly went under. The motor sputtered. Tuck worked the throttle to bring it back to life.

They were already going up the face of another wave, steeper than the last. If the wind caught them at the top, they would flip. Tuck suddenly remembered a surfing move from his youth. The cut-back. There was no way they could continue into the wind and into the waves. Halfway up the face of the wave, he twisted the throttle and threw the motor sideways. It coughed as if expelling a hairball, then roared, sending them across the face of the wave.

"What you doing?" Kimi shouted.

Tuck didn't answer. He was looking for the pocket, the place where the face of the wave would stay the same. If only the motor could maintain speed.

The wave was creeping up on them, looming above their backs, but then they were high enough for the wind to catch them. Just enough boost. Just enough speed. The boat flattened out on the face of the wave. They were surfing, a thirty-foot wall of water waiting to crush them from behind should Tuck lose the pocket.

Strangely, Tuck felt elated. It was a small victory, maybe even a temporary one, but they were running with the storm and he was in control of something for the first time since the plane crash. He watched the angle of the boat on the face of the wave, gauged its speed, its steepness, and made the adjustments that would keep them alive. The black water seemed to eat up the flashlight beams, but he could see the wave becoming steeper and rising higher as it climbed the ocean shelf toward the hungry reef.

18

Land Ho

The island was little more than a coral cupcake with a guano frosting. Not a hundred yards wide at its widest point and only five feet above sea level at its highest, it served as a resting place for seabirds, a nesting place for turtles, and purchase for forty-eight coconut palms. The foliage and coconuts had all been torn from the palms, and the storm-driven waves breaking on the surrounding reef frothed over the island, beating against the trunks and washing away the precious topsoil. Heavy as they were, some of the palms were being undermined by the sea and would soon wash away.

Of the three travelers, only Roberto knew the island was there. As a young bat, he had stopped there to rest after leaving Guam, his birthplace, on his way to someplace where the mangoes were sweet and the natives did not consider fruit bat a delicacy. But right now he was too busy hiding inside Kimi's dress, screeching and clawing and generally trying to keep warm, to mention to the navigator that the reason they were suddenly riding the face of an increasingly steep fifty-foot wave was because they were about to crash over a reef.

By the time Tucker Case realized what was happening, they were inside an immense tube of water, surfing inside of the curl of the wave. The flashlights refracted off the green water, illuminating the tube, making it appear as if they were inside a giant seething Coke bottle. Tuck tried to keep the boat pointed toward the narrow circle of blackness where the bottle cap would go, where they would have to go to escape. He'd seen films of surfers shooting the curl on the North Shore of Hawaii. It could be done. He clung to that vision, even as the wave passed over the reef and collapsed upon them.

The boat rolled once, twice, three times, then tossed end over end and spun just under the surface as the wave frothed over the island. Kimi and Tuck were wound against the boat by their lifelines, beaten against the trunks of the palms, tossed and battered against the boat. For Tucker there was no up, no down, no way to know when he might take a breath of life-giving air or suck seawater and die. He held his breath until he felt as if he would explode, then was slammed between the boat and a tree and he let go.

Roberto's wing claws cut deep furrows into Kimi's ribs as he scrambled for air. The navigator had taken a glancing blow across the forehead as the boat rolled over him and was knocked unconscious.

Tuck felt himself pulled away from the boat, spun for a moment, then the pressure of the lifeline around his waist. He could see the lights attached to the boat, still shining, the only visual input in the sensory chaos. The boat had caught on something and he was trailing out behind it. Something bumped against his ribs and he reached for it instinctively, catching a handful of Kimi's dress. Roberto was clinging to Kimi's head, growling into the wind.

They had passed through the island and come out on the other side. The boat had caught on the last palm tree before they were swept out to sea again.

Tuck caught his lifeline with one hand, then wrapped his other arm around Kimi's chest. Slowly, working against the streaming current, more like a river now that the waves had been broken by the reef and the island, he pulled them back to the boat.

The boat was afloat, but barely, held up by the Styrofoam underseats and the air trapped in the gas tank. Only an inch or two of gunwale showed above the water. Tuck crawled in, took one deep breath, then dragged the lifeless navigator in after him. Roberto scrambled on Kimi's head to escape the sea and was almost taken by the wind. Tucker caught the giant bat by the throat and lifted him from Kimi's head to his own back, wincing as Roberto's claws penetrated his shirt. Then he hung the navigator over the side and began pumping the water out of his lungs.

After a few seconds, he flipped him again and administered mouth-to-mouth until Kimi coughed and vomited up a stream of seawater. Tuck held his head.

"You okay?"

Kimi nodded as he sucked in painful lungfuls of air. Once he had his breath, he said, "Roberto?"

Tuck pointed to the little dog face that was looking over his shoulder.

Kimi managed a smile. "Roberto! Come." He took the bat from Tuck's back and held him to his chest.

They were safe, relatively; sheltered by the island from the monster swells, they had only the wind and the rain to deal with. The tarpaulin was gone. The boat was full of water, but it was afloat. Miraculously, the flashlights were still attached. Tucker could see the tree that had caught them. He fell back into the bow, hooking his armpits over the gunwales, then slipped into a state of exhausted unconsciousness that could almost be called sleep.

19

Water, Water

At first light the coconut palm that had saved them finally gave up and tipped over, releasing the boat to the sea. The outgoing tide carried the skiff and its sleeping passengers through a break in the reef to the open ocean.

Tuck, sitting chest deep in seawater in the bow, was dreaming of being lost in the desert when a flying fish smacked him in the side of the head. Startled, he reached up instinctively, as one might slap at a biting mosquito, and caught the fish in his right hand. He opened his eyes. In his mind he was still in the desert, dying of thirst, and the fact that he was now holding on to something that looked like a trout with wings seemed a cruel surrealist joke. He looked around, saw the boat, Kimi slumped in the back, ocean and sky, and nothing else—there was no land in sight.

He threw the fish at Kimi. It bounced off the navigator's forehead and into the sea. Kimi screamed and sat up abruptly. Roberto—sunglasses akimbo—poked his head out the neck of Kimi's dress and screeched at Tucker.

"What you do that for?" Kimi said.

"Nice piece of navigation," Tuck said. Then he mocked Kimi's broken English. "You smell storm? You see storm in sky?"

"Oh, you big-time pilot. Why you not check weather? What kind of dumb fuck American try to go two hundred miles in outboard, huh?"

"You told me it was no problem."

"You paying Kimi big money. Not a problem."

"Well, it's a fucking problem now, isn't it?"

Kimi stroked Roberto's head to calm him. "Stop yelling. You scare Roberto."

"I don't care about Roberto. We're half-sunk in the middle of the Pacific and we don't have a motor. I'd say we have a problem."

Kimi stopped ministering to Roberto and looked up. "No motor?" He turned and looked back at the empty motor board. There were marks where the clamps had raked across it as the motor pulled off in the tumble. He turned back to Tuck and grinned sheepishly. "Whoops."

"We're dead," Tuck said.

Kimi looked back again where the motor should have been, just to make sure that it was still gone. "I ask that man, 'Is motor on good?' He say, 'Oh yes, is clamp on very tight.' I pay him good money and he lie. Oh, Kimi is very mad."

Roberto barked in agreement.

"Stop it!" Tucker shouted. Roberto ducked into Kimi's dress again. "We've got to get some of this water out of here. We have no motor. We can't go anywhere. We're adrift, lost . . ."

"Alive," Kimi interrupted. "I get you out of typhoon alive and you just yell and say bad things. I quit. You get new navigator. Roberto say you mean, nasty, Chevy-driving, milk-drinking, American dog fucker."

"I don't drink milk," Tuck said. Ha! Won that round.

"That what he say."

"Roberto does not talk!"

"Not to you, dog fucker. You no . . ." Kimi paused in mid-rant and retrieved the coffee can, which had been tied to the boat with a string, and started furiously scooping water out of the boat. "You right. Now we bail."

"What?" Tuck looked up to see Kimi was looking, wide-eyed, out to sea. Tuck followed his gaze to a spot twenty yards in front of the boat where a triangular fin was describing slow arcs in the swells.

"Hurry," Kimi shouted. "He coming in."

Tucker reached for his pack, causing the bow to dip under the water by a foot. Before he could adjust his weight to counterbalance the boat, the shark came over the gunwale, snapping its jaws like a man-eating puppet.

Tuck stood up to escape the jaws and the bow lurched deeper underwater. The shark slid into the boat as Tuck went backward over the side.

Fear bolted through his body as if the water had been electrified.

He wanted to move in all directions at once. He kicked hard and came up a few feet from the boat to see the shark slide back into the water.

"Get in boat!" Kimi screamed. He was standing with his feet wide, trying to keep the boat from capsizing.

Tuck kicked so hard that he raised out of the water to the waist, then he fell toward the boat, catching the gunwale with one hand. Kimi shifted his weight to counterbalance and Tuck pulled himself in just as something hit his foot. He jerked his foot so hard he nearly went out of the boat on the opposite side, then he twisted in time to see the shark sliding down into the water with his shoe in its mouth.

"Behind you!" Kimi screamed.

Another shark rose up at Tuck's back. He swung around and punched it on the snout as hard as he could, taking the skin off of his knuckles on the shark's sandpaper skin. The shark slid away.

The motion in the bow caused the stern to dip underwater and the next attack came at Kimi. He tossed Roberto into the air as the shark came into the boat. Roberto spread his wings and soared into the sky. Kimi reached down and came up with the rubber fuel line.

Tucker looked for anything they could use as a weapon, then remembered the folding knife he had put in his pocket the night before. It was still there.

Kimi was slapping the shark with the rubber hose and backing his way up onto the huge gas tank that made up the midsection of the boat. Tuck opened the knife, then lunged forward at the navigator. "Kimi!"

Kimi reached back and Tuck fit the handle of the knife into his hand. The shark had worked half of its nine-foot body into the boat. Its tail thrashed at the water to power the shark up onto the gas tank. Kimi scrambled backward. Roberto swooped and screeched in the air above.

Kimi's right foot found purchase on the screw cap of the gas tank and he sat up. Tuck thought he was going to strike the shark with the knife, but instead he cut the gas line and squirted a stream of gas into the shark's gaping mouth. The shark thrashed and slid off the side of the boat.

Kimi brandished the knife in the air. "Yeah, fuckface, you run away. That not taste so sweet as Kimi, huh?" He fell back onto the gas tank and took a deep breath. "We show that shark who the boss."

Tuck said, "Kimi, there's more." He pointed to set of fins approaching from the stern.

20

Leadership's a Bitch

The storm had been easy on the Shark People. A little thatch lost from a roof here and there, a cookhouse blown over, some breadfruit and coconuts stripped from the trees, but not enough to cause hardship. Some seawater had washed into the taro patch, but only time would tell if it was enough to kill the crop. The Shark People went slowly about the business of cleaning up, the women doing most of the work while the men sat in the shade of the men's house, drinking alcoholic *tuba* and pretending to discuss important religious matters. Mainly they were there to pass the heat of the day and get good and drunk before dinner.

Malink, the high chief of the Shark People, was late rising. He awoke shivering and afraid, trying to figure out how to interpret a strange dream. He rolled off of his grass sleeping mat, then rose creakily and ambled out of the hut to relieve himself at the base of a giant breadfruit tree.

He was a short, powerfully built man of sixty. His hair was bushy and gone completely white. His skin, once a light butterscotch, had been burned over the years to the dark brown of a tarnished penny. Like most of the Shark men, he wore only a cotton loincloth and a wreath of fresh flowers in his hair (left there by one of his four daughters while he slept). The image of a shark was tattooed on his left pectoral muscle, a B-26 bomber on the other.

He went back into the hut and pulled a steel ammo box out of the rafters. Inside lay a nylon web belt with a holster that held a portable phone, his badge of leadership, his direct line to the Sorcerer. The only time he had ever used it was when one of his daughters had come down with a fever during the night. He had pushed the button and the Sorcerer had come to the village and given her medicine. He was afraid to use the phone now, but the dream had told him that he must deliver a message.

Malink would have liked to go down to the men's house and discuss his decision for a few hours with the others, but he knew that he couldn't. He had to deliver the dream message. Vincent had said so, and Vincent knew everything.

As he pushed the button, he wished he had never been born a chief.

The High Priestess was also sleeping late, as she always did. The Sorcerer jostled her and she pulled the sheets over her head.

"What?"

"I just got a call from Malink. He says he's had a message from Vincent."

The High Priestess was awake now. Wide awake. She sat upright in bed and the Sorcerer's eyes fell immediately to her naked breasts. "What do you mean he's had a message from Vincent? I didn't give him any message."

The Sorcerer finally looked up at her face. "He was terrified. He said that Vincent came to him in a dream and told him—get this—to tell me that 'the pilot was alive and on his way, and to wait for him.' "

She rubbed the sleep out of her eyes and shook her head. "I don't get it. How did he know about a pilot coming? Did you say something?"

"No, did you?"

"Are you kidding? I'm not stupid, Sebastian, despite what you might think."

"Well, how did he find out? The guards don't know anything. I haven't said anything."

"Maybe it's a coincidence," she said. "Maybe he was just having bad dreams from the storm. Vincent is all he thinks about. It's all any of them think about."

The Sorcerer stood and backed away from the bed, eyeing her suspiciously. "Coincidence or not, I don't like it. I think you need to have an audience with the Shark People and give them a direct message from Vincent. This whole operation depends on us being the voice of Vincent. We can't let them think that they can reach him directly." He turned and started out of the room.

"Sebastian," she said and the Sorcerer paused and looked over his shoulder at her. "What about the pilot? What if Malink is right about the pilot being on his way?"

"Don't be stupid, Beth. The only way to control the faithful is to not become one of them." He turned to leave and was struck in the back of the head by a high-velocity whiskey tumbler. He turned as he dropped to the floor grasping his head.

The High Priestess was standing by the bed wearing nothing but a fine golden chain at her hips and an animal scowl. "You ever call me stupid again and I'll rip your fucking nuts off."

~~~~~~

21

How the Navigator Got from There to Here

Watching the sharks circle the boat, Tuck felt as if he was being sucked down the vortex of a huge bathroom drain.

"We need a better weapon," Tuck said. He remembered a movie once where Spencer Tracy had battled sharks from a small boat with a knife lashed to an oar. "Don't we have any oars?"

Kimi looked insulted. "What wrong with *me*?"

"Not whores. *Oars*!" Tucker pantomimed rowing. "For rowing."

"How I know what you talking about? Malcolme always say oars. 'Bloody oars,' he say. No, we don't have oars."

"Bail," Tuck said.

The navigator began scooping water with the coffee can as Tuck did his best to bail with his hands.

A half hour later the boat was only partially full of water and the sharks had moved on to easier meals. Tucker fell back onto the bow to catch his breath. The sun was still low in the morning sky, but already it burned his skin. The parts of his body not soaked with seawater were soaked with sweat. He dug into the pack and pulled out the liter bottle of water he had bought the day before. It was half-full and it was all they had.

Tuck eyed the navigator, who was bailing intently. He'd never know if Tuck drank all of the water right now. He unscrewed the cap and took a small sip. Nectar of the gods. Keeping his eye on Kimi, he a took a large gulp. He could almost feel his water-starved cells rejoicing at the relief.

As he bailed, Kimi sang softly in Spanish to Roberto, who clung to his back. Whenever he tried to hit a high note, his voice cracked like crumpled parchment. Salt was crusted at the corners of his mouth.

"Kimi, you want a drink?" Tucker crawled onto the gas tank and held the bottle out to the navigator.

Kimi took the bottle. "Thank you," he said. He wiped the mouth of the bottle on his dress and took a deep drink, then poured some water into his palm and held it while Roberto lapped it up. He handed the bottle back to Tucker.

"You drink the rest. You bigger."

Tucker nodded and drained the bottle. "Who's Malcolme?"

"Malcolme buy me from my mother. He from Sydney. He a pimp."

"He bought you?"

"Yes. My mother very poor in Manila. She can't feed me, so she sell me to Malcolme when I am twelve."

"What about your father?"

"He not with us. He a navigator on Satawan. He meet my mother in Manila when he is working on a tuna boat. He marry her and take her to Satawan. She stay for ten years, but she not like it. She say women like dirt to Micronesians. So she take me and go back to Manila when I am nine. Then she sell me to Malcolme. He dress me up and I make big money for him. But he mean to me. He say I have to get rid Roberto, so I run away to find my father to finish teach me to be a navigator. They hear of him on Yap. They say he lost at sea five year ago."

"And he was the one that taught you to navigate?" Tucker knew it was a snotty question, but he had no idea what to say to someone whose mother had sold him to a pimp.

Kimi didn't catch the sarcasm. "He teach me some. It take long time to be navigator. Sometime twenty, thirty year. You want learn, I teach you."

Tucker remembered how difficult it had been to learn Western navigation for his pilot's license. And that was using sophisticated charts and instruments. He could imagine that learning to navigate by the stars—by memory, without charts—would take years. He said, "No, that's okay. It's different for airplanes. We have machines to navigate now."

They bailed until the sun was high in the sky. Tuck could feel his skin baking. He found some sunscreen in the pack and shared it with Kimi, but it was no relief from the heat.

"We need some shade." The tarp was gone. He rifled the pack, looking for something they could use for shade, but for once Jake Skye's bag of tricks failed them.

By noon Tuck was cursing himself for pouring out the gallon of fresh water during the storm. Kimi sat in the bottom of the boat, stroking Roberto's head and mumbling softly to the panting bat.

Tuck tried to pass the time by cleaning his cuts and applying the antibiotic ointment from Jake's first-aid kit. By turning his back and crouching, he was able to create enough privacy to check on his damaged penis. He could see infection around the sutures. He imagined gangrene, amputation, and consequently suicide. Then, looking on the bright side, he realized that he would die of thirst long before the infection had gone that far.

~~~~~~

22

Finding Spam

The octopus jetted across the bottom, over a giant head of brain coral, and tucked itself into a tiny crevice in the reef. Sarapul could see the light purple skin pulsing in the crevice three fathoms down. He took a deep breath and dove, his spear in hand.

The octopus, sensing danger, changed color to the rust brown of the coral around it and adjusted its shape to fit the crannies of its hiding place. Sarapul caught the edge of the crevice with his left hand and thrust in his spear with his right. The spear barely pierced one of the octopus's tentacles and it turned bright red in a chromatic scream, then released its ink. The ink expanded into a smoky cloud in the water. Sarapul dropped his spear to wave the ink away before making another thrust. But his air was gone. He left his spear in the crevice and shot to the surface. The octopus sensed the opening and jetted out of the crevice to a new hiding place before Sarapul knew it was gone.

Sarapul broke the surface cursing. Only three fathoms, eighteen feet, and he couldn't stay down long enough to tease an octopus out of its hole. As a young man, he could dive to twelve fathoms and stay down longer than any of the Shark men. He was glad that no one had been there to see him: an old man who could barely feed himself.

He pulled off his mask and spit into it, then rinsed it with seawater. He looked out to sea, checking for any sign of the sharks that lived in abundance off the reef. There was a boat out there, perhaps half a mile off the reef, drifting. He put on his mask and looked down to get a bearing on his spear so he could retrieve it later. Then he swam a slow crawl toward the drifting boat.

He was winded when he reached the boat and he hung on the side for a few minutes, bobbing in the swell, while he caught his breath. He made his way around to the bow and pulled himself up and in. A huge black bat flew up into his face and winged off toward the island. Sarapul cursed and said some magic words to protect himself, then took a deep breath and examined the bodies.

A man and a woman—and not long dead. There was no smell and no swelling of the bellies. The meat would still be fresh. It had been too long since he'd tasted the long pig. He pinched the man's leg to test the fat. The man moaned. He was still alive. Even better, Sarapul thought. I can eat the dead one and keep the other one fresh!

PART TWO

Island of the Shark People

23

Deus Ex Machina

The Sky Priestess first appeared in 1944 on the nose of a B-26 bomber. Conjured out of cans of enamel by a young aviator named Jack Moses, she lay cool and naked across the aluminum skin, a red pump dangling from a dainty toe, a smile that promised pleasure that no mortal woman could offer. As soon as Moses laid the final brushstroke on her black-seamed stocking, he knew there was something special about this one, something electric and alive that would break his heart when they flew her off to the Pacific. He caught a kiss in his palm and placed it gently on her bottom, then backed down the ladder to survey his work.

He stood on the tarmac for perhaps half an hour, just looking at her, charmed, wishing that he could take her home, or to a museum, or lift her off the skin of the bomber and put her on the ceiling of a cathedral.

Jack Moses didn't notice the major standing at his side until the older man spoke.

"She's something," the major said. And although he wasn't sure why, he removed his hat.

"Ain't she," Moses said. "She's off to Tinian tomorrow. Wish I was going with her."

The major reached out and squeezed Moses's shoulder; he was a little short of breath and the Sky Priestess had set off a stag film in his head. "Put some clothes on her, son. We can't have muffin showing up on a newsreel."

"Yes, sir. I don't have to put a top on her, do I?"

The major smiled. "Son, you put a top on her, I'll have you court-marshaled."

"Yes, sir."

Moses saluted the major and scampered back up the ladder with his brushes and his red enamel and painted a serpentine scarf between her legs.

A week later, as a young pilot named Vincent Bennidetti was leading his crew across the runway to take the Sky Priestess on her first mission, he turned to his navigator and said, "I'd give a year's pay to be that scarf."

A half century away, Beth Curtis pinned a big red bow into her hair, then, one at a time, worked sheer black-seamed stockings up her legs. She stood in front of the mirror and tied the red scarf around her waist, letting the ends trail long between her legs. She stepped into the red pumps, did a quick turnaround in the mirror, and emerged from her bungalow to the sound of the Shark People's drums welcoming her, the Sky Priestess.

Vincent Bennidetti and his crew flew the Sky Priestess on twelve missions and sank six Japanese ships before a fusillade from a Japanese destroyer punctured her wing tanks and took out her right engine. But even as they were limping back toward Tinian, trailing smoke and fuel, the crew of the Sky Priestess knew she watched over them. They were, after all, charmed. For the price of a blown kiss or a pat on the bottom, the Sky Priestess had ushered them into battle like a vicious guardian angel, shielding them even as the other bombers in their squadron flamed into the sea around them. She had shown them where to drop their bombs, then led them through the smoke and the flak back to Valhalla. Home. Safe.

The copilot chattered over the intercom to the navigator, airspeed, fuel consumption, and now descent rate. If they lost any more airspeed, the B-26 would stall, so Captain Vinnie was bringing her down into sweet, thick lower air at the rate of a hundred feet per minute. But the lower they flew, the faster the fuel would burn.

"I'm going to level her off at two thousand," Captain Vinnie said.

The navigator did some quick calculations and came back with: "At two thousand we'll be short of base by three hundred miles,

Captain. I recommend we level at three thousand for a safer bailout."

"Oh ye of little fucking faith," Vincent said. "Check your charts for somewhere we can ditch her."

The navigator checked their position on the charts. There was a flyspeck atoll named Alualu about forty nautical miles to the south. And it showed that it was now in American hands. He relayed the information to the captain.

"The chart shows an uncompleted airstrip. We must have chased the Japs out before they finished it."

"Give me a course."

"Sir, there might not be anything there."

"Ya fuckin' mook, look out the window. You see anything but water?"

The navigator gave him the course.

Vincent patted the throttles and said, "Come on, sweetheart. You get us there safe and I'll build you a shrine. "

Sarapul was heading for the beach and the men's drinking circle when he heard the drums welcoming the Sky Priestess. That white bitch was stealing his fire again. He'd been thinking all afternoon about what he would say at the drinking circle: how the Shark People needed to return to the old ways and how he had just the ritual to get everyone started. Nothing like a little cannibalism to get people thinking right. But now that was all ruined. Everyone would be out on the airstrip, drumming and chanting and marching around like a bunch of idiots, and when the Sky Priestess finally left and the men finally did show up at the drinking circle, all they would talk about was the wonderful words of Vincent. Sarapul wouldn't be able to get a word in edgewise. He took the path that led away from the village and made his way toward the runway. After all, the Sky Priestess might pass out some good cargo and he didn't want to miss out on his share.

Sarapul had been permanently banished from the village of the Shark People ever since one of the chief's grandchildren had mysteriously disappeared and was later found in the jungle with Sarapul, who was building a child-sized earthen oven (an *oom*) and gathering various fragrant fire woods. Oh, the men tolerated him at the nightly drinking circle, and he was allowed to share in the village's take of shark meat, and the members of his clan saw to it that he got part of the wonderful cargo passed out by the Sorcerer and the Sky Priestess, but he was forbidden to enter the village when women and children were present. He lived alone in his little hut on the far side of the island and was regarded by the Shark People as little more than a monster to frighten children into behaving: "You stay inside the reef or old Sarapul will catch you and eat you." Actually, scaring children was the only real joy Sarapul had left in life.

As he emerged from the jungle, the old cannibal saw the torches where the Shark People waited in a semicircle around a raised platform. He stopped in a grove of betel nut palms, sat on the ground, and watched. He heard a click from the PA speakers mounted on the gate across the runway and the Shark People stopped drumming. Two of the Japanese guards appeared out of the compound and Sarapul felt the hair rise on his neck as they rolled back the gate and fifty years of residual hatred rose in his throat like acid. The Japanese had killed his wife and children, and if there was any single reason to return to the old ways of the warrior, it was to take revenge on the guards.

Music blared out of the PA speakers: Glenn Miller's "String of Pearls." The Shark People turned toward the gate and dropped to their knees. Pillars of red smoke rose from either side of the gate and wafted across the runway like sulfurous serpents. The distant whine of airplane propellers replaced the big band sound from the PA and grew into a roar that ended with a flash and explosion that sent a mushroom cloud of smoke a hundred feet into the night sky.

And half-naked, the Sky Priestess walked out of the smoke into the moonlight.

Chief Malink turned to his friend Favo and said, "Excellent *boom*."

"Very excellent *boom*, " Favo said.

"There it is," the copilot said.

The B-26 was sputtering on her last few drops of fuel. Vincent nosed her over and started his descent. "There's a strip cut right across the center of the island. Let's hope we didn't bomb the shit out of it when the Japs had it."

His last few words seemed unusually loud as the engine cut out.

"No go-around, boys. We're going down. Rig for a rough one and be ready for extreme dampness if we come in short."

Vincent could see patches of dirt on the airstrip, as well as fingers of vines and undergrowth from the jungle trying to reclaim the clearing.

"You going in gear up?" the copilot asked, thinking that they might have a better chance of survival going over a bomb crater if they skidded in on the plane's belly.

"Gear down," Bennidetti said, making it a command. "We might be able to land her gear up, but she'd never take off again."

"Gear down and locked," the copilot said.

They glided in about ten feet over the reef. A dozen Shark men who were standing on the reef dove underwater as the airplane passed over them as silent and ominous as a manta ray. Bennidetti flared the B-26 to drop the rear gear first and they bounced over a patch of ferns and began the rocket slide down the coral gravel airstrip. Without the engines to reverse thrust, Vincent had only the wheel brakes to stop the bomber. He applied them gingerly at first, then, realizing that the runway was obscured by vines that might be covering a bomb crater, laid into them, causing the wheels to plow furrows into the gravel and filling the still air with a thick white cloud of dust.

"We still burning?" Vincent asked the copilot over the rumble.

The copilot looked out the window. "Can't see anything but a little black smoke."

The bomber rolled to a stop and a cheer went up from the crew.

"Everybody out. Now," Vincent ordered. "We still might have fire.

They stumbled over each other to get out of the plane into the dust cloud. Bennidetti led them away at a run. They were a hundred yards from the plane before anyone looked back.

"She looks okay, Captain. No fire."

That set off a round of cheering and backslapping and when they turned around again they saw group of native children approaching them from the jungle led by a proud ten-year-old boy carrying a spear.

"Let me handle this," Vincent told the crew as he dug into his flight suit pocket for a Hershey bar.

"Hey, squirts, how you doing?"

The boy with the spear stood his ground, keeping his eye trained on the downed bomber while the other children lost their nerve and backed away like scolded puppies.

"We're Americans," Vincent said. "Friendly. We are bringing

you many good things." He held the chocolate bar out to the spear boy, who didn't move or take his eyes off of the airplane.

Vincent tried again. "Here, kid. This stuff tastes good. Chocolate." He smacked his lips and mimed eating the candy bar. "You savvy American, kid?"

"No," the boy said. "I no speak American. I speak English."

Vincent laughed. "Well, I'm from New York, kid. We don't speak much English there. Go tell your chief that Captain Vincent is here with presents for him from a faraway and most magical place."

"Who she?" the kid asked, pointing to the image of the Sky Priestess. "She your queen?"

"She works for me, kid. That's the Sky Priestess. She's bringing presents for your chief."

"You are chief?"

Vincent knew he had to be careful here. He'd heard of island chiefs refusing to deal with anyone but Roosevelt because he was the only American equal to their status.

"I'm higher than chief," Vincent said. "I'm Captain Vinnie Fuckin' Bennidetti, Bad-ass of Brooklyn, High Emperor of the Allied Forces, Pilot of the Magic Sky Priestess, Swinging Dick of the Free Fuckin' World, and Protector of the Innocent. Now take me to your chief, squirt, before I have the Sky Priestess burn you to fucking ashes."

"Christ, Cap'n!" the bombardier said.

Vincent shot him a grin over his shoulder.

The kid bowed his head. "Christ, Cap'n. I am Malink, chief of the Shark People."

The Sky Priestess came out of the smoke and took her place in the middle of the semicircle of Shark People. Women kept their eyes to the ground even as they pushed their children forward, hoping that they would be the next to be chosen. The Sky Priestess threw the tails of her scarf over her shoulder and the music from the PA system stopped abruptly. The Shark People fell to their knees and waited for her words, the words of Vincent. It had been months since anyone had been chosen.

Malink rose and approached the Sky Priestess with a coconut shell cup of the special *tuba* they had made for her. He was as stunned by her now as when he had first seen her painted on the side of Vincent's plane.

She drained the cup and handed it back to the chief, who bowed over it.

"Still tastes like shit," she said.

"Tastes like shit!" the Shark People chanted.

Beth Curtis turned her head to suppress a smile and a belch. When she turned back to Malink, her eyes were fury.

"Who speaks for Vincent?"

"The Priestess of the Sky," Malink answered.

"Who brings the words and cargo from Vincent?"

"The Priestess of the Sky, " Malink repeated.

"And who takes the chosen to Vincent?"

"The Priestess of the Sky," Malink said again, backing away a step. He'd never seen her so angry.

"And who else, Malink?"

"No one else."

"Damn straight no one else!" She spat so violently she nearly disengaged the bow from her hair. "You told the Sorcerer that Vincent came to you in a dream. This is not true."

The Shark People gasped. Despite what the Sky Priestess and the Sorcerer thought, Malink had told none of his people about the dream. But Malink was confused. He *had* dreamed of Vincent. "Vincent said that the pilot is coming. That he is still alive."

"Vincent speaks only through me."

"But—"

"No coffee or sugar for a month," the Sky Priestess said. She pulled her scarf from her shoulders and the music began again. The Shark People watched as she walked away. There was an explosion across the runway and the Sky Priestess disappeared into the smoke.

24

Valhalla: From the Runyonese

Vincent Bennidetti was sitting at an oversized table dealing five-card draw to five other guys and relating the story of the crash landing of the Sky Priestess in hopes that the tale would distract his opponents from his creative shuffling.

"So the squirt says to me, he says, 'I'm Malink, chief of the Shark People,' and he puffs up his little chest like I'm supposed to be impressed and drop down and kiss his ring, except he ain't wearing any ring; in fact, he ain't wearing nothing but a loincloth and a little hat made of palm leaves, so I says, 'Honored and charmed I'm sure, Chief.' And I gives him a grade A Hershey bar as a peace offering to assure that the kid doesn't get any ideas about ventilating me with his spear. Although I have a roscoe handy in my flight suit, in Manhattan it is considered very bad luck indeed to shoot a kid unless he deserves it, so I am trying to take the diplomatic route.

"So the squirt chief takes the sweet and slaps a lip over a morsel and his little mug splits in a grin so big that I'm figuring I know now how his tribe gets named Shark People. And before I know it the kid yells something to his pals and they vamoose to the jungle while I watch the squirt's spear and he keeps a peeper peeled at the Sky Priestess like any minute she's gonna jump off the plane and do the bump and grind across the airstrip.

"Now we are sure that Sky Priestess is not burning or blowing up, Sparky goes back in and sings Mayday on the radio until I am thinking that even Marconi is sorry he ever invented the machine (another distinguished Italian genius, if I may point out, and it would be impolite for anyone, at this juncture, to mention Mussolini, as I will have to delay the game whilst I pop him in the beezer, thank you), and finally HQ comes back on and requests more than somewhat sternly that we cease broadcasting our position, as they will send someone as soon as they can unless the Japs find us first, in which case it has been an honor serving with us.

"Call and raise a buck.

"So the squirt asks me do I kill Japs? And I tell him that I am killing so many Japs I have to come rest on his island for a few days to give the Japs a chance to send in reinforcements for me to kill, when out of the jungle comes a whole platoon of native guys, mostly real old guys, carrying baskets of fruit and coconuts and dried fish which they are laying at my feet after doing enough bowing and chanting to fill a year of encores on Broadway.

"And the kid says, 'You more powerful than Father Rodriquez. Japs kill him.' From which I figure where the kid learns to speak English and why I am seeing no young guys, because it is well known that the Japs have killed any missionaries they find and have taken most of the able-bodied native guys which they do not kill off to build airstrips and boat landing ramps and other Jap military stuff.

" 'Yeah,' I tells the kid, 'too bad about Father Rodriquez, and all the other guys that don't make it, but Vincent and the Sky Priestess is here now and you got nothing to worry about.' Then I inquire as to if there are any available dolls on the island and the kid jabbers something to one of the old guys, who wobbles off and comes back about ten minutes later with a line of young native dolls who are wearing skirts on their bottom but are nothing but bounce and bosoms on the top, except for the odd garnish of flowers here and there for fragrance and color.

"I swear on my mother's grave (should she pass away before I get home) that I am looking at more brown curves than I have seen since I fly over the Mississippi at ten Gs, and they are by no means an unpleasant sight, but as soon as I pick out one of the young dolls and give her my best Tyrone Power wink, she starts bawling like I have broken her heart and runs into the jungle followed, posthaste, by the other lovelies until the airstrip is, once again, strictly stag.

" 'What goes?' I ask the kid. And he explains that because I am a god the dames are most frightened that I will destroy them. Then the squirt starts bawling himself, and I am beginning to feel very low indeed, as I can see that the little guy has taken my god action and it is six to five that he thinks he is on the destruction express along with the dames, and some explanation and consolation are then needed to caulk the kid's waterworks and generally ease his mind.

"So I sits down with the kid under the wing of the Sky Priestess and by and by along comes an old native guy with a jug of the local hooch, of which I am somewhat dubious and which tastes like matchheads mixed with dishwater but smooths out considerably after the first four or five belts, and soon the mood becomes most festive and a good time is had by all (except for Sparky, who is bending over the runway looking at everything he drinks for the second time).

"Now all of this time I am thinking that the kid is running a game on me about being chief until he explains that the Japs killed his father and his older brother as examples and he is next in line, so he is chief whether he likes it or not. And now he is worried that his people will not have enough to eat, as the Japs have taken most of the fruit and coconuts and destroyed all the canoes and cargo, like rice, which the late Father Rodriquez brings in, and my heart is breaking for the kid, who should be playing stickball and stealing candy and other assorted kid activities instead of worrying about a whole population of citizens. So I look at my guys eating all the food the kid gives us, and my heart is feeling very heavy indeed, so I tell him not to worry, as Vincent and the Sky Priestess will see that his people get everything they need and I gives the kid a pack of Luckys and my Zippo to seal the promise. Then, as soon as Sparky finishes doing the rainbow yawn, I tells him to get on the radio to a friend of mine who is in the quartermaster corps, and I gives him a list of things to place on the PT boat which is coming to get us.

"So as the evening wears on, the kid is telling me stories of how the island was made by a dame from Yap who rides on a turtle with a basketful of dirt which she dumps in the ocean, making the island, which must have been quite some basket, and she tells all the children she is having on the island (although the kid says nothing about her having an old man) that she isn't going to give them a good reef for fishing, so they are going to be eating sharks. And although the people of all the other islands are afraid of sharks, here the sharks are afraid of the people. 'They will be called the Shark People,' the dame with the dirt says.

"And I says, 'Yeah, I know that dame.' That, in fact, I take her to the races one day and she is such good luck that I win the trifecta for five Gs. And I can see the kid is most impressed, even though he wouldn't know a G from a G-string. So I begins to lay it on a bit thick and by the time we have consumed all of the local bug juice and most of the fruit and fish, the kid is convinced that if I am not the Second Coming, I am at least pinch-hitting that day.

"By now I am feeling I am in serious need of female company and I mention this to the kid, who says maybe there is something he can do, as there is one doll in the village whose job it is to change the oil of the unmarried native guys (I am at once reminded of a costume optional dancer named Chintzy Bilouski, who performs a similar service for myself and many other unmarried male citizens in the Broadway district) and it seems that this native doll has been short of work of late, as all of the young unmarried guys are either killed or taken away. And the kid says he will approach this doll on my behalf if I promise that she will not burst into flames or be otherwise harmed and as long as I keep it quiet. As these are similar terms I agree to with Chintzy Bilouski (and a sawbuck cheaper, in fact), I tell the kid to lead the way, which he does. And soon we are in a big grass house by the beach, which he calls the bachelors' house, and which is clearly intended to house many citizens, but is currently only the home of one doll, who is by no means hard on the peepers and who proceeds immediately to catch up on any work she has been missing in a most enthusiastic and friendly manner, if you know what I mean.

"So, to make a long story short, the guys and I spend three more days telling stories to the kid and drinking bug juice and creeping to the bachelors' house until the PT boat shows with some mechanics and welders and all the supplies I have requested from my pal the quartermaster. And the islanders all line up while I pass out many machetes and knives and chocolate bars and various other luxuries from Uncle Sam. And that night they throw a big party in my honor with much drinking and dancing and a swell time is had by one and all. But as we are ready to leave, the kid chief comes up all leaky-eyed, asking why am I leaving and will I come back and what will his people do without me. So I promise him I will be back soon with many wonderful things and to save me a spot in the bachelors' house, but until then, every time he sees a plane, he and his people will know that me and the Sky Priestess are looking out for them.

"Then when we are back at base I am working something with the colonel to run a recon mission to inspect the airstrip for emergency use. No bombs. I am thinking we will fill the Sky Priestess up with medicine and supplies for the Shark kid and his people as soon as permission comes through. And I'm fully intending to come through, as I gives the kid my word and he believes it, but how am I to know that on our very next bombing run a squadron of Zeros will surprise us and fill the Sky Priestess with all manner of cannon and machine gun slugs, sending us down in a ball of flames and killing me and everyone aboard quite dead."

The guy with the beard cleared his throat and said, "That was a swell story the first dozen times we heard it, Vinnie, but are you going to talk or play cards?"

"Bite me, Jewboy, it ain't like we haven't had to fight the yawns through your loaves and fishes epic a hundred fuckin' times." Then Vincent flashed him a feral grin. "And since it is now your bet, I will advise you to fold, as I am now holding a hand that is so hot it is about to burst into flames like the proverbial bush."

The guy with the beard held up a punctured palm to silence Vincent. "You're holding a pair of eights, Vinnie."

"I hate fuckin' playing with you," Vincent said.

25

We Ask the Gods for Answers and They Give Us Questions

Tucker Case heard the beating of wings above his head and suddenly there was a familiar little face in front of him. Roberto was hanging upside down from the harness ropes around Tuck's chest. He never thought he'd be glad to see the little vermin.

"Roberto! Buddy!" Tuck smiled at the bat.

Roberto squeaked and bent forward to lick Tucker's face.

Tucker sputtered. He could smell papaya on the bat's breath.

"How about climbing up there and gnawing through these ropes, little guy?"

Roberto looked at him quizzically, then laid a big lick on him, right across the lips.

"Ack! Bat spit!"

Tuck heard a weak voice from above. "He no gnaw rope. His teeth too little," Kimi said.

Roberto took flight and landed on Kimi's head and began licking and clawing him ecstatically.

Kimi was suspended about two feet above Tucker and about five feet away. It hurt his neck, but he could see the navigator dangling if he stretched. "You're alive!" Tucker said. "I thought you were dead."

"I am bery thirsty. Why you put us in tree?"

"I didn't. It was an old island guy. I think he's going to eat us."

"No, no, no. No cannibal in these islands for many years."

"Good. You tell him that when he comes back."

Kimi struggled against his bonds and set himself spinning. "These ropes hurt on my arms. Someone put us in crab harness."

"I figured that out," Tuck said. He craned his neck and eyed

Kimi's harness. "Maybe I can swing to you and catch on to your harness. If I can get hold of it, I might be able to untie you."

"Good plan," Kimi said.

"Yankee know-how, kid."

As Tuck started to swing his arms and legs, he felt the harness tighten around his chest. Soon he was swinging in a wide elliptical pattern that brought him within a foot of Kimi, but the harness was so tight he could barely breathe. Weakened from lack of food and water, he gave up. "I can't breathe," he gasped.

"That good plan, though," Kimi said. "Now I have Roberto bring that knife over by door of house and I cut the ropes. Okay?"

"Roberto can fetch?"

"Yes."

"Why didn't you say so?"

"I want to see Yankee know-how."

Sarapul tried to run back to his hut, but the pain in his ancient knees wouldn't allow him to move faster than a slow amble. If only he could absorb the power of an enemy or two, perhaps the pain would subside and his strength would return along with his courage. It was courage he needed now. Instead, he had questions.

Why, if Malink dreamed a message from Vincent, did the white bitch say that he did not? And if Vincent had sent a pilot, why did the Sky Priestess not know about him? And if Vincent had not sent a pilot, who is hanging in the breadfruit tree?

In the old days Sarapul would have asked the turtle, his clan animal, for an answer to his questions. Then he would have watched the waves and listened to the wind for an answer, perhaps he would have gone to a sorcerer for an interpretation. But he was too deaf and blind to see a sign now. And the only sorcerer left was the white man who lived behind the big fence and gave medicine to the Shark People: Vincent's Sorcerer. Sarapul didn't believe in Vincent any more than he believed in the god Father Rodriquez had worn around his neck on a chain.

Father Rodriquez had said that the old ways—the taboos and the totem animals—were lies and that the skinny white god on the cross was the only real god. Sarapul was prepared to believe him, especially when he offered everyone a piece of the body of Christ. But Christ tasted like dried pounded taro and Father Rodriquez lost the old cannibal as a convert when he said that you would be thrown into fire forever if you ate anyone besides the stale starchy god on the cross.

Then the Japanese came and cut off Father Rodriquez's head and threw his god on a chain into the sea. Sarapul knew for sure then that the Father had been lying all along. The Japanese raped and killed his wife and made his two sons work building the airstrip until they became sick and died. He asked the Turtle why his family had been taken away, and when the sign came in the form of a cloud shaped like an eel, the sorcerer said that it had happened because the Shark People had broken the taboos, had eaten their totem animals and taken fish from the forbidden reef: They were being punished.

The next night Sarapul killed a Japanese soldier and built an *oom* to bake him in, but none of the Shark People would help him. Some were afraid of the god of Father Rodriquez and the rest were afraid of the Japanese. They took the body and fed it to the sharks who lived at the edge of the reef.

In the morning the Japanese lined up the old sorcerer and a dozen children and machine-gunned them. And Sarapul lost his mind.

Then the American planes came, dropping their bombs and fire from the sky for two days, and when the explosions stopped and the smoke cleared, the Japanese left, taking with them all the coconuts and breadfruit on the island. A week later Vincent arrived in the Sky Priestess.

Sarapul still had the machete that the flyer had given him. It was more than he had ever gotten from Father Rodriquez's god, but the cannibal did not believe that Vincent was a god. Even if Vincent had scared away the Japanese and brought the food that saved the Shark People, Sarapul had angered the old gods before and he would not do it again.

When the white Sorcerer arrived, he too talked of the god on the cross and although the Shark People took the food and medicine he gave them and even attended his services, they would not forsake Vincent, their savior. The god on the cross had let them down before. Eventually, the white Sorcerer turned to Vincent too. But Sarapul clung to the old ways, even when the Sky Priestess returned with her red scarf and explosions. It was all just entertainment: Christ was just a cracker, Vincent was just a flyer, and he, Sarapul, was a cannibal.

Still, he did not blame Malink for banishing him or for clinging to Vincent's promises. Vincent was the god of Malink's childhood, and Malink clung to him in the same way that Sarapul clung to the old ways. Faith grew stronger when planted in a child. Sarapul knew that. He was mad, but he was not stupid.

Until now he had never put an ounce of faith in Vincent, but this dream of Malink's vexed him. He would have to figure things out before he ate the man in his breadfruit tree. He had to talk to Malink now.

The cannibal took the path that led into the village. He crept between the houses where the sweet rasp of snoring children wafted through the woven grass walls like the sizzle of frying pork, through the smoke of dying cook fires, past the bachelors' house, the men's house, and finally to the beach, where the men sat in a circle, drinking and talking softly, the moon spraying their shoulders with a cold blue light.

The men continued to talk as Sarapul joined the circle, politely ignoring the creak and crackle of his old joints as he sat in the sand. Some of the younger men, those who had grown up with the disciplinary specter of the cannibal, subtly changed position so they could reach their knives quickly. Malink greeted Sarapul with a nod, then filled the coconut shell cup from the big glass jug and handed it to him.

"No coffee or sugar for a month," Malink said. "Vincent is angry."

Sarapul drained the cup and handed it back. "How about cigarettes?"

"The Sorcerer says that cigarettes are bad."

"Vincent smoked cigarettes," Sarapul pointed out. "He gave you the lighter."

The young men fidgeted at the firsthand reference to Vincent. It disturbed them when the old men spoke of Vincent as if he was a person. Malink reached inside the long flat basket where he kept the lighter along with his other personal belongings. He touched the Zippo that Vincent had given him.

"Cigarettes aren't good for us," he repeated.

"Then they should give us cigarettes for punishment," Sarapul insisted.

Malink pulled a copy of *People* magazine from his basket, drawing everyone's attention away from the cannibal. The old chief tore a small square from the masthead page and handed it to Abo, a muscular young man who tended the tobacco patch for the Shark People.

"Roll one," Malink said. Abo began filling the paper with tobacco from his basket.

Malink opened the magazine on the sand in front of him and squinted at the pages in the moonlight. Everyone in the circle leaned forward to look at the pictures.

"Oprah's skinny again," Malink pronounced.

Sarapul scoffed and the men angrily looked up, the young ones looking away quickly when they saw who had made the noise. Abo finished rolling the cigarette and held it out to Malink. The chief gestured to Sarapul and Abo gave the smoke to the old cannibal. Their hands brushed lightly in the exchange and Sarapul held the young man's gaze as he licked his finger as if tasting a sweet sauce. Abo shuddered and backed to the outside of the circle.

Malink lit the cigarette with the sacred Zippo, then he returned to his magazine. "There will be no more *People* for a while, not with the Sky Priestess mad at us."

A communal moan rose up from the men and the drinking cup was filled and passed.

"We are cut off," Malink added.

Sarapul shrugged. "All the people in this book, they shit. It does not matter. They die. It does not matter. If we put them all in a big boat and sank it, you would not even know for six months when the Sky Priestess gives you her old copy, and it still would not matter. This is stupid."

"But look!" Malink pointed to a picture of a man with unnaturally large ears, "This man is a king and he wishes to be a tampon. It is quoted."

Sarapul scrunched up his face, his wrinkles folding over each other like venetian blinds, while he tried to figure out what, exactly, a tampon was. Finally he said, "I was a tampon once, back in the old days, before you were born. All warriors became tampons. It was better then."

"You have never been a tampon," Malink stated, although he couldn't be sure. "Only a king may be a tampon. And now, without *People*, we will never know if this man who would be a tampon succeeded. It has been a dark day."

The cup had come around again to Sarapul and he drained it before answering. "Tell me of this dream you had."

"I should not speak of it." Malink pretended to be engaged in the magazine.

Sarapul pushed on. "The Sky Priestess said that Vincent spoke to you of a pilot. Is that true?"

Malink nodded. "It is true. But it is only a dream or the Sorcerer would have known."

Sarapul was torn now. This was his chance to discredit the Sorcerer and his white bitch, but if he told Malink about the man in the tree, then he would lose his chance to taste the long pig again. Then again, he found them first, and he was willing to share the meat. "What if your dream was true?"

"It was just a dream. Vincent speaks to us only through the Sky Priestess now. She has spoken."

"Vincent smoked and she says smoking is bad. Vincent was an enemy of the Japanese and now she has Japanese guards inside the fence. She lies."

Some of the men moved away from the circle. It was one thing to drink with a cannibal, but it was quite another to tolerate a heretic. (Of the twenty men in the circle, three of the elders were named John, four who had been born during Father Rodriquez's tenure were named Jesus [Hey-zeus], and three of the younger men were named Vincent.) They were a group that honored the gods, whoever the gods might be that week.

"The Sky Priestess does not lie," Malink said calmly. "She speaks for Vincent."

Sarapul pinched the flame of his cigarette with his ashy fingers, then popped the stub into his mouth and began to chew as he grinned. "Your dream was true, Malink. I have seen the pilot. He is on Alualu and he is alive."

"You are old and you drink too much."

"I'll show you." Sarapul leaped to his feet to show that he was not drunk, and in doing so scared the hell out of the younger men. "Come with me," he said.

26

Swing Time

Kimi had freed his hands and feet with the knife, only to find that he could not reach the rope suspending him from the middle of his back. Now he was forced to follow Tuck's plan of swinging like a human pendulum until he could grab the pilot's rope and cut him down. Roberto hung upside down from a nearby branch, wondering why his friends were behaving like fighting spiders.

Tucker found he could only hold his head up for a few seconds at a time before dizziness set in, so he watched the navigator's swinging shadow to gauge his distance. "One more time, Kimi. Then grab the rope." It bothered him some that when he was cut loose he would fall six feet and land face-first in the coral gravel, but he was learning to take things as they came and figured he would deal with that on the way down.

"I hear someone," Kimi said. On the apex of his arc, he grabbed for Tuck's rope, missed, and accidentally raked the knife across the pilot's scalp.

"Ouch! Shit, Kimi. Watch what you're doing." Tuck braced himself for the next attack, which never came. He looked up to see that Kimi's arc had been stopped in mid-swing. A rotund gray-haired native had caught the navigator around the waist and was prying the knife out of his hand.

Tuck felt the hope drain out of him. The leathery old cannibal stood amid a group of twenty men. All of them seemed to be waiting for the fat guy to say something. It was time for a last-ditch effort.

"Look, you motherfuckers, people are expecting me. I'm supposed to be flying medical supplies for a big-time doctor, so if you fuck with me you're all going to die of the tropical creeping crud and I won't give you so much as a fucking aspirin."

The native released Kimi into the hands of two younger men and regarded Tuck. "You pilot?" He said in English.

"Damn right I am. And I'm sick and infected and stuff, so if you eat me you're going to die like a gut-shot dog—and in addition I would like to add that I don't taste anything like Spam." Tuck was breathless from the diatribe and he was starting to black out from trying to hold his head back.

The native said something in his own language, which Tuck took to be "Cut him down," because a second later he found himself falling into the arms of four strong islanders who lowered him to the ground.

Tucker's arms and legs burned as the blood rushed back into them. Above him he saw a circle of moonlit brown faces. He managed to grab enough breath to squeak, "Soon as I'm on my feet, your asses are mine. You all might as well just go practice falling down for a while so you'll be used to it. Just order the body bags now 'cause when I'm done, you're going to look like piles of chocolate pudding. They'll be cleaning you up with shovels—you . . ." Tuck's breath caught in his throat and he passed out.

Malink looked at his old friend Favo and smiled. "Excellent threat," he said.

"Most excellent threat," Favo said.

Sarapul pushed his way through the kneeling men. "He's dead. Let's eat him."

"He no like that," Kimi said. "Not even for free."

The Sorcerer heard the lab door open and turned from his microscope just in time to catch her as she ran into his arms.

"Did you see, 'Bastian? Was I great or what?"

He held her for a second, smelling the perfume in her hair. "You were great," he said. When he released her, there were two pink spots on his lab coat from the rouge she had rubbed on her nipples.

She skipped around the lab like a little girl. "Malink was shaking in his shoes," she said. Well, not in his shoes, but you know what I mean." She stopped and looked into the microscope. "What's this?"

He watched a delicate line of muscle run down the back of her thigh and postulated what kind of genetics went into preserving a body like that on Chee-tos and vodka. He thought a lot about genetics lately. "I'm doing the last of the tissue typing. I should be finished in a couple of days."

She said, "Did you like 'String of Pearls' better than 'In the Mood'?"

High Priestess of the nonsequiter, Sebastian thought. "It was perfect. You were perfect."

She moved away from the microscope and paced around the table, frowning now, as if she was working on an equation in her head. "I've been thinking about 'Pennsylvania 6-5000,' putting the ninjas in top hats and tails in kind of a chorus line. You know, they could carry me across the runway and pause and shout the chorus. There's no singing on the recording; they would just have to shout. I mean, if we have to have them around, they might as well do something." She stopped pacing and turned to him. "What do you think?"

It took Sebastian a second to realize that she was serious. "I'm not sure that would be a good idea. The Shark People are suspicious of the nin—, the guards. I wish Akiro would have listened to me and found some non-Japanese. This business with Malink's dream is a sign that our credibility is slipping."

"That's what I'm saying. If we show that they're under the control of the Sky Priestess—"

"I don't think it's a good idea, Beth."

She dismissed the thought with a wave. "Fine. We can talk about it later."

Sebastian wanted to stop himself before he ruined her ebullient mood, but he pressed on despite himself. "Don't you think that no coffee or sugar for a month was a little harsh?"

"You really don't get it, do you? I'll give it all back after a week, 'Bastian, and they'll love me for it. Generosity of the gods: The Sky Priestess taketh away and the Sky Priestess giveth back. It's how these things work. You put a few people on a boat, then you drown every living creature on the planet—the people on the boat are pretty goddamn grateful." She flipped the end of her red scarf over her shoulder.

"I wish you wouldn't talk like that."

"You make the rules and you play the game, 'Bastian. What's wrong with that?"

He turned from her and pretended to go through some notes. "I guess you're right," he said, but he felt acid rising from his stomach. She was calling it a game.

She came up behind him, pushed her breasts into his back, and reached around inside his lab coat. "Poor baby. You still feel like you did the right thing by burning your Beatles records."

"Beth, please."

She unzipped his khakis and snaked her hand in his fly. "Deep down, you feel like John Lennon got what he deserved, don't you, sweetheart? Saying he was more popular than Jesus. That loony-toon Chapman was the instrument of God, wasn't he?"

He whirled on her and grabbed her shoulders. "Yes, dammit." His face had gone hot. He could feel the veins pulse in his forehead, in his crotch. "That's enough, Beth."

"No, it's not." She ripped open the front of his trousers and fell back on the lab table, pulling him on top of her. "Come on, show me the wrath of the Sorcerer."

27

Girl Talk

Sepie washed the pilot's hair in a bowl with pounded coconut and brackish water. She had been taking care of the unconscious white man for two days and it was starting to get tedious. She was mispel of the bachelors' house, and washing and ministering to a sick and stinky white man was not in her job description. This was women's work.

There are legends in the islands, and some of the old men swear they are true, that the women who service the bachelors' houses, the mispels, were taken to the secret island of Maluuk, known only to the high navigators, where they were trained in the art of pleasuring a man.

After months of training, a mispel was required to pass a test before she was allowed to return to her home island to take over the duty of tending to the sexual needs of the men of the bachelors' house. The test? She was sent into the ocean with a ripe brown coconut clutched between her thighs, and there she floated, in heavy surf, for the entire circuit of the tides. Should the coconut pop loose or the mispel touch it with her hands, she failed the test (although there was some leeway in the event of shark attack). It is said that the inner thighs of the mispels of old were as strong as net cable. The second part of the test required the girl to find a delicate dragonfly orchid with a straight stem, and while her teachers looked on, she would lower herself over the flower until it disappeared inside of her, then rise again after a few minutes, leaving the stem unbent and the petals unbruised. The mispel held a position of honor, respected and revered among the islanders. She was not required to do housekeeping, cooking, or weaving, and while the other women toiled in taro fields from the time they could walk, a mispel was allowed to nap in the shade, conserving her energy for her nocturnal duties. A mispel often ended her tour of duty by marrying a man of high status. No stigma followed her into married life, and she would be sought out to the end of her days by the other women for advice on handling men.

Sepie, however, had not been chosen because of any special skill, nor had she passed through any vigorous concubinal boot camp. Sepie had been marked for mispel from the moment of her menses, when she emerged from the women's house with her lavalava tied a bit too high and showing a bit too much cappuccino thigh, her skin rubbed with copra until she glistened all over, and her breasts shining like polished wooden tea cups. She had painted her lips with the juice of crushed berries and peppered her long black hair with scores of sweet jasmine blossoms. She giggled coquettishly in the presence of all the men, danced dangerously close to the taboo of speaking to them in public, risked beatings by refusing to fall to her knees when her male cousins passed, and went about her chores with a wiggly energy that had caused more than one of the distracted village boys to fall out of a breadfruit tree during harvest. (She broke ankles as well as hearts.) Sepie was all titter and tease, a lazy girl who excelled at leisure, a natural at invoking and denying desire, a wet dream deferred. At fifteen she took up residence in the bachelors' house and had lived there for four years.

When Malink and the men brought the flyer and the man in the dress to her, she knew she was in for some trouble.

"Take care of them," Malink said. "Feed them. Help to make them strong."

Sepie kept her head bowed while Malink spoke, but when he finished she took his hand and led him into the bachelors' house, gesturing to the other men to lay the flyer and his friend on the ground outside. The men smiled among themselves, thinking that old Malink was going inside to receive a special favor from the mispel. What, in fact, he was receiving was an ass chewing.

"Why don't you take them to your house, Malink? I don't want them here."

"It's a secret. If my wife and daughters find out they are here, then everyone will know."

"I'm the only one who can keep a secret in the bachelors' house. Take them to old Sarapul's house. No one goes there."

"He wants to eat them." Malink couldn't remember ever having to argue with a woman and he wasn't at all prepared for it.

"You're chief. Tell him not to. I will not cook for them. If I feed them, they will shit. I'm not going to clean it up."

"Sepie, what will you do when you marry and have children? You will have to do these things then. I am asking you as your chief to do these things."

"No," Sepie said.

Malink sighed. "I am asking you to do these things because these men have been sent to us by Vincent."

Sepie didn't know what to say. She had heard the Sky Priestess chastise Malink in front of the people, but she had been more concerned with losing coffee and sugar for a month than with the actual offense. "You will tell the men to cook for them?"

"Yes."

"And they will carry them to the beach and wash them if they shit?"

"I will tell them. Please, Sepie."

No man had ever said "please" to her before, let alone the chief. It was not a courtesy that women deserved. For the first time she realized how desperate Malink really was. "And you will tell Abo to wash his dick when it is his turn."

"What does that have to do with this?"

"He is stinky."

"I will tell him."

"And you will tell Favo to quit making me put beads in his ass."

"Favo does that?"

"He said he learned it from the Japanese."

"Really? Favo?"

"Yes."

"But he's old, and he has a wife and many grandchildren."

"He says it makes his spear stronger."

"He does? I mean, does it work?" Malink had momentarily forgotten why he was here.

"I don't like it. It is evil and unclean."

"You're talking about my old friend Favo, right? He's the one you're talking about?"

"I told him only bachelors were suppose to stay here, but he says his wife doesn't understand him. His hands are like the skin of a shark."

"What kind of beads?"

"Tell him," Sepie said.

"Okay," Malink said in English. Then to himself he said: "Old Favo." He shook his head as he walked out of the bachelors' house. "Beads."

Sepie watched him go, wishing that she had asked for more favors.

Outside the men were grinning when Malink stepped into the moonlight. He hitched up his loincloth and averted his eyes from theirs.

"Take them inside. You must cook and clean for them. Don't let the woman do it. It is too important for her."

As the men carried Tuck and Kimi into the bachelors' house, Favo ambled up to Malink. "How was it?"

Malink looked at his old friend and noticed for the first time that Favo wore a long string of ivory beads around his neck. "I have to go home now," Malink said.

Sepie was, once again, swabbing up the wooden floor where the pilot had urinated on himself, when she heard the other one speak for the first time. The men had propped the Filipino up in the corner, where he had sat drinking the coconut milk and fish broth that she had been pouring into the pilot, but except for a few grunts when he made his way outside to urinate, the man in the dress had been quiet for two days. Sepie had learned to ignore him. He didn't smell as bad as the pilot, and she sort of liked his flowered dress. She'd said a prayer to Vincent for a dress just like it.

"Where is Roberto?" the Filipino said.

Sepie jumped. It didn't surprise her so much that he had spoken, but that he had spoken in her language. Although the words were clipped, the way someone from Iffallik or Satawan might speak.

"He's right here," she said. "Your friend stinks. You should take him outside and wash him in the sea."

"That's not Roberto. That's Tucker. Roberto is shorter." Kimi crawled over to Tuck and laid his hand on the flyer's forehead. "He has bad fever. You have medicine?"

"Aspirin," Sepie said. Malink had given her a bottle of the tablets to crush into the flyer's broth, but after he gagged on the first dose she had stopped giving it to him.

"He is more sick than aspirin. He needs a doctor. You have a doctor?"

"We have the Sorcerer. He does our medicine. He was a doctor before the Sky Priestess came."

Kimi looked at her. "What island is this?"

"Alualu."

"Ha! We have to get doctor for Tucker. He owes me five hundred dollars."

Sepie's eyes went wide. No wonder he wears such a fine dress. Five hundred dollars! She said, "The chief says I have to be secret about this man. Everyone knows he is here. The boys get drunk and talk. But I can't get the doctor."

"Why are you taking care of him? You are just a girl."

"I am not just a girl. I am mispel."

Kimi scoffed. "There are no mispels anymore."

Sepie threw down the rag she was using to wipe the floor. "What do you know? You are a man in a dress, and I don't believe you have five hundred dollars."

"It was a nice dress before the typhoon," Kimi said. "Wash-and-wear. No dry cleaning."

Sepie nodded as if she knew what he was talking about. "It is a very pretty dress. I like it."

"You do?" Kimi picked at the crushed pleats around his legs. "It's just an old thing I picked up in Manila. It was on sale. You really like it?"

Sepie didn't understand. Among her people, if you admired someone's else possession, manners bound them to give it to you. How could this silly man speak her language and still not know her customs. And he wasn't even looking at her that way all men looked at her.

"What island do you come from?"

"Satawan," Kimi said. "I am a navigator."

Sepie scoffed. "There are no more navigators."

Just then the doorway darkened and they looked up to see Abo, the fierce one, entering the bachelors' house. He was lean and heavily muscled and he wore a permanent scowl on his face. The sides of his head were shaved and tattooed with images of hammerhead sharks. He wore his hair tied into a warrior's topknot that had gone out of fashion a hundred years ago.

"Has the pilot awakened?" he growled.

Sepie looked down and smiled coyly. Abo was the one boy in the bachelors' house who didn't seem to accept the communal nature of her position. He was always jealous, enraged, or brooding, but he brought her many presents, sometimes even copies of *People* that he stole from the men's drinking circle. Sepie thought she might marry him someday.

"He is too sick for this," Kimi said. "We need to take him to the doctor."

"Malink says he must stay here until he is well."

"He is dying." Kimi said.

Abo looked at Sepie for confirmation.

"Well, he smells dead," she said. The sooner they sent the pilot to the Sorcerer, the sooner she could get back to spending her days swimming and preening. "Malink will be angry if he dies," she added for good measure.

Abo nodded. "I will tell him." He pointed to Kimi. "You come with me."

Kimi got up to leave, then turned back to Sepie when he reached the doorway. "If Roberto comes, tell him I'll be right back."

Sepie shrugged. "Who is Roberto?"

"He's a fruit bat. From Guam. You can tell by his accent."

"Oh, him. I think Sarapul ate him," Sepie said casually."

Kimi turned and ran screaming into the village.

Malink looked up from his breakfast, a banana leaf full of fish and rice, to see Abo coming down the coral path toward his house. Malink's wife and daughters shuffled to the cookhouse at the sight of the fierce one.

"Good morning, Chief," Abo said.

"Food?" Malink answered, gesturing with his breakfast.

Abo had already eaten, but it would have been rude not to accept. "Yes."

Malink's wife poked her head out of the cookhouse and saw the chief nod. In a second she was giving her own breakfast to Abo, who neither thanked her or acknowledged her presence.

"The pilot is sick," Abo said. "Very bad fever. Sepie and the girl-man say that he will die soon without the Sorcerer's help."

Malink suddenly lost his appetite. He set his breakfast on the ground and one of his daughters appeared out of nowhere to take it to the cookhouse, where the women shared what was left.

"And what do you think?" Malink asked.

"I think he is dying. He smells of sickness. Like when Tamu was bitten by the shark and his leg turned black."

Malink rubbed his temples. How to handle this? The Sky Priestess was angry with him for even dreaming of the pilot. What would happen if he suddenly showed up with him?

"What about the girl-man?"

"He is not sick, but he has gone crazy. He runs around the village looking for Sarapul."

Malink nodded. "Catch him and tie him up. Make a litter and take the pilot to the betel nut trees by the runway. Leave him there."

"Leave him there?"

"Yes, quickly. And bring the litter back with you. Make it look as if he walked to the runway. Send a boy to me when it is done. Go now."

Abo put down his food and ran off down the path.

Malink went into his house and pulled the ammo box out of the rafters. Inside, next to the portable phone, he found the Zippo that Vincent had given him. He clicked it open, lit it, and sat it on the floor while it burned. "Vincent," he said, "It's your friend Malink here. Please tell the Sky Priestess that this is not my fault. Tell her that you have sent the pilot. Please tell her for your friend Malink so she will not be angry. Amen."

His prayer finished, Malink snapped the lighter shut, put it away, then took the portable phone and went outside to wait for the boy to tell him everything was in place.

28

Choose Your Own Nightmare

Tucker Case rolled through a fever dream where he was tossed in great elastic waves of bat-winged demons—crushed, smothered, bitten, and scratched—and there, amid the chaos, a pink fabric softener sheet passed by the corner of his eye, confirming that he had been stuffed into a dryer in the laundromat of Hell. He tumbled toward the pink, ascended out of the clawing mass, and awoke gasping, with no idea where he was.

The pink was a dress on a heart-faced woman who said, "Good morning, Mr. Case. Welcome back to the world."

A man's voice: "After your message and the typhoon, we thought for sure you'd been lost at sea." He was a white blur with a head, then a lab coat wrapped around a tall, smiling middle-aged man, gray and balding, a stethoscope around his neck.

The doctor had his arm around the heart-faced woman. She too was smiling, with the aspect of an angel, the vessel of human kindness. Together they looked as if they had walked off of fifties television.

The man said, "I'm Dr. Sebastian Curtis, Mr. Case. This is my wife, Beth."

Tuck tried to speak, but emitted only a rasping squeak. The woman lifted a plastic cup of water to his lips and he drank. He eyed the IV bag running into his arm.

"Glucose and antibiotics," the doctor said. "You've got some badly infected wounds. The islanders found you washed up on the reef."

Tucker did a quick inventory of his limbs by feel, then looked at them lest he had lost a leg that was still giving off phantom feeling. He raised his head to look at his crotch, which was sending pulses of pain up through his abdomen.

The woman gently pushed him down. "You're going to be fine. They found you in time, but you're going to need more rest. 'Bastian can give you something for the pain if you need it."

She smiled beatifically at her husband, who patted Tuck's arm. "Don't be embarrassed, Mr. Case. Beth is a surgical nurse. I'm afraid the catheter will have to stay in for a few days."

"There was another guy with me," Tuck said. "A Filipino. He was piloting the boat."

The doctor and his wife shot each other a glance and the "Ozzie and Harriet" calm shattered into panic, but only for a second, then they were back to their reassuring cooing. Tuck wasn't even sure he had seen the break.

"I'm sorry, but the islanders didn't find anyone else. He must have been lost in the storm."

"But the tree. He was hung in the tree . . ."

Beth Curtis put her finger gently on his lips. "I'm sorry you lost your friend, Mr. Case, but you need to get some rest. I'll bring you something to eat in a little while and we'll see if you can hold down some solid food."

She pulled her hand away and put her arm around her husband's waist as he pushed a syringe of fluid into Tuck's IV tube. "We'll check on you shortly," the doctor said.

Tucker watched them walk away and noticed that for all her "Little House on the Prairie" purity, Beth Curtis had a nice shape under that calico. Then he felt a little sleazy, as if he'd been caught horning on a friend's mom. Like the time, drunk and full of himself, he'd hit on Mary Jean Dobbins.

To hell with solid food. Gin—in large quantities over a tall column of ice—that's the rub. Tonic to chase away the blues of bad dreams and men lost at sea.

Tuck looked around the room. It was a small hospital ward. Only four beds, but amazingly clean considering where it was. And there was some pretty serious-looking equipment against the walls: technical stuff on casters, stuff you might use in complicated surgery or to set the timing on a Toyota. He was sure Jake Skye would know what it was. He thought about the Learjet, then felt himself starting to doze.

Sleep came with the face of a cannibal, leg-jerk dreams, and finally settled in on the oiled breasts of a brown girl brushing against his face and smelling of coconut and flowers. There was a scratch and scuttle on the tin roof, followed by the bark of a fruit bat. Tuck didn't hear it.

The pig thief had been caught and Jefferson Pardee had to find a new lead story. He sat at his desk pouring over the notes he'd written on a yellow legal pad, hoping that something would jump out at him. In fact, there wasn't a lot of jumping material there. The notes read: "They caught the pig thief. Now what?"

You could run down the leads, pound the pavement, check all your facts with two sources, then structure your meticulously gathered information into the inverted pyramid form and what you got was: The pig's owner had gotten drunk and beat up his wife, so she sold his pig to someone on the outer islands and bought a used stun gun from an ensign with the Navy Cat team. The next time her husband got rough, a group of Japanese tourists found him by the side of the road, sizzling in the dirt like a strip of frying bacon. Mistaking him for a street performer, the tourists clapped joyously, took pictures of each other standing beside the electrocuted man, and gave his wife five dollars. The whole intrigue had been exposed when police found the pig-stealing wife in front of the Continental Hotel charging tourists a dollar apiece to watch her zap her husband's twitching supine body. The stun gun was confiscated, no charges were pressed, and the wife beater was pronounced unharmed by a Peace Corps volunteer, although he did need to be reminded several times of his name, where he lived, and how many children he had.

The mystery was solved and the *Truk Star* had no lead story. Jefferson Pardee was miserable. He was actually going to have to go out and find a story or, as he had done so many time before, make one up. The *Micro Spirit* was in port. Maybe he'd go down to the dock and see if he could stir up some news out of the crew. He slid his press card into the band of his Australian bush hat and waddled out the door and down the dusty street to the pier where rock-hard, rope-muscled islanders were loading fifty-five-gallon drums into cargo nets and hoisting them into the holds of the *Micro Spirit*.

The *Micro Spirit* and the *Micro Trader* were sister ships: small freighters that cruised the Micronesian crescent carrying cargo and passengers to the outer islands. There were no cabins other than those of the captain and crew. Passengers traveled and slept on the deck.

Pardee waved to the first mate, a heavily tattooed Tongan who stood at the rail chewing betel nut and spitting gooey red comets over the side.

"Ahoy!" Pardee called. "Permission to come aboard."

The mate shook his head. "Not until we finish loading this jet fuel. I'll come down. How you doing, Scoop?"

Pardee had convinced the crew of the *Micro Spirit* to call him "Scoop" one drunken night in the Yumi Bar. He watched the mate vault over the railing at the bow and monkey down a mooring line to the dock with no more effort than if he was walking down stairs. Watching him made Pardee sad that he was a fat man.

The mate strolled up to Pardee and pumped his hand. "Good to see you."

"Likewise," Pardee said. "Where you guys in from?"

"We bring chiefs in from Wolei for a conference. Pick up some tuna and copra. Same, same."

Pardee looked back at the sailors loading the barrels. "Did you say jet fuel? I thought the Mobil tankers handled all the fuel for Continental." Continental was the only major airline that flew Micronesia.

"Mobil tankers won't go to Alualu. No lagoon, no harbor. We going to Ulithi, then take this fuel special order to the doctor on Alualu."

Pardee took a moment to digest the information. "I thought the *Micro Trader* did Yap and Palau States. What are you going all the way over there for?"

"Like I say, special order. Moen has jet fuel, we here in Moen, doctor wants jet fuel soon, so we go. I like it. I never been Alualu and I know a girl on Ulithi."

Pardee couldn't help but smile. This was a story in itself. Not a big one, but when the *Trader* or the *Spirit* changed schedules it made the paper. But there was more of a story somewhere in those barrels of jet fuel, in the rumor of armed guards, and in the two pilots that had passed through Truk on the way to No One's Island. The question for Pardee was: Did he want to track it down? Could he track it down?

"When do you sail?" he asked the mate.

"Tomorrow morning. We get drunk together tonight Yumi Bar. My boys carry you home if you want. Hey?" The mate laughed.

Pardee felt sick. That was what they knew him for, a fat, drunken white man who they could carry home and then tell stories about.

"I can't drink tonight. I'm sailing with you in the morning. I've got to get ready."

The mate removed the betel nut cud from his cheek and tossed it into the sea, where tiny yellow fish rose to nip at it. He eyed Pardee suspiciously. "You going to leave Truk?"

"It's not that big a deal. I've gone off-island before for a story."

"Not in ten years I sail the *Spirit*."

"Do you have room for another passenger or not?"

"We always have room. You know you have to sleep on deck?"

Pardee was beginning to get irritated. He needed a beer. "I've done this before."

The mate shook his head as if clearing his ears of water and laughed. "Okay, we sail six in morning. Be on dock at five."

"When do you come back this way?"

"A month. You can fly from Yap if you don't want to come back with us."

"A month?" He'd have to get someone to run the paper while he was gone. Or maybe not. Would anyone even notice he was gone?

Pardee said, "I'll see you in the morning. Don't get too drunk."

"You too," the mate said.

Pardee made his way down the dock, feeling every bit of his two hundred and sixty pounds. By the time he made it back to the street, he was soaked with sweat and yearning for a dark air-conditioned bar. He shook off the craving and headed for the Catholic high school to ask the nuns if they had any bright students who might keep the paper running in his absence.

He was going to do it, dammit. He'd be on the dock at five if he had to stay up all night drinking to do it.

29

Safe in the Hands of Medicine

"How are you feeling today?" Sebastian Curtis pulled the sheet down to Tuck's knees and lifted the pilot's hospital gown. Tucker flinched when the doctor touched the catheter. "Better," Tuck said. "That thing is itching, though."

"It's healing." The doctor palpated the lymph nodes in Tucker's crotch. His hands were cold and Tuck shivered at the touch. "The infection is subsiding. This happened to you in the plane crash?"

"I fell back on some levers while I was trying to get a passenger out of the plane."

"The hooker?" The doctor didn't look up from his work.

Tuck wanted to throw the sheets over his head and hide. Instead, he said, "I don't suppose it would make a difference if I said I didn't know she was a hooker."

Sebastian Curtis looked up and smiled; his eyes were light gray flecked with orange. With his gray hair and tropical tan, he could have been a retired general, Rommel maybe. "I'm not really concerned with what the woman was doing there. What does concern me is that you had been drinking. We can't have that here, Mr. Case. You may have to fly on a moment's notice, so you won't be able to drink or indulge in any other chemical diversions. I assume that won't pose a problem."

"No. None," Tuck said, but he felt like he'd been hit with a bag of sand. He'd been craving a drink since he'd regained consciousness. "By the way, Doc, since we're going to be doing business together, maybe you should call me Tucker."

"Tucker it is," Curtis said. "And you can call me Dr. Curtis." He smiled again.

"Swell. And your wife's name is?"

"Mrs. Curtis."

"Of course."

The doctor finished his examination and pulled the sheet back up to Tuck's waist. "You should be on your feet in a few days. We'll move you to your bungalow this afternoon. I think you'll find everything you need there, but if you do need anything, please let us know."

A gin and tonic, Tuck thought. "I'd like to find out what happened to the guy who was piloting my boat."

"As I told you, the islanders found you and a few pieces of your boat." There was a finality in his voice that made it clear that he didn't want to talk about Kimi or the boat.

Tuck pressed on. Respect for authority had never been his long suit. "I guess I'll ask around when I get out of here. Maybe he washed up on a different part of the island. I remember being hung in a tree with him by an old cannibal."

Tuck saw a frown cross the doctor's face like a fleeting shadow, then the professional smile was back. "Mr. Case, there haven't been any cannibals in these islands for a hundred years. Besides, I will have to ask you to stay inside the compound while you are here. You'll have access to beaches and there's plenty of room to roam, but you won't be having any contact with the islanders."

"Why, I mean if they saved me?"

"The Shark People have a very closed society. We try not to intrude on that any more than is necessary for us to do our work."

"The Shark People? Why the Shark People?"

"I'll explain it all to you when you are feeling better. Right now you need to rest." The doctor took a syringe from a metal drawer by the wall and filled it from a vial of clear fluid, then injected it into Tuck's IV. "When do you think you'll be ready to fly?"

Tuck felt as if a veil of gauze had been thrown over his mind. Everything in the room went soft and fuzzy. "Not real soon if you keep giving me that stuff. Wow, what was that? Hey, you're a doctor. Do you think we taste like Spam?"

He was going to ask another question, but somehow it didn't seem to matter anymore.

The Sorcerer stormed into the Sky Priestess's bungalow, stripped off his lab coat, and threw it into the corner. He went to the open kitchen, ripped open the freezer, pulled out a frosty fifth of Absolut, and poured a triple shot into a water glass that froze and steamed like dry ice in the humidity. "Malink lied," he said. Then he tossed back half the glass and grabbed his temples when the cold hit his brain.

The Sky Priestess looked up from her magazine. "A little stressed, darling?" She was lying out on the lanai, naked except for a wide-brimmed straw hat, her white skin shining in the sun like pearl.

The Sorcerer joined her and fell onto a chaise lounge, a hand still clamped on his temples. "Case says there was another man with him on the island. He said an old cannibal hung them in a tree."

"I heard him," the Sky Priestess said. "He's delirious?"

"I don't think so. I think Malink lied. That they found the boat pilot and didn't tell us."

She moved next to him on the chaise lounge and pried the glass of vodka out of his hand. "So send the ninjas on a search mission. You're paying them. They might as well do something."

"That's not an option and you know it."

"Well, then go yourself. Or call Malink on it. Tell him that you know there was another man and you want him brought here chop-chop."

"I think we're losing them, Beth. Malink wouldn't have dared lie to me a month ago. It's that dream. He dreams that Vincent is sending them a pilot, then you tell him it's not true, then a pilot washes up on the reef."

The Sky Priestess drained the glass of vodka and handed it back to him empty. "Yeah, nothing fucks up a good religion like the intervention of a real god."

"I wish you wouldn't talk that way."

"So what are you going to do, after you get a refill, I mean?"

The Sorcerer looked up at her as if noticing her for the first time. "Beth, what are you doing out here? The Priestess of the Sky does not have a tan."

She reached under the chaise lounge and came up with a plastic bottle of lotion. "SPF 90. Relax, 'Bastian, this stuff would keep me creamy white in a nuclear flare. You want to rub some on me?" She pushed her hat back on her head so he could see the predator seriousness in her eyes.

"Beth, please. I'm on the cusp of a crisis here."

"It's not a crisis. It's obvious why the Shark People are getting restless."

"It is?"

"No one has been chosen in over two months, 'Bastian."

He shook his head. "Case isn't ready to fly."

"Well, get him ready."

30

Fashion Statements

Kimi sat under a coconut palm outside of the bachelors' house sulking. His flowered dress was gone and he wore a blue *thu*, the long saronglike loincloth worn by the Shark men. Gone too was his blond wig, his high heels, and his best friend, Roberto, who he had not seen since the cannibal tree. Now it looked as if he had no place to sleep. Sepie had thrown him out.

Sepie came out of the bachelors' house wearing Kimi's floral dress and glared at him. She paused on the coral pathway. "I am not a monkey," she said. Then she picked up a stone from the path and hurled it at him, barely missing his head.

Kimi scuffled to the leeward side of the tree and peeked around. "I didn't say you were a monkey. I said that if you didn't shave your legs, you would soon look like a monkey."

A rock whizzed by his face so close he could feel the wind of it. She was getting more accurate with each throw. "You know nothing," she said. "You are just a girl-man."

Kimi dug a stone from the sand at his feet and hurled it at her, but his heart wasn't in it and it missed her by five feet. In English he said, "You just a poxy oar with a big mouth." He hoped this verbal missile hit closer to home. They were the last words of Malcolme, Kimi's pimp back in Manila. In retrospect, Malcolme's mistake had been one of memory. He had forgotten that the overly made-up little girl standing in front of him with a machete was, in fact, a wiry young man with the anger of hundreds of beatings burning in his memory.

"I no have the pox," Kimi said to Malcolme, whose look of surprise remained fixed even as his head rolled into the corner of the hotel room, where a rat darted out and gently licked his shortened neck.

"I no have the pox," Sepie said in English, punctuating her statement with a thrown lump of coral.

"I know," Kimi said. "I'm sorry I say that." He skulked off down the beach.

Sepie stood outside the bachelors' house watching him, totally disarmed. No man had ever apologized to her before.

Kimi hadn't meant to hurt her feelings. Sometimes it takes a thick skin to trade beauty tips with a girlfriend. Sepie was naturally pretty, but she didn't understand fashion. Why bother to put on a pretty dress if you're going to have monkey legs and tufts of hair hanging out from under your arms making it look like bats hanging there?

Bats. Kimi missed Roberto.

The Shark men wouldn't talk to him, the women ignored him, except for Sepie, who was angry at him now, and even Tucker had been taken away to the other side of the island. Kimi was lonely. And as he walked down the beach, past the children playing with a trained frigate bird, past the men lounging in the shade of an empty boathouse, his loneliness turned to anger. He turned up the beach and took a path into the village to look for a weapon. It was time to go see the old cannibal.

Outside each of the houses, near the cook sheds, stood an iron spike—a pick head that was driven into the ground and used to husk coconuts. Kimi stopped at one house and yanked on the spike, but it wouldn't budge. He moved between the houses, vacant now in the early morning, the women working in the taro field, the men lounging in various patches of shade. He peeked into a cook shed, and there, by the pot that held the crust of this morning's rice, he found a long chef's knife. He looked around to make sure that no one was watching, then bolted into the shed and snatched the knife, fitting it into his *thu* so that only the handle protruded at the small of his back.

Ten minutes later he was hiding in a patch of giant ferns, watching the old cannibal roll coconut husk fibers into rope on his leathery old thighs. He sat with his back against a palm tree, his legs straight out in front of him, pulling the fibers that had been soaked and separated out of a basket and measuring by feel the right amount to add to the coil of cord that was building on the ground beside him. From time to time he stopped and took a drink from a jar of milky liquid that Kimi was sure was alcoholic *tuba*. Good, he was drunk.

Kimi moved slowly around the house, staying in the undergrowth of ferns and elephant ears, careful not to kick up any of the coral gravel that rang like broken glass if you didn't place your feet carefully.

Once he was behind the old man, he drew the knife from the small of his back and moved forward to kill that man who had eaten his friend.

From the window of his new quarters Tucker Case watched the Japanese guards move through the compound carrying palm fronds and broken branches, detritus of the typhoon, which they piled in an open space at the side of the hangar to dry in the sun. They were dressed like a police SWAT team, in black coveralls with baseball caps and paratrooper boots, and if he squinted, they looked like giant worker ants cleaning out the nest. From time to time one of the guards would look toward his bungalow, then quickly turn away when he saw Tucker standing in the window in his pajamas. He had given up waving to them after the first hour of being ignored.

He'd been in the one-room bungalow for four days now, but this was the first time he'd felt well enough to get up and move around, other than to use the bathroom, which to his surprise, had hot and cold running water, a flush toilet, and a shower stall made of galvanized metal. The walls were tightly woven grass between a sturdy frame of teak and mahogany logs; the floor was unfinished teak, sanded smooth and pink; and the furniture was wicker with brightly colored cushions. A ceiling fan spun languidly above a double bed that was draped with a canopy of mosquito netting. The windows looked out on the compound and hangar on one side and through a grove of palm trees to the ocean on the other. He could see several bungalows perched near the beach, a small dock, and the cinderblock hospital building, its tin roof arrayed with antennae, solar electric panels, and a massive satellite dish.

Tuck backed away from the window and sat down on the wicker couch. A few minutes on his feet and he felt exhausted. He was twenty pounds lighter than when he had left Houston and there wasn't a six-inch patch of skin on his body that didn't have some kind of bandage on it. The doc had said that between the cuts on his arms, knees, and scalp, he had taken a hundred sutures. The first time he looked in the little mirror in his bathroom, he thought he was looking at a human version of the mangy feral dog he'd seen on Truk. His blue eyes lay like dull ice in sunken brown craters and his cheeks were drawn into his face like a mummified bog man's. His hair had been bleached white by the sun and stuck out in straw-dry tufts between pink patches where the doctor had shaved his scalp to stitch him up. He took small comfort in the fact that there were no women around to see him. No real women, anyway. The doctor's wife, who came several times a day to bring him food or to change his bandages, seemed robotic, like some Stepford/Barbie hybrid with the smooth sexless carriage of a mannequin and a personality pulled out of an Eisenhower-era soap commercial. She made the straight-laced cosmetic reps from his past seem like a tribe of pillbox nympho hose hunters.

There was a tap on the door and Beth Curtis breezed in carrying a wooden serving tray with plates of pancakes and fresh fruit. "Mr. Case, you're up. Feeling better today?"

She set the tray down on the coffee table in front of him and stepped back. Today she was in pleated khaki pants and a white blouse with puffed shoulders. Her hair was tied back with a big white bow at the back of her neck. She might have just walked out of a Stewart Granger safari movie.

"Yes, better," Tuck said, "But I wore myself out just walking to the window."

"Your body is still fighting off the infection. The doctor will be by soon to give you some antibiotics. For now you need to eat." She sat on the chair across from him.

Tuck cut a divot out of the stack of pancakes with a fork and speared it through a piece of papaya. After the first bite, he realized how hungry he really was and began wolfing down the pancakes.

Beth Curtis smiled. "Have you had a chance to look over the manuals for the airplane?"

Tuck nodded, his mouth still full. She'd left the operations manuals on his bed two days ago. He'd leafed through them enough to know that he could fly the thing. He swallowed and said, "I used to fly a Lear 25 for Mary Jean. This one is a little faster and has longer range, but basically it's the same. Shouldn't be a problem."

"Oh, good," she said, sporting one of her plastic smiles. "When will you be able to fly?"

Tucker put down his fork. "Mrs. Curtis, I don't mean to be rude, but what in the hell is going on around here?"

"Regarding what, Mr. Case?"

"Well, first, regarding the man I came to this island with. I was sick, but I wasn't hallucinating. We were strung up in a tree by an old native guy and cut down by a bunch of others. What happened to my friend?"

She shifted in her chair, and the wicker crackled like snapping rat bones. "My husband told you what the islanders told us, Mr. Case. The natives live on the other side of the island. They have their own society, their own chief, their own laws. We try to take care of their medical needs and bring a few souls into the fold, but they are a private people. I'll ask them about your friend. If I find out anything, I'll let you know." She stood and straightened the front of her slacks.

"I'd appreciate that," Tuck said. "I promised him I'd get him back to Yap and I owe him some money. The natives didn't find my backpack, did they? My money was in it."

She shook her head. "Just the clothes you had on. We burned them. Fortunately, you and Sebastian are about the same size. Now, if you'll excuse me, Mr. Case, I have some work to do. Sebastian will be along in a bit with your medicine. I'm glad you're feeling better." She turned and walked out the door into the blinding sunlight.

Tucker stood and watched her walk across the compound. The Japanese guards stopped their work and leered at her. She spun on them and waited, her hands on her hips, until one by one they lost their courage and returned to their work, not embarrassed but afraid, as if meeting her direct gaze might turn them to frost. Tuck sat down to his half-eaten pancakes and shivered, thinking it must be the fever.

A half hour later the doctor entered the bungalow. Tucker was spread out on the couch descending into a nap. They'd been doing this since they'd moved him to the bungalow, tag-teaming him, one showing up at least every hour to check on him, bring him food or medicine, change the sheets, take his temperature, help him to the bathroom, wipe his forehead. It looked like concerned care, but it felt like surveillance.

Sebastian Curtis took a capped syringe from his coat pocket as he crossed the room.

Tuck sighed. "Another one?"

"You must be feeling like a pin cushion by now, Mr. Case. I need you to roll over."

Tuck rolled over and the doctor gave him the injection. "It's either this or the IV. We've got this infection on the run, but we don't want it to get a foothold again."

Tuck rubbed his bottom and sat up. Before he could say anything, the doctor stuck a digital thermometer in his mouth.

"Beth tells me that you're worried about your friend, the one you say came to the island with you?"

Tuck nodded.

"I'll check into it, I promise you. In the meantime, if you're feeling up to it, Beth and I would like you to join us for dinner. Get to know each other a little. Let you know what's expected of you." He pulled the thermometer out of Tuck's mouth and checked it but made no comment. "You up for dinner tonight?"

"Sure," Tuck said. "But . . ."

"Good. We'll eat at seven. I'll have Beth bring you down some clothes. I'm sorry about the hand-me-downs, but it's the best we can do for now." He started to leave.

"Doc?"

Sebastian turned. "Yes."

"You've been out here, what, thirty years?"

The doctor stiffened. "Twenty-eight. Why?"

"Well, Mrs. Curtis doesn't look . . ."

"Yes, Beth is quite a bit younger than I am. But we can talk about all that at dinner. You should probably rest now and let those anti-biotics do their work. I need you healthy, Mr. Case. We have a round of golf to play."

"Golf?"

"You do play, don't you?"

Tuck took a second to catch up with the abrupt change of subject, then said, "You play golf here?"

"I *am* a physician, Mr. Case. Even in the Pacific we have Wednesdays." Then he smiled and left the bungalow.

31

Revenge: Sweet and Low in Calories

Sarapul twisted the last of the fibers into his rope and drew his knife to trim the ragged end. It was a good knife, made in Germany, with a thin flexible blade that was perfect for filleting fish or cutting microthin slices from coconut stems to keep the *tuba* running. He'd had the knife for ten years and he kept it honed and polished on a piece of tanned pig hide. The blade flashed blue as he picked it up and he saw the face of vengeance reflected in the metal.

Without turning, he said, "The young ones are going to kill you."

Kimi stopped, his knife held ready to strike the old man in the neck. "You ate my friend."

Sarapul gripped his knife blade down so he might turn and slash at the same time. There was no quickness in his bones, though. The Filipino would kill him before he got halfway around. "Your friend is with the white Sorcerer and Vincent's bitch. Malink took him away."

"Not that one. Roberto. The bat."

"Bats are taboo. We don't eat bats on Alualu."

Kimi lowered his knife an inch. "You are not supposed to eat people either, but you do."

"Not people I know. Come over here where I can see you. I am old and my neck won't turn that far around."

Kimi walked a crescent around the tree and crouched at ready in front of the old man.

Sarapul said, "You were going to kill me."

"If you ate Roberto."

"I like that. Nobody kills anybody anymore. Oh, the young ones are talking about killing you, but I think Malink will talk them out of it."

Kimi cleared his throat. "Were you going to eat me when they killed me?"

"Someone brought that up at the drinking circle. I don't remember who."

"Then how do I know you did not eat Roberto?"

"Look at me, little one. I am a hundred years old maybe. Sometimes I go to the beach to pee and the tides change before my water comes. How would I catch a bat?"

Kimi sat down on the ground across from the old man and dropped his knife in the gravel. "Something happened to Roberto. He flew off."

"Maybe he found a girl bat," Sarapul said. "Maybe he will come back. You want a drink?" The old cannibal offered his jar of *tuba* to Kimi, who leaned forward and snatched it before retreating out of knife range.

Kimi took a sip and grimaced. "Why are they going to kill me?"

"They say you are a girl-man and that you make Sepie forget her duties as mispel. And they don't like you. Don't worry, no one kills anyone anymore. It is just drunk talk."

Kimi hung his head. "Sepie sent me away from the bachelors' house. She is mad at me. I have nowhere to go."

Sarapul nodded in sympathy, but said nothing. He'd been exiled for so long that he'd gotten used to the alienation, but he remembered how he had felt when Malink had first banished him.

"You speak our language pretty good," Sarapul said.

"My father was from Satawan. He was a great navigator. He taught me."

"You're a navigator?" In the old days the navigators stood above even the chiefs—and just below the gods. As a boy, Sarapul idolized the two navigators of Alualu. The long-dead dream of his boyhood surfaced and he remembered learning from them, watching them draw star charts in the sand and stand at the beach lecturing on tides and currents and winds. He had wanted to be a navigator, had begun the training, for in the rigid caste system of the Yapese islands it was the one way for a man to distinguish himself. But one of the navigators had died of a fever and the other was killed in a fight before he could pass on his knowledge. The navigators and warriors were ghosts of the past. If this girl-man was a navigator, then the bachelors were piss ants to talk of killing him. Sarpul felt infused with an energy he hadn't felt in years.

"I can show you something," Sarapul said. He tried to climb to his feet and fell back into a crouch. Kimi took him by a bony arm and helped him up. "Come," Sarapul said.

The old man led Kimi down the path to the beach and stopped at the water's edge. He began to sing, his voice like dried palm leaves rattling in the wind. He waved his arms in arcs, then threw them wide to the sky so that his chest looked as if it might crack open like a rotten breadfruit. And the wind came up.

He took handfuls of sand and cast them into the wind, then clapped his hands and resumed singing until the palms above them were waving in the wind. Then he stopped.

"Now we wait," he said. He pointed out to sea. "Watch there."

A column of fog rose off the ocean at the horizon and boiled black and silver into a huge thunderhead. Sarapul clapped his hands again and a lightning bolt ripped out of the cloud and across the sky like a jagged white fissure in blue glass. The thunderclap was instant, deafening, and crackled for a full ten seconds.

Sarapul turned to Kimi, who was staring at the thunderhead with his mouth open. "Can you do that?"

Kimi shook off his astonishment with a shiver. "No, I never learned that. My father said he could send the thunder, but I didn't see him do it."

Sarapul grinned. "Ever eat a guy?"

Kimi shook his head. "No."

"Tastes like Spam," Sarapul said.

"I heard that."

"I can teach you to send the thunder. I don't know the stars, though."

"I know the stars," Kimi said.

"Go get your things," Sarapul said.

32

The Missionary Position

The guards came for Tucker at sunset, just as he was slipping into the cotton pants and shirt the doctor had left for him. The doctor's clothes were at least three sizes too big for him, but with the bandages he had to put them over, that was a blessing. He still had his own sneakers, which he put on his bare feet. He asked the guards to wait and they stood just inside his door, as straight and silent as terra-cotta soldiers.

"So, you guys speak English?"

The guards didn't answer. They watched him.

"Japanese, huh? I've never been to Japan. I hear a Big Mac goes for twelve bucks."

He waited for some response and got none. The Japanese stood impassive, silent, small beads of sweat shining through their crew cuts.

"Sorry, guys, I'd love to hang around with you chatterboxes, but I'm due for dinner with the doc and his wife."

Tuck limped to the guards and offered each an arm in escort. "Shall we go?"

The guards turned and led him across the compound to one of the bungalows on the beach. The guards stopped at the steps of the lanai and Tuck dug into his pants pockets. "Sorry guys, no cash. Have the concierge put a couple of yen on my bill."

The doctor came through the french doors in a white ice cream suit, carrying a tall iced drink garnished with mango. "Mr. Case, you're looking much better. How are you feeling?"

"Nothing wrong with me one of those won't cure."

Sebastian Curtis frowned. "I'm afraid not. You shouldn't drink alcohol with the antibiotics I have you on."

Tucker felt his guts twist. "Just one won't hurt, will it?"

"I'm afraid so. But I'll make you one without alcohol. Come in. Beth is making a wonderful grouper in ginger sauce."

Tucker went though the french doors to find a bungalow decorated much like his own, only larger. There was an open kitchen nook where Beth Curtis was stirring something with a wooden spoon. She looked up and smiled. "Mr. Case, just in time. I need someone to taste this sauce." She was wearing a cream-colored Joan Crawford number with middle linebacker shoulder pads and buff-colored high heels. The dress was straight out of the forties, but Tuck had been around Mary Jean long enough to know that Mrs. Curtis had dropped at least five hundred bucks on the shoes. Evidently, missionary work paid pretty well.

She held a hand under Tuck's chin as she presented the spoon. The sauce was sweet citrus with a piquant bite to it. "It's good," he said. "Really good."

"No fibbing, Mr. Case. You're going to have to eat it."

"No, I like it."

"Well, good. Dinner will be ready in about a half hour. Now, why don't you men take your drinks out on the lanai and let a girl do her magic."

Sebastian handed Tuck an icy glass filled with an orange liquid and garnished with mango. "Shall we?" he said, leading Tuck back outside.

They stood at the railing, looking out at the moon reflecting in the ocean.

"Would you be more comfortable sitting, Mr. Case?" the doctor asked.

"No, I'm fine. And please call me Tuck. Anyone calls me Mr. Case more than three times, I start thinking I'm going to get audited."

The doctor laughed, "We can't have that. Not with the kind of money you're going to be making. But legally, you know, it's tax-free until you take it back into the United States."

Tuck stared out at the ocean for a moment, wondering whether it was time to give this gift horse a dental exam. There was just too damn much money showing on this island.

The equipment, the plane, Beth Curtis's clothes. After Jake Skye's lecture, Tuck had imagined that he might encounter some sweaty drug-smuggling doctor with a Walther in his belt and a coke whore wife, but these two could have just flown in from an upscale church social. Still, he knew they were lying to him. They had referred to the Japanese as their "staff," but he'd seen one of them carrying an Uzi out behind the hangar. He was going to ask, he really was, but as he turned to face the doctor, he heard a soft bark at the end of the lanai and looked up to see a large fruit bat hanging from the edge of the tin roof. Roberto.

The doctor said, "Tucker, about the drinking."

Tuck pulled his gaze away from the bat. The doctor had seen him. "What drinking?"

"You know that we saw the reports on your—how should I put it?"

"Crash."

"Yes, on your crash. I'm afraid, as I told you, we can't have you drinking while you're working here. We may need you to fly on very short notice and we can't risk that you might not be ready."

"That was an isolated incident," Tuck lied. "I really don't drink much."

"Just a momentary lapse of judgment, I understand. And it may seem a bit draconian, but as long as you don't drink or go out of the compound, everything will be fine."

"Sure, no problem." Tuck was watching the bat over the doctor's shoulder. Roberto had unfurled his wings and was turning in the sea breeze like an inverted weather vane. Tuck tried to wave him off behind the doctor's back.

"I know this may all seem very limiting, but I've worked with the Shark People for a long time, and they're very sensitive to contact with outsiders."

"The Shark People? You said you'd explain that."

"They hunt sharks. Most of the natives in Micronesia won't eat shark. In fact, it's taboo. But the reef fish here often have a high concentration of neurotoxin, so the natives developed shark as a food source. You would think that the sharks, being higher on the food chain, would have a higher concentration of the toxin, wouldn't you?"

"You'd think," Tuck said, having no idea whatsoever what the doctor was talking about.

"They don't, though. It's as if something in their system neutralizes the toxin. I've done a little research in my spare time."

"I've seen a lot of shark shows on the Discovery Channel. They go on and on about how harmless sharks are. It's bullshit. Half of these stitches you put in me are because of a shark attack."

"Maybe they don't have cable," the doctor said.

Tuck turned to him, amazed. "A joke, Doc?"

The doctor looked a little embarrassed. "I'm going to go see how dinner is coming along. I'll be right back." He turned and went into the house.

Tucker bolted to the end of the lanai where Roberto was hanging. "Shoo. Go away."

Roberto made a trilling noise and tried to catch Tuck's drink with his wing claw.

"Okay, you can have the mango, but then you have to get out of here." Tucker held out the piece of cut mango and the fruit bat took it in his wing claw and slurped it down.

"Now get out of here," Tucker said. "Go find Kimi. Shoo, shoo."

Roberto tilted his head and said, "Back off on these people, Tuck. You push them too hard, they'll pull your plug. Just keep your eyes open."

Tuck moved away from the bat with stiff jerking steps out of the line dance of the undead. The bat had said something. It was a tiny voice, high but raspy, the voice of a chain-smoking Topo Gigio, but it was clear. "You didn't talk," Tucker said.

"Okay," said Roberto. "Thanks for the mango."

Roberto took off, the beat of his wings like the shuffle of a deck of leather cards. Tuck backed though the french doors into a wicker emperor's chair and sat down.

"Come sit," Beth Curtis said as she carried a tray to the table. "Dinner's ready."

"What kind of drugs have you been giving me, Doc?"

"Broad-spectrum antibiotics and some Tylenol. Why?"

"Any chance they could cause hallucinations?"

"Not unless you were allergic, and we'd know that by now. Why?"

"Just wondering."

Beth Curtis came to him and patted his shoulder. Her nails, he noticed, were perfect. "You had a fever when they brought you in. Sometimes that can give a person bad dreams. I think you'll feel a lot better after a good meal."

She helped him up and led him to the table, which was set with a white tablecloth and black linen napkins around a centerpiece of orchid sprigs arranged in a crystal bowl. A whole grouper stared up between fanned slices of plantain on a serving tray, his eye a little dry but clear and accusing.

Tuck said, "If that thing starts talking, I want to be sedated—and right now."

"Oh, Mr. Case." Beth Curtis rolled her eyes and laughed as they sat down to dinner.

Tuck could almost feel his body absorbing the nourishment. He told them the story of his journey to the island, exaggerating the danger aspect and glossing over his injuries, Kimi, and his craving for alcohol. He didn't mention Roberto at all. By the time Tucker was in the typhoon, the Curtises were well into their second bottle of white wine. Beth's cheeks were flushed and her eyes sparkled with enthusiasm for Tuck's every word.

Tuck really intended to ask about Kimi, their cryptic messages, the guards, the rules for his employment, and of course, where the hell all the money came from, but instead he found himself playing to Beth Curtis like a comedian on a roll and he left the bungalow at midnight quite taken with both himself and the doctor's wife.

The Curtises stood arm in arm at the door as the guards escorted Tucker back to his quarters. Halfway across the compound, he did a giddy turn and waved to them, feeling as if *he* had been the one to consume two bottles of wine.

"What do you think?" the Sorcerer asked his wife.

"Not a problem," she said, keeping a parade smile pointed Tuck's way.

"I really expected him to be a little more resistant to our conditions."

"As if he's in a position to bargain. The man has nothing, is nothing. He shatters this little illusion we've given him and he has to face himself."

"He looks at you like you're some sort of beatific vestal virgin. I don't like it."

"I can handle that. You just get flyboy ready to do his job."

"He'll be able to fly within a week. He brought up his navigator again while we were outside."

"If he's here, you'd better find him."

"I'll speak to Malink tonight. The *Micro Spirit* is due in day after tomorrow. If we find the navigator, we can send him back on the ship."

"Depending on what he's seen," she said.
"Yes, depending on what he knows."

Tucker Case entered his bungalow feeling satisfied and full of himself. Someone had turned on the lights in his absence and turned down the bed. "What, no mint on the pillow?"

He changed into a pair of the doctor's pajama bottoms and grabbed a paperback spy novel from a stack someone had left on the coffee table.

They had a TV. There had been a TV in the Curtises' bungalow. He'd have to ask them to get him one. No, dammit, demand a television. What did Mary Jean always say? "You can sell all day, but if you don't ask for the money, you haven't made a sale." Good food, good money, and a great aircraft to fly—he'd stumbled into the best gig on the planet. I am the Phoenix, rising from the ashes. I am the comeback kid. I am the entire 1980 gold-medal-winning U.S. Olympic hockey team. I am the fucking walrus, coo-coo ka-choo.

He went into the bathroom to brush his teeth, caught his reflection in the mirror. His mood went terminal. I am never going to get laid again as long as I live. I should have pressed them about Kimi. I didn't even ask about what in the hell kind of cargo I'm going to be flying. I am a spineless worm. I'm scum. I'm the *Hindenburg*, I'm Michael Milken, Richard Nixon. I'm seeing ghosts and bats that talk and I'm stuck on an island where the only woman makes Mother Theresa look like a lap dancer in a leper colony. I am the man who put the *F* in failure, the *P* in pathetic, the *G* in gullible. I am the ringworm poster boy of Gangrene City. I'm an insane, unemployed bus driver for the death camp cartel.

Tuck went to bed without brushing his teeth.

33

Chasing the Scoop

Natives slept side by side, crisscrossed, and piled on the deck of the *Micro Spirit* until—with a *thu* showing here, or a lavalava there, streams of primary color among all that gelatinous brown flesh—it looked as if someone had dropped a big box of candy in the hot sun and they had melted together and spilled their fillings. Amid the mess, Jefferson Pardee, rolled and pitched with the ship, finding three sleeping children lying on him when the ship moved to starboard, a rotund island grandmother washing against him when the ship listed to port. He'd been stepped on three times by ashy callused feet, once on the groin, and he was relatively sure he could feel lice crawling in his scalp.

Unable to sleep, he stood up and the mass moved amoebalike into the vacated deck space. A three-quarter moon shone high and bright, and Pardee could see well enough to make his way through to the railing, only stepping on one woman and evoking colorful island curses from two men. Once at the rail, the warm wind washed away the cloying smell of sweat and the rancid nut smell of copra coming from the holds. The moon's reflection lay in the black sea like a tossing pool of mercury. A pod of dolphins rode the ship's bow wave like gray ghosts.

He took several deep breaths, relieved himself over the side, then dug a bent cigarette out of his shirt pocket. He lit it with a disposable lighter and exhaled a contrail of smoke with a long sigh. Thirty years in the tropics had given him a high tolerance for discomfort and inconvenience, but the break in routine was maddening. Back on Truk, he'd be toweling off the smell of stale beer and the residue of an oily tumble with a dollar whore, preparing to pass out with a volume of Mencken under his little air conditioner. No thought of the day to come or the one just passed, for one was like the next and they were all the same. Just cool cloudy sleep that made him feel, if only for a minute, like that young Midwestern boy on an adventure, exhausted from passion and fear, rather than a fat old man worn down by ennui.

And here, in the salt and the moonlight, on the trail of a story or maybe just a rumor, he felt the fungus growing in his lungs, the pain in his lower back, the weight of ten thousand beers and half a million cigarettes and thirty years of fish fried in coconut oil pressing on his heart, and none of it—none of it—was so heavy as the possibility of dashed hopes. Why had he opened himself up to a future and failure, when he had been failing just fine already?

"You can't sleep?" the mate said.

Pardee hadn't heard the wiry sailor move to the rail. He was drinking a Bud tallboy, against regulations, and Pardee felt a craving twist like a worm in his chest at the sight of the can.

"You got another one of those?"

The mate reached into the deep front pocket of his shorts, pulled out another beer, and handed it to Pardee. It was warm, but Pardee popped the top and drank off half of it in one gulp.

"How long before we make Alualu?" Pardee asked.

"Three, maybe four hour. Sunrise. We drop you on north side of island, you swim in."

"What?" Pardee looked down to the black waves, then back at the mate.

"The doctor no let anyone go on the island except to bring cargo. You have to swim in on other side of island. Maybe half mile, maybe less."

"How will I get back to the ship?"

"Captain say he will swing back around the island when we leave. Captain say he wait half an hour. You swim back out. We pick you up."

"Can't you send a boat?"

"No boat. No break in reef except on south side where we unload. We have many fuel barrel and crates. You will have seven, maybe eight hour."

Pardee had seen the *Spirit* arrive in Truk lagoon a thousand times; the ship was always surrounded by outboards and canoes filled with excited natives. "Maybe I can get one of the Shark People to ferry me." He did not want to get in that water, and he certainly didn't want to swim half a mile to shore, wasn't sure he could.

"Shark People no have boat. They no leave island."

"No boats?" Pardee was amazed. Living in these islands without a boat was akin to living in Los Angeles without a car. It wasn't done; it couldn't be done.

The mate patted Pardee's big shoulder. "You be fine. I have mask and fins for you."

"What about sharks?"

"Sharks afraid around there. On most island people afraid of shark. On Alualu shark afraid of people."

"You're sure about that?"

"No."

"Oh, good. Do you have another beer?"

Three hours later the rising sun lay like a silver tray on the horizon and Jefferson Pardee was having swim fins duct-taped to his feet by the first mate. The deck bustled with excited natives eating rice balls and taro paste, smoking cigarettes, shitting over the railings, and milling around the ship's store, trying to buy Cokes and Planter's cheese balls, Australian corned beef, and, of course, Spam. A small crowd had gathered around to watch the white man prepare for his swim. Pardee stood in his boxer shorts, maggot white except for his forearms and face, which looked like they'd been dipped in red barn paint. The mate stuffed Pardee's clothes and notebook into a garbage bag and handed it to him, then slathered the journalist with waterproof sunscreen, a task on par with basting a hippo. Pardee snarled at a group of giggling children and they ran off down the deck screaming.

Pardee heard the ship's big screws grind to a halt and the mate unhooked a chain gate set in the railing. "Jump," he said.

Pardee looked at the crystal water forty feet below. "You're out of your fucking mind. Don't you have a ladder?"

"You can't climb ladder with fins."

"I'll take the fins off until I get in the water."

"No. Straps broken. You have to jump."

Pardee shook his head and the flesh on his shoulders and back followed suit. "It's not gonna happen."

Suddenly the children Pardee had frightened came running around the bridge like a squealing pack of piglets. Two little boys broke formation and ran toward the journalist, who looked around just as he felt four tiny brown hands impact with his back.

Pardee saw sky, then water, then sky, then the island of Alualu laying on the sea like a bad green toupee, then the impact with the water took his breath, ripped the mask from his face, and forced streams of brine into his sinuses strong enough to bring blood.

Before he could even find the surface, he heard the ship's screws begin to grind as the *Micro Spirit* steamed away.

Two excited boys shook Malink awake. "The ship is here and the Sorcerer is coming!" The old chief sat up on his grass sleeping mat and wiped the sleep from his eyes. He slept on the porch of his house, part of the stone foundation that had been there for eight hundred years. He stood on creaking morning legs and went to the bunch of red bananas that hung from the porch roof. He tore off two bananas and gave them to the boys.

"Where did you see the Sorcerer?"

"He comes across Vincent's airstrip."

"Good boys. You go eat breakfast now."

Malink went to a stand of ferns behind his house, pulled aside his *thu*, and waited to relieve himself. This took longer every day it seemed. The Sorcerer had told Malink that he had angered the prostate monster and the only way to appease him was to quit drinking coffee and *tuba* and to eat the bitter root of the saw palmetto. Malink had tried these things for almost two full days before giving up, but it was too hard to wake up without coffee, too hard to go to sleep without *tuba*, saw palmetto made his stomach hurt, and he seemed to have a headache all the time. The prostate monster would just have to remain angry. Sometimes the Sorcerer was wrong.

He finished and straightened his *thu*, passed a thundering cannonade of gas, then went back to the sitting spot on the porch to get his cigarettes. The women had made a fire to boil water for coffee; the smoke from the burning coconut husks wafted out of the corrugated tin cookhouse and hung like blue fog under the canopy of breadfruit, mahogany, and palm trees.

Malink lit a cigarette and looked up to see the Sorcerer coming down the coral path, his white lab coat stark against the browns and greens of the village.

"*Saswitch*" (good morning), Malink said. The Sorcerer spoke their language.

"*Saswitch*, Malink," the Sorcerer said. At the sound of his voice

Malink's wife and daughters ran out of the cookhouse and disappeared down the paths of the village.

"Coffee?" Malink asked in English.

"No, Malink, there is no time today."

Malink frowned. It was rude for anyone to turn down an offer of food or drink, even the Sorcerer. "We have little Tang. You want Tang? Spacemen drink it."

The Sorcerer shook his head. "Malink, there was another man here with the pilot you found. I need to find him."

Malink looked at the ground. "I no see any other man." The Sorcerer didn't seem angry, but just the same, Malink didn't like lying to him. He didn't want to anger Vincent.

"I won't punish anyone if something happened to him, if he was hurt or drowned, but I need to know where he is. Vincent has asked me to find him, Malink."

Malink could feel the Sorcerer staring a hole in the top of his head. "Maybe I see another man. I will ask at the men's house today. What he look like?"

"You know what he looks like. I need to find him now. The Sky Priestess will give back the coffee and sugar if we can find him today."

Malink stood. "Come, we find him." He led the Sorcerer through the village, which appeared deserted except for a few chickens and dogs, but Malink could see eyes peeking out from the doorways. How would he explain this when they asked why the Sorcerer had come? They passed out of the village, went past the abandoned church, the graveyard, where great slabs of coral rock kept the bodies from floating up through the soil during the rainy season, and down the overgrown path to Sarapul's little house.

The old cannibal was sitting in his doorway sharpening his machete.

Malink turned to the Sorcerer and whispered, "He rude sometime. He very old. Don't be mad."

The Sorcerer nodded.

"*Saswitch,* Sarapul. The Sorcerer has come to see you."

Sarapul looked up and glared at them. He had red chicken feathers stuck in his hair, two severed chicken feet hung from a cord above his head. "All the sorcerers are dead," Sarapul said. "He is just a white doctor."

Malink looked at the Sorcerer apologetically, then turned back to Sarapul. "He wants to see the man you found with the pilot."

Sarapul ran his thumb over the edge of his machete. "I don't know what happened to him. Maybe he went swimming and a shark got him. Maybe someone eat him."

Sebastian Curtis stepped forward. "He won't be hurt," he said. "We are going to send him out on the ship."

"I want to go to the ship," Sarapul said. "I want to buy things. Why can't we go to the ship?"

"That's not the issue here, old man. Vincent wants this man found. If he's dead, I need to know."

"Vincent is dead."

The Sorcerer crouched down until he was eye-to-eye with the old cannibal. "You've seen the guards at the compound, Sarapul. If the man isn't at the gate in an hour, I'm going to have the guards tear the island apart until they find him."

Sarapul grinned. "The Japanese? Good. You send them here." He swung his machete in front of the sorcerer's face. "I have a present for them."

Curtis stood. "An hour." He turned and walked away.

Malink ambled along behind him. "Maybe he is right. Maybe the man drown or something."

"Find him, Malink. I meant it about the guards. I want this man in an hour."

"He is gone," Sarapul said. "You can come out."

Kimi dropped out of the rafters of Sarapul's little house. "What is he talking about—guards?"

"Ha!" Sarapul said. "He knows nothing. He didn't even know I had this." Sarapul reached down and pulled out a headless chicken he had been sitting on. "He is no sorcerer."

"He said there were guards." Kimi said.

Sarapul laid his chicken on the ground. "If you are afraid, you should go."

"I have to find Roberto."

"Then let them send the guards," Sarapul said, brandishing his machete. "They can die just like this chicken."

Kimi stepped back from the old cannibal, who was on the verge of foaming at the mouth. "We friends, right?"

"Build a fire," Sarapul said. "I want to eat my chicken."

34

Water Hazard

Jefferson Pardee was trying desperately not to look like a sea turtle. He'd managed to find the surface, catch his breath, and put his mask on. Blood from his nose was now swishing around inside it like brandy in a snifter. After locating the floating garbage bag that contained his clothes and propping it under his chest as a life preserver, his main focus was not to look like a turtle. To a shark living in the warm Pacific waters off Alualu, sea turtles were food. Not that there was any real danger of a shark making that particular mistake. Even a mentally challenged shark would figure out that sea turtles did not wear boxer shorts printed in flying piggies, and no turtle would be yattering streams of obscenities between chain-smoker gasps of breath. Still, a couple of harmless white-tipped reef sharks smelled blood in the water and cruised by to check out the source, only to retreat, regretting that in one hundred and twenty million years on the planet they had never evolved the equipment to laugh.

The surf was calm and the tide low, and considering Pardee's buoyancy, the swim should have been easy. But when Pardee saw the two black shadows cruise by below him, his heart started playing a sternum-rattling drum solo that kept up until he barked his knees on the reef. An antler of coral caught the plastic bag, stopping Pardee's progress long enough for him to notice that here on the reef the water was only two feet deep. He flipped over on his back, then sat on the coral, not really caring that it was cutting into his bottom. Waves lapped around him as he fought to catch his breath. He lifted his mask and let the blood run down his face and over his chest to expand into a rusty stain in the water. Tiny blue and yellow reef fish rose around him looking for food and nipping at his skin, tickling him like teasing children.

He looked toward the beach, perhaps two hundred yards away. Inside the reef the danger of sharks was minimal—minimal enough that he would sit here and rest for a while. He watched the waves breaking softly around him, lapping against his back, and realized, with horror, that he was going to have to do this again in a few hours, against the waves and probably the tide. He'd have to find someone with a boat; that was all there was to it.

Ten minutes passed before his heart slowed down and he was able to steel his courage enough to swim the final leg. He picked out a stand of coconut palms above a small beach and slid across the reef toward the island. He kicked slowly, scanning the water around him for any sign of sharks. Except for a moment of temporary terror when a manta ray with a seven-foot wingspan flew out of the blue and passed below him, the swim to the beach was safe and easy. If manta rays are going to be harmless, they should look more harmless, Pardee thought. Fuckers look like aquatic Draculas.

He sat in the wash at the water's edge and was tearing the tape that held the fins on his feet when he heard a sharp mechanical click behind him. He turned to see two men in black pointing Uzis at his head. Pardee grinned. "*Konichi-wa*," he said. "You guys have a dry cigarette? I seem to have torn my garbage bag."

A seven iron, Tuck, thought. After all these years I need a seven iron.

Tucker Case did not play golf. He'd tried it once, and although he'd enjoyed the drinking and driving the little electric car into the lake, he just didn't get the appeal. It seemed—and he'd examined the game closely because his father had loved it—an awful lot like a bunch of rich white guys in goofy clothing walking around on an absurdly large lawn hitting absurdly small white balls with crooked sticks. If the greens were at opposite ends of the same fairway and foursomes had to play against each other, defending their own green while assaulting the opponents' and risking getting hit with a ball or a club at close quarters, well, then you'd have a game. If the game was scored on how quickly one got through the eighteen holes instead of the fewest strokes and they dropped small-block Chevys into the little carts, why, then you'd have yourself a game. (Maybe put those little *Ben-Hur* food processors on the wheels and make it legal to hamstring competitors.) But traditional golf, as it was, had always left Tuck cold. Strange, then, that he absolutely yearned for a seven iron, or maybe a shotgun.

Tuck had been up since before dawn, awakened rudely and kept awake by what seemed like eight million roosters. It was now ten o'clock and they were still going strong. What joy to feel the *thwack* of a seven iron on red feathers, the satisfying impact of balanced metal on poultry (suddenly silenced and somewhat tenderized for your trouble). He saw himself wading into a bucket of roosters, swinging his seven iron madly (but always keeping his head down and his left arm straight), dealing death and destruction like the Colonel's own avenging angel. Welcome to Tucker Case's chicken death camp, my little feathered friends. Now, kindly prepare to have your nuggets knocked off.

Tucker Case was not a morning person.

He decided that he'd give them five more minutes to shut up, then he was going to get dressed and go borrow a seven iron from the doc. Five minutes later he was preparing to leave when Beth Curtis knocked and opened his door without waiting for an answer. She was wearing disposable surgical blues and a hairnet; she wore no makeup and the vapid housewife smile was gone from her eyes.

"Mr. Case, we need you to be ready to fly in two hours. Can you do it?"

"Uh, sure. I guess. Where are we going?"

"Japan. The navigational settings should already be programmed into the plane's computer. I need you to have your pre-flight finished and the Lear fueled and on the runway, ready to go."

Tucker felt as if he was talking to a different person than the one he had seen for the last week. There was no hint of the soft femininity, just hard business.

"I haven't had time to go over the controls for the Lear."

"You took the job, didn't you? Can you fly it?"

Tuck nodded.

"Then be ready in two hours." She turned and marched toward the hospital building. Tuck started to follow her, then noticed movement through the trees, down by the beach: men unloading fuel drums from a longboat onto the pier. He could see a white freighter anchored outside the reef.

"Mrs. Curtis!" he called.

She turned and regarded him like an annoying insect. "Yes, Mr. Case."

"That ship. You didn't tell me there was a ship."

"It doesn't concern you. They are simply delivering some supplies. Now please, prepare the plane."

"But if they're delivering supplies, why do we need to ...?"

"Mr. Case," she barked, "do your job. The doctor needs me." She threw open the hospital door and stepped inside.

"Ask him if I can borrow his seven iron," Tuck said weakly.

Tuck shuffled back toward his bungalow. Just a few seconds in the sun had given him a headache and he felt as if he would pass out any second. He was going to fly again. He was sick and dizzy and suffered from talking bat hallucinations and he was going to get to do the only thing he had ever been any good at. It scared the hell out of him.

It had been fifty years since men with guns had entered the village of the Shark People. As the four guards went from house to house, Malink walked the paths of the village, his cordless phone in hand so the people could see that he had things under control. He'd been calling the Sorcerer since the four Japanese had arrived in the village, but he'd only gotten the answering machine. He had told everyone to go inside their houses and not to resist the guards, and even now the village seem deserted, except for the sobs of a few frightened children. He could hear the guards kicking their way through the coconut husks that had been piled in the cookhouses for fuel.

Suddenly Favo was at his side. Favo, who had seen the coming of the Japanese during the war, had seen the killing. "Why does Vincent allow this?"

Malink really didn't have an answer. He had lit the Zippo and asked Vincent that very morning. "It is the will of the Sorcerer, so it must be the will of Vincent. They want the girl-man."

"We should fight," Favo said. "We should kill the guards."

"Spears against machine guns, Favo? Should the children grow up without fathers like we did? No, they will find the girl-man and they will go away."

"The girl-man has gone to live with Sarapul. Did you tell them?"

"I told them. I took the Sorcerer there."

The guards came out of the old church and crunched in single file down the path toward Favo and Malink. The old men stood their ground, making the guards walk into a stand of ferns to get around them. They made no eye contact and said nothing. Favo hurled a curse at them, but it had been too long since he had spoken Japanese and it was not a language suited for swearing. He ended up telling them that their truck tires smelled of sardines, which elicited no response whatsoever.

"Excellent curse," Malink said, trying to raise his friend's spirits.

"It needs work. English is the best for swearing."

"They have machine guns, Favo."

"Fuckin' mooks," Favo said.

"Amen," Malink said, crossing himself in the sign of the B-26 bomber.

The two old men fell in behind the guards, following them from house to house, waiting outside on the path so the villagers could see them when they were roused out of their houses.

For the guards' part, it was a wholly unsatisfying endeavor. They had been looking forward to kicking in some doors, only to find that the Shark People had no doors. There were no beds to throw over, no back rooms to burst into, no closets, no place, in fact, where a man could hide and not be exposed by the most perfunctory inspection. And the doctor had told them that no one was to be hurt. They did not want to make a mistake. For all the appearance of military efficiency, they were screwups to a man. One, a former security guard at a nuclear power plant, had been fired for taking drugs; two were brothers who had been dismissed from the Tokyo police department for accepting Yakuza bribes; the fourth, from Okinawa, had been a jujitsu instructor who had beaten a German tourist to death in a bar over a gross miscarriage of karaoke. The man who had recruited them, put them in the black uniforms, and trained them made it clear that this was their last chance. They had two choices: succeed and become rich or die. They took their jobs very seriously.

"He might be in the trees," Favo said in Japanese. "Look in the trees!"

The guards scanned the trees as they marched, which caused them to bump into each other and stumble. Above them there was a fluttering of wings. A glout of bat guano splatted across the Okinawan's forehead. He threw the bolt on his Uzi and the air was filled with the staccato roar of nine millimeters ripping through the foliage. When at last the clip was empty, palm fronds settled to the ground around them. Frightened children screamed in their mothers' arms, and Favo, who was lying next to his friend with his arms thrown over his head, snickered like an asthmatic hyena.

The guards scuffled for a moment, not sure whether to disarm their companion or shove their clips home and begin the massacre. Above the crying, the scuffle, the snickering, and the tintinnabulation of residual gunfire, a girl giggled. The guards looked up. Sepie stood in the doorway of the bachelors' house, naked but for a pair of panties she'd recently acquired from a transvestite navigator. "Hey, sailors," she said, trying out a phrase she'd also acquired from Kimi, "you want a date?" The guards didn't understand the words, but they got the message.

"Go inside, girl," Malink scolded. Women, even the mispel, were not permitted to show their thighs in public. Not even when swimming, not when bathing, not when crapping on the beach, not ever.

"Go back inside," Favo said. "When they go away, you will be beaten."

"I have been beaten before," Sepie said. "Now I will be rich."

"Tell her," Favo said to Malink.

Malink shrugged. His authority as chief worked only as long as his people willingly obeyed him. The key to retaining their respect was to find out what they wanted to do, then tell them to do it. He levied the most severe punishment he knew. "Sepie, you may not touch the sea for ten days."

She turned and wiggled her bottom at him, then disappeared into the bachelors' house. The stunned guards ceased their scuffle and moved tentatively toward the doorway, looking to each other for permission.

"This is your fault," Malink said to Favo. "You shouldn't have started giving her things."

"I didn't give her things," Favo said.

"You gave her things for"—and here Malink paused, trying to catch himself before losing a friend—"for doing favors for you."

35

Free Press, My Ass

Jefferson Pardee sat on a metal office chair in the corner of a windowless cinder-block room. The guard stood by the metal door, his machine gun trained on Pardee's hairy chest. The reporter was trying to affect an attitude of innocence tempered with a little righteous indignation, but, in fact, he was terrified. He could feel his heartbeat climbing into his throat and sweat rolled down his back in icy streams. He'd given up on trying to talk to the guards; they either didn't speak English or were pretending they didn't.

He heard the throw of the heavy bolt on the door and expected the other guard to return, but instead a woman wearing surgical garb entered the room. Her eyes were the same color as the surgical blues and even in the oppressive heat she looked chilly.

"At last," Pardee said. "There's been some kind of mistake here." He offered his hand, trying not to show how unsteady he was, and the guard threatened him with the Uzi. "I'm Jefferson Pardee from the *Truk Star*."

She nodded to the guard and he left the room. Her voice was friendly, but she wasn't smiling.

"I'm Beth Curtis. My husband runs the mission clinic on this island." She didn't offer her hand. "I'm sorry you've been treated this way, Mr. Pardee, but this island is under quarantine. We've tried to limit the contact with the outside until we have a better handle on this epidemic."

"What epidemic? I haven't heard anything about this?"

"Encephalitis. It's a rare strain, airborne and very contagious. We don't let anyone off island who's been exposed."

Jefferson Pardee exhaled a deep sigh of relief. So this was the big story. Of course he'd promise not to say a word, but *Time* magazine would kill for this. He'd leave out the part about being taken prisoner in his flying piggy boxers. "And the guards?"

"World Health Organization. They've also given us an aircraft and lab equipment, as I'm sure you've seen."

He'd seen an awful lot of lab equipment as he was led through the little hospital, but the aircraft was still a rumor. He decided to go for the facts. "You have a new Learjet, is that correct?"

"Yes." She seemed genuinely taken aback by his comment. "How did you know?"

"I have my sources," Pardee said, wishing he wore glasses so he could take them off in a meaningful way.

"I'm sure you do. Information is like a virus sometimes, and the only way to find a cure is to trace it to the source. Who told you about the jet?"

Pardee wasn't giving anything for free. "How long have you known about the encephalitis?"

For the first time Pardee noticed that Beth Curtis had been holding her right hand behind her back the entire time they had been talking. He noticed because when the hand appeared, it was holding a syringe. "Mr. Pardee, this syringe contains a vaccine that my husband and I have developed with the help of the World Health Organization. Because you took it on yourself to sneak onto Alualu, you have exposed yourself to a deadly virus that attacks the nervous system. The vaccine seems to work even after exposure to the disease, but only if administered in the first few hours. I want to give you this vaccine, I really do. But if you insist on drawing out this little game of liar's poker, then I can't guarantee that you won't contract the disease and die a horrible and painful death. So, that said, who told you about the jet?"

Pardee felt the sweat rising again. She hadn't raised her voice, there wasn't even a detectable note of anger there, but he felt as if she was holding a knife to his throat. Okay, to hell with the adventurous journalist. He could still get a byline based on what she'd already told him. "I talked to a pilot who passed through Truk a few months ago."

"A few months ago? Not more recently?"

"No. He said he was going to fly a jet for some missionaries on Alualu. I came out to check it out."

"And that was all you heard? Just that we had a jet?"

"Yes, it's pretty unusual for a missionary clinic to have money for a jet, wouldn't you say?"

She smiled. "I guess it is. So how did you plan to get off the island after you got your story?"

"The *Micro Spirit* was going to pick me up on the other side of the island. That's it. I was just curious. It's an occupational hazard."

"Who knows you're here, besides the crew of the *Spirit*?"

Pardee considered her question; what would be the best answer. Surely she wouldn't let him die of some dreaded disease, but how stupid would he have been to come out here without telling anyone? "The people who work for me at the *Star* and a friend of mine at AP who I called for some background before I left."

"Oh, that's good," she said, still smiling. Pardee couldn't help but feel pleased with himself. It had been a long time since he'd gotten any approval—or attention for that matter—from a beautiful woman.

She uncapped the syringe. "Now, before I give you the vaccine, a few medical questions, okay?"

"Sure. Shoot."

"You smoke and drink to excess, correct?"

"I indulge from time to time. Another occupational hazard."

"I see," she said. "And have you ever had a test for HIV?"

"A month ago. Clean as a whistle." This was true. He'd been motivated to take the test by a creepy rash on his stomach that turned out to be caused by skin-burrowing mites. The medic with the Navy CAT team had given him an ointment that cleared it up in a few days.

"Have you ever had hepatitis, cancer, or kidney disease?"

"Nope."

"How about your family? Anyone with a history of kidney disease or cancer?"

"Not last time I heard. I haven't talked with my family in twenty-five years."

She seemed especially pleased at that. "And you're not married? No children?"

"No."

"Very good," she said. She plunged the needle into his shoulder and pushed the plunger.

"Ouch. Hey, you could have warned me. Aren't you supposed to swab that with alcohol first or something?"

She stepped to the door and smiled again. "I don't think infection is going to be a problem, Mr. Pardee. Now don't panic, but in a minute or so you are going to go to sleep. I can't believe you bought that bit about the encephalitis. People get stupid living in the tropics, don't you think?"

She went out of focus and the lines of the room started to heave as if the entire structure was breathing. "What was in . . . ?" His tongue was too heavy; the words wouldn't come.

"You don't have a staff and you didn't call anyone at AP, Mr. Pardee. That was a stupid lie. We'll have to put 'self-importance' down under cause of death."

Pardee tried to stand, but his legs wouldn't obey him. He slid off the chair and his legs splayed straight out in front of him.

Beth Curtis bent over him, pushed her lips into a pout, and baby-talked. "Oh, are his wittle wegs all wobbly?" She stood up straight and put her hands on her hips. To Pardee her face floated like the moon through clouds.

She said, "You're probably thinking that I'm being unusually cruel to tease a dying man, but you see, you're not dying right now. Soon, but not right now."

Pardee tried to form a question, but the room seemed to go liquid and crash over him like a black wave.

Sebastian Curtis walked down the dock to where the crew of the *Micro Spirit* was unloading fuel drums from a longboat. He was wearing his white lab coat over Bermuda shorts and a Hawaiian shirt, a stethoscope hung from his neck like a medallion of power.

The *Micro Spirit's* first mate, who was drinking a Coke while supervising the unloading, jumped up on the dock to meet the doctor. "Good morning."

"Good morning," Curtis said. "Are you in charge here?"

"I'm the first mate."

Curtis regarded the tattooed Tongan. "Mr. Pardee will be staying with us for a while. He's asked me to tell you not to wait for him."

"That don't bother you?" the mate asked. It seemed strange to him after the effort Pardee had made to sneak onto the island.

"No, of course not. In fact, we've offered to fly Mr. Pardee to Hawaii when he finishes his work."

The mate had never heard Pardee's name in the same sentence as the word "work." It didn't sound right. Still, he had his job to do and the doctor was paying double freight for these barrels. He said, "Is he going to pay his fare?"

Curtis smiled and pulled a wad of bills out of the pocket of his shorts. "Of course. He asked me to give you the money. How much is it?"

"From Truk, one way, is three hundred."

The doctor counted out a stack of twenties and held it out to the mate. "Here's six hundred. Mr. Pardee asked me to pay the round-trip fare, since that's what he originally contracted for."

The mate stared at the stack of bills. He had known Jefferson Pardee for ten years and had never even known the man to buy a beer; now he was just giving him three hundred extra dollars? Three hundred dollars that the company and the captain didn't know about. "Okay," he said. He snatched the money out of the doctor's hand and shoved it into his pocket before the crew could see.

He would get the whole crew drunk and they would toast the generosity of Jefferson Pardee.

36

Return to the Sky

The Lear 45 was a working corporate issue, the seats up-holstered in muted blues and grays, facing each other over small worktables. For some reason Tucker had expected something more unusual: bright carnival colors with a monkey in a flight attendant outfit perhaps; a stark metal interior stripped for cargo; maybe stainless steel over enamel with a lot of complicated medical gizmos. Nope, this was the standard, run-of-the-mill station wagon model of your basic four-million-dollar jet.

He slid into the pilot's seat and a rage of adrenaline coursed through him, as if his body was reliving the crash of the pink Gulfstream. He fought the urge to bolt, let the adrenaline jag settle to a low-grade nausea, then started his preflight checklist. Everything looked normal; the instruments and controls were in place. He snapped on the power for the gauges and nothing happened: no lights, no LEDs, nothing.

He felt the plane move as someone came up the retractable steps and suddenly one of the guards reached around him and inserted a cylindrical key into a socket on the instrument board. The guard turned the key several times and the cockpit whirred to life.

"This thing has a main power cutoff?" Tuck said to the guard.

The guard removed the key and walked off the plane without saying a word.

"Nice chatting with you," Tuck said. He'd never seen a plane with an ignition key and he was sure that this one was not factory-issue. Why? Who would steal a jet airplane? Who could? I could, that's who. The doctor had installed the key to keep him from repeating his performance in Seattle. The missionary bastard didn't trust him.

Tuck checked the navigation computer. It was, as Beth Curtis had told him, set for an airfield in southern Japan. He watched as the LEDs on the nav computer came on, indicating that it was acquiring the satellites it needed to locate his position. When three were lit, his longitude and latitude flashed on the screen; when a fourth satellite was acquired, he had his current altitude: eight feet above sea level. He thought of Kimi navigating by the stars and felt a twinge of guilt for not trying harder to find him. He resolved to look for the navigator personally when he got back to Alualu.

He ran through the checklist and threw the autostart switches for the engines. As the twin jets spooled up, Tuck felt his anxiety float away like an exorcised ghost. This is where he was supposed to be. This is what he did. For the first time in weeks he felt like his head was clear.

He pushed the controls through their full range of motion and checked out the window to make sure that the flaps and ailerons were moving as well. Beth Curtis was coming across the compound toward the plane. At least he thought it was Beth Curtis. She wore a sharp, dark business suit with nylons and high heels. Her hair was pulled back into a severe bun and she wore wire-frame aviator sunglasses. She carried a small plastic cooler in one hand and an aluminum briefcase in the other. She looked like one of Mary Jean's corporate killer attorneys. Her third identity in as many days.

She walked into the plane and the guard pushed the hatch shut behind her. She stashed the cooler and briefcase in the overhead, then climbed into the cockpit and strapped herself in the copilot's seat.

"Any problems?" she said.

"You look nice today, Mrs. Curtis."

"Thank you, Mr. Case. Are we ready?"

"Tuck. You can call me Tuck. I need you to look out the window and tell me if the flaps and ailerons move when I move the controls."

"They look fine. Shall we go?"

Tuck released the ground brakes and taxied out onto the runway. "I need to pick up some sunglasses while we're in Japan."

"I'll get you some. You won't be leaving the plane."

"I won't?"

"We'll only be on the ground for a few minutes, then we'll be coming back."

"Look, Mrs. Curtis, I know you think that because of the circumstances that brought me here that I'm a total fuckup, but I am really good at what I do. You don't have to treat me like a child."

She looked at him and took off her sunglasses. Tuck wished he had sunglasses so he could whip them off like that.

She said, "Mr. Case, I'm putting my life in your hands right now. How much more confidence would you like?"

Tuck didn't really know how to answer. "I guess you're right. Sorry. You could be a little less mysterious about what's going on here. I know that we're not flying supplies, not with this plane and the kind of money you're paying me."

"If you really want to know, I can tell you. But if I tell you, I'll have to kill you."

Tuck looked from the instruments to catch her expression. She was grinning, a deep silly grin that crinkled the corners of her eyes.

He looked at the instruments. "I'm going to take off now. Okay?"

"And I haven't even shown you the best way to fight boredom on our little island."

Tuck concentrated on the gauges and the runway. He said, "What church do you and your husband work for?"

"Methodist."

"You'll have to tell me about it."

"What's there to tell? Methodists rock!" she said, then she giggled like a little girl as Tuck pulled the plane into the sky.

Malink joined the drinking circle late, hoping that everyone would be drunk enough to forget what had gone on that day. He'd spent most of the afternoon at Favo's house, afraid even to face his wife and daughters, but when the sun was well boiled in the sea, he knew he had to join the other men or face the consequences of *tuba*-poisoned theories and rumors aspiring to truth. He sneaked into an open spot in the circle and sat on the sand, even though several younger men moved so he could sit on a log with his back to the tree. He threw an open pack of Benson & Hedges into the center of the circle and Favo divided up the smokes among the men. Some lit up, others broke them into sections to chew with betel nut, and a few tucked them behind their ears for later. The distraction was short-lived and one of the Johns, an elder, said, "So why did Vincent send the Japanese into our houses?"

Malink waved him off as he drank from the coconut shell cup and made a great show of enjoying his first drink before handing the cup to Abo, who was pouring. Then he stalled another few seconds by lighting a Benson & Hedges with the Zippo, making sure everyone saw it and remembered, then after a long drag he said, "I'm fucked if I know." He said this in English—English being the best language for swearing.

"It is not good," said John.

"They came to the bachelors' house," said Abo, who, as usual, was angry. "They looked at our mispel's thighs."

"We should kill them," said one of the younger men who had been named for Vincent.

"And eat them!" someone added—and it was as if the air had been pulled on the circle before it could inflate to well-rounded violent mob.

Everyone turned to see Sarapul walking out of the shadows. For once, Malink was glad to see him. The old cannibal seemed to have a spring in his step, seemed younger, stronger.

"I need an ax," Sarapul said. The men who owned axes all stared into the sand or examined their fingernails.

"What for?" Malink asked.

"I can't tell you. It's a secret."

"You're not going to start headhunting, are you?" Malink said. "We've put up with your talk of eating people, but I draw the line at headhunting. No headhunting while I'm chief."

Everybody grunted in agreement and Malink was glad to have been able to assert his authority in a way that no one could dispute. An anthropologist had once come to the island and given him a book about headhunters. Malink felt very cosmopolitan discussing the topic.

Sarapul looked confused. He'd never read the headhunting book, had never read any book, but he did have a Classic Comics version of *The Count of Monte Cristo*, which a sailor had given him in the days before the Shark People were forbidden to meet visiting ships. He'd made Kimi read it to him every night. Sarapul liked the thread of revenge and murder that ran through the story.

Sarapul said, "What is this headhunting? I just want to cut a tree."

"Cutting trees is taboo," said one of the younger men.

"I will get special dispensation," Sarapul said, using a term he had learned from Father Rodriquez.

Malink shook his head. "We don't have that anymore. We only had that when we were Catholics."

"I need an ax," Sarapul said, as if he might do better if he started over. "And I need permission from the great Chief Malink to cut a tree."

Malink scratched a mosquito bite and looked at his feet. It was true that he could give permission to break a taboo, and Sarapul had distracted the circle before they ganged up on him. "You may cut one tree, on your side of the island, and you must show it to me before you cut it. Now, who has an ax?"

Everyone knew who owned axes, but nobody volunteered. Malink chose one of the young Vincents. "You, go get your ax." Then to Sarapul he said: "Why do you need to cut a tree?"

Sarapul considered holding out, but decided that a credible lie would be better. "My house is falling down from the girl-man climbing in the rafters."

It was the wrong answer to give in front of a group of men whose houses had been rifled only hours ago. Malink cradled his head in his hands.

The toughest part of the landing for Tuck was restraining himself from leaping out of the seat and demanding high-fives from the woman. It was perfect. He was back. Never mind the ghosts, the talking bats, the three-hour flight with a woman who could have been the model for the new Multiple Personality Barbie. *She's elegant, she's fashionable, and she's the reason that Ken has no genitals! Have fun, but remember to hide the sharp stuff!* Never mind all that. He was a pilot.

They were somewhere in southern Japan, a small jetport, probably private, with no tower and only a few hangars. Tuck had gotten them there by following the nav computer, which, he found in midflight, had only two coordinates programmed into it: Alualu and this airfield.

"What happens if we have a problem and have to divert?" he asked Beth.

"Don't worry about it," she said. She had spent most of the flight grilling him about the navigational instruments, as if she wanted to know enough to be able to check the course herself. He complied, feeling insulted by the whole conversation.

Another Lear was spooling up on the tarmac and Beth Curtis instructed him to taxi to it. As the jet bumped to a stop and he prepared to shut down, she pulled her briefcase and cooler out of the overhead and turned to him. "Stay here. We'll take off in a few minutes."

"What about loading supplies?"

"Mr. Case, please just prepare the plane for departure. I won't be long."

Two men in blue coveralls crossed the tarmac from the other jet and lowered the hatch for her. Tuck watched out the window as she met a third Japanese man in a white lab coat. She handed him the cooler and a folder from the briefcase, then traded bows with him and quickstepped back to the Lear. One of the men in blue coveralls followed her into the plane with a cardboard box, which he strapped into one of the passenger seats.

"*Domo,*" Beth Curtis said.

He bowed quickly, left the plane, and sealed the hatch. She stashed the briefcase in the overhead again climbed into the copilot's seat.

"Let's go."

"That's it?"

"That's it. Let's go."

"We should top off the fuel tanks while we're here."

"I understand why you might be a little nervous about that, Mr. Case, but we have plenty of fuel to make it back."

"One box. That's all we're picking up?"

"One box."

"What's in it?"

"It's a case of '78 Bordeaux. Sebastian loves it. Let's go."

"But I have to use the bathroom. I thought . . ."

"Hold it," Beth Curtis said.

"Bitch."

"Exactly. Now don't you need to do your checklist thingy?"

37

Bombs and Bribes

The itching started a week after the first flight. It began on his scalp and a few days later, as the wounds on his arms, legs, and genitals healed, Tucker would have stripped off his skin to escape it. If there had been some other distraction, something to do besides sit in his bungalow waiting to be called for a flight, it might have been bearable, but now the doctor came only once a day to check on him, and he hadn't seen Beth Curtis since they landed. He read spy novels, listened to the country western radio station out of Guam until he thought that if he heard one more wailing steel guitar, he'd rip the rest of his hair out. Sometimes he lay under the mosquito netting, acutely aware of his comatose member, and tried to think of all the women he had had, one by one, then all the women he had ever wanted, including actresses, models, and famous figures from history (the Marilyn Monroe/Cleopatra double-team-in-warm-pudding scenario kept him distracted for almost an hour). Twice a day he cooked himself a meal. The doctor had set him up with a double hot plate and a pantry full of canned goods, and occasionally one of the guards dropped off a parcel of fruit or fresh fish. Mostly, though, he itched.

Tuck tried to engage Sebastian Curtis in conversation, but there were few subjects about which the missionary was not evasive, and most reminded him that he had left some pressing task at the clinic. Questions about Kimi, the guards, the lack of cargo, his personal history, his wife, the natives of the island, or communication with the outside world evoked half-answers and downright silence.

He asked the doctor for some cortisone, for a television, for access to a computer so he could send a message back to Jake Skye, and while the doctor didn't say no outright, Tuck was left empty-handed except for a suggestion that he ought to go swimming and a reminder of how much money he was making for reading spy novels and scratching at scabs. Tuck wanted a steak, a woman (although he still wasn't sure he could do anything but talk to her), and a chilled bottle of vodka. The doctor gave him some fins, a mask and snorkel, and a bottle of waterproof sunscreen.

When, one morning, Tuck spent an empty hour trying to will his member to life by mentally wrapping his fifth-grade teacher, Mrs. Nelson, in Saran Wrap, only to find his fantasy foiled by her insistence that he had no lead in his Number 2 pencil, he grabbed the snorkeling gear and made his way to the beach.

Two of the guards followed at a distance. They were always there. When he looked out the window, if he tried to take a walk, if he wanted to check on the Lear, they clung to him like stereo shadows. They stood over him as he sat in the sand, pulling the fins on.

"Why don't you guys go put on some trunks and join me? Those jumpsuits have to be pretty uncomfortable." It wasn't the first time he'd tried to talk to them, and it wasn't the first time he'd been ignored. They just stood there, as silent as meditating monks. Tuck hadn't been able to discern if they understood a word of English.

"Okay, then, I'm going to do the Cousteau thing, but later let's get together for some raw fish and karaoke?" He gave them a wink.

No reaction.

"Then let's play some cards and talk about how you guys recite haiku while blowing each other every night?" Tuck thought that might do it, but still there was no reaction.

As he started toward the water, Tuck said, "I heard the Japanese flag was modeled after a used sanitary napkin. Is that true?" He looked over his shoulder for a response and his fin caught and bent double on a rock. An instant later he was facedown on the beach, sputtering to get the sand out of his mouth, and the guards were laughing.

"Asshole," he heard one say, and he was on his feet and looming over the Japanese like a giant rabid duck.

"Just back off, Odd Job!"

The guard who had spoken stood his ground, but his companion backed away looking lost without his Uzi.

"What's the matter, no submachine gun? You chickenshits so busy crawling up my back that you forgot your toys?" Tuck poked the guard in the chest to punctuate his point.

The guard grabbed Tuck's finger and bent it back, then swept the pilot's feet out from under him and drew a Glock nine-millimeter pistol from a holster at the small of his back and pressed the barrel to Tucker's forehead hard enough to dent the skin. The other guard barked something in Japanese, then stepped forward and kicked Tuck in the stomach. Tucker rolled into a ball in the sand, instinctively throwing one arm over his face and clenching the other at his side to protect his kidneys as he waited for the next blow. It didn't come. When he looked up, the guards were walking back to the compound.

Getting them to leave him alone had been the desired result, but the process was a little rougher than he'd expected. Tuck wiggled his finger to make sure it wasn't broken and examined the boot toe print under his rib cage. Then the anger unlocked his imagination and plans for revenge began. The easiest thing to do would be to tell the doctor, but Tuck, like all men, had been conditioned against two responses: You don't cry and you don't rat. No, it would have to be something subtle, elegant, painful, and most of all, humiliating.

Tuck almost skipped into the water, running on his newfound energy: adrenalized vengeance. He paddled around at the inside edge of the reef, watching anemones pulse in the current while small fish in improbable neon colors darted in and out of the coral. The ocean was as warm as bathwater, and after a few minutes with his face in the water, he felt detached from his body and the color and movement below became as meaningless as the patterns in a campfire. The only reminder that he was human was the sound of his breath rushing through the snorkel and the images of cold revenge in his mind.

He looked down the ragged curve of the reef and saw a large shadow moving across the bottom, but before fight-or-flight panic could even set in, he saw it was the shadow of a loggerhead turtle flying through the water like a saurian angel. The turtle circled him and cruised by close enough for Tuck to see the movement in the creature's silver-dollar-sized eye as it studied him, and a message there: "You don't belong here," it said. And that part of Tuck that had recognized the saltwater as its mother rebelled and he felt alien and vulnerable and cold, and a little rude, as if he had been attending a black-tie dinner only to realize as dessert was served that he was wearing pajamas. It was time to go.

He lifted his head, took a bearing on the chain-link fence that ran to the edge of the beach, and started a slow crawl toward shore. As the water went shallow, he banged his knee on a submerged rock, then stood and slogged through the lapping surf as his fins tried to drag him back off the beach. Once clear of the water, he fell in the sand and tore the fins off his feet. He threw them up the shore without looking and a half a breath later a deafening explosion lifted him up and he landed ten feet away, stunned and breathless, as damp sand and pieces of swim fin rained down upon him.

Tucker stormed through the clinic door trailing sand and water across the concrete floor. "Mines! You have fucking land mines on the fucking beach?"

Sebastian Curtis was seated at a computer terminal. He quickly clicked off the screen and swiveled in his chair. "I heard the explosion, but birds and turtles have set them off before. Was anyone hurt?"

"Other than I'm going to hear a high-pitched wail for the rest of my life and my sphincter won't relax until I'm dead a couple of years, no, no one was hurt. What I want to know is why you have mines on the beach."

"Calm down, Mr. Case. Please sit down." The doctor gestured to a folding metal chair. "Please." He looked sad, not at all confrontational, not like the kind of man who would mine a tropical beach. "I suppose there are some things you need to know. First, I have something for you." He opened a drawer under the keyboard, withdrew a check, and handed it to Tuck.

Tucker's rage dropped a level when he looked at the amount. "Ten grand? What's this for?"

"Call it a first-flight bonus. Beth said you did very well."

Tucker fingered the check, then brushed the sand off it and read it again. If he had any self-respect, he'd throw it in the doctor's face. He didn't, of course. "This is great, Doc. Ten grand for picking up a case of wine. I'm not even going to ask you what was in the cooler she gave that guy, but I was almost killed on the beach a few minutes ago."

"I'm very sorry about that. There's a lot of Japanese ordnance scattered around the island. The area at the edge of the fence used to be a minefield. The staff and the natives all know not to go there."

"Well, you might have mentioned it to me."

"I didn't want to alarm you. I told a couple of members of the staff to keep an eye on you and steer you away from there. I'll speak to them."

"They've been spoken to. I spoke to them myself. And I'm a little tired of being watched by them."

"It's for your own safety, as I'm sure you can see now."

"I'm not a child and I don't expect to be treated like one. I want to go where I want, when I want, and I don't want to be watched by a bunch of ninjas."

The doctor sat bolt-upright in his chair. "Why do you refer to them as ninjas? Who told you to call the staff that?"

"Look at them. They're Japanese, they wear all black, they know martial arts—hell, the only thing they're missing are T-shirts that say, 'Ask me about being a ninja.' I call them that because that's what they look like. They sure as hell aren't medical staff."

"No, they're not," Sebastian said, "but I'm afraid they are a necessary evil, and one that I can't do much about."

"Why not? It's your island."

"This island belongs to the Shark People. And even this clinic isn't mine, Mr. Case. As I'm sure you've guessed, we are not financed by the Methodist Mission Fund."

"Yeah, I kinda figured that."

"We do have some very powerful corporate sponsors in Japan, and they have insisted that we keep a small contingent of security men on the island if we want to keep our funding."

"Funding for what, Doc?"

"Research."

Tuck laughed. "Right. This is the perfect environment for research. No sense using some sterile high-tech facility in Tokyo. Do your R and D out on the asshole of the Pacific. Come clean. What's really going on?"

The doctor pointed to the check Tucker was holding. "If I tell you, Mr. Case, that's the last one of those you will see. You make the choice. If you want to work here, you have to work in the dark. There is no compromise. It's research, it's secret, and the people who are paying for it want it to stay that way or they wouldn't have hired the guards and they wouldn't allow me to pay you so well." He pushed back his gray hair and stared into Tucker's eyes, not threatening, not challenging, but with the compassion of a physician concerned about the welfare of a patient. "Now, do you really want to know what we're doing here?"

Tuck looked at the check, looked back at the doctor, then looked at the check. If it was good, it was the largest amount of money he'd ever possessed at one time. He said, "I just want the guards to lighten up, give me some room to breathe."

The doctor smiled. "I think we can do that. But I need your word that you won't try to leave the compound."

"To go where? I've seen this island from the air, remember? I can't be missing much."

"I'm only interested in your safety."

"Right," Tucker said, as sincerely as he could muster. "But I want a TV. I'm going nuts sitting around in that room. If I read one more spy novel, I'll qualify for a Double-O number. You guys have a TV, so I know you have one of those satellite dishes hooked up. I want a TV."

Again the doctor smiled. "You can have ours. I'm sure Beth won't mind."

"You gave him *what*?" The Sky Priestess looked up from a copy of *Us* magazine. She was draped in a white silk kimono that was untied and cascaded around her into a shimmering pool at the foot of her chair. Her hair was pinned up with ivory chopsticks inlaid with ebony dragons.

The Sorcerer stood in the door of her chambers. He'd felt rather proud of himself until the tone in her voice struck him like an ice pick in the neck.

"Your television. But it's only temporary. I'll have another one waiting for you at the airstrip on the next flight."

"Which is when?"

"As soon as I can set up an order. I promise, Beth."

"Which means that I also have to do a performance without my soaps. I depend on my soaps to practice my sense memories, Sebastian. How do you expect me to play a goddess if I can't find my emotional moment?"

"Maybe, just this once, you could try emotions that don't come by satellite feed."

She dropped her magazine and bit her lip, looking off to the corner of the room as if considering it. "Fine. Give him the TV."

"I gave him ten thousand dollars, as well."

Her eyes narrowed. "What does he get if he blows himself up again, a night with the Sky Priestess?"

"If I can bargain him down to that," the Sorcerer said. He turned and walked out of the room smiling to himself.

~~~~~~

38

Native Customs

Tucker Case spent the next week watching the compound, trying to get a clue to what was going on. The doctor had brought the TV as he promised, and even loaned Tucker a seven iron, but since then Tuck had only seen him from a distance, making his way back and forth from the clinic to one of the small bungalows at the other side of the beach. The guards still watched him, following him at a distance when he went for a swim or a search-and-destroy mission for roosters, but there had been no sign of Beth Curtis.

If indeed the doctor was doing some sort of research, there was no hint as to what it involved. Tuck tried stopping by the clinic several times, only to find the door locked and no response when he knocked.

Boredom worked on Tuck, pressed down on him like a pile of wet blankets until he felt as if he would suffocate under the weight. In the past he had always fought boredom with alcohol and women, and the trouble that ensued from that combination filled the days. Here there was nothing but spy novels and bad Asian cooking shows (the doctor had refused to let him hook up to the satellite dish) and although he was pleased that he now knew nine different ways to prepare beagle, it wasn't enough. He needed to get out of the compound, if for no other reason than because they told him he couldn't.

Fortunately, over the years, Tuck had acquired an encyclopedic knowledge of women-in-prison movies, so he had at his disposal a plethora of escape strategies. Of course, many of them weren't applicable. He immediately rejected the idea of seducing and shiving the large lesbian matron, and faking menstrual cramps would only get him sent to the clinic with a Mydol IV, but strangely enough, as he was acting out the gratuitous shower scene, his plan burst forth: soap-slathered, silicone-enhanced, and in total defiance of time, gravity, and natural proportion . . .

The shower drain opened directly onto the coral gravel below.

He could see it down there, the ground, and a small hermit crab scuttling to escape the soapy water. He'd lost weight, but not enough to slide down the drain. The entire bottom of the shower was no more than a tray of galvanized metal. He bent, grasped the edge, and lifted. It didn't come free, but it moved. A little time, a little patience, and he'd have it free. Planning and patience. Those were the keys to a successful escape.

So he could get out of the bungalow without being seen. The next obstacle would be the fence.

Tuck found out early on that the fence around the compound was electrified. He'd found a rooster stuck to the wires, doing a convulsive imitation of the funky chicken while its feathers smoldered and sparks shot from its grounded foot. Satisfying as the discovery was, Tuck realized that there would be no going over the fence, and the gate to the airfield was locked with a massive chain and padlock. The only way past the fence was around it, and the only place to get around it was at the beach. Sure, he could swim out and come in farther down the beach, but how far did the minefield extend? He began testing it by hitting rocks into the minefield with his seven iron under the auspices of practicing his swing. He managed to produce several impressive craters and scare the guards with the explosion before finding the edge of the minefield some fifty yards down the beach. He decided to risk it.

He picked up a coconut on his way back to the bungalow, then climbed into bed and waited for darkness to fall.

After the sun set and the three-quarter moon rose, Tuck waited for the guard to peek through the window, then as he heard him crunch away, began building the decoy (a trick he learned from *Falling Fingers: Leper Bimbos Behind Bars II*). Two pillows and a coconut head made for a reasonable likeness, especially when viewed by moonlight through mosquito netting. He slipped out of bed and crawled below window level to the bathroom, where he had left his mask, fins, and a candle.

He shoved a towel under the door to keep the light from leaking out, then lit the candle and began working the metal shower tray out of its frame. After five minutes of tugging, stopping for a moment when he heard the guard's boots crunching outside, he released the shower tray and leaned it up on its side.

Tuck blew out the candle and dropped to gravel four feet below, then reached back and pulled his fins and mask through the opening. The coral gravel felt like broken glass on his tender feet, but he decided to endure the pain rather than risk the noise of shoes. Tuck heard the guard coming again and dropped to the ground where he could look out under the bungalow into the courtyard.

The guard thumped up the steps, paused as he looked through the window, then, satisfied that Tucker was asleep, walked across the compound to the guards' quarters and sat in a folding chair outside the door.

Tuck checked behind him, then scrambled out of the crawl space into the grove of coconut palms. He paused and caught his breath, then planned his path to the beach. He would have to cover fifty yards between his bungalow and the clinic, fifty yards that weren't completely open but visible from where the guard sat. He could hop from tree to tree, but if the guard happened to be looking that way, he was done.

A lizard scampered up the tree he was leaning on and Tuck felt his heart stop. What was he thinking? There could be scorpions out here, sharks and barracudas and other creepy stuff in the dark ocean. And what happened when he got to the other side of the fence? More sand and scorpions and possibly hostile natives. He was waiting, thinking about how easy it would be to crawl back through the shower and go to bed, when a lighter flared across the compound and he saw the guard's face illuminated orange, and Tuck bolted for the rear of the clinic building, hoping the lighter would blind the guard long enough for him to cover the fifty yards.

Halfway across, he dropped a fin, then fell to the ground beside it and looked up. The guard was smoking peacefully, watching blue streams of smoke rise in the moonlight.

Tuck grabbed the fin and crawled on his belly the final ten yards to the clinic, fighting the urge to cry out as the gravel dug into his elbows. A hermit crab scuttled over his back sending a bolt of the electric willies shooting up his spine to speed him to cover.

The guard didn't look up. Tuck climbed to his feet, dusted himself off, and made his way to the beach.

A light breeze rattled the palm leaves and Tuck could hear the surf crashing out on the reef, but at the shore the waves lapped only shin high. Tuck waded into the warm water carrying his fins. When he was waist deep, he crouched and slipped them on, then paddled out on his back, looking back toward shore.

There were lights on in both of the Curtises' bungalows. He could see Beth Curtis moving past the windows. She appeared to be naked, but from this distance he couldn't tell for sure. He tore himself away and swam out past the surf line to make his way down the beach.

It was an easy swim to the fence, the biggest challenge being to keep his mind off what might be lurking under the dark water. He swam another hundred yards down the beach, then started toward shore. When his hand brushed a rock, he reached down and pulled off his fins. He gritted his teeth as he put his feet down to stand, expecting the shooting pain of an urchin or a ray. He cursed himself for not bringing his sneakers.

As he slogged up the beach, Tuck heard a rustling in the trees and looked up to see a flash of color in the moonlight. He ran up the beach, dove behind a log at the high-tide line, and lay there watching as tiny crabs clicked and crawled around him.

She emerged from the trees only ten yards from where Tucker lay. She was wearing a purple lavalava, which she unwrapped and dropped on the sand.

Tuck stopped breathing. She walked by him, only a few feet away, her body oiled and shining in the moonlight, her long black hair playing behind her in the breeze. He risked lifting his head and watched her walk into the water up to her knees and begin washing, splashing water on her thighs and bottom.

From the time he had left Houston he had carried images in his head of what it would be like to live on a tropical island. Those images had been buried by cuts and scrapes, typhoons and humidity, sharks and ninjas and enigmatic missionaries. This was why he had come: a naked island girl washing her mocha thighs on a warm moonlit beach.

He felt a stirring under him and almost leaped to his feet, thinking he was lying on some sea creature. Then he realized that the stirring came from within. It had been so long since he'd felt signs of an erection that he didn't recognize it at first. He almost burst out laughing. It still worked. He was still a man. Hell, he was more than just a man, he was Tucker Case, secret agent, and for the first time in months, he was packing wood.

The girl walked out of the water and Tuck ducked his head as she passed. He watched her wrap the lavalava around her hips and disappear into the trees. He waited until she was gone, then followed her, enjoying the tension in his trunks as he crept into the trees.

Malink looked up from pouring *tuba* for the men at the drinking circle to see Sepie coming down from the village. This was an outrage and an embarrassment. No women were allowed near the drinking circle. It was a place for men.

"Go home, Sepie!" Malink barked. "You are not to be here."

Sepie ignored him and kept coming, her hips swaying. Several of the young married men looked away, feeling regret that they wouldn't be bedding down in the bachelors' house tonight. "There's a white man following me."

Malink stood. "You talk nonsense. Now go home or you'll have another week away from the ocean." He noticed that the ends of her hair were wet and drops ran off her legs. She'd already broken her punishment for talking with the Japanese guards.

"Fine," Sepie said. "I don't care if a white man is sneaking around in the bushes. I just though you would want to know."

She flipped her hair as she turned and made her way back up the beach. As she passed the tree that Tuck had ducked behind, she said in English, "The fat loud one is chief. You go talk to him. He tell you who I am." And she walked on, head high, without looking back.

Tuck felt his face flush and his ego deflate along with the swelling in his pants. Busted. She'd known he was there all along. Some secret agent. He'd be lucky to get back into the compound without getting caught.

He watched the men on the beach passing around the communal cup. From the way they moved he could see that some of them were pretty drunk. He remembered the warning of Jefferson Pardee about not drinking with these latent warriors, but they looked harmless, even a little silly with their loincloths and shark tattoos. One young man reached to take the cup from the old guy who was pouring and fell on his face in the sand. That did it. Tuck stepped out from behind his tree and started toward the circle. Whatever was being poured from those jugs was probably not gin and tonic, but it would definitely get you fucked up, and getting fucked up sounded pretty good right now.

"*Jambo,*" Tuck said, using a greeting he'd heard in a Tarzan movie.

The whole group looked up. One man actually let out an abbreviated scream. The fat old guy stood up, a fire in his eyes that cooled as Tuck moved out of the shadows.

Mary Jean had always said, "Doesn't matter if it's a senator or a doorman. No one is immune to a warm smile and a firm handshake."

Tuck held out his hand and smiled. "Tucker Case. Pleased to meet you."

Malink allowed the white man to shake his hand. As the others looked on, still stunned, Malink said, "You are looking better than the last time I saw you. The Sorcerer made you well."

Tuck's eyes were trained on the three-gallon jugs of milky liquid at the center of the circle. "Yeah, I'm feeling on top of the world. You guys think you could spare a sip of that jungle juice?"

"Sit," Malink said, and he waved the young men aside to make space for Tuck on one of the sitting logs. Tuck stepped in and sat as Favo handed him the coconut shell cup. Tuck downed the contents in one gulp and fought to keep from gagging. It tasted of sulfur, sugar, and a tint of ammonia, but the alcohol was there, and the familiar warmth was coursing through him before he'd even stopped shuddering from the taste.

"Good. Very good." Tuck smiled and nodded around the circle. The Shark men smiled and nodded back.

Malink sat beside him. "We thought you died."

"So did I. How about another belt?"

Malink looked embarrassed. "The cup must come around again."

"Fine, fine. Drink up, boys," Tuck said, smiling and nodding like a madman.

"How you come here?" Malink asked.

"A little stroll, a little swim. I wanted to get out and meet some people. You know, get to know the local customs. Gets pretty boring up at the clinic."

Malink frowned. "You are the pilot. We see you fly the plane."

"That's me."

"Vincent said you would come."

"Who's Vincent?"

The men, who had been whispering among themselves, fell silent. The pouring and drinking stopped as they waited for Malink's reply.

"Vincent is pilot too. He come long time ago, bringing cargo. He send the Sky Priestess until he come back. You see her with the Sorcerer. At hospital. She have yellow hair like yours."

Tuck nodded, as if he had any idea what the chief was talking about. Right now he just wanted to see the cup finish its lap and get back to him. "Yeah, right. I've seen her. She's the doctor's wife."

Abo, who was drunk and for once not angry, laughed and said, "She is nobody's wife, you fuckin' mook. She's the Sky Priestess."

Tuck froze. A plane crash and a talking bat rose like demons, ruining his oncoming buzz.

Malink looked apologetic. "He is young and drunk and stupid. You not fuckin' mook."

"Where'd you hear that?" Tuck asked. "Where'd you hear 'fuckin' mook'?"

"Vincent say that. We all say that."

"Vincent? What's Vincent look like?"

The young men looked to Favo and Malink. Favo spoke. "He is American. Have dark hair like us, but his nose point. Young. Maybe as old as you."

"And he's a pilot? What's he wear?"

"He wear gray suit, sometimes a jacket with fur here." Favo mimed a collar and lapels.

"A bomber jacket."

Malink smiled. "Yes, Sky Priestess is bomber."

Tuck snatched the cup from one of the Johns and drained it, then handed it back. "Sorry. Emergency." He looked at Malink. "And this Vincent said I was coming?"

Malink nodded. "He tell me in a dream. Then Sarapul find you and your friend on the reef."

"My friend? Is he around?"

"We no see him now. He go to live with Sarapul on other side of island."

"Take me to him."

"We drink *tuba* now. Go in morning?"

"I have to be back before morning. And you can't tell anyone that I was here."

"One more," Malink said. "The *tuba* is good tonight."

"Okay, one more," Tuck said.

39

Showtime

The Sky Priestess rolled over in bed and slapped the beeping intercom as if it was a mouthy stepchild. "I'm sleeping here," she said.

"Get in character, Beth. We have an order, due in Japan in six hours."

"Why don't these fuckers ever call at a civilized hour?"

"We guarantee freshness. We have to deliver."

"Don't grow a sense of humor on me at this point, Sebastian. The shock might kill me. Who's the chosen?"

"Sepie, female, nineteen, a hundred and ten pounds."

"I know her," the Sky Priestess said. "What about our pilot?"

"I'm putting two of the staff on him to make sure he stays in his bungalow."

"He's still going to hear it. Are you sure you don't want to sedate him?"

"Use your head, Beth. He has to fly. We'll do it with smaller explosions. Maybe he'll sleep through it."

She was wide awake now and starting to feel the excitement and anxiety of a performance. "I'll be ready in twenty minutes. Have the ninjas start my music."

Tuck had Favo in a headlock and was administering affectionate noogies to the old man's scalp. "I love this fuckin' guy. This fuckin' guy is the best. I love all you fuckin' guys."

Malink had never seen noogies and wondered why this bizarre

ritual had never showed up in the party scenes in *People*. He prided
himself on understanding white people's habits, but this was a new
one. Favo didn't seem to be enjoying the ritual nearly as much as
Tuck was. The *tuba* had all been drunk. Maybe it was time to rescue
his friend.

"Now we go find the girl-man," Malink said.

Tuck looked up, still holding Favo, whose eyes were starting to
bug out a little. " 'Kay," the pilot said.

Malink led them into the village, his bowlegged gait more wobbly than normal. A dozen Shark men and Tucker crashed and staggered behind him. As they passed by the bachelors' house and onto
the trail that led to Sarapul's side of the island, the music started:
big band sounds with easy liquid rhythms echoed through the jungle. The Shark men stopped in their tracks and when the music
paused, just for a second, they shouted, "Pennsylvania 6-5000!" and
the music began again.

"What's that?" Tucker asked.

Women and children were stirring from their sleep, creeping off
into the bushes to pee, rubbing sleepy eyes and stretching creaky
backs. Malink said, "The Sky Priestess is coming."

"Who?" Tuck finally released Favo, who he had been dragging
by his head. The old man gasped, then grinned and sat splayed-
legged on the trail.

"We have to go," Malink said. "You should go back now."

The music paused and Malink, along with the rest of the Shark
People, shouted, "Pennsylvania 6-5000!"

"Go now," Malink ordered, once again the chief. "The Sky
Priestess comes. We must get ready." He turned and strode back
into the village. The other Shark men scattered, leaving Tucker
standing on the trail by himself.

Tuck heard the sound of large prop planes mixing with the big
band music. The Shark People were draining out of the village onto
the trails that led to the runway. Within seconds, the village was
deserted. Tuck staggered back to the beach where he'd left his fins
and mask. As he stepped over the logs of the drinking circle, there
was an explosion and he thought for a moment that he'd found
another land mine until he realized that the sound had come from
the direction of the runway.

Not trusting himself to find the path through the village, Tucker
decided to follow the beach back to the compound. After he'd gone
a hundred yards or so, he saw something white lying on the beach

and bent to pick it up. A long spiral notebook. The moon was high in the sky and he could see a name printed on the cover in bold permanent marker: JEFFERSON PARDEE.

Beth Curtis, dressed in surgical greens, waved the guards away from Tuck's door and knocked. She waited a few seconds and knocked again, then walked in. She could just make out a sleeping figure through the mosquito net.

"Case, get up. We've got to fly."

The body did not stir. "Case?" She pulled aside the netting and poked the sleeping figure. A green coconut rolled out of the bed and thumped at her feet. "You sleep with a coconut? You pathetic bastard."

She jumped back and a groggy Tucker Case groaned. "What?"

"Wake up. We fly in half an hour."

Tuck rolled over and blinked through the hangover fog. The sun was coming up and the roosters were going off all over the island. The room was only half-lit.

"What time is it?"

"It's time to go. Get the plane ready." Beth Curtis walked out.

Tuck rolled out of bed, crawled to the bathroom, and emptied his stomach into the bowl with a trumpeting heave.

40

Unfriendly Skies

Tuck spooled up the jets as he watched the guards scramble around the Lear. Each time one walked past the nose, Tuck flipped on the radar and chuckled. The microwave energy wasn't enough to boil the guards in their skins, which was Tuck's fantasy, but he could be reasonably certain that they would never have any children and he might have planted the seeds of a few choice tumors. Once in Houston a maintenance man made the mistake of walking in front of Mary Jean's jet with an armload of fluorescent bulbs meant for the hangar, and Jake Skye had shown Tucker a little trick.

"Watch this, Jake had said." He flipped on the radar and the bulbs, bombarded by the microwaves from the radar, lit up in the maintenance man's arms. The poor guy threw the bulbs in the air and ran off the field, leaving a pile of glass shards and white powder behind. It was the second-coolest thing Tucker had ever seen, the first being the time they had used the Gulfstream's jets to sandblast the paint off a Porsche whose owner insisted on parking on the tarmac. Tuck was waiting for one of the guards to walk behind the jets when Beth Curtis came on board.

She wore her business suit and carried the briefcase and the cooler, but this time she sat in one of the passenger seats in the back and fell asleep before they took off. Tuck took the opportunity to suck some oxygen from the emergency supply to help cut through his hangover.

When they were five hundred miles out over the Pacific, Tuck peeked into the passenger compartment to make sure Beth Curtis was still sleeping. When he was sure she was still out, he checked the fuel gauges, then pushed the yoke forward and dropped the Lear down to level off at a hundred feet.

Traveling at almost six hundred miles per hour at only a hundred feet off the water did exactly what Tuck had hoped it would. He was absolutely ecstatic with an adrenaline rush that chased his hangover back to the Dark Ages. He dropped another fifty feet and laughed out loud when some salt spray dashed the windscreen.

It was a clear sunny day with only a few wispy columnar clouds rising off the water. Tuck flew under and through them as if they were enemy ghosts. Then a speck appeared on the horizon. A second later Tuck recognized it as a ship and pulled the jet up to two hundred feet. Suddenly something rose off the ship's deck. A helicopter, going out to spot and herd schools of tuna for the factory ship. Tuck pulled up on the yoke, but the helicopter rose directly into his path. There wasn't even time to key the radio to warn the pilot. Tuck threw the Lear into a tight turn while pulling the jet up and whizzed by the helicopter close enough to see the pilot's eyes go wide. He could just make out men shaking fists at him from the deck of the factory ship.

"*Eee-haa!*" he shouted (a bad habit he'd picked up in Texas cowboy bars, and if this wasn't cowboy flying, what was?). He steered the jet back on course and leveled off at two hundred feet. He was still dangerously low and burning fuel four times faster than he would at altitude, but hell, a guy had to have some fun. He wasn't paying for the fuel, and there hadn't been much low-level flying when he'd worked for Mary Jean. People on the ground might have trouble remembering the numbers on the side of the plane to report to the FAA, but you don't soon forget a pink jet flying close enough to the ground to cool your soup.

"What in the hell was that?" Beth Curtis appeared in the cockpit doorway. "Why are we so low?"

A wave of panic akin to being caught smoking in the boys' room swept over Tuck, but he couldn't think fast enough to come up with a viable lie. He said, "You haven't surfed until you've surfed in a Learjet."

Much to his amazement, Beth Curtis said, "Cool!" and strapped herself into the copilot's seat.

Tuck grinned and eased the jet down to fifty feet. Beth Curtis clapped her hands like an excited child. "This is great!"

"We can't do it for long. Burns too much fuel."

"A little while longer, okay?"

Tuck smiled. "Maybe five more minutes. We can catch a tailwind at altitude that'll save us some time and fuel."

"Is this what you were doing the night you crashed?"

Tuck winced. "No."

"Because I could understand if it was. What a rush!" She reached out and grabbed his shoulder affectionately. "I love this. How could you let me sleep through this?"

"We can surf some more on the way back," Tuck said. And with that his resolve was gone. He'd planned to ask her about the music and explosions from last night. He'd planned to ask her about Jefferson Pardee's notebook, which he carried in his back pocket, but he didn't want to break this mood. It had been too long since he'd had any attention from a beautiful woman, and he gave himself to it like a jonesing junkie.

"I'm sorry," she said, "but you'll have to wait here." Beth Curtis retrieved her briefcase and cooler from the back of the plane and met the dark-suited Japanese on the tarmac. There was another Lear spooling up nearby and a couple of workmen in coveralls waited beside a large cardboard carton.

Tuck watched as Beth Curtis handed the cooler to one of the suits, who ran to the waiting Lear. Within seconds, the door was pulled shut and the other Lear was taxied out to the runway. Another one of the suits handed Beth a thick manila envelope, which she stashed in her briefcase. She turned and ran back into the plane. She stepped into the cockpit and put her briefcase behind the copilot's seat. "I'll be right back, ten minutes max. I've got to make sure these guys get my TV on board unbroken."

"TV?"

"Thirty-two-inch Trinitron," she said with a smile. "To replace the one that you're using."

"I want a thirty-two-inch Trinitron," Tuck said to her back, but she was already out the door.

He looked out the window to make sure she was busy with the television, then pulled her briefcase from behind the seat and threw the latches. To his amazement, it was unlocked. He removed the manila envelope. Under it lay a small automatic pistol. He could take it, but then what? Hold it on Beth Curtis until she confessed to whatever she and the doctor were doing? And what was that? Research?

There was no law against that. He left the gun untouched and opened the envelope.

He wasn't sure what he expected to find: research notes, bearer bonds, stock certificates, cash, something that would shed some light on all this clandestine behavior for sure. What he found was four issues of *People* magazine and four issues of *Us*. Beth Curtis was smuggling American cheese out of Japan and that was it.

He put the envelope back into the briefcase and slid it behind the seat, then pulled Jefferson Pardee's notebook out of his pocket. Perhaps there was something inside that would tell him how the notebook had gotten to a beach some seven hundred miles from where its owner was supposed to be.

He flipped though the pages where Pardee had scribbled phone numbers, dates, and a few notes, but the only things he recognized were his own name, the names of Sebastian Curtis and his wife, and the word "Learjet," followed by "Why? How? Who paid?" and "Find other pilot." Pardee was obviously asking the same questions that were circling in Tuck's mind, but what was this about another pilot? Had Pardee come to Alualu looking for the answers? And if he did, where was he now?

"What's that?" Beth Curtis said as she came through the cockpit door.

Tuck flipped the notebook shut and stuffed it in his back pocket. "Some flight notes. I'm used to keeping a log for the FAA. I guess I brought this along out of habit." In the midst of the lie, he almost panicked. If she asked where he had gotten the notebook in the first place, he was dead. Maybe better to confront her here in Japan anyway—while he knew where the gun was.

She said, "I didn't realize there was any paperwork to flying a plane."

"More than you'd think," Tuck said. "I'm still getting used to how this plane handles. I'm just writing down things I need to remember, you know, climb rates and engine exhaust pressures, fuel consumption per hour at altitude, stuff like that." Right, he thought. Baffle her with bullshit.

"Oh," she said with what Tuck thought was indifference until she reached behind her seat and pulled out her briefcase.

He held his breath, waiting for the gun to appear. She took out an issue of *People* and opened it on her lap. She didn't look away from the magazine until they were well over the Pacific, heading home.

"You know, we haven't seen much of you lately. Maybe you should come up to the house and have dinner with Sebastian and me tonight." She had slipped on her fifties housewife personality.

Tuck had been thinking about Pardee's notebook and where he'd found it. He wanted to get back to the village tonight. If Pardee had come to Alualu, maybe the old chief knew something about it.

"I'm a little tired. We got a pretty early start. I think maybe I'll just fix up something quick at my place and get to bed early."

She yawned. "Maybe tomorrow night. Around seven. Maybe we can try out my new TV."

"That'll be fine." Tuck said. "I have a few things I'd like to discuss with you and the doc anyway."

"Good," she said. "I think we should spend more time together. Now explain to me what all these gauges mean."

41

What's a Kidney?

Privacy is a rare commodity on a small island and secrets weigh heavy on their keepers. Malink was weary with the burden of too many secrets. If he could only go to the drinking circle and let his secrets out, let the coconut telegraph carry his secrets to the edges of the island and let him walk light. But that wasn't going to happen. Secrets sought him out now, even from the old cannibal.

He stood with Sarapul and Kimi examining an eighty-four-foot breadfruit tree with a trunk you couldn't get your arms around. Kimi held an ax on his shoulder, waiting for Malink's judgment.

"Why so big?" Malink asked. "This tree will give much breadfruit."

"This is the tree," Sarapul said. "The navigator has chosen it."

Kimi said, "We will plant ten trees to take its place, but this is the one."

"Why do you need such a big tree?"

"I can't tell you," Sarapul said.

"You will tell me or you won't cut the tree."

"If I tell you, will you promise not to tell anyone else?"

Malink sighed. Yet another secret. "I will tell no one."

"Come. We'll show you."

Sarapul led Malink and Kimi through the jungle to an overgrown spot piled with dried palm leaves. Malink leaned on a tree while the old cannibal pulled away the palm fronds to reveal the prow of a canoe. Not just any canoe. A forty-foot-long sailing canoe. Malink hadn't seen one since he was a small boy.

"This is why we need the tree," Sarapul said. "I have hidden it here for many years, but the hull is rotten and we need to fix it."

Malink felt something stir in him at the sight of the big eye painted on the prow. Something that went back to a time before he could remember, when his people sailed thousands of miles by the eye of the canoe and the guidance of the great navigators. Lost arts made sad by this reminder. He shook his head. "No one knows how to build a sailing canoe anymore, Sarapul. You are so old you don't remember what you've forgotten."

"He can fix it," Sarapul said, pointing to Kimi.

Kimi grinned. "My father taught me. He was a great navigator from Satawan."

Malink raised a grizzled eyebrow. "That is where you learned our language?"

"I can fix it. And I can sail it."

"He's teaching me," Sarapul said.

Malink felt the stirring inside him grow into excitement. There was something here he hadn't felt since the arrival of Vincent. This was a secret that lifted him rather than weighing him down. But he was chief and dignity forbade him from shouting joy to the sky.

"You may cut the tree, but there is a condition."

"You can't tell anyone," Sarapul said.

"I will not tell anyone. But when the canoe is fixed, you must teach one of the young ones to be a navigator." He looked at Kimi. "Will you do that?"

Kimi nodded.

"You have your tree, old man," Malink said. "I will tell no one." He turned and walked and fell into a light bowlegged amble down the path.

Kimi called to him, "I hear my friend, the pilot, was in the village last night."

Malink turned. The coconut telegraph evidently ran even to Sarapul's little corner of the island. "He asked about you. He said he will come back."

"Did he have a bat with him?"

"No bat," Malink said. "Come tonight to the drinking circle. Maybe he will come."

"I can't," Kimi said. "The boys from the bachelors' house hate me."

"They hate the girl-man," Malink said, "not the navigator. You come."

After a nutritious dinner of canned peaches and instant coffee, Tuck checked the position of the guards, turned out the lights, and built his coconut-headed surrogate under the mosquito netting. Only the second time and already it seemed routine. There was none of the nervousness or anxiety of the night before as he crawled below window level to the bathroom and pried up the metal shower tray.

He dropped through the opening and was reaching up to grab his mask and fins when he heard the knock on the front door and froze.

He heard the door open and Beth Curtis call, "Mr. Case, are you asleep already?"

He couldn't let her see the dummy in his bed. "I'm in the bathroom. Just a second."

He caught the edges of the shower opening and vaulted back into the bathroom. The metal tray fell back over the opening, sounding like the Tin Man trying to escape from a garbage can.

He heard Beth Curtis pad to the bathroom door. "Are you all right in there?"

"Fine," Tuck said. "Just dropped the soap." He snagged a bar of soap off the sink and placed it in the bottom of the shower tray, then threw open the bathroom door.

Beth Curtis stood there in a long red silk kimono that was open in a narrow canyon of white flesh to her navel. Whatever Tuck was going to say, he forgot.

"Sebastian wanted me to bring you this." She held out a check. Tuck tore his eyes from her cleavage and took the check.

"Five thousand dollars. Mrs. Curtis, this is really more than I bargained for."

"You deserve it. You were very sweet to take the time to explain all the instrumentation to me." She leaned over and kissed him on the forehead, keeping the warm pressure of her lips there a little too long. Tuck imagined her tongue darting though his skull and licking his brain's pleasure center. He could smell her perfume, something deep and musky, and his eyes locked on her breasts, which were completely exposed when she leaned forward. He felt as if he had been staring at an arc welder and that creamy powdered image would travel across his field of vision for hours. A chasm of silence opened up and wrenched his attention back into the room.

"This is very generous," he said. "But it could have waited. It's not like I have anywhere to spend it."

"I know. I just wanted to thank you again. Personally, without

Sebastian around. And I thought you might be able to explain some of the finer points of flying a jet. It's all so exciting."

Never a man of strong resolve, the combination of sight, scent, and flattery activated Tuck's seduction autopilot. He glanced toward the bed and the switch clicked off. Sexual response was replaced by the dummy Tuck shaking its coconut head. He looked back at her and locked on her eyes—only her eyes. "Maybe tomorrow," he said. "I'm really bushed. I was just going to catch a shower and go right to bed."

For an instant her pouty smile disappeared and her lips seemed to tighten into a red line, then just as quickly the smile was back, and Tuck wasn't sure he'd seen the change at all.

"Well, tomorrow, then," she said, pulling the front of her kimono together as if she had only just noticed that it had fallen open. "We'll see you at seven." She turned at the door and threw Tuck a parade queen wave as she left, once again the darling of the Eisenhower era.

When she was safely out of the bungalow, Tuck ran to the bed and picked up the green coconut. "What in the hell was that about?"

The coconut didn't answer. "Fine," Tuck said, fitting the head back on the sleeping dummy. "I am not impressed. I am not shaken, nor am I stirred. Weirdness is my business." Even as he said it, he dismissed the hallucination as his own good sense manifesting a warning, but the duel cravings for a drink and a woman yanked at his insides like dull fishhooks. He turned off the light and let the cravings lead him out the bathroom hatch to the moonlit sea.

Forty minutes later he took his place in the circle of the Shark men. Chief Malink stood and greeted Tuck with a jarring backslap. "Good to see you, my friend. How's it hanging?"

"It hangs with magnificent splendor," Tuck said, his programmed response to the truck drivers and cowboys who used that expression, although he wondered where Malink had heard it. "But I'm a little parched," he said.

A fat young man named Vincent was pouring tonight and he handed Tucker the coconut cup with a smile. Tuck sipped at first, fighting that first gag, then gulped down the coconut liquor and gritted his teeth to keep it from coming back up.

The older men in the group seemed festive and yattered back and forth in their native language, but Tuck noticed that the younger men were sulking, digging their toes into the sand like pouting little boys.

"Why so glum, guys? Someone kill your dog?"

"No," Malink said, not quite understanding the question. "We eat a turtle today."

Having your dog killed must mean something different here than it means back in Texas, Tuck realized.

Malink sensed Tuck's confusion. "They are sad because the Sky Priestess has chosen the mispel from their house and she will be gone many days now."

"Mispel?"

"The girl you followed last night is mispel of the bachelors' house."

"Sorry to hear that, guys," Tuck said, acting as if he had the slightest idea what a mispel or being chosen was. He figured that maybe it had something to do with PMS. Maybe when the women started getting cranky with the old Sky Priestess cramps, they just checked her into a special "chosen" hut until she mellowed out. He waited until the cup came around the circle before he brought it up again. "So she was chosen by the old Sky Priestess, huh? Tough luck there. Did you try giving her chocolate? That takes the edge off sometimes."

"We give her special tuba when she comes," Malink said.

"Tastes like shit!" several of the men chanted.

Abo, the fierce one, said, "I am chosen and now Sepie is chosen. I will marry her."

Several of the other young men seemed less than pleased at Abo's announcement.

"Come on, man," Tuck said. "You might need a little attitude adjustment, but you're not chosen."

"I am," Abo insisted. "Look." He turned his back to the group and ran his finger across a long pink scar that ran diagonally across his ribs. "The Sky Priestess chose me for Vincent in the time of the ripe breadfruit."

Tuck stared at the scar, stunned, hoping that what he was thinking was as far off as his PMS theory had been. "The Sky Priestess? That was the music last night, all the noise?"

"Yes," Malink said, "Vincent brings her in his airplane. We never see it, but we hear it."

"And when someone is chosen, then does the jet always fly the next day?"

Malink nodded. "No one was chosen for a long time until Vincent sent you to fly the white airplane. We thought Vincent was angry with us."

Tuck looked to Abo, who seemed satisfied that the chief was backing him up. "Where do you go when you are chosen?"

"You go to the white house where the Sorcerer lives. There are many machine."

"And then what? What happens in the white house?"

"It is secret."

Tuck was across the circle in Abo's face. "What happens there?"

Abo seemed frightened and turned away. Tuck looked around at the other men. "Who else here has been chosen?"

The fat kid who had been pouring twisted so Tuck could see the scar on his back.

"What's your name, kid?"

"Vincent."

"I should have known. Vincent, what happens in the white house?"

Young Vincent shook his head. Tuck turned to Malink. "What happens?"

Malink shook his head. "I don't know. I have not been chosen."

A familiar voice called out of the dark, "They make them sleep."

Everyone turned to see Kimi coming down the path from the village. The old cannibal creaked along behind him.

Abo barked a reproach to Kimi in his native tongue. Kimi barked back something in the same language. Tuck didn't have to know the language to know that Kimi had told the fierce one to fuck off.

"Kimi, are you okay?" Tuck barely recognized the navigator. He was wearing the blue loincloth of the Shark men and he seemed to have put on some muscle. Tuck was genuinely delighted to see him. The navigator ran to him and threw his arms around the pilot. Tuck found himself returning the embrace.

Several of the young men had stood and were glaring at Kimi. One of the jugs of *tuba* had been kicked over, but no one seemed to notice the liquor running out on the sand.

"Kimi, do you know what's going on here?"

"A pretty white woman with yellow hair. She come out of the fence and take the girl away. They will put her to sleep and when she wakes up she will have a cut here." He drew his finger across the back of his ribs.

"No!" Abo screamed. He leaped over the crouching Malink to get to Kimi. Without thinking, Tuck swung around and caught Abo under the jaw with a roundhouse punch. Abo's feet flew out from under him and he landed on his back. Tuck rubbed his hand. Abo tried to struggle to his feet and Malink barked an order to two of the young Vincents. Reluctantly, they restrained their friend. "Vincent has sent the pilot," Malink reminded them.

Tuck turned back to Kimi. "What happens then?"

"You owe me five hundred dollars."

"You'll get it. What happens then?"

"The chosen has to stay in bed for many days. There are tube stuck in them and they are in much pain. Then they come back."

"That's it?"

"Yes," Kimi said.

Malink stood now and addressed Kimi. "How do you know this?"

Kimi shrugged. "Sepie tells me."

Malink turned to Abo, who had stopped struggling and now looked terrified. "She said she would not tell. The girl-man put a spell on her."

Tuck stood rubbing his knuckles, watching this little tropical opera and feeling like someone had snapped on a light and found him french-kissing a maggoty corpse. The cooler, the surgical garb, the flights on short notice, the second jet waiting on the tarmac in Japan, the guards, the secrecy, the money. How had he been so fucking stupid?

Malink was hurling a string of native curses at Abo, who looked as if he would burst into tears any second.

"You dumb motherfuckers!" Tuck shouted.

Malink stopped talking.

"She's selling your kidneys. The doc is taking out your kidneys and selling them in Japan."

This revelation didn't have quite the effect that Tuck thought it would. In fact, he seemed to be the only one concerned about it at all.

"Did you hear me?"

Malink looked a little embarrassed. "What is a kidney?"

PART THREE

Coconut Angel

42

~~~~~~

Bedfellows

Just before dawn, Tuck crawled through the bottom of the shower like a homesick cockroach, scuttled out of the bathroom under the mosquito netting and into bed. There were things to do, big things, important things, maybe even dangerous things, but he had no idea what they were and he was too tired and too drunk to figure them out now. He had tried, he had really tried to convince the Shark men that the doctor and his wife were doing horrible things to them, but the islanders always came back with the same answer: "It is what Vincent wants. Vincent will take care of us."

To hell with them, Tuck thought. Dumb bastards deserve what happens to them.

He rolled over and pushed the coconut-headed dummy aside. The dummy pushed back.

Tuck leaped out of bed, tripped in the mosquito netting, and scooted on his butt like a man backing away from a snake.

And the dummy sat up.

Tuck couldn't see the face in the predawn light filtering into the bungalow, just a silhouette behind the mosquito netting, a shadow. And the shadow wore a captain's hat.

"Don't think I don't know what you're thinking because I'll give you six to five I do." The accent was somewhere out of a Bowery Boys movie, and Tuck recognized the voice. He'd heard it in his head, he'd heard it in the voice of a talking bat, and he'd heard it twice from a young flyer.

"You do?"

"Yeah, you're thinking, 'Hey, I never wanted to find a guy in my bed, but if you got to find a guy in your bed, this is the guy I'd want it to be,' right?"

"That's not what I was thinking."

"Then you shoulda taken odds, ya mook."

"Who are you?"

The flyer threw back the mosquito netting and tossed something across the room. Tuck flinched as it landed with a *thump* on the floor next to him.

"Pick it up."

Tuck could just see an object shining by his knee. He picked up what felt like a cigarette lighter.

"Read what it says," the shadow said.

"I can't. It's dark."

Tuck could see the flyer shaking his head dolefully.

"You know, I saw a guy in the war that got his head shot off about the hat line. Docs did some hammering on some stainless steel and riveted it on his noggin and saved his life, but the guy didn't do nothing from that day forward but walk around in a circle yanking his hamster and singing just the 'row' part of 'Row, Row, Row Your Boat.' They had to tape oven mitts on him to keep him from rubbing himself raw. Now, I'm not saying that the guy didn't know how to have a good time, but he wasn't much for conversation, if you know what I mean."

"That was a beautiful story," Tuck said. "Why?"

"Because the steelhead hamster-pulling 'row' guy was a genius compared to you. Light the fuckin' lighter, ya mook."

"Oh," Tuck said and he flipped open the lighter and sparked it. By the firelight he could read the engraving: VINCENT BENNIDETTI, CAPTAIN U.S.A.F.

Tuck looked back at the flyer, who was still caged in shadow, even though the rest of the room had started to lighten. "You're Vincent?"

The shadow gave a slight bow. "Not exactly in the flesh, but at your fuckin' service."

"You're Malink's Vincent?"

"The same. I gave the chief the original of that lighter."

"You could have just said so. You didn't have to be so dramatic." Tuck was glad he was a little drunk. He didn't feel frightened. As strange as it all was, he felt safe. This guy—this thing, this spirit— had more or less saved his life at least twice, maybe three times.

"I got responsibilities, kid, and so do you."

"Responsibilities?" Now Tuck was frightened. It was a conditioned response.

"Yeah, so when you get up later today, don't go storming into the doc's office demanding the facts. Just go swimming. Cool off."

"Go swimming?"

"Yeah, go to the far side of the reef and swim away from the direction of the village about five hundred yards. Keep an eye out for sharks outside of the reef."

"Why?"

"A guy appears out of nowhere in the middle of the night saying all kinds of mystical shit and you ask why?"

"Yeah. Why?"

"Because I said so," Vincent said.

"My dad always said that. Are you the ghost of my dad?"

The shade slapped his forehead. "Repeat after me—and don't be getting any on you, now—one and two and three and 'Row, row, row, row, row . . .'" He started to fade away with the chant.

"Wait," Tuck said. "I need to know more than that."

"Stay on the sly, kid. You don't know as much as you think you do."

"But . . ."

"You owe me."

Two armed ninjas followed Tuck to the water. He watched them, looking for signs of microwave poisoning from the radar blasts, but he wasn't sure exactly what the signs would be. Would they plump noticeably, perhaps explode without fork holes to release the inner pressure? That would be cool. Maybe they'd fall asleep on the beach and wake up a hundred times larger, yearning to do battle with Godzilla while tiny people whose words didn't match their mouth movements scrambled in the flaming rubble below? (It happened all the time in Japanese movies, didn't it?) Too good for them.

He pulled on his fins and bowed to them as he backed into the water. "May your nads shrivel like raisins," he said with a smile.

They bowed back, more out of reflex than respect.

The far side of the reef and five hundred yards down: The ninjas were going to have a fit. He'd never gone to the ocean side of the reef. Inside was a warm clear aquamarine where you could always see the bottom and the fish seemed, if not friendly, at least not dangerous. But the ocean side, past the surf, was a dark cobalt blue, as deep and liquid as a clear night sky. The colorful reef fish must look like M&Ms to the hunters of the deep blue, Tuck thought. The outer edge of the reef is the candy dish of monsters.

He kicked slowly out to the reef, letting the light surge lift and drop him as he watched the multicolored links in the food chain dart around the bottom. A trigger fish, painted in tans and blues that seemed more at home in the desert, was crunching the legs off of a crab while smaller fish darted in to steal the floating crumbs. He pulled up and looked at the only visible break in the reef, a deep blue channel, and headed toward it. He'd have to go out to the ocean side and swim the five hundred yards there, otherwise the breaking surf would dash him against the coral when he tried to swim over the reef.

He put his face in the water and kicked out of the channel until the bottom disappeared, then, once past the surf line, turned and swam parallel to the reef. It was like swimming in space at the edge of a canyon. He could see the reef sloping down a hundred and fifty feet to disappear into a blue blur. He tried to keep his bearing on the reef, let his eye bounce from coral fan to anemone to nudibranch to eel, like visual stepping-stones, because to his left there was no reference, nothing but empty blue, and when he looked there he felt like a child watching for a strange face at the window, so convinced and terrified it would come that any shape, any movement, any play of light becomes a horror. He saw a flash out the side of his mask and whipped around in time to see a harmless green parrot fish munching coral. He sucked a mouthful of water into his submerged snorkel and choked.

He hovered in a dead man's float for a full minute before he could breathe normally and start kicking his way up the reef again, this time resolved to faith. Whatever, whoever Vincent was, he had saved Tuck's life, and he knew things. He wouldn't have gone to the trouble to have Tuck eaten by barracudas.

Tuck ticked off his stepping-stones, trying to gauge how far he had come. He would have to go out farther to see past the rising surf and use the shore as a reference, and besides, what was above the water's surface was irrelevant. This was a foreign world, and he was an uninvited guest.

Then another flash, but this time he fought the panic. Sunlight on something metal about thirty feet down the slope of the reef. Something waving in the surge near the flash. He rested a second, gathered his breath, and dove, swooping down to grab the object just as he recognized what it was: a set of military dog tags on a beaded metal chain. He shot to the surface and hovered as he caught his breath and read: SOMMERS, JAMES W. James Sommers was a Presbyterian, according to the dog tag. Somehow Tuck didn't think that a thousand-yard swim was worth finding a pair of dog tags. But there was the swath of fabric still down there. Tuck hadn't gotten a good look at it.

He tucked the tags into the inside pocket of his trunks and dove again. He kicked down to the swath of cloth, holding his nose and blowing to equalize the pressure on his ears, even as the air in his lungs tried to pull him to the surface, away from his prize. It was some kind of printed cotton. He grasped at it and a piece came away in his hand. He pulled again, but the cloth was wedged into a crevice in the reef. He yanked and the cloth came away, revealing something white. Out of breath, he shot to the surface and examined the cloth. Flying piggies. Oh, good. He'd risked his life for Presbyterian dog tags and a flying piggies print.

One more dive and he saw what it was that had wedged into the crevice: a human pelvic bone. Whatever else had been here had been carried away, but this bone had wedged and been picked clean. Someone wearing flying piggies boxers had become part of the food chain.

The swim back to the channel seemed longer and slower, but this time Tuck forgot his fear of what might lurk behind the vasty blue. The real danger lay back on shore.

And how does one, over dinner, proffer the opinion that one's employers are murdering organ thieves? "Stay on the sly," Vincent had said. And so far he seemed to know what he was talking about.

43

Boiling the Puppets

"Oh, come in, Mr. Case. Sebastian is out on the lanai." She wore a white raw silk pant suit, cut loose in the legs and low at the neck, a rope of pearls with matching earrings. Her hair was tied back with a white satin bow and she moved before him like the ghost of good housekeeping. "How do you feel about Pacific lobster?"

"I like it," Tuck said, looking for some sign from her that she knew that he knew. There was no acknowledgment of her appearance in his room last night or that she had any suspicion of him at all. Tuck said, "I feel like I'm taking advantage coming to dinner empty-handed. I ought to have you and the doc over to my place some evening."

"Oh, do you cook too, Mr. Case?"

"A few things. My specialty is blackened Pez."

"A Cajun dish?"

"I learned to make it in Texas, actually."

"A Tex-Mex specialty, then."

"Well, a fifth of tequila does make it taste a little better."

She laughed, a polite hostess laugh, and said, "Can I get you something to drink?"

"You mean a drink or some liquid?"

"I'm sorry. It does seem constraining, I'm sure, but you understand, you might have to fly."

She had a large glass of white wine on the counter where she had been working. Tuck looked at it and said, "But performing major surgery under the influence is no problem, right?" That was subtle, Tuck thought. Very smooth. I am a dead man.

Her eyes narrowed, but the polite smile never left her lips. "Sebastian," she called, "you'd better come in, dear. I think Mr. Case has something he wants to discuss with us."

Sebastian Curtis came through the french doors looking tall and dignified, his gray hair brushed back, his tan face striking against the gray. To Tuck he looked like any number of executives one might see at a yacht club, a retired male model perhaps, a Shakespearean actor finally finished with the young prince and lover roles, seasoned and ready to play Caesar, Lear, or more appropriately, Prospero, the banished wizard of *The Tempest*.

Tuck, still in his borrowed clothes, baggy and rolled at the cuffs, felt like a beggar. He fought to hold on to his righteous indignation, which was an unfamiliar emotion to him anyway.

Sebastian Curtis said, "Mr. Case. Nice to see you. Beth and I were just talking about how pleased we are with your work. I'm sure these impromptu flights are difficult."

"Mr. Case was just suggesting that we keep an eye on our alcohol consumption," Beth Curtis said. "Just in case we might have to perform an emergency surgery."

The jovial manner dropped from the doctor like a veil. "And just what kind of surgery might you be referring to?"

Tuck looked at the floor. He should have thought this through a little more. He fingered the dog tags in his pocket. The plan was to throw them on the table and demand an explanation. What had happened to the skeleton, the owner of the tags? And for that matter, what would happen to Tucker Case if he threw this in their faces? Mary Jean used to say, "In negotiations, always leave yourself a way out. You can always come back later."

Go slow, Tuck told himself. He said, "Doc, I'm concerned about the flights. I should know what we're carrying in case we're detained by the authorities. What's in the cooler?"

"But I told you, you're carrying research samples."

"What kind of samples?" It was time to play a card. "I'm not flying again until I know."

Sebastian Curtis shot a glance at his wife, then looked back to Tucker. "Perhaps we should sit down and have a talk." He pulled a chair out for Tucker. "Please." Tuck sat. The doctor repeated the gesture for his wife and then sat down next to her, across the table from Tuck.

"I've been on Alualu for twenty-eight years, Mr. Case."

"What does that have to do . . . ?"

Curtis held up a hand. "Hear me out. If you want answers, you have to take them in the context that I give them."

"Okay."

"My family didn't have the money for medical school, so I took a scholarship from the Methodist Missions, on the condition that I work for them when I graduated and go where they sent me. They sent me here. I was full of myself and full of the Spirit of the Lord. I was going to bring God and healing to the heathens of the Pacific. There hadn't been a Christian missionary on the island since World War II, and I was warned that there might be a residual Catholic influence, but the Methodists have liberal ideas about spreading the Word of God. A Methodist missionary works with the culture he finds. But I didn't find a Catholic population here. What I found was a population that worshipped the memory of an American pilot and his bomber."

"A cargo cult," Tuck said, hoping to move things along.

"Then you know about them. Yes, a cargo cult. The strongest I'd ever heard of. Fortunately for me, it wasn't based on the hatred of whites like the cargo cults in New Guinea. They loved Americans and everything that came from America. They took my medicine, the tools I brought, food, reading material, everything I offered them, except, of course, the Word of God. And I was good to them. The natives on this island are the healthiest in the Pacific. Partly because they are so isolated that communicable diseases don't reach them, but I take some credit for it as well."

"So that's why you don't let them have any contact with the ship when it arrives?"

"No, well, that is one of the reasons, but mainly I wanted to keep them away from the ship's store."

"Why?"

"Because the store offered them things that I couldn't or wouldn't give them, and the store only accepted money. Money was becoming an icon in their religion. I heard drums in the village one night and went into the village to find all the women crouched around a fire holding wooden bowls with a few coins in the bottom. They were oiled and waving their heads as if in a trance, and as the drummers played, the men, wearing masks fashioned to look like the faces on American currency, moved around behind the women, copulating with them and chanting. It was a fertility ceremony to make the money in the bowls multiply so they could buy things from the ship's store."

"Well, it does sound better than getting a job," Tuck said.

Curtis didn't see the humor. "By forbidding them to have contact with the ship, I thought I could kill the cargo cult, but it didn't work. I would talk of Jesus, and the miracles that he performed, and how he would save them, and they would ask me if I had seen him. Because they had seen their savior. Their pilot had saved them from the Japanese. Jesus had just told them that they had to give up their customs and taboos. Christianity couldn't compete. But I still tried. I gave them the best care I could. But after five years, the Methodist Missions sent a group of officials to check on my progress. They cut my funding and wanted to send me home, but I decided to stay and try to do the best I could without their support."

"He was afraid to leave," Beth Curtis said.

Sebastian Curtis looked as if he was going to strike his wife. "That's not true, Beth."

"Sure it is. You hadn't been off this island in years. You forgot how to live with real people."

"They are real people."

As amusing as it was to watch the perfect couple illusion go up in flames before his eyes, Tuck put out the fire. "A Learjet and millions in electronics. Looks like you did pretty good with no funding, Doc."

"I'm sorry." And he looked as if he was. "I tried to make it on what the islanders could raise by selling copra, but it wasn't enough. I lost one of my patients, a little boy, because I didn't have the funds to fly him to a hospital that could give him the care he needed. I tried harder to convert the natives, thinking I might get another mission to sponsor us, but how can you compete with a Messiah people have actually spoken to?"

Tuck didn't answer. Having spoken to the "Messiah" himself, he was convinced already.

Sebastian Curtis drained his glass of wine and continued. "I sent letters to churches, foundations, and corporations all over the world. Then one day a plane landed out on the airstrip and some Japanese businessmen got out. They wouldn't fund the clinic out of charity, but if I could get every able-bodied islander to give blood every two weeks, then they would help. And every two weeks the plane came and picked up three hundred pints of blood. I got twenty-five American dollars for every pint."

"How'd you talk the natives into it? I've given blood. It's not that pleasant."

"They were coming on a plane, remember? Airplanes are a big part of these people's religion."

"If you can't beat 'em, join 'em, huh?"

"They always brought something on the plane for the natives. Rice, machetes, cooking pots. I got all the medicines I needed and I was able to get the materials to build most of this compound."

Beth Curtis stood up. "Oh, as much as I love hearing this story, I think we should eat. Excuse me." She went to the kitchen area, where a large pot was boiling on the stove, reached into a wooden crate on the floor, and came up with a large live lobster in each hand. The giant sea bugs waved their legs and antennae around looking for purchase. Beth Curtis held them over the pot, puppeting them. "Oh, Steve, you got us a room with a hot tub. How wonderful," she made the left lobster say.

"Yes, I'm very romantic," she said in a deeper voice, bouncing the bug with the words. "Let's go in now. I'm a little tense."

"Oh, you're wonderful." Then she dropped the lobsters into the boiling water.

A high-pitched squeal came from the pot and Beth Curtis went to the crate for another victim.

"Beth, please," the doctor said.

"I'm just trying to lighten things up a little, 'Bastian. Be still."

She held the second lobster over the pot, then looked at Tucker as she began her narration. "This is the crazed doctor talking. There's always a crazed megalomaniacal doctor. It's traditional."

Sebastian Curtis stood up. "Stop it, Beth!"

She affected a German accent. "You see, Mr. Bond, a man spends too much time on an island alone, he changes. He loses his faith. He begins to think of ways to improve his lot. My associates in Japan came to me with a proposal. They would send me to a seminar in San Francisco to brush up on organ transplant surgery. I would no longer be selling blood for pocket change. They would send me specific orders for kidneys, and I could deliver them within hours for a cool half-million apiece. A dying man will pay a lot for a healthy kidney. In San Francisco I met a woman, a beautiful woman." Beth came out of character for a moment, grinned, and bowed quickly, then went back to terrorizing the lobster. "I brought her here, and it was she who devised the plan to get the natives to comply with having their organs removed. Not only beautiful, but a genius as well, and she had a degree as a surgical nurse. She used her abundant charms on the natives"—she held the lobster where it could have a good view of her cleavage—"and the savages were more than happy to donate a kidney. Meanwhile, I have become rich beyond my wildest dreams, and as for you, Mr. Bond, now it's time for you to die." She dropped the lobster into the pot and began to shake with a diabolical laugh. She stopped laughing abruptly and said, "They should be ready in about ten minutes. Salad, Mr. Case?"

Tuck couldn't think. Somewhere in that little puppet show of the damned was a confession to cutting out people's organs and selling them like so much meat, and the doctor's wife not only didn't seem to have any regrets about it, she was absolutely gleeful. Sebastian Curtis, on the other hand, had his head down on the table, and when he did look up, he couldn't make eye contact with Tuck. A minute passed in uncomfortable silence. Beth Curtis seemed to be waiting for someone to shout "Encore!" while the good doctor gathered his wits.

"What I'd like you to understand, Mr. Case, is that I—we— couldn't have taken care of these people without the funds we've received for what we do. They would have no modern medical care at all."

Tuck was thinking again, trying to measure what he could say and what he wasn't willing to reveal. He couldn't let them know that he knew anything at all about the Shark People, and, as Vincent had implied, he'd better find out more before he threw down the dog tags and Pardee's notebook. The doc was obviously stretched pretty tight by the situation, and Mrs. Curtis—well, Mrs. Curtis was just fucking scary. Play it chilly. They'd brought him here because they thought he was as twisted as they were. No sense in ruining his image.

"I understand." Tuck said. "I wish you'd been a little more up front about it, but I think I get all the secrecy now. But what I want to know is: Why can't I drink if you guys do? I mean, if you guys can perform major surgery when you're half in the bag, then I can fly a plane."

Beth said, "We wanted to help you with your substance abuse problem. We thought that if you weren't exposed to other drinkers that you'd relapse when you went back home."

"Very thoughtful of you," Tuck said. "But when exactly am I supposed to go home?"

"When we're finished," she said.

The doctor nodded. "Yes, we were going to tell you, but we wanted you to become used to the routine. We wanted to see if you could handle the job first. We're going to do the operations until we have a hundred million, then we will invest it on behalf of the islanders. The proceeds will assure we can continue our work and that the Shark People will be taken care of as long as they are here."

Tuck laughed. "Right. You're not taking anything for yourself. This is all a mercy mission."

"No, we may leave, but there'll be enough to keep someone running this clinic and shipping in food and supplies forever. And then there's your bonus."

"Go," Tuck said. "Go ahead."

"The plane."

Tuck raised an eyebrow. "The plane?"

"If you stay until we finish our work, we will sign the plane over to you, plus your salary and any other bonuses you've accumulated. You can go anywhere in the world you want, start a charter business if you want, or just sell it and live comfortably for the rest of your life."

Tuck shook his head. Of all the weirdness that had gone on so far, this seemed like the weirdest, if only because the doctor seemed so earnest. It might have had something to do with the fact that it was one of those things that a guy hopes all his life he is going to hear, but convinces himself that it's never going to happen. These people were going to give him his own Learjet.

He didn't want to do it, he fought not to do it, he strained, but nevertheless, Tuck couldn't stop himself from asking. "Why?"

"Because we can't do it without you, and this is something that you can't get any other way. And because we'd rather keep you than have to find another pilot and lose the time."

"What if I say no?"

"Then, you understand, we'd have to ask you to leave and you would keep the money that you've already earned."

"And I can just go?"

"Of course. As you know, you are not our first pilot. He decided to move on. But then again, we didn't make him this offer."

"What was your first pilot's name?"

The doctor shot a look at his wife. She said, "Giordano, he was Italian. Why?"

"The aviation community is pretty small. I thought I might know him."

"Do you?" she said and there was too much sincerity in the question for Tuck to believe that she didn't know the answer.

"No."

Sebastian Curtis cleared his throat and forced a smile. "So what do you think? How would you like to own your own Learjet, Mr. Case?"

Tuck sat staring at the open wine bottle, measuring what he could say, what answer they not only wanted to hear, but had to hear if he was going to leave the island alive. He extended his hand for the doctor to shake. "I think you've got yourself a pilot. Let's drink to the deal."

An electronic bell trilled from the bedroom and the doctor and his wife exchanged glances. "I'll take care of it," Beth Curtis said. She stood and put her napkin on the table.

"Excuse me, Mr. Case, but we have a patient in the clinic who requires my attention." Then the whiplash mood swing from officious to acid. "She presses that buzzer so much you'd think it was attached to her clit."

Sebastian Curtis looked at Tuck and shrugged apologetically.

44

Revealed: The Perfect Couple

Back at his bungalow, an argument went on in the still-sober brain of Tucker Case.

I am scum. I should have told them to shove it.

But they might have killed you.

Yeah, but I would have at least had my integrity.

Your what? Get real.

But I'm scum.

Big deal. You've been scum before. You've never owned a Learjet before.

You actually think they'll give me the jet?

It could happen. Stranger things have happened.

But I should do something about this.

Why? You've never done anything before.

Well, maybe it's time.

No way. Take the jet.

I'm scum.

Well, yes, you are. But you're rich scum.

I can live with that.

The dog tags and Jefferson Pardee's notebook lay on the coffee table, threatening to set off another fusillade of doubt and condemnation. Tuck lay back on the rattan couch and turned on the television to escape the noise in his mind. Skinny Asian guys were beating the snot out of each other in a kickboxing match from the Philippines. The Malaysian channel was showing how to fillet a schnauzer. The cooking show reminded him of surgery, and surgery reminded him that there was a beautiful island girl lying in the clinic, recovering from an unnecessary major surgery that he could have prevented. Definitely kickboxing.

He was just getting into the rhythm of the violence when the bat came through the window and made an awkward swinging landing on one of the bungalow's open rafters. Tuck lost his breath for a minute, thinking there might just be a wild animal in his house. Then he saw the sunglasses.

Roberto steadied himself into a slightly swinging upside-down hang.

Tuck sighed. "Please just be a bat in sunglasses tonight. Please."

Thankfully, the bat said nothing. The sunglasses were sliding off his nose.

"How do you fly in those things?" Tuck said, thinking out loud.

"They're aviators."

"Of course," Tuck said. The bat had indeed changed from rhinestone glasses to aviators, but once you accept a talking bat, the leap to a talking bat with an eyewear wardrobe is a short one.

Roberto dropped from the rafter and took wing just before he hit the floor. Two beats of his wings and he was on the coffee table, as awkward in his spiderlike crawl as he was graceful in the air. With his wing claw, he raked at Jefferson Pardee's notebook until it was open to the middle, then he launched himself and flew out the window.

Tuck picked up the notebook and read what Pardee had written. Tuck had missed this page when he had looked at the notebook before. This page had been stuck to the one before it; the bat's clawing had revealed it. It was a list of leads that Pardee had made for the story he had been working on. The second item read: "What happened to the first pilot, James Sommers? Call immigration in Yap and Guam." Tuck flipped through the notebook to see if he had missed something else. Had Pardee found out? Of course he had. He'd found out and he'd followed Sommers to the last place anyone had seen him. But where was Pardee? His notebook hadn't come to the island without him.

Tuck went through the notebook three more times. There were some foreign names and phone numbers. Something that looked like a packing list for a trip. Some notes on the background of Sebastian Curtis. Notes to check up on Japanese with guns. The word "Learjet" underlined three times. And nothing else. There didn't seem to be any organizational form to the notes. Just random facts, names, places, and dates. Dates? Tuck went through it once more. On the third page in, all by itself, was printed: "Alualu, Sept. 9."

Tuck ran to the nightstand drawer, where the Curtises had left him a calendar. He counted back the days to the ninth and tried to put events to days. The ship had arrived on the ninth, and the morning of the tenth he had made his first flight. Jefferson Pardee could be lying in the clinic right now, wondering where in the hell his kidney was. If he was, Tuck needed to see him.

Tuck looked in the closet for something dark to wear. This was going to be different than sneaking out to the village. There were no buildings between the guards' quarters and the clinic, no trees, nothing but seventy-five yards of open compound. Darkness would be his only cover.

It was a tropical-weight wet suit—two-mil neoprene—and it was two sizes two big, but it was the only thing in the closet that wasn't khaki or white. In the 80-degree heat and 90-percent humidity, Tuck was reeling from the heat before he got the hood on. He stepped into the shower and soaked himself with cold water, then peeled the hood over his head and made his escape through the shower floor, dropping onto the wet gravel below.

In the movies the spies—the Navy SEALS, the Special Forces, the demolition experts—always sneak through the night in their wet suits. Why, Tuck wondered, don't they squish and slosh and make squeaking raspberry noises when they creep? Must be special training. You never hear James Bond say, "Frankly, Q, I'll trade the laser-guided cufflink missiles for a wet suit that doesn't make me feel like a bloody bag of catsick." Which is how Tuck felt as he sloshed around the side of the clinic and peeked across the compound at the guard on duty, who seemed to be looking right at him.

Tuck pulled back around the corner. He needed a diversion if he was going to make it to the clinic door unseen. The moon was bright, the sky clear, and the compound of white coral gravel reflected enough light to read by.

He heard the guard shout, and he was sure he'd been spotted. He flattened against the wall and held his breath. Then there were more Japanese from across the compound, but no footsteps. He ventured a peek. The guard was gesturing toward the sky and brushing his head. Two other guards had joined him and were laughing at the guard on duty. He seemed to get angrier, cursing at the sky and wiping his hand on his uniform. The other guards led him inside to calm him down and clean him up.

Tuck heard a bark from the sky and looked up to see the silhouette of a huge bat against the moon. Roberto had delivered a guano air strike. Tuck had his diversion.

He slipped around the front of the building, grabbed the doorknob, and turned. It was unlocked. Given Beth Curtis's irritation at being buzzed and the amount of wine she'd consumed, Tuck had guessed that she'd get tired locking and unlocking the door. What did Mary Jean always say? "Ladies, if you do your job and assume that everyone else is incompetent, you will seldom be disappointed." Amen, Tuck thought.

He squished into the outer room of the clinic, which was dark except for the red-eyed stare of a half-dozen machines and the dancing glow of a computer screen running a screen saver. He'd try to get into that later, but now he was interested in what, or who, lay in the small hospital ward, two rooms back.

He sloshed into the examination/operating room by the light of more LED eyes and pushed through the curtain to the four-bed ward. Only one bed held a patient—or what looked like a patient. The only light was a green glow from a heart monitor that blipped away silently, the sound turned off. Whoever was in the bed was certainly large enough to be Jefferson Pardee. There were a couple of IVs hanging above the patient. Probably painkillers after such major surgery, Tuck thought.

He moved closer and ventured a whisper. "Pst, Pardee."

The lump under the covers moved and moaned in a distinctly unmasculine voice. "Pardee, it's Tucker Case. Remember?"

The sheet was thrown back and Tuck saw a thin male face in the green glow. "Kimi?"

"Hi, Tucker." Kimi looked down at the other person under the covers. "You remember Tucker? He all better now."

The pretty island girl said, "I take care of you when you sick. You stink very much."

Tuck backed off a step. "Kimi, what are you doing here?"

"Well, she like pretty thing, and I like pretty thing. She tired of having many mans and so am I. We have a lot in common."

"He the best," Sepie added with an adoring smile at Kimi.

Kimi handed the smile off to Tuck. "Once you be a woman, you know how to make a woman happy."

Tuck was getting over the initial surprise and began to smell the smoke of his beautiful island girl fantasy as it caught fire and burned to ash. He hadn't realized how much time he'd spent thinking about this girl. She, after all, was the one who had revived his manhood. Sort of.

"You right," Kimi said. "Women are better. I am lesbian now."

"You shouldn't be doing this. This girl just had major surgery."

"Oh, we not doing nothing but kissing. She very hurt. But this make it better." Kimi held his arm up, displaying an IV line. "You want to try? Put in you arm and push button. It make you feel very very nice."

"That's for her, Kimi. You shouldn't be using it."

"We share," Sepie said.

"Yes, we share," Kimi said.

"I'm very happy for you. How in the hell did you get in here?"

"Like you get out. I swim around mimes and come here to see Sepie. No problem."

"You don't want to let them catch you. You've got to go. Now."

"One more push." Sepie held the button, ready to administer another dose of morphine to Kimi.

Tuck grabbed it from her hand. "No. Go now. How did you know about the mines?"

"I have other friend. Sarapul. I teach him how to be a navigator. He know a lot of things too. He a cannibal."

"You're a cannibal lesbian?"

"Just learning. How come you have rubber suit? You kinky?"

"Sneaky. Look, Kimi, have you seen a fat white guy, an American?"

"No, but Sarapul see him. He see the guards take him from the beach. He not here?"

"No. I found his notebook. I met him on Truk."

"Sarapul say he see the guards bring him to the Sorcerer. He say it very funny, the white man wear pigs with wings."

Tuck felt his face go numb. All that was left of Pardee was a pelvic bone wedged in the reef, stripped of flesh and wrapped in flying piggy shorts. Oh, there might be the odd kidney left alive in someone in Japan, a kidney that he had delivered. Had the fat man died on the operating table during the operation, the surgery too much for his heart? Or was he put under and never meant to wake up?

Tuck suddenly felt that getting into the doctor's computer was more important than ever. He grabbed Kimi's arm and pulled the IV needle out of his vein. The navigator didn't resist, and he didn't seem to feel it.

"Kimi, see if you can get that back in Sepie's arm and come with me."

"Okay boss."

Tuck looked down at the girl, who had evidently picked up on the panic in his voice. Her eyes were wide, despite the morphine glaze. "Don't buzz the doctor until after we're gone. This button will let you have only so much morphine, and Kimi's used some of yours. But if it hurts, you still have to wait, okay?"

She nodded. Kimi crawled out of the bed and nearly fell. Tuck caught him by the arm and steadied him.

"I am chosen," Sepie said. "When Vincent comes, he will give me many pretty things."

Tuck brushed back her hair with his fingers. "Yes, he will. You sleep now. And thank you for taking care of me when I was sick."

Kimi kissed the girl and after a minute Tuck pulled him away and led him through the operating room to the office section of the clinic. In the glow of the computer screen, Tuck said, "Kimi, the doctor and his wife are killing people."

"No, they not. They sent by Vincent. Sepie say Vincent come from Heaven to bring people many good things. They very poor."

"No, Kimi, they are bad people. Like Malcolme. They are taking advantage of Sepie's people. They are just pretending to be working for a god."

"How you know? You no believe in God."

Tuck took the boy by the shoulders. He was no longer angry or even irritated, he was afraid, and for the first time ever, not just for himself. "Kimi, can you swim back around the mines?"

"I think."

"You've got to go to the other side of the island and you can't come back. If the guards find you I'm pretty sure you'll be killed."

"You just want Sepie for yourself. She tell me you follow her."

"I'll check on her and I'll meet you at the drinking circle tomorrow night—tell you how she's doing. I won't touch her, I promise. Okay?"

"Okay." Kimi leaned against the wall by the door.

Tuck studied him for a moment to try and determine just how fucked up he was. It wasn't a difficult swim. Tuck had done it stone drunk, but he'd been wearing fins and a mask and snorkel. "You're sure you can swim?"

Kimi nodded and Tuck cracked the door. The moon had moved across the sky throwing the front of the clinic in shadow. The guard across the compound was reading a magazine by flashlight. "When you get outside, go left and get behind the building." The navigator stepped out, slid down the side of the building and around the corner. Tuck heard him trip and fall and swear softly in Filipino.

"Shit," Tuck said to himself. He glanced at the computer. It would have to wait. He slid out the door, palming it shut behind him, then followed the navigator around the building. He heard the guard shout from across the compound, and for once in his life, Tuck made a definitive decision. He grabbed the navigator under the arms and ran.

45

Confessions Over Tee

Tucker Case dreamed of machine-gun fire and jerked as the bullets ripped into his back. He tossed forward into the dirt, mouth filling with sand, smothering him as the life drained out of a thousand ragged wounds, and still the guns kept firing, the rhythmic reports pounding like a violet storm of timpanis, like a persistent fist on a rickety door.

"Just let me die!" Tuck screamed, most of the sound caught by his pillow.

It was a persistent fist on a rickety door. "Mr. Case, rise and shine," said a cheery Sebastian Curtis. "Ten minutes to tee time."

Tuck rolled into the mosquito netting, became entangled, and ripped it from the ceiling. He was still wearing his wet suit and the fragile netting clung to it like cobwebs. He arrived at the door looking like a tattered ghost fresh out of Davy Jones's locker.

"What? I can't fly. I can't even fucking walk. Go away." Tuck was not a morning person.

Sebastian Curtis stood in the doorway beaming. "It's Wednesday," he said. "I thought you might want to play a few holes."

Tuck looked at the doctor through bloodshot eyes and several layers of torn mosquito netting. Behind Curtis stood one of the guards, sans machine gun, with a golf bag slung over his shoulder. "Golf?" Tuck said. "You want to play golf?"

"It's a different game here on Alualu, Mr. Case. Quite challenging. But then, you've been practicing, haven't you?"

"Look, Doc, I didn't sleep well last night . . ."

"Could be the wet suit, if you don't mind my saying. Here in the tropics, you want fabrics that breathe. Cotton is best."

Tuck was beginning to come around, and as he did, he found he was focusing an intense hatred on the doctor. "I guess we know who got laid last night."

Curtis looked down and smiled coyly. He was actually embarrassed. Tuck couldn't quite put it together. The doc didn't seem to have any problem with killing people or taking their organs—or both—but he was blushing at the mention of sex with his wife. Tuck glared at him.

Curtis said, "You'd better change. The first tee is out in front of the hangar. I'll go down and practice a few drives while you get dressed."

"You do that," Tuck said. He slammed the door.

Twenty minutes later Tuck, his hair still wet from the shower, joined Curtis and the guard in front of the hangar. He was feeling the weight of three nights with almost no sleep, and his back ached from dragging Kimi across the compound, then towing him in the water to the far side of the minefield. The guard had never caught up to them, but he had come to the edge of the water and shouted, waving his machine gun until Tuck and Kimi were out of sight.

"We'll have to share a set of clubs," Curtis said. "But perhaps now that you've decided to stay, we can order you a set."

"Swell," Tuck said. He couldn't be sure, but he thought the guard might be the same one that had chased them to the beach. Tuck sneered at him and he looked away. Yep, he was the one.

"This is Mato. He'll be caddying for us today."

The guard bowed slightly. Tuck saluted him with a middle finger. If the doctor saw the gesture, he didn't comment. He was lining the ball up on a small square of AstroTurf with a rubberized pad on the bottom. "We have to hit off of this. At least until someone invents a gravel wedge." He laughed at his own joke.

Tuck forced a smile.

"The Shark People covered this entire island with gravel hundreds of years ago. Keeps the topsoil from being washed away in typhoons. This first hole is a dogleg to the left. The pin is behind the staff's quarters about a hundred yards."

"Doc, now that we've come clean, why don't we call them the guards?"

"Very well, Mr. Case. Would you like honors?"

"Call me Tuck. No, you go ahead."

Curtis hit a long bad hook that arced around the guards' quarters and landed out of sight in a stand of palm trees behind the building.

"I have to admit that I may have a bit of an advantage. I've laid out the course to accommodate my stroke. Most of the holes are doglegs to the left."

Tuck nodded as if he understood what Curtis was talking about, then took the driver from the doctor and hit his own shot, a grounder that skipped across the gravel to stop fifty yards in front of them. "Oh, bad luck. Would you like to take a McGuffin?"

"Blow me, Doc," Tuck said as he walked away toward his ball.

"I guess not, then."

The pins were bamboo shafts driven into the compound, the holes were lined with old Coke cans with the tops cut off. The best part about it was that Tuck was able to deliver several vicious high-velocity putts into the shins of Mato, who was tending the pins. The worst part was that now that Curtis considered Tuck a confidant, he decided to open up.

"Beth is quite a woman, isn't she? Did I tell you how we met?"

"Yeah."

"I was at a transplant symposium in San Francisco. Beth is quite the nurse, the best I've ever seen in an operating room, but she wasn't working as a nurse when I met her."

"Oh, good," Tuck said.

Curtis seemed to be waiting for Tucker to ask. Tucker was waiting for the guard to rat him out for sneaking out of the compound last night.

"She was a dancer in North Beach. An exotic dancer."

"No shit." Tuck said.

"Are you shocked?" Curtis obviously wanted him to be shocked. "No."

"She was incredible. The most incredible woman I had ever seen. She still is."

"But then, you've been a missionary on a remote island for twenty-eight years," Tuck said.

Curtis picked his club for the next shot: the seven iron. "What's this?"

"Looks like blood and feathers," Tuck said.

Curtis handed the club to Mato for him to clean it. "Beth did a dance with surgical tubing and a stethoscope that took my breath away."

"Pretty common," Tuck said. "Choke you with the surgical tubing and use the stethoscope to make sure you haven't done the twitching fish."

"Really?" Curtis said. "You've seen a woman do that?"

Tuck put on his earnest young man face. "Seen? You didn't notice the ligature marks on my neck when you examined me?"

"Oh, I see," Curtis said. "Still, I, at least, had never seen anything like it. She . . ." Curtis couldn't seem to return to his story. "The wet suit this morning. Was that a sexual thing? I mean, most people would find it uncomfortable."

"No, I'm just trying to lose a little weight."

Curtis looked serious now. "I don't know if that's such a good idea. You're still very thin from your ordeal in getting here."

"I'd like to get down to about eight pounds," Tuck said. "There's a big Gandhi revival thing going on back in the States. Guys who look like they're starving have to beat the babes off with a stick. Started with female fashion models, but now it's moved to the men."

Curtis look embarrassed. "I guess I'm a bit out of touch. Beth tries to keep up with what's going on in the States, but it, well, seems irrelevant out here. I guess I'll be glad when this is all over and we can leave the island."

"Then why don't you just leave? You're a physician. You could open up a practice in the States and pull down a fortune without all this."

Curtis glanced at the guard, then looked back to Tuck. "A fortune maybe, but not a fortune like we're accumulating now. I'm too old to start over at the bottom."

"You've got twenty-eight years' experience. You said yourself that the people you take care of are the healthiest in the Pacific. You wouldn't be starting over."

"Yes, I would. Mr. Case—Tuck—I'm a doctor, but I'm not a very good one."

Tuck had met a number of doctors in his life, but he had never met one who could bear to admit that he was incompetent at anything. It was a running joke among flight instructors that doctors made the worst students. "They think they're gods. It's our job to teach them that they're mortal. Only pilots are gods."

This guy seemed so pathetic that Tuck had to remind himself that the good doctor was at least a double murderer. He watched

Curtis hit a nice hundred-yard bloodstained seven iron to within ten feet of the pin, which was set up on a small patch of grass near the beach.

Tuck chased down his own skidding *thwack* of a nine iron that had landed between the roots of a walking tree, an arboreal oddity that sat atop a three-foot teepee of tangled roots and gave the impression that it might move off on its own power at any moment. Tuck was hoping that it would.

The caddie followed Tuck, and when they were out of earshot of the doctor, he turned to face the stoic Japanese. "You can't tell him, can you?"

The guard pretended not to understand, but Tuck saw that he was getting it, even if only by inflection. "You can't tell him and you can't fucking shoot me, can you? You killed the last pilot and that got you in a world of trouble, didn't it? That's why you guys follow me like a bunch of baby ducks, isn't it?" Tuck was guessing, but it was the only logical explanation.

Mato glanced toward the doctor.

"No," Tuck said. "He doesn't know that I know. And we're not going to tell him, are we? Just shake your head if you're getting this."

The guard shook his head.

"Okay, then, here's the deal. I'll let you guys look like you're doing your job, but when I wave you off, you're gone. You hear me? I want you guys off my ass. You tell your buddies, okay?"

The guard nodded.

"Can you speak any English at all?"

"*Hai.* A rittle."

"You guys killed the pilot, didn't you?"

"He tly to take prane." Mato looked as if the words were painful for him to form.

Tuck nodded, feeling heat rise in his face. He wanted to smash the guard's face, knock him to the ground, and kick him into a glob of goo. "And you killed Pardee, the fat American man."

Mato shook his head. "No. We don't."

"Bullshit!"

"No, we . . . we . . ." He was searching for the English word.

"What?"

"We take him, but not shoot."

"Take him where? To the clinic?"

The guard shook his head violently. Not saying no, but trying to say that he couldn't say.

"What happened to the fat man?"

"He die. Hospital. We put him water."

"You took his body to the edge of the reef, where the sharks would find it?"

The guard nodded.

"And the pilot? You put him in the same place?"

Again the nod.

"What's going on. Are you going to hit or not?"

Tuck and the guard looked up like two boys caught trading curses in the schoolyard. Curtis had come back down the fairway to within fifty feet of them.

Tuck pointed to his ball. "Kato here won't let me move that out for a shot. I'll take the penalty stroke, Doc. But hell, we don't have mutant trees like that in Texas. It's unnatural."

Curtis looked sideways at Tuck's ball, then at Mato. "He can move it. No penalty. You're a guest here, Mr. Case. We can let you bend a few rules." Curtis did not smile. Suddenly he seemed very serious about his golf.

"We're partners now, Doc," Tuck said. "Call me Tuck."

46

Beans and Succubus

Tuck's other partner showed up at his bungalow that evening as he was sitting down to a plate of pork and beans. She didn't knock, or call out, or even clear her throat politely to let him know she was there. One minute Tuck was studying a gelatinous white cube of unidentifiable carbon-based life-form awash in a lumpy puddle of boiled legumes and tomato sauce, and the next the door opened and she was standing there wearing nothing but a red scarf and sequined high heels. Tuck dropped his spoon. Two partially used beans dribbled out of his open mouth, tracing contrails of sauce down the front of his shirt.

She executed a single flamenco heel stomp and Tuck watched the impact move up her body and settle comfortably in her breasts. She threw her arms wide, struck a pose, and said, "The Sky Priestess has arrived."

"Yes, she has," Tuck said with the glassy-eyed stupifaction of a newly converted Moonie. He'd seen something like her before, either on the hood of a Rolls-Royce or on a bowling trophy, but in the flesh the image was much more immediate, awe-inspiring even.

She pirouetted and the tails of the scarf trailed around her like affectionate smoke. "What do you think?"

"Uh-huh," Tuck said, nodding.

"Come here."

Tuck stood and moved toward her in the mindless shuffle step of a zombie compelled by the promise of living flesh. His brain stopped working, his entire life energy shifted to another part of his body, and it led him across the room to within an inch of her. It wasn't the first time this had happened to him, but before he had always retained the power of speech and most of his motor functions.

"What's wrong with you?" she said. "Bolts in your neck too tight?"

"My entire body has an erection."

She took him by the front of the shirt and backed him across the room to the bed, then pushed him down and pulled his pants down to his knees. She vaulted onto him in a straddle and he reached up for her breasts. She caught his wrists.

"No. You'll fuck up my makeup."

And he noticed—like an accident victim might notice a butterfly in the grille of the bus that is running over him—that her nipples had been rouged to an unnatural pink.

He tried to sit up and she shoved him back down, then took him in her hand, nicking him with a red fingernail, making him wince, and guided him inside of her. He reached for her hips to drive her down and got his hands slapped for the effort.

And she fucked him—precise and mechanical as a machine, a single pounding motion repeated and lubricated and repeated again—until her breath rasped in her throat like hissing hydraulics and she arched her back and stalled, and misfired, then dieseled for a stroke or two, and she climbed off. Somewhere in all that he had come and she had looked at him once.

He lay there looking at the remnants of torn mosquito netting over the bed, breathing hard, feeling a little dizzy, and wondering what had just happened. She went to the bathroom, then returned a few seconds later and threw him a towel, which she had obviously used herself.

"We're flying in three or four hours. Be ready."

"Okay." Was he supposed to say something? Didn't this signify some sort of change that should be acknowledged?

"I want you to watch me, but you can't let them see you. Wait a few minutes and go out by the hangar where you can see the airstrip. It's a great show. Theater makes it all possible, you know. Ask the Catholics. They survived the Middle Ages by putting on performances in a language that no one understood on grand stages that were built by the pennies of the poor. That's the problem with religion today. No theater."

This must be her version of cuddling. "Performance?"

"The appearance of the Sky Priestess," she said as if she was talking to a piece of toast. She walked to the door, then paused and looked over her shoulder. Almost as an afterthought she said, "Tucker," and when he looked up she blew him a kiss. Then she was out the door and he heard her shout, "Cue the music!"

A big band sound blasted across the island, sending a shiver rattling through Tuck's body as if a chill ghost from the forties had jitterbugged over his spine.

47

Grand Theft Aircraft

The Shark men were breaking into their second jug of *tuba* when the music started. They all looked to Malink. Why hadn't he told them there was going to be an appearance of the Sky Priestess?

Malink thought fast, then grinned as if he had known this was coming all along. "I wanted it to be a surprise," he said. Why hadn't this been announced by the Sorcerer? Was he still angry because Malink had not produced the girl-man on demand? Was Vincent himself angry at Malink for something? Certainly Malink's people would be angry at him for not giving them the time to prepare the drums and the bamboo rifles of Vincent's army—and the women, oh, the women would be shitting coconuts over not having time to oil their skins and paint their faces and put on their ceremonial grass skirts.

As Malink trudged to the airstrip he tried to formulate some explanation that would work with everyone. As if it wasn't difficult enough being chief with no coffee to drink in the morning—he'd had a headache for two weeks from caffeine withdrawal—now his role as religious leader was giving him problems. Leading a religion is tough work when your gods start stirring for real and messing up your prophecies. And what if he did come up with an explanation, only to have the Priestess of the Sky say something that contradicted him? She was supposed to be Vincent's voice, but that voice had been angry lately, so he didn't dare ask her for help as he had in the past. Not in front of his people.

He came out of the jungle just in time to see the flash of the explosions. The Sky Priestess walked out of the smoke and even from a hundred yards away, Malink could tell by her step that she was pleased. Malink breathed a sigh of relief. She was carrying magazines for them. If his people were happy with what she said, then he could use the old "will of Vincent" argument for not preparing them.

He could have never guessed the real reason the Sorcerer had not forewarned him of the appearance of the Sky Priestess. At the time when he normally called the warning, the Sorcerer had been watching through the window as the Sky Priestess pumped away on Tucker Case.

Tuck waited five minutes before he pulled up his pants and slid out the door of his bungalow, nearly running into Sebastian Curtis. The doctor, normally cool, was soaked with sweat and looked past Tuck to the clinic. "Mr. Case. I thought you'd be preparing the plane. Beth did tell you that you have a flight?"

Tuck fought the urge to bolt. He hadn't had enough time to build up any remorse about having sex with the doctor's wife, and he didn't excel at remorse in the first place. "I was on my way to do the preflight. It doesn't take long."

The doctor didn't make eye contact. "You'll forgive me if I seem distracted. I have to perform major surgery in a few minutes. You should go watch Beth's little show."

"What's all the music and explosions?"

"It's how we retrieve our donors. Beth will explain her theory of religion and theater to you, I'm sure. Excuse me." He pushed past Tucker and looked at his shoes as he walked toward the clinic.

"Aren't you going to watch?" Tuck said.

"Thank you, but I find it nauseating."

"Oh," Tuck said. "Then I'll go check out the Lear. Great game today, Doc."

"Yes," Curtis said. He resumed his stiff-armed walk to the clinic, his fists balled so hard at his sides that Tuck could see them shaking.

The guards were gathered at the edge of the hangar. Mato looked up quickly and made eye contact long enough for Tuck to see that he was nervous. Tuck wished he had asked him if the other guards spoke English.

"*Konichi-wa*, motherfuckers," Tuck said, covering his linguistic bases.

None of the guards responded. Except for Mato, their eyes were trained on Beth Curtis dancing across the airstrip to Benny Goodman's "Sing, Sing, Sing." One of the guards hit a button by the hangar and the music stopped as Beth Curtis stepped onto a small wooden platform on the far side of the runway. With the speakers silenced, Tuck could hear the drums of the Shark People. Some were marching around in formation holding lengths of bamboo painted red as rifles. Beth Curtis raised her hands, a copy of *People* in each, and the drums stopped.

Tuck couldn't hear what she was saying, but she was waving her arms around like a soapbox preacher, and the crowd of natives moved, and flinched, and hung on her every word. She paused at one point and handed the magazines down to Malink, who backed away from the platform with his head bowed.

Tuck didn't find anything about her performance nauseating, but it was nothing if not strange. Why all the pomp and circumstance? You have six guys with machine guns, you can pretty much go rip a kidney out anytime you want to.

He needed to think, and he didn't particularly want to see whom she would pick. Whoever it was, their face would be in his head all the way to Japan and back. He went into the hangar, lowered the door on the Lear, climbed into the dark plane, and lay down in the aisle between the seats. He couldn't hear the sound of the Sky Priestess or the natives *oohing* and *ahhhing*, and here among the steel and glass and plastic and upholstery, it felt like home. Here he could hear the sound of his own mind; here in his very own Learjet, the weirdness was all outside. But for the lack of a key he would have taken the plane right then.

The guard kicked Tuck in the thigh much harder than was needed to wake him. Tuck looked up to see the face of the guard who had beaten him on the beach. He had a scar that ran up his forehead tracing a bare streak into his scalp and Tuck had started to think of him as Stripe, the evil little monster from the movie *Gremlins*. Tuck's anger was immediate and white-hot. Only the Uzi stopped him from getting his ass kicked again.

The guard dangled the key to the Lear's main power cutoff. It was time to go. Tuck limped to the cockpit and strapped himself into the pilot's seat. Stripe inserted the power key into the instrument console, twisted it, and stepped back to watch as Tuck started the power-up procedure.

The other ninjas pulled the Lear out of the hangar by a large T-bar attached to the front wheel. When the plane was safely out of the hangar, Tuck started to spool up the jets. Stripe remained with the Uzi at port arms.

Tuck made a big show of going though the checklist, testing switches and gauges. He frowned and clicked the radar switch a couple of times. He looked back at Stripe. "Go check the nose. Something's not right."

The guard shook his head. Tuck mimed his instructions again and Stripe nodded, then he motioned through the window for another of the guards to join them on board. Evidently, they weren't going to leave him unguarded in the plane with the power key in. Stripe turned over the guard duty to the other ninja and appeared at the front of the plane. Tuck motioned for him to get closer to the nose. Stripe did. Tuck turned on the radar. "And a lovely brain tumor for you, you son of a bitch." Stripe seemed to actually feel the microwave energy and he jumped back from the plane. Tuck grinned and gave him the okay sign. "I hope your tiny little balls are boiling," he said aloud. The guard behind him didn't seem to understand what Tuck was saying, but he nudged him with the barrel of his Uzi and pointed. Beth Curtis, in her dark Armani, was coming across the compound with briefcase and cooler in hand.

She stepped into the plane and nodded to the guard. Instead of leaving, he took a seat back in the passenger compartment. Beth strapped herself into the copilot's seat.

"We taking him in for shore leave?" Tuck said.

"No. He's just along for the ride tonight."

"Oh, right." Tuck powered up the jets and eased the Lear out of the compound onto the runway.

Beth Curtis was silent until they were at altitude, cruising toward Japan. Tuck did not engage the autopilot, but steered the Lear gradually, perhaps a degree a minute, to the west.

"So what did you think?"

"Pretty impressive, but I don't get it. Why the whole show to bring in someone for surgery? Why not just send the guards?"

"We're not taking their kidneys, Tucker. They're giving them."

Tuck didn't want to give away what he had learned from Malink and Sepie about the "chosen." He said, "Giving them to who? A naked white woman?"

She laughed, reached into her briefcase, and brought out an eight-by-ten color photograph. "To the Sky Priestess." She held the photograph where Tuck could see it. He had to steer manually. If he hit the autopilot now, the plane would turn back toward Japan, the only preset in the nav computer. The photograph was in color but old. A flyer stood by the side of a B-26 bomber. On the side of the bomber was the painting of a voluptuous naked woman and the legend SKY PRIESTESS. It could have been a painting of Beth Curtis as she had looked when she arrived at Tuck's bungalow. He recognized the flyer as well. It was the ghost flyer he'd been seeing all along. He felt his face flush, but he tried to stay cool. "So who's that?"

"The flyer was a guy named Vincent Bennidetti," Beth said. "The plane was named the Sky Priestess. All the bombers had nose art like that in World War II. We found the picture in the library in San Francisco."

"So what's that got to do with our operation? You're dressing up like the picture on an airplane."

"No, *I am* the Sky Priestess."

"I'm sorry, Beth. I still don't get it."

"This is the pilot that the Shark People worship. The cargo cult that 'Bastian told you about."

Tuck nodded and tried to look surprised, but he was watching his course without seeming to do so. If he had figured it right, they would be over Guam in fifteen minutes and the American military would force them down. The Air Force was very cranky about private jets flying though their airspace.

"The natives on Alualu worship this Vincent guy," Beth said. "I speak for Vincent. They come to me when we play the music and I give them everything. In return, I choose one of them for the honor of the mark of Vincent, which, of course, is the scar they get from the operation."

"Like I said, you've got armed guards. Why not just take what you want?"

She looked shocked that he would ask. "And get out of show business?" Then she smiled and reached over and gave his crotch a squeeze.

"When I met Sebastian in San Francisco, he was drunk and throwing money around. One minute he was so dignified and erudite, the next he was like a little naive child. He told me about the cargo cult and I came up with the idea of not just doing this to support the clinic, but to get really filthy rich. We had to keep the people happy if we were going to do this in big numbers."

"So you thought all of this up?"

"It's the reason I'm here."

"But Sebastian said you were a"—Tuck caught himself before he said "stripper"—"surgical nurse."

"I was. So what? Did I get any respect for that? Did I get any power? No. To the doctors I was just a piece of ass who could handle surgical instruments and close a patient when they needed to get to the golf course. Did Sebastian tell you I used to strip?"

"He mentioned something about it in passing."

"Well, I did. And I was good."

"I can imagine," Tuck said. A few more minutes and they should be joined by an F-16.

She smiled. "Fuck nursing. I was just a piece of meat to the men I worked with, so I decided to go with it. I was pushing thirty and all single women my age were walking around with a desperate look in their eye and a biological clock ticking so loud you thought it was the crocodile from *Peter Pan*. If I was going to be treated like meat, I was going to make money at it. And I did. Not enough, but a lot more than I would have made nursing."

"Do tell," Tuck said. He couldn't remember ever saying "Do tell," and it sounded a little strange hearing it.

She looked out the window as if she had fallen into some reverie. Then, without looking back, she said, "What's that island?"

Tuck tensed. "I couldn't say."

She sighed. "Islands are amazing."

"I always say that."

She seemed to come out of her trance and looked at the instrument board. Tuck acted as if he was concentrating on flying the plane. He glanced at Beth Curtis. Her mouth had tightened into a line.

She reached into the briefcase and came out with the Walther automatic.

"What's that for?" Tuck said.

"Get back on course."

"I am on course."

"Now!"

"But I am on course. Look." He pointed to the nav computer, which still showed the coordinates of the airstrip in Japan, although it wasn't engaged with the autopilot.

"No, you're not." She pointed to the compass. "You're at least ninety degrees off course. Turn the plane to Japan now or I'll shoot you."

Tuck was tired of it. "Right. And you'll fly the plane? There's a difference between being able to read a compass and making a landing."

"I didn't say I would kill you. I'm good with this. You'll still be able to fly with one testicle. Now that would be a shame for both of us. Please turn the plane."

Tuck engaged the autopilot and let the Lear bring itself around to the course to Japan.

"Sebastian said you might try something like that," she said. "I told him I could handle you. I can, can't I? Handle you, I mean."

Tuck was quiet for a minute, berating himself for overestimating the efficiency of the military. Then finally he said, "You are a nefarious, diabolical, and evil bitch."

"And?"

"That's all."

"I'm impressed. 'Nefarious' has more than two syllables. I am a good influence on you."

"Fuck you."

"You will," she said.

48

Too Many Guns

Back at the drinking circle, Malink opened a copy of *People* reverentially and read by kerosene lamp while the other men huddled to get a look at the pictures.

"Cher is worst-dressed," Malink announced.

"Too skinny," said Favo. "I like Lady Di."

Malink cringed. In the picture Lady Di was wearing a string of pearls, obviously the reason for Favo's preference. Malink turned the page.

"*Celestine Raptors of Madison County* is number one movie in country," Malink read.

"I want to see a movie," Favo said. "You must tell the Sky Priestess to tell Vincent to bring a movie."

"Many movies," said Abo. "And many delicious light and healthy snacks with NutraSweet registered trademark," he added in English. "Vincent will bring many snacks."

Malink was turning to the moving story of a two-thousand-pound man who, after being forklifted out of his house, had dieted down to a svelte fourteen hundred when the sound of a machine gun rattled across the island. Malink put down the magazine and held up his hand to quiet the men. They waited and there was another burst of gunfire. A few seconds later they heard shouting and looked down the beach to see Sarapul running as fast as his spindly old legs would carry him.

"Come help!" he shouted. "They shot the navigator!"

➡

The Uzi was pressed so hard into Tuck's side that he felt as if his ribs were going to separate any second. The guard crouched behind him in the cockpit hatchway, while out on the tarmac Beth Curtis exchanged the cooler for another manila envelope. She seemed to be in a much better mood when she climbed back into the copilot's seat.

"Home, James."

Tuck tossed his head toward the back of the plane where the guard was taking his seat. "I guess you weren't taking any chances about me taking off while you were out of the plane."

"Do I look stupid?" she said. A smile there, no hint of a challenge.

"No, I guess not." Tuck pushed up the throttles and taxied the Lear back out to the runway.

Again Beth Curtis reached over and gave him a light squeeze to the crotch. She put on her headset so she could talk to him over the roar of the engines as they took off. "Look, I know this is hard for you. Trust is something you build, and you haven't known me long enough to learn to do that."

Tuck thought, It would help if you weren't changing personalities every five minutes.

"Trust me, Tucker. What we are doing is not hurting the people of Alualu. There are people in India who are selling off their organs for less than the price of a used Toyota pickup. With what we make, we can be sure that these people are always taken care of, and we can take care of ourselves in the meantime."

"If people are selling their organs on the cheap, then how are you—we—making so much money?"

"Because we can do it to order. Transplant isn't just a matter of blood type, you know. Sure, in a pinch—and usually it is a pinch—you can go on just blood type, but there are four other factors in tissue typing. If they match, along with blood type, then you have a better chance of the body not rejecting the organ. Sebastian has a database of the tissue types of every native on the island. When there's a need for an exact match, the order comes in over the satellite and we run it through the database. If we have it, the Sky Priestess calls the chosen."

"Don't the people have to be the same race?"

"It helps, but it seems that the people of Alualu have a very similar genetic pattern to the Japanese."

"They don't look Japanese. How do you know this?"

"Actually, it was figured out by an anthropologist who came to the island long before I did. He was studying the language and genetics of the islanders to determine where they migrated from. Turns out there are both linguistic and genetic links to Japan. They've been diluted by interbreeding with natives from New Guinea, but it's still very close."

"So you guys opened up Kidneys 'R' Us and started making a mint."

"Except for the scar, their lives don't change, Tucker. We've never lost a patient to a botched operation or infection."

But bullets, Tuck thought, are another matter. Still, there was nothing he could do to stop them, and if he had to do nothing, a great salary and his own jet were pretty good compensation. He'd spent most of his life not doing anything. Was it so bad to be paid for what you're good at?

He said, "So it doesn't hurt them? In the long run, I mean."

"Their other kidney steps up production and they never notice the difference."

"I still don't get the Sky Priestess thing."

She sighed. "Control the religion and you control the people. Sebastian tried to bring Christianity to the Shark People—and the Catholics before him—but you can't compete with a god people have actually seen. The answer? Become that god."

"But I thought Vincent was the god."

"He is, but he will bring wonderful cargo in the Sky Priestess. Besides, it breaks the boredom. Boredom can be a lethal thing on a small island. You know about that already."

Tuck nodded. It wasn't so bad now. The fear of being murdered had gone a long way toward breaking his boredom.

Beth Curtis leaned over and kissed him lightly on the temple. "You and I can fight the boredom together. That's one of the reasons I chose you."

"*You* chose me?" In spite of himself, he was thinking about her naked body grinding away above him.

"Of course I chose you. I'm the Sky Priestess, aren't I?"

"I'm not so sure it was you," Tuck said, thinking about the ghost pilot.

She pushed away and looked at him as if he had lost his mind.

49

The Bedside Manner of Cannibals

Tuck slept through most of the day, then woke up with a pot of coffee over a spy novel. He looked at the words and his eyes moved down the pages for half an hour, but when he put it down he had no idea what he had read. His mind was torn by the thought of Beth Curtis showing up at his door. Whenever a guard crunched across the gravel compound, Tuck would go to the window to see if it was her. She wouldn't come here during the day, would she?

He had promised Kimi that he would check on Sepie and meet him at the drinking circle, but now he was already a day late on the promise. What would happen if Beth Curtis came to his bungalow while he was out? She couldn't tell the doc, could she? What would her excuse be for coming here? Still, Tuck was beginning to think that the doc wasn't really the one running the show. He was merely skilled labor, and so, probably, was Tucker himself.

Tuck looked at the pages of the spy novel, watched a little Malaysian television (today they were throwing spears at coconuts on top of a pole while the Asian stock market's tickers scrolled at the bottom of the screen in thin-colored bands), and waited for nightfall. When he could no longer see the guard's face across the compound, he made a great show of yawning and stretching in front of the window, then turned out the lights, built the dummy in his bed, and slipped out through the bottom of the shower.

He took his usual path behind the clinic, then inched his way up on the far side and peeked around the front. Not ten feet away a guard stood by the door. He ducked quickly around the corner. There was no way into the clinic tonight. He could wait or even try to intimidate the guard, now that he knew they were afraid to shoot him. Of course, he wasn't sure *they* knew they were afraid to shoot him. What if Mato was the only one?

He slid back down the side of the building and through the coconut grove to the beach. The swim had become like walking to the mailbox, and he was past the minefield in less than five minutes. As he rounded the curve of the beach, he saw a light and figures moving around it. The Shark men had brought a kerosene lamp to the drinking circle. How civilized.

Some of the men acknowledged his presence as he moved into the circle, but the old chief only stared into the sand between his feet. There was a stack of magazines at his side.

"What's going on, guys?"

A panic made its way around the circle to land on Abo, who looked up and said, "Your friend is shot by the guards."

Tuck waited, but Abo looked away. Tuck jumped in front of Malink. "Chief, is he telling the truth? Did they shoot Kimi? Is he dead?"

"Not dead," Malink said, shaking his head. "Hurt very bad."

"Take me to him."

"He is at Sarapul's house."

"Right. I'll look it up in the guidebook later. Now take me to him."

Old Malink shook his head. "He going to die."

"Where is he shot?"

"In the water by the minefield."

"No, numbnuts. Where on his body?"

Malink held his hand to his side. "I say, 'Take him to the Sorcerer,' but Sarapul say, 'The Sorcerer shoot him.'" Malink then looked Tuck in the eye for the first time. His big brown face was a study in trouble. "Vincent send you. What do I do?"

Tuck could sense a profound embarrassment in the old man. He had just admitted in front of the men in his tribe that he didn't have a clue. The loss of face was gnawing at him like a hungry sand crab.

Tuck said, "Vincent is pleased with your decision, Malink. Now I must see Kimi."

One of the young Vincents stood up. Feeling very brave, he said, "I will take you."

Tuck grabbed his shoulder. "You're a good man. Lead on."

The young Vincent seemed to forget to breathe for a moment, as if Tuck had touched him on the shoulders with a sword and welcomed him to a seat at the Round Table, then he came to his senses and took off into the jungle. Tuck followed close behind, nearly clotheslining himself a couple of times on branches that the young Vincent ran right under. The coral gravel on the path tore at Tuck's feet as he ran.

When they emerged from the jungle, Tuck could see a light coming out of Sarapul's hut, which Tuck recognized from his day in the cannibal tree. He turned to young Vincent, who was terrified. He had charged the dragon, but had made the mistake of stopping to think about it.

"Kimi's with the cannibal?"

Young Vincent nodded rapidly while bouncing from foot to foot, looking like he would wet himself any second.

"Go on," Tuck said. "Go tell Malink to come here. And have a drink. You're wigging out."

Vincent nodded and ran off.

Tuck approached the door slowly, creeping up until he could see the old man crouched over Kimi, trying to pour something into his mouth from a coconut cup.

"Hey," Tuck said, "how's he doing?"

Sarapul looked around and gestured for Tuck to enter the house. Tuck had to bend to get through the low door, but once inside the ceiling opened to a fifteen-foot peak. Tuck knelt by Kimi. The navigator's eyes were closed, and even in the orange light of Sarapul's oil lamp, he looked pale. He was uncovered and a bandage was wrapped around his middle.

"Did you do this?" Tuck asked Sarapul.

The old cannibal nodded. "They shoot him in water. I pull him in."

"How many times?"

Sarapu held up a long bent finger.

"Both sides? Did it go through?" Tuck gestured with his fingers on either side of his hip.

"Yes," Sarapul said.

"Let me see."

The old cannibal nodded and unwrapped Kimi's bandage. Tuck rolled the navigator gently on his side. Kimi groaned, but didn't wake. The bullet had hit him about two inches above the hip and about an inch in. It had passed right though, going in the size of a pencil and exiting the size of a quarter. Tuck was amazed that he hadn't bled to death. The old cannibal had done a good job.

"Don't take him to the Sorcerer," Sarapul said. "The Sorcerer will kill him. He is the only navigator." The old cannibal was pleading while trying to remain fierce. A sob betrayed him. "He is my friend."

Tuck studied the wound to give the old cannibal a chance to gather himself. He couldn't remember any vital organs being in that area. But the wounds would have to be stiched shut. Tuck wasn't sure he had the stomach for it, but Sarapul was right. He couldn't take Kimi to Curtis.

"Do you guys have anything you use to kill pain?"

The cannibal looked at him quizzically. Tuck pinched him and he yelped. "Pain. Do you have anything to stop pain?"

"Yes. Don't do that anymore."

"No, for Kimi."

Sarapul nodded and went out into the dark. He returned a few seconds later with a glass jug half-full of milky liquid. He handed it to Tuck. "Kava," he said. "It make you no ouch."

Tuck uncapped the bottle and a smell like cooking cabbage assaulted his nostrils. He held his breath and took a big slug of the stuff, suppressed a gag, and swallowed. His mouth was immediately numb. "Wow, this ought to do it. I need a needle and some thread and some hot water. And some alcohol or peroxide if you have it."

Sarapul nodded. "I put Neosporin on him."

"You know about that? Why am I doing this?"

Sarapul shrugged and left the house. Evidently, he didn't keep anything inside but his skinny old ass.

Kimi moaned and Tuck rolled him over. The navigator's eyes fluttered open.

"Boss, that dog fucker shot me."

"Curtis? The older white guy?"

"No. Japanese dog fucker." Kimi drew his finger across his scalp in a line and Tuck knew exactly who he meant.

"What were you doing, Kimi? I told you that I'd check on Sepie and meet you." Tuck felt a pleasant numbness moving into his limbs. This kava stuff would definitely do the trick.

"You didn't come. I worry for her."

"I had to fly."

"Sarapul say those people very bad. You should come live here, boss."

"Be quiet. Drink this." He held the jug to Kimi's lips and tipped it up. The navigator took a sip and Tuck let him rest before administering another dose.

"That stuff nasty," Kimi said.

"I'm going to stitch you up."

The navigator's eyes went wide. He took the jug from Tuck and gulped from it until Tuck ripped it out of his hands. "It won't be that bad."

"Not for you."

Tuck grinned. "Haven't you heard? I've been sent here by Vincent."

"That what Sarapul say. He say he don't believe in Vincent until we come, but now he do."

"Really?"

Sarapul came through the door with an armload of supplies. "I don't say that. This dog fucker lies."

Tuck shook his head. "You guys were made for each other."

Sarapul set down a sewing kit and a bottle of peroxide, then crouched over the navigator and looked up at Tuck. "Can you fix him?"

Tuck grinned and grabbed the old cannibal by the cheek. "Yum," Tuck said.

"Sorry," Sarapul said.

"I'll fix him," Tuck said. Silently he asked for help from Vincent.

"I can't feel my arms," Kimi said. "My legs, where are my legs? I'm dying."

Sarapul looked at Tuck. "Good," he said. "More kava."

Tuck picked up the jug, now only a quarter full. "This is great stuff."

"I'm dying," Kimi said.

Tuck rolled the navigator over on his side. "Kimi, did I tell you I saw Roberto?"

"See, I didn't eat him," Sarapul said.

"Where?" Kimi asked.

"He came to my house. He talked to me."

"You lie. He only speak Filipino."

"He learned English. Can you feel that?"

"Feel what? I am dying?"

"Good," Tuck said and he laid his first stitch.

"What Roberto say? He mad at me?"

"No, he said you're dying."

"I'm dying, I'm dying," Kimi wailed.

"Just kidding. He didn't say that. He said you're probably dying." Tuck kept Kimi talking, and before long the navigator was so convinced of his approaching death he didn't notice that Tucker Case, self-taught incompetent, had completely stitched and dressed his wounds.

~~~~~~

50

Don Quixote at the
Miniature Golf Course

He was sleeping, dreaming of flying, but not in a plane. He was soaring over the warm Pacific above a pod of humpback whales. He swooped in close to the waves and one of the whales breached, winked at him with a football-sized eye, and said, "You da man." Then the whale smiled and blew the dream all to hell, for while Tuck knew himself to indeed "be da man" and while he didn't mind being told so, he also knew that whales couldn't smile and that bit of illogic above all the others broke the dream's back. He woke up. There was music playing in his bungalow.

"Dance with me, Tucker," she said. "Dance with me in the moonlight."

The smooth muted horns of "Moonlight Serenade" filled the room from a portable boom box on his coffee table. Beth Curtis, wearing a sequined evening gown and high-heeled sandals, danced an imaginary partner around the room. "Oh, dance with me, Tucker. Please."

She glided over to the bed and held her hand out to him. He gave her the coconut man's head, rolled over, and ducked under the sheet. "Go away. I'm tired and you're insane."

She sat on the bed with a bounce. "You old stick in the mud." A pouty voice now. "You never want to have any romance."

Tuck feigned sleep. Pretty well, he thought.

"I brought champagne and candles. And I made cookies."

This is me sleeping, Tuck thought. This is exactly how I behave when I sleep.

"I twisted up a joint of skunky green bud the size of your dick."

"I hope you got help carrying it," he said, still under the covers.

"I rolled it on the inside of my thigh the way the women in Cuba roll cigars."

"Don't tell me how you licked the paper."

She slapped him on the bottom. "Come on, dance with me."

He rolled over and pulled the sheet off his face. "You're not going to go away, are you?"

"Not until you dance with me and have some champagne."

Tuck looked at his watch. "It's five in the morning."

"Haven't you ever danced till dawn?"

"Not vertically."

"Oh, you nasty boy." Coy now, as if anything short of being caught at genocide could make her blush. The song changed to something slow and oily that Tuck didn't recognize.

"This is such a good song. Let's dance." She swooned. She actually swooned. Swooning, Tuck noticed, looked very much like an asthma attack wheezed in slow motion. A rooster crowed, and seven thousand six hundred and fifty-two roosters responded in turn.

"Beth, it's morning. Please go home."

"Then you're not going to dance with me?"

"No."

"All right, I guess we'll skip the dancing, but I want you to know that I'm very disappointed." She stood up, pulled the evening gown over her head, and dropp1 it to the floor. The sequins sizzled against the floor like a dying rattlesnake. She wore only stockings underneath.

Tuck said, "I don't think this is such a good idea," but there was no conviction in his voice and she pushed him back on the bed.

Tuck was staring up at the ceiling, his arm pinned under her neck, silently mouthing his mantra, "After this, I will not bone the crazy woman. After this, I will not bone the crazy woman. After . . ." Boy, how many times had he said that? Maybe things were getting better, though. In the past it had always been "I will not get drunk and bone the crazy woman." He had been only sleepy this time.

He tried to worm his arm out from under her, then used the "old snuggle method." He rolled into her for a hug and when she responded with a sleepy moan and tried to kiss him, the space under her neck opened up and he was free. It worked as well on murdering bitch goddesses as it did on Mary Jean ladies. Better even, Beth didn't wear near as much hair spray, which can slow a guy down. God, I'm good.

He rolled out of bed and crept into the bathroom. While he peed, he softly chanted, "Yo, after this, I will not bone the crazy woman." It had taken on a rap cadence and he was feeling very hip along with the usual self-loathing. His scars made him think of Kimi's wound, and suddenly he was angry. He padded naked back to the bed and jostled the sleeping icon. "Get up, Beth. Go home."

And someone pounded on the door. "Mr. Case, tee time in five."

Tuck clamped his hand over Beth's mouth, lifted her by her head in a single sweeping move from the bed to the bathroom, where he released her and shut the door. Fred Astaire, had he been a terrorist, would have been proud of the move.

Tuck grabbed his pants off the floor, which is where he kept them, pulled them on, and answered the door. Sebastian Curtis had a driver slung over his shoulder. "You might want to put on a shirt, Mr. Case. You can get burned, even this early."

"Right," Tuck said. He was looking at the caddie. Today Stripe carried the clubs. The guard sneered at him. Tuck smiled back. Stripe, like Mato before him, was doing caddie duty unarmed. Time to play a little round for the navigator, he thought. He winked at Stripe.

"I'll be right there." Tuck closed the door and went to the bathroom to tell Beth to wait until he'd gone before coming out, but when he opened the door, she was gone.

"Did you know that over ninety percent of all the endangered species are on islands?" the doctor said.

"Nope," Tuck said. He picked his ball up and put it on the rubberized mat, then turned to Stripe. "Dopey, give me a five iron."

They were on the fourth hole and had crisscrossed the compound pretending to play golf for an hour. Tuck swung and skidded the ball fifty yards across the gravel. "Heads up, Bashful," Tuck said as he threw the club back to Stripe.

"Islands are like evolutionary pressure cookers. New species pop up faster and go extinct more quickly. It works the same way with religions."

"No kidding, Doc?" They still had fifty yards to get to where Sebastian's first shot lay. Tuck had hit three times.

"The cargo cults have all the same events associated with the great religions: a period of oppression, the rise of a Messiah, a new order, the promise of an endless time of peace and prosperity. But instead of developing over centuries like Christianity or Buddhism, it happens in just a few years. It's fascinating, like being able to see the hands of the clock move right before your eyes and be a part of it."

"So you must totally get off when daylight savings time comes around."

"It was just a metaphor, Mr. Case."

"Call me Tuck." They had reached Tuck's ball and he placed it on the AstroTurf mat. "Sneezy, give me the driver."

Sebastian cleared his throat. "That looks more like a nine iron to me. You've only got fifty yards to the pin."

"Trust me, Doc. I need a driver for this one."

Stripe snickered and handed him the driver. Tuck examined it, one of the large-headed alloy models that had become so popular in the States—all metal. Tuck grinned at Stripe. "So, Doc, I guess you shitcanned the Methodist thing to watch the clock spin." Tuck lined up the shot and took a practice swing. The club whooshed through the air.

"Have you ever had faith in anything, Mr. Case?"

Tuck took another practice swing. "Me? Faith? Nope."

"Not even your own abilities?"

"Nope." Tuck made a show of lining up the shot again and making sure his hips were loose.

"Then you shouldn't make jokes about it."

"Right," Tuck said. He tensed and put his entire weight behind the club, but instead of hitting the ball, he swung it around like a baseball bat, slamming the head into Stripe's cheek, shattering the bone with a sickening *thwack*. The guard's feet went out from under him and he landed with a crunch in the coral.

"Christ!" Sebastian yelled. He grabbed the club and wrenched it from Tuck's grasp. "What in the hell are you doing?"

Tuck didn't answer. He bent over the guard until he was only inches from his face and whispered, "Fore, motherfucker."

A second later Tuck heard a mechanical click and the guard who had been tending the pin had an Uzi pressed to his ear.

Sebastian Curtis was bent over Stripe, pulling his eyes open to see if his pupils would contract. "Take Mr. Case to his bungalow and stay with him. Send two men with a stretcher and find Beth. Tell her to—" Curtis suddenly realized that the guard was only getting about a third of what he said. "Bring my wife."

"I'll get back to you on that faith thing, Doc," Tuck said.

51

Where Losers Flourish

The Sorcerer paced back and forth across the lanai. "I want to find another pilot, Beth. We can't let him act that way and get away with it."

The Sky Priestess yawned. She was draped across the wicker emperor's chair, wearing a towel she'd wrapped above her breasts at the Sorcerer's request. He said he needed to think. "Did you ask him why he did it?"

"Of course I asked him. He said he was trying to liven up the game."

"Worked, didn't it?"

"It's not funny, Beth. We're going to have trouble with him."

The Sky Priestess stood up and put her arms around the Sorcerer. "You have to have a little faith in me," she said. "I can handle Tucker Case." She didn't want to have this conversation. Not yet. She hadn't told the Sorcerer about Tuck going off course. She had plans for the fair-haired pilot.

The Sorcerer pulled away from her and backed up to the rail. "What if I don't like the way you handle him?"

"And what's that supposed to mean?"

"You know what it means."

She approached him again, this time untucking the towel so it dropped as she stepped into his arms. Her nipples just brushed the front of his shirt. " 'Bastian, if what happened today proved anything, it proved that Tucker Case is a troglodyte. He's no threat to you. I'm attracted to finesse, not force. Case reacts to force with force. That's why he hit Yamata. You use a gentle touch with a guy like that and he's helpless."

Sebastian Curtis turned away from her. "I'm not taking the guards off his house, not for a while anyway."

"You do what you think is best, but it's not good policy to make an enemy of someone whose services you require. So what if he hates the ninjas? I hate the ninjas. You hate the ninjas. But we need them, and we need a pilot. We're not likely to be as lucky next time."

"Lucky? The man's a reprobate."

"Tucker Case is a loser. Losers flourish on islands, away from competition. You taught me that." Flattery might work where seduction seemed to be failing.

"I did?"

She unzipped his pants. "Sure, that monologue about ninety percent of the endangered species living on islands. That's because they would have died out years ago from real competition. Losers, like Tucker Case."

"I was talking about unique ecosystems, like the Galápagos, where evolution is speeded up. The way the religions take hold."

"Same difference."

He yanked her hand out of his pants and pushed her away. "What's that make us, Beth? What does that make me?"

The Sky Priestess was losing on all fronts. There was an element here that she was not in control of, an unknown variable that was affecting the Sorcerer's mood. When sex and flattery don't work, what next? Ah, team spirit. "It makes us the fittest, 'Bastian. It makes us superior."

He looked at her quizzically.

Easy now, she thought. You're getting him back. She walked slowly back to the emperor's chair and sat down daintily, then threw a leg over either arm and leaned back spread-eagle. "A quiz, 'Bastian, a quiz on evolution: Why, after all these years, with all the fossil evidence, doesn't anyone know for sure what happened to the dinosaurs? Don't answer right away. Think." She fiddled with her left nipple while she waited, and finally a smile came over his face. He really did have great teeth. She had to give him credit for keeping up his dental hygiene all these years on the island.

"No witnesses," he said finally.

"We have a winner. But more precisely, no surviving witnesses. Losers can only flourish until a dominant species appears, even on an island."

A shade of concern crossed his face. "But dinosaurs ruled the Earth for sixty million years. You can hardly call them losers."

Could he be any more difficult? "Look, Darwin, there are absolutely no dinosaurs getting laid tonight. Pick your team."

52

Don't Know Much About History

Tuck twisted the guts out of the stick pen and pried off the end cap with a kitchen knife, making, in effect, a perfect compact blowgun. He found a piece of notebook paper in the nightstand and seated himself on the wicker couch so he had a good diagonal view of the guards posted outside his door. He tore off a small piece of the paper with his teeth, worked it into a sufficiently gooey ball, then fit it into the pen tube and blew. The spit wad sailed through the window and curved harmlessly away from the guards.

Too much moisture. He squeezed the next one between his fingers before loading, then let fly to strike the nearest guard in the neck. He brushed at his neck as if waving off an insect, but otherwise didn't react.

More moisture.

Tuck had taught himself deadly accuracy with the spitball blowgun at a time when he was supposed to be learning algebra. In contradiction to what his teacher had told him, he had never needed to know algebra in later life, but mastery of the spitball was going to come in handy, although this skill had not ended up on his permanent record, as had, presumably, his failure of algebra.

The third wad struck the guard in the temple and stuck. He turned and cursed in Japanese. Tuck had prechewed a follow-up shot that took the guard in the neck. The guard gestured with his Uzi.

"Go ahead, fuckstick. Shoot me," Tuck said, a gleam in his eye. "Explain to the doc how you shot his pilot over a spit wad." He tore off another piece of paper with his teeth and chewed it while the guard glared.

The corrugated steel storm shutters above the windows were held open with a single wooden strut. The guard clipped the strut and the shutter fell with a clang.

Tuck moved to the next window down. He leaned out and fired. A splat in the forehead of guard number two, another strut knocked out, another clanging shutter.

One window to go, this one demanding a shot of almost twenty-five feet. Tuck popped his head out and blew. A spiderweb of spittle trailed behind the projectile as it traveled down the lanai. It struck the first guard on the front of his black shirt and he ran toward Tuck, leading with his Uzi. Tuck ducked back inside and the final shutter fell.

Tuck heard the guard at each shutter, latching it down.

Mission accomplished.

With the guards peeking in the window every two minutes, he would have never been able to pull off the coconut dummy switch. And even in the ambient moonlight, he'd have never made it to the bathroom unnoticed. Of course, he couldn't have closed the windows. That would have been suspicious.

"Good night, guys. I'm turning in." He stood, blowgun waiting, but the shutters remained latched. He quickly turned off the lights and crawled into bed, where he constructed the coconut man and waited until he heard the guards start to talk and smelled tobacco smoke from their cigarettes. Then he tiptoed to the bathroom and made his escape.

He half-expected the shower bottom to be nailed down. Beth Curtis had used it to escape only this morning. Maybe she hadn't figured that he knew about it. No, she was nuts, but she wasn't stupid. She knew he knew. She even knew that he knew she knew. So why hadn't she told Sebastian? And she hadn't said anything about their little detour to Guam either—or maybe she had. Sebastian hadn't sent a big postflight check like before. Tuck made a mental note to ask the doc about the check the next time they were on the golf course.

For now he snatched up his flippers and mask and headed for the beach. Before entering the water, he pulled a bottle of pills from his pocket—antibiotics left over from his dickrot—and made sure that the cap was on tight. This might be the only chance he'd have to get medicine to Kimi.

He swam around the minefield and went straight into the village and down the path toward Sarapul's house. Women and children were still sitting around outside their houses, the women weaving on small looms by kerosene lantern, the children playing quietly or finishing up dinners off banana leaf plates. Only the smallest children looked at Tuck as he passed. The women turned away, determined, it seemed, not to make eye contact with the strange American. Yet there was no alarm in their actions and no fear, just a concerted effort to not notice him. Tuck thought, This must be what New York was like before the white man came. And with that in mind, he stared at a spot in the path exactly twelve feet in front of him and denied their existence right back. It was better this way. He never knew when he might have to fly one of their body parts to Japan.

He made his way quickly up the path and soon he could see a glow near Sarapul's house. He broke into the clearing and saw the old cannibal and Kimi sitting around a fire, working on something. Sewing, it looked like.

"Kimi," Tuck said, "you shouldn't be up."

Kimi looked up from his work. There was a huge piece of blue nylon draped over his and Sarapul's laps. "I feel better. You fixed me, boss."

Tuck handed him the pills. "Take two of these now and two a day until they're gone."

"Sarapul give me kava. It make the hurt stop."

"These aren't for the hurt. These are for infection. Take them, okay?"

"Okay, boss. You want to help?"

"'What are you guys making?"

"I'll show you." Kimi started to rise and his face twisted with pain.

Sarapul pushed him back down. "I will show." The old cannibal snatched up the kerosene lantern and gestured for Tuck to follow him into the jungle.

Tuck looked back at Kimi. "You take those pills. And don't move around much, I'm not sure how well those stitches will hold. You had a big hole in you."

"Okay, boss."

Sarapul disappeared into the jungle. Tuck ran after him and almost ran him over coming out of a patch of small banana trees into an area that cleared into walking trees, mangroves, and palms. About fifty yards ahead, Sarapul stopped near the beach. He stood by what appeared to be a large fallen tree, but when Tuck got closer he saw it was a long sailing canoe. Sarapul grinned up at Tuck, the light from the lamp making him appear like some demon from the dark island past. "The *palu*—the navigator—he make. I help." Sarapul ran the light down the length of the canoe. Tuck could see that one of the tall gunwales was darkened and glazed with age, while the other had been hewn recently and was bright yellow. He could smell the fresh wood sap.

There was an outrigger the size of a normal canoe and a platform across the struts. As canoes went, it was a huge structure, and hewing the hull from a single piece of wood with hand tools had taken an incredible amount of work, not to mention skill.

"Kimi did this? This is gorgeous."

Sarapul nodded, his eyes catching the fire of the lamp. "This boat broken since before the time of Vincent. Kimi is great navigator."

"He is?" Tuck had his doubts, given the storm, but then again, as Kimi had said, they had survived a typhoon in a rowboat. And this craft was no accident; this was a piece of art. "So you guys are sewing a sail for this?"

"We finish soon. Then *palu* will teach me to sail. The Shark People will go to sea again."

"Where'd you get the nylon for the sail? I can't see Dr. Curtis thinking this is a good idea."

Sarapul climbed into the canoe and dug under a stack of paddles and lines, each hand-braided from coconut fiber, until he came up with a tattered mass of nylon straps, Velcro, and plastic buckles with a few shreds of blue nylon hanging here and there.

"My pack. You guys used my pack?"

"And tent inside."

"Do you have the stuff that was inside? There were some pills that can help Kimi."

Sarapul nodded. He led Tuck back through the jungle to his house. Kimi had gone inside and was lying down.

"Boss, I don't feel so good."

"Hang on. I might have some more medicine." Actually, Tuck had never been sure of all the things that Jake Skye had loaded into the pack.

Sarapul retrieved a palm frond basket from the rafters and handed it to Tucker. Tuck found the antibiotics he had been looking for, as well as painkillers and aspirin. Even what was left of his cash was in the basket. All the pills were still dry. Tuck doled out a dose and handed them to the navigator. "Take these when you have pain, and these take like the other ones, twice a day, okay?"

"You good doctor, boss."

"You did a hell of a job on that boat."

Kimi seemed distressed. "You not tell Sorcerer or Vincent's white bitch."

"No, I won't tell them."

Kimi seemed to breathe easier. "Roberto come today. He say you must see the canoe. But he say you should no tell the Sorcerer."

"Roberto told you that."

"He talk funny now," Kimi said. "Like you, kinda. In American. He tell me Sepie is okay. She come home soon."

"I couldn't get in to see her. There was a guard on the clinic."

"Dog fuckers," Kimi said.

Then Tuck told the navigator about the golf game and watched as the old cannibal held him while he laughed, then curled with pain. "I better sleep now, boss. You come back. I take you sailing."

"You got it." Tuck backed out of the house and waited until Sarapul joined him with the lamp. "You know which pills to give him?"

Sarapul nodded. Tuck started down the path toward the village, but pulled up a minute later when he heard the cannibal running after him.

"Hey, pilot. Vincent send you to us, huh?"

"I don't know."

"You tell Vincent I wasn't going to eat you. Okay?"

Tuck smiled. "I'll try to smuggle you some Spam next time I come."

Sarapul smiled back.

As he came up on the drinking circle, Tuck stopped and checked his watch. He didn't want to be gone more than a couple of hours. There was little danger that he'd be called to fly, at least not without the warning appearance of the Sky Priestess, but Beth Curtis might show up at his bungalow at any time. Funny, he didn't think of the Sky Priestess and Beth as the same person.

The Shark men were applying new coats of red paint to their bamboo rifles by the light of a kerosene lamp. They moved around on the logs and Tuck took a seat by Malink. Without a word, the young man who was pouring handed Tuck the cup. He drained it and handed it back.

"What's the deal with the rifles?" Tuck asked Malink.

"Vincent's army," Malink said. "Vincent said we must always be ready to fight the enemies of the United States of America."

"Oh," Tuck said. "Why red?"

Malink looked at Tuck as if he was something he had stepped in. "It is the color of Vincent's brother."

"Yeah?" Tuck didn't get it.

"Vincent's brother, Santa Claus. Red is his color. You must know that."

Tuck couldn't help it. He let his mouth fall open. "Santa Claus is Vincent's brother?"

"Yes, Santa Claus brings excellent cargo for everyone, but only once a year. He comes in a sleigh on the snow. You know, right?"

"Right. But I don't get the connection."

Malink looked as if it was all he could do not to tell Tuck how incredibly dense he really was. "Well, we have no snow, so Vincent will come in a plane. Not once a year. When Vincent come, he will bring cargo every day. More than he gives through the Sky Priestess. More than Santa Claus."

"And Vincent told you this, that he was Santa's brother?"

Malink nodded. "His skinny brother, he say. So we make rifles red." Malink watched for signs that Tuck was getting it. Tuck wasn't giving them. "Even Father Rodriguez know about Santa Claus," Malink insisted.

"Okay," Tuck said, "how about moving that cup around the circle a little faster, guys?"

"Vincent will bring us real rifles when he come. We must be always ready to fight," Malink said.

"Who?" Tuck asked. "Have you guys ever been attacked?"

"Once," Malink said. "When I was boy, some guys from New Guinea come in canoe. We no like those guys. We go in our canoes to kill them."

"And what happened?"

"It got dark."

"And?"

"We come home. Those guys from New Guinea pretty lucky no one know how to navigate in the dark."

"No *palu*?" Tuck asked, using the native word for "navigator."

"Japanese kill them. No *palu* left, except maybe one."

"That's why you didn't turn Kimi over to the Sorcerer?"

Malink nodded and trouble crossed his brow. "I am thinking, if Vincent send you, how come the Sorcerer not know you here? And how you not know Santa Claus?"

Tuck noticed that the men had stopped painting their rifles and talking among themselves to listen to his answer. There was pressure here, beyond whether he'd be able to drink or not. He told them what they needed to hear. "Vincent called me from the land of armored possums to come to the island of the Shark People. I am a flyer, as Vincent was a flyer. He does not tell me everything, and he does not tell the Sorcerer everything. Vincent is sometimes mysterious, but we must trust his judgment."

Malink smiled. "Let us drink to this flyer. Then we go to sleep." To Tuck, Malink said: "Tomorrow is the hunt."

~~~~~~

53

How the Shark People Got Their Name

When the pounding came at his door just after dawn, Tuck prepared himself mentally to meet the smiling face of Sebastian Curtis, who would be overly cheerful at the prospect of trouncing the pilot at another round of gravel golf, but when he opened the door, there was Beth Curtis wearing a long-sleeved white cotton dress and a huge sun hat with a brim that fell over her face like a lampshade.

Tuck had on hand-me-down boxer shorts that showed more of his morning bulge than he was comfortable with. Strange, a month ago he was ready to sell his soul for this physiological phenomenon, and today it was an embarrassment.

"Good morning," he said. "I was expecting the doc."

"Oh, did you two have plans?"

"No, I just . . . never mind. Would you like to come in for some coffee?" He gestured to the small kitchen nook.

"Why don't you make yourself a cup and bring it with you? I have something to show you."

"Sure. Just give me a second."

She waited by the door while he threw a pot of water on the stove, dressed quickly and combed his hair, then poured the water over some coffee grounds and stirred in some powdered milk. "I'm ready. What's up?"

"I want to show you something on the other side of the island."

"Outside of the compound?"

"Near the village. I think you'll enjoy it."

Tuck walked with her out into the morning sun, nursing his

coffee as they went. There were no guards in sight anywhere. The wide gate to the runway was open.

"Where's the ninjas?"

"You call them that too? That's funny." She laughed, but because he couldn't see her face under the hat, he couldn't tell if there was any sincerity in it.

She put her hand on his arm and let him lead her across the runway like a Victorian lady under escort.

"Do you ever miss your family?" she asked as they walked.

Tuck was taken by surprise. "My family? No. We parted on less than favorable terms. I fell out of contact with them long before I came out here."

"I'm sorry. Really. Is it difficult for you?"

Tuck thought she might be joking. "My mother and my uncle are my only real family. They married after my father was killed. I wasn't pleased."

"You're kidding. I thought they only did that in West Virginia. Aren't you from California?"

"She married my father's brother, not her brother. Still, I don't miss them."

"What about your friends?"

Tuck thought for a second. Things had changed for him since he'd last seen Jake Skye. In a way he'd taken on some responsibility. He was acting on his own, without a net. He wished that he could tell Jake about it. "Yeah, I miss my friends sometimes."

"Me too, Tucker. I'd like to be your friend."

"You have Sebastian."

"Yes, I do, don't I."

They walked in silence until they entered the village, which was deserted except for a few dogs and too many roosters. "Where is everybody?" Tuck reminded himself not to let it appear that any of this was familiar to him. "Is this where the natives live?"

"They're all at the beach. Today is the day of the hunt."

"The hunt?"

"You'll see. It's a surprise."

As they passed the bachelors' house, Tuck peeked through he door. He could see someone sleeping inside. Beth led the way to the beach and Tucker looked back. Sepie stood in the doorway wearing only a bandage around her ribs. She waved and Tuck risked a quick smile and turned away. They were going to give him away. One hint of recognition and he was screwed.

The women, children, and old men were all lined up on the beach. Tuck had never seen most of the women and children. There must have been three hundred people there. The only familiar face was Favo, the old man from the drinking circle, who showed no recognition when he looked at Tuck. The younger men were out in the water, standing knee deep on the reef in the light low-tide surf. Each of the men held a five-foot-long stick with a rope tied at one end. They wore long knives tucked into cords tied around their waists.

"Fishing?" Tuck asked.

"Just watch," Beth said. "This is how the Shark People got their name."

Tuck spotted Malink coming out of the jungle with four other men. Each carried a large plastic bucket.

"They make the buckets out of net floats from the huge factory ships," Beth Curtis said. "The plastic is tougher than anything they can make."

"What's in them?" Tuck watched as each man swam out to the reef holding a bucket on his head.

"Pig and chicken blood."

Two men helped Malink onto the reef and took his bucket from him. Malink looked out to sea and said something in his native language, then looked to the people on the beach as if to say, "Ready."

The chief shouted a command to the men in the water and they dumped the buckets of blood. Soon they were all knee deep in crimson surf and the bloodstain swept out into the ocean in a great cloud.

"Isn't that dangerous?" Tuck asked.

"Of course. It's insane."

Interesting choice of words. Tuck was surprised that no one seemed to notice or make a big deal of Beth's presence. "Why aren't they drumming and kowtowing to you?"

"They aren't allowed to when I'm dressed like this. It's a rule. I need my privacy at times."

"Of course," Tuck said.

A fin appeared in the water about twenty yards out from the reef. Someone shouted and Tuck recognized Abo from his warrior's topknot. Malink nodded and Abo dove into the water and swam toward the shark. Before he was ten yards out, the fin turned toward him.

More fins appeared and as Malink nodded, more young men dove into the water with their sticks.

"Shit, this is suicide," Tuck said. He watched as the first shark made a pass at Abo, who moved out of its way like a bullfighter.

"You've got to stop this." Tuck couldn't remember ever feeling such panic for another human being.

Beth Curtis squeezed his arm. "They know what they're doing."

The shark circled and made a second pass at Abo, but this time the young warrior didn't move out of the way. He shoved his stick into the shark's jaws as if it was a bit, then flipped himself on the shark's back and wrapped the cord just behind the pectoral fins, then back to the other end of the stick so it wouldn't come out. The water boiled around Abo as the shark thrashed, but Abo stayed on and, holding the stick like handlebars, he pulled back to keep the shark from diving and steered him into the shallow water of the reef, where the other men waited with their knives drawn.

A roar went up from the crowd on the beach as Abo turned the shark over to the slaughterers and held up his arms in triumph. The men on the reef slit the shark's belly and cut off a huge hunk of the liver, which they handed to Abo. He bit into it, tearing out a ragged chunk and swallowing as blood ran down his chest.

Soon others were steering sharks onto the reef and the water beyond was alive with fins. The red cloud expanded as the sharks died and bled and more came to take their place. The gutted sharks were brought onto the beach, where the women continued the butchering, handing pieces of the raw flesh to the children as treats or prying out serrated teeth and giving them to little boys as trophies.

One of the men actually stood up on the back of a huge hammerhead that he was steering to the reef and nearly castrated himself on the dorsal fin as he fell. But the shark was held fast and died on the reef with the others.

In half an hour the shark hunt was over. The sea was red with blood for a thousand yards in all directions and the beach was littered with the corpses of a hundred sharks: black tips, white tips, hammerheads, blue, and mako. Some of the deadliest creatures had been taken like they were guppies in a net, and not one of the Shark People was hurt, although Tuck noticed that many were bleeding from abrasions on the inside of their thighs where they had rubbed against the sharks' skin during their ride. The Shark People were ecstatic, and every one of them was drenched in blood.

Tuck was stunned. He'd never seen such courage or such slaughter before, and he was getting the willies thinking about all the time he had spent swimming in these waters at night.

Malink walked up the beach dragging a leopard shark by its gills. His Buddha belly was dripping in blood. He looked up at Tucker and risked a smile.

"That's the chief," Beth Curtis said. "He's really too old for this, but he won't stay on shore."

"Do the sharks ever get any of them?"

"Sometimes. Usually just a bite. A lot of sutures, but no one's been killed since I've been on the island."

No one hunting sharks, anyway, Tuck thought. A little girl who had been helping her mother shyly peeked over the carcass of a big hammerhead, then ran up to Tucker and quickly touched him on the knee before retreating to the safety of her mother.

"That's strange," Beth Curtis said. "The women and girls won't have anything to do with a white man. Even when they come to Sebastian, they talk to him through a brother or husband—and he speaks their language."

Tuck didn't answer. He was still looking at the little girl's back. She had a massive pink scar that ran like a smile from her sternum, under her arm, to her backbone at exactly the place where the kidney would be. Tuck felt sick to his stomach.

"I think I've seen enough, Beth. Can we go?"

"Can't deal with the sight of blood?"

"Something like that."

As they walked back through the village, Tuck noticed a woman and a little boy sitting outside of one of the cookhouses. The mother was holding the boy and singing to him softly as she rocked him. Both of his eyes were bandaged with gauze pads. Tucker approached the woman and she pulled the child to her breast.

Beth Curtis caught Tuck's arm and tried to pull him back. Tuck shook her off and went to the woman.

"What's wrong with him?" Tuck asked.

The woman slid across the gravel, away from him.

"Tucker!" Beth Curtis said, "Leave her alone. You're scaring her."

"It's okay," Tuck whispered to the woman. "I'm the pilot. Vincent sent me."

The woman seemed to calm down, and although her eyes went wide with wonder, she managed a small smile.

Tuck reached out and touched the child's head. "What's wrong with him?"

The woman held out the boy as if presenting him for baptism.

"He is chosen," she said. She looked at the Sky Priestess for approval.

Tuck stood and backed away from her. He was afraid to look at Beth, afraid that he might strangle her on the spot. Instead, calmly, deliberately, although it took all his effort to keep from shaking, he said, "We'd better get back." He led the way through the village and back to the compound.

54

Selling Tucker

The Sky Priestess threw the straw hat across the room, then tore at the high-buttoned collar of the white dress. She was losing him. She hated that more than anything: losing control. She ripped the dress down the front and wrestled out of it.

She stormed across the room, the dress still trailing from one foot, and pulled a bottle of vodka from the freezer. She poured herself a tumbler and drank half of it off while still holding the bottle, then refilled the glass while her temples throbbed with the cold. She carried the bottle and glass to a chair in front of the television, sat down, and turned it on. Nothing but static and snow. Sebastian was using the satellite dish. She threw the vodka bottle at the screen, but missed and it bounced off the case, taking a small chip out of the plastic.

"Fuck!" She keyed the intercom next to her chair. " 'Bastian! Dammit!"

"Yes, my sweet." His voice was calm and oily.

"What the fuck are you doing? I want to watch TV."

"I'm just finishing up, sweetheart."

"We need to talk." She tossed back another slug of vodka.

"Yes, we do. I'll be up in a moment."

"Bring some vodka from your house."

"As you wish."

Ten minutes later the Sorcerer walked into her bungalow, the picture of the patrician physician. He handed her the vodka and sat down across from her. "Pour me one, would you, darling?"

Before she could catch herself, she'd gotten up and fetched him a glass from the kitchen. She handed it to him along with the bottle.

"Your dress is torn, dear."

"No shit."

"I like the look," the Sorcerer said, "although I'd have preferred to tear it off you myself."

"Not now. I think we have trouble."

The Sorcerer smiled. "We did, but as of tonight at midnight, our troubles are over. How was your walk this morning, by the way?"

"I took Case to see the shark hunt. I thought it would keep him from getting island fever, something different to break the boredom."

"As opposed to fucking him."

She wasn't going to show any surprise, not after he'd laid a trap like that. "No, in addition to fucking him. It was a mistake."

"The shark hunt or the fucking?"

She bristled, "The shark hunt. The fucking was fine. He saw the boy whose corneas we harvested."

"So."

"He freaked. I shouldn't have let him connect the people with the procedure."

"But I thought you could handle him."

He was enjoying this entirely too much for her taste. "Don't be smug, 'Bastian. What are you going to do, lock him in the back room of the clinic? We need him."

"No, we don't. I've hired a new pilot. A Japanese."

"I thought we'd agreed that . . ."

"It hasn't worked using Americans, has it? He starts tonight."

"How?"

"You're going to go pick him up. The corporation assures me that he's the best, and he won't ask questions."

"I'm going to pick him up?"

"We have a heart-lung order. You and Mr. Case need to deliver it."

"I can't do it, 'Bastian. I can't do a performance and a heart-lung tonight. I'm too jangled."

"You don't have to do either, dear. We don't have to do the surgery. We'll make less money on it, but we only have to deliver the donor."

"But what about doing the choosing?"

"You've done that already. You chose when you went to bed with our intrepid Mr. Case. The heart-lung donor is Tucker Case."

Tuck needed a drink. He looked around the bungalow, hoping that someone had left a stray bottle of vanilla extract or aftershave that might go well with a slice of mango. Mangoes he had, but anything containing ethyl alcohol was not to be found. It would be hours before darkness could cover his escape to the drinking circle, where he intended to get gloriously hammered if he could look any of the Shark People in the eye and keep his stomach. *Sorry, you guys. Just had to take the edge off of the guilt of blinding a child to get my own airplane.*

He tried to distract himself by reading, but the moral certainties of the literary spy guys only served to make him feel worse. Television was no help either. Some sort of Balinese shadow puppet show and Filipino news special on how swell it was to make American semiconductors for three bucks a day. He punched the remote to off and tossed it across the room.

Frustration leaped out in a string of curses, followed by "All right, Mr. Ghost Pilot, where in the hell are you now?"

And there was a knock on the door.

"Kidding," Tuck said. "I was kidding."

"Tucker, can I come in?" Beth Curtis said.

"It's open." It was always open. There was no lock on it.

He looked away as she entered, afraid that, like the face of the Medusa, she might turn him to stone—or at least that part of him unaffected by conscience. She came up behind him and began kneading the muscles in his shoulders. He did not look back at her and still had no idea if she might be naked or wearing a clown suit.

"You're upset. I understand. But it's not what you think."

"There's not a lot of room for misinterpretation."

"Isn't there? What if I told you that that boy was blind from birth. His corneas were healthy, but he was born with atrophied optic nerves."

"I feel much better, thanks. Kid wasn't using his eyes, so we ripped them out."

He felt her nails dig into his trapezius muscles. "Ripped out is hardly appropriate. It's a very delicate operation. And because we did it, another child is able to see. You seem to be missing that aspect of what we're doing here. Every time we deliver a kidney, we're saving a life."

She was right. He hadn't thought about that. "I just fly the plane," he said.

"And take the money. You could have this same job back in the States. You could be flying the organs of accident victims on Life Flight jets and accomplishing the same thing, except you wouldn't be making enough to pay the taxes on what you make here, right?"

No, not exactly, he thought. Back in the States, he couldn't fly anything but a hang glider without his license. "I guess so," he said. "But you could have told me what you were doing."

"And have you thinking about the little blind kid at five hundred miles per hour. I don't think so." She bent over and kissed his earlobe lightly. "I'm not a monster, Tuck. I was a little girl once, with a mother and a father and a cat named Cupcake. I don't blind little kids."

Finally he turned in the chair to face her and was grateful to see that she was wearing one of her conservative Donna Reed dresses. "What happened to you, Beth? How in the hell do you get from 'Here, Cupcake' to the Murdering Bitch Goddess of the Shark People?" He immediately regretted saying it. Not because it wasn't true, but because he'd given away the fact that he knew it was. He braced himself for the rage.

She moved to the couch and sat down across from him. Then she curled into a ball, her face against the cushions, and covered her eyes. He said nothing. He just watched as her body quaked with silent sobs. He hoped this wasn't an act. He hoped that she was so offended that she would take his murder accusation for hyperbole.

Five full minutes passed before she looked up. Her eyes were red and she'd managed to smear mascara across one cheek. "It's your fault," she said.

Tuck nodded and tried not to let a smile cross his lips. She was playing another part, and she didn't do the victim nearly as well as she did the seduction queen. He said, "I'm sorry, Beth. I was out of line."

She seemed surprised and broke character. Evidently, he'd stepped on her line, the one she'd been thinking of while pretending to cry. A second for composure and she was back at it. "It's your fault. I only wanted to have a friend, not a lover. All men are that way."

"Then you must not have gotten the newsletter: 'Men Are Pigs.' Next issue is 'Water Is Wet.' Don't miss it."

She fell out of character again. "What are you saying?"

"You might have been a victim once, but now that's just a distant memory you use to rationalize what you do now. You use men because you can. I can't figure out what happened in San Francisco, though. A woman who looks like you should have been able to find an easier way to fuck her way to a fortune. The doc must have been a cakewalk for you."

"And you weren't?"

Tuck felt as if someone had injected him with a truth serum that was lighting up his mind, and not with revelations about Beth Curtis. The light was shining on him.

"Yeah, I guess I was a cakewalk. So what? Did you think for a minute that you might try not to go to bed with me?

"Other than when I found out that you'd almost torn your balls off, not for a minute." She was gritting her teeth.

"And how big a task do you think you took on? It's not like you were corrupting me or anything. I've been on the other end of the game for years. I know you, Beth. I am you."

"You don't know anything." She was visibly trying not to scream, but Tuck could see the blood rising in her face.

He pushed on. "Freud says I'm this way because I was never hugged as a child. What's your excuse?"

"Don't be smug. I could have you right now if I wanted." As if to prove her point, she placed her feet at either end of the coffee table and began to pull up her dress. She wore white stockings and nothing else underneath.

"Not interested," Tuck said. "Been there, done that."

"You're so transparent," she said. She crawled over the table and did a languid cat stretch as she ran her hands up the inside of his thighs. By the time her hands got to his belt buckle, she was face-to-face with him, almost touching noses. Tuck could smell the alcohol on her breath. She flicked her tongue on his lips. He just looked in her eyes, as cold and blue as crystal, like his own. She wasn't fooling anyone, and in realizing that, Tuck realized that he also had never fooled anybody. Every Mary Jean lady, every bar bimbo, every secretary, flight attendant, or girl at the grocery store had seen him coming and let him come.

Beth unzipped his pants and took him in her hand, her face still only a millimeter from his, their eyes locked. "Your armor seems to have a weak spot, tough guy."

"Nope," Tuck said.

She slid down to the floor and took him into her mouth. Tuck suppressed a gasp. He watched her head moving on him. To keep himself from touching her he grabbed the arms of the chair and the wicker creaked as if it was being punished.

"That's a pretty convincing argument," said the male voice. Tuck looked up to see Vincent sitting on the couch where Beth had been a minute ago.

"Jesus!" Tuck said. Beth let out a muffled moan and dug her nails into his ass.

"Wrong!" Vincent said. "But never play cards with that guy." . The flyer was smoking a cigarette, but Tuck couldn't smell it. "Oh, don't worry. She can't hear me. Can't see me either, not that she's looking or anything."

Tuck just shook his head and pushed up on the arms of the chair. Beth took his movement for enthusiasm and paused to look up at him. Tuck met her gaze with eyes the size of golf balls. She smiled, her lipstick a bit worse for the wear, a string of saliva trailed from her lips. "Just enjoy. You lost. Losers flourish here." She licked her lips and returned to her task.

"Dame makes a point," Vincent said. "I give you three to one she brings you around to her way of thinking. Whatta ya say?"

"No." Tuck waved the flyer off and shut his eyes.

"Oh, yes," Beth said, as if speaking into the microphone.

Vincent flicked his cigarette butt out the window. "I'm not distracting you, am I? I just dropped in to take up on the dame's side, as she is unable to speak for herself at present."

Tuck was experiencing the worst case of bed spins he'd ever had—in a chair. Sexual vertigo.

"Of course," Vincent continued, "this is kinda turning into a religious experience for you, ain't it? Go with what you know, right? You let her run the show, you got no decisions to make and no worries ever after. Not a worry in the world. You got my word on that. Although, if it was me, I'd check out her story just to be safe. Look in the doc's computer maybe."

Beth was working her mouth and hands like she was pumping water on an inner fire that was consuming her with each second that passed. Tuck heard his own breath rise to a pant and the wicker chair crackle and creak and skid on the wooden floor. He was helping her now, wanting her to quench that flame and that was all there was.

"You think about it," Vincent said. "You'll do the right thing. You owe me, remember." He faded and disappeared.

"What does that mean?" Tuck said, then he moaned, arched his back, and came so hard he thought he would pass out, but she kept on and on until he couldn't stand the intensity and had to push her away. She landed on the floor at his feet and looked up like an angry she-cat.

"You're mine," she said. She was still breathing hard and her dress was still up around her waist. "We're friends."

It came out like a command, but Tuck heard a note of desperation below the panting and the ire, and he felt a wrenching pain in his chest like nothing he'd ever felt before. "I know you, Beth. I am you," he said. But not anymore, he thought. He said, "Yes, we're friends."

She smiled like a little girl who'd been given a pony for her birthday. "I knew it," she said. She climbed to her feet and smoothed down her skirt, then bent and kissed him on the eyebrow. He tried to smile.

She said, "I'll see you in a few hours. We're flying out at nine. I have to go see to Sebastian."

Tuck zipped up his pants. "And get ready for your performance?" he said.

"No, this isn't a medical flight. Just supplies."

Tuck nodded. "Beth, was that little boy blind from birth?"

"Of course," she said, looking offended. She was more convincing as the Sky Priestess.

"You go see to Sebastian," Tuck said.

After she had left, Tuck looked at the ceiling and said, "Vincent, just in case you're listening, I'm not buying your bullshit. If you want to help me, fine. But if not, stay out of my way."

~~~~~~

55

Pay No Attention to That Man Behind the Computer

Tuck went into the bathroom and washed his face, then combed his hair. He studied his face in the mirror, looking for that scary glint that he'd seen in Beth Curtis's eyes. He wasn't her. He wasn't as smart as she was, but he wasn't as crazy either. He cringed with the realization that he had spent most of his adult life being a jerk or a patsy and sometimes both simultaneously. And it was no small irony to have had an epiphany during a blow job. Vincent, whatever he was, had been playing some kind of game from the beginning, mixing lies and truth, helping him only to get him into trouble. There was no grand bailout coming, and if he was going to find out what was really being planned for him, he had to get into the computer.

The best time to sneak into the clinic was right now, in broad daylight. He hadn't seen any of the guards all day and Beth was "seeing to Sebastian." If he got caught, he'd simply say he was trying to get the weather for tonight's flight. If the doc could e-mail and fax all over the world, then surely he would have access to weather services. It didn't matter; he didn't think he'd have a hard time convincing the doc that he was just being stupid. His entire life had set up the cover.

He grabbed some paper and a pencil from the nightstand and stuffed them into his back pocket. While he was in there, he might as well see if he could pick up the coordinates for Okinawa. If he could sneak them into the nav computer on the Lear, he might just be able to get the military to force the jet down there. He didn't have a chance in hell of getting there on his own navigational skills.

He stepped out on the lanai and gave a sidelong glance to the guards' quarters to make sure no one was just inside the door watching his bungalow. Satisfied, he walked to the clinic and tried the door. It was unlocked.

He checked the compound again, saw nothing, and slipped into the clinic. He was immediately met by the sound of voices coming from the back room. Male voices, speaking Japanese. He tiptoed through the door that led into the operating room and opened it a crack. The door to the far side was open. He could see all the ninjas gathered around one of the hospital beds playing cards. It was visiting day for Stripe. He palmed the door shut and went to the computer.

There had been a time when Tuck was so ignorant of computers that he thought a mouse pad was Disney's brand of sanitary napkin, but that was before he met Jake Skye. Jake had taught him how to access the weather maps, charts, and how to file his flight plans through the computer. In the process Tuck had also learned what Jake considered the most important computer skill, how to hack into someone else's stuff.

The three CRTs were all on, two green over black and one color. Tuck focused on the color screen. It was friendlier and it was displaying a screen saver he recognized, a slide show of dolphins. He moved the mouse and the familiar Windows screen appeared. There was a cheer from the back room and Tuck nearly drove the mouse off the top of the desk. Must have been a good hand.

He expected to see obscure medical programs, something he'd never figure out, but it looked like the doc used the same stuff everyone in the States did. Tuck clicked on the database icon and the program jumped to fill the screen. He opened a file menu; there were only two. One was named SUPPLIES, the other TT. Tissue types? He clicked it. The ENTER PASSWORD field opened. "Shit."

Jake had always told him that people used obvious passwords if you knew the people. Something they wouldn't forget. Put yourself in their place, you'll figure out their passwords, and don't eliminate the possibility that it may be written on a Post-it note stuck to the computer. Tuck looked for Post-it notes, then open the desk drawers and riffled through the papers for anything that looked like a password. He pushed out the chair and looked under the desk. Bingo! There were two long numbers written on tape on the bottom of the desk drawer. He pulled the paper and pencil from his pocket and copied them down, then entered the first one in the password field.

<INVALID PASSWORD> was the response

Tuck typed in the second number.

<INVALID PASSWORD>

Look for the obvious. Tuck typed SKY PRIESTESS.

<INVALID PASSWORD>

The guards were laughing in the other room. Tuck typed in VIN-
CENT.

<INVALID PASSWORD>

DOCTOR.

<INVALID PASSWORD>

It would be something that the doc would be sitting here thinking about. It would be on his mind.

Tuck typed BETH.

<INVALID PASSWORD>

BETHS TITS.

Wait a minute. This was the doc thinking. He typed BETHS
BREASTS.

The file scrolled open, filling the screen with a list of names
down the left side followed by rows and columns of letters and numbers. All of the names Tuck could see were native. Across the top
were five columns that must be the tissue types and blood types,
next to those, kidney, liver, heart, lung, cornea, and pancreas. Christ,
it was an inventory sheet. And the heart, lung, liver, and pancreas
categories convinced him once and for all that there was no benev-
olent intention behind the Curtises' plan. They were going to the
meat market with the Shark People until the village was empty.

Tuck typed in SEPIE in the FIND field. An x had been placed in
all the organ categories except kidney. There he found an H and a
date. H? Harvested. The date was the day they harvested it.

He typed in PARDEE, JEFFERSON. No "x's" in any of the columns,
but two H's under heart and lungs. Of course the other organs
weren't marked. They'd been donated to the sharks and were no
longer available. There was nothing under SOMMERS, JAMES. That too
made sense. How would they get the organs to Japan without a pilot.
Tuck wished he'd gotten the little blind boy's name. He couldn't take
the time to scroll though all three hundred or so names looking for
missing corneas. He typed in CASE, TUCKER. There were H's marked
under the heart and lung category. The harvest date was today.

"You fuckers," he said. There was a shuffling in the back room
and he stood so quickly the chair rolled back and banged into a
cabinet on the other side of the office. The database was still up on

the screen. Tuck reached out and punched the button on the monitor. It clicked off as Mato came through the door.

"What are you guys doing here?" Tuck said.

Mato pulled up. He seemed confused. He was supposed to be doing the yelling.

"We're flying tonight," Tuck said. "Do you guys have the plane fueled up?"

Mato shook his head. "Then get on it. I wondered where you were."

Mato just looked at him.

"Go!" Tuck said. "Now!"

Mato started to slink toward the door, obviously not comfortable with leaving Tuck in the clinic. Another guard came into the office and when Mato looked up, Tuck snatched his paper and pencil from the desk. He dropped the pencil and when he bent to pick it up, he hit the main power switch on the computer. The computer would reboot when turned on and the doctor would only know that it had been turned off. He'd never suspect that someone had been into the donor files.

"Let's go, you guys."

Tuck pushed past Mato out the office door, shoving the paper in his pocket as he went.

Tuck made quite a show of the preflight on the Lear, demanding three times that the guard with access to the key to the main power cutoff turn it on so he could check out the plane. The guard wasn't buying it. He walked away from Tuck snickering. Tuck checked under the instrument panel. Maybe there would be some obvious way to hot-wire the switch. He'd been lucky with the computer. The switch and all the wires leading into it were covered by a steel case. He couldn't get into it with a blowtorch, and frankly, he had no idea which wires did what. It probably wasn't even a simple switch, but a relay that lead to another switch. There'd be no way to wire around it.

He left the hangar and went back to his bungalow. Unless he found some way to get off the island, he was going to be short a couple of lungs and a heart come midnight. Beth would have at least one guard on the plane with her, probably two, given the circumstances. And he had no doubt that she'd shoot him in the crotch and make him fly to Japan anyway. There had to be another way. Like a boat. Kimi's boat. Didn't these guys travel thousands of miles over the Pacific in canoes like that? What could the doc do? He'd been so careful about safeguarding the island that the guards didn't even have a boat to chase him with.

Tuck put on his shorts and took his fins and mask to the bathroom. He knotted the ends of his trouser legs and started filling them with supplies. A shirt, a light jacket, some disinfectant, sunscreen, a short kitchen knife. He found a small jar of sugar in the kitchen, dumped the sugar into the sink, and filled the jar with matches and Band-Aids. When he was ready to seal it, he saw the slip of paper he'd written on in the office sticking from the pocket of the trousers and shoved it into the jar as an afterthought. He topped off the pants bag with a pair of sneakers, then pulled the webbed belt tight to cinch it all up. He could swim with the pants legs like water wings. The wet clothing would get heavy, but not until he hit the beach on the far side of the minefield. To Tuck's way of thinking, once he was past the minefield he was halfway there. Then all he had to do was convince the old cannibal to give him the canoe, enough food and water to get somewhere, and Kimi to navigate. Where in the hell would they go? Yap? Guam?

One step at a time. First he had to get out of the compound. He checked the guards' positions. Leaning out the window, he could see three—no, four—at the hangar. He waited. He'd never tried to make the swim while it was still light. They'd be able to see him in the water from as far away as the runway. He just had to hope that they didn't look in that direction.

The guards were rolling barrels into the hangar to hand-pump the jet fuel into the Lear. Two on each barrel, four out in the compound, bingo. One guy had to be in the hangar cranking the pump. And Stripe was in the clinic. Showtime!

Tuck went into the bathroom, lifted the hatch, threw down the pants bag and his swimming stuff, and followed it through.

He weighed sneaking against running, stealth against speed, and decided to go like a newborn turtle for the water. The only people who might see him were the Doc and Beth, and they were probably in the process of pushing the twin beds together and doing the Ozzie and Harriet double-skin sweat slap—or whatever sort of weird shit they did. He hoped it was painful.

He broke into a dead run across the gravel, feeling the coral dig at his feet and the ferns whip at his ankles but keeping his focus on the beach. As he passed the clinic, he thought he saw some movement out of the corner of his eye, but he didn't turn. He was Carl Lewis, Michael Johnson, and Edwin Moses (except he was white and slow), a single head turn could cause him to lose his stride and the race—and boy, does that beach seem farther when you're running than when you're sneaking. He almost tumbled when he hit the sand, but managed a controlled forward stumble that put him face-first in four inches of water. The baby turtle had made it to the water, but now he faced a whole new set of dangers at sea, not the least of which was trying to swim with a pair of stuffed khakis around his neck.

He kicked a few feet out into the water, put on his fins and mask, and began the swim.

He'd been furious from the moment he heard the pilot's voice in the clinic and he had fought the cloud of painkillers and the pressure in his head to get to him. Yamata watched the pilot stumble into the water before he tried shouting for the others. The shout came out little more than a grunt through his wired jaw, and his crushed sinuses allowed little sound to pass through his nose. His gun was in the guards' quarters, the others were at the hangar, and his hated enemy was escaping. He decided to go for his gun. The others might want to take the pilot alive.

56

Escape

Kimi was trying to call up thunder and was having no luck at all. He'd been chanting and waving his arms for half an hour and there still wasn't a cloud in the sky.

"You're not holding your arms right," Sarapul said. He was lying under a palm tree, chewing a betel nut and offering constructive criticism to the navigator. Sepie lay nearby watching.

"I am too," Kimi said. "I'm holding them the same way you do."

"Maybe it doesn't work for Filipinos."

"It's because I'm shot," Kimi said. "If I wasn't shot, I could do this."

Sarapul scanned the horizon. Not even a bird. "That's it. It's because you're shot." He spit out a red stream of betel nut juice. "And you're not holding your arms right."

Kimi resumed chanting and waving his arms.

"Hey!" Sarapul said.

"What? Did you hear thunder? I knew I could do it."

"No. Be quiet. Someone is calling you."

Kimi listened. Someone was calling him, and they were getting closer. He limped down the beach toward the voice and saw Tucker Case coming around the island.

"Hey, boss, what you doin' out here during the day? The Sorcerer gonna be plenty mad at you."

Tuck was out of breath. "He is mad. I need your boat, Kimi. And I need you to navigate for me."

"Not his ship," Sarapul said. "My ship."

"The doc is going to kill me if I don't get off the island. Can I use your boat?"

The old cannibal was silent for a moment, thinking. "Where you go?"

"I don't know. Guam, Yap, anywhere."

"Can I come?"

"Yes, yes, if I can use your boat."

"Okay, we leave five days. Right, Kimi?"

Kimi looked at Tuck. "It not be good sailing for five days."

"I have to go now, Kimi."

"Can Sepie come?"

Sepie stepped back, surprised. "You want to take me? Women don't sail."

"You come," Kimi said. "Okay, boss?" he said to Tuck.

Tuck nodded. "Whatever. Sepie, go tell Malink that I need everyone to bring drinking coconuts. Many drinking coconuts with the husks taken off. Bananas, mangoes, papaya, and dried fish if he has any."

"There is plenty shark meat," Sepie said.

"I need it now, Sepie. Go. Tell Malink that Vincent demands it."

Sarapul began to chop at the underbrush in front of the sailing canoe to clear a path to the water. "Put down palm leaf to slide ship on," he told Tuck. Tuck began to gather long palm fronds and lay them down in a path to the water.

"Kimi, can you go get the things from my pack? There's things we can use."

"What about Roberto?"

"Call for him, but go get the stuff. The money too."

"Okay, boss."

Ten minutes later Tuck looked up to see Malink leading a line of Shark People through the jungle. All were carrying baskets of food and husked green coconuts.

"You are leaving?"

"Yes, I have to go, Chief."

"You are taking our ship and our navigator."

"And our mispel," Abo added from behind Malink.

"I have to go, Malink. The Sorcerer and the Sky Priestess are going to kill me."

"But Vincent send you. How they hurt you?"

"They don't really believe in Vincent. They use him to get you to give up the chosen, Malink. They're going to start killing off your people too."

"They no kill the chosen. Chosen are for Vincent."

"No. I told you before. They take out your organs and sell them to be put inside of other people."

Malink scoffed. "You can no put one man kidney in other man."

"It was in *People* magazine. Didn't you see it? Demi Moore, Melanie Griffith, Mariel Hemingway, all of them? You didn't read about it?"

Recognition lit up Malink's face. "Boob job!"

"Yes," Tuck said. "Where do you think they get those boobs?"

"Oh, no."

"Yes."

"He speaks the truth," Malink said to the islanders. "It was in *People*. Put the food in the boat."

He took Tuck aside. "You will come back?"

"I'll try."

"And bring our navigator."

"I'll try, Malink. I really will."

"You try."

"Tide," Kimi called. "We go now."

The center of the canoe was filled with coconuts, fruit, and bundles of dried shark meat wrapped in banana leaves. Kimi directed the men to get on either side of the canoe and push it over the mat of palm fronds to the water. When it was afloat, Tuck lifted Sepie in, then climbed in himself. Kimi, standing on the outrigger platform, started to hoist the sail. It was the shape of a tortilla chip stood on end with a bite taken out at the top. Tuck recognized the pieces of his pack sewn into the nylon patchwork.

"Where is Sarapul?" Kimi said.

"Here!" The old cannibal was running out of the jungle, seeming stronger now than Tuck had ever seen him. He had gone back for his spear, a long shaft of mahogany with a wickedly barbed metal tip. Tuck caught the old man by the forearm and pulled him out of the surf and into the canoe.

The canoe was already fifty yards from the shore. Sarapul took the long oar at the rear and steered it toward the channel as Kimi stood on the outrigger platform and manipulated the sail.

The Shark People stood on the beach looking stunned. A few waved. Malink looked forlorn, Abo heartbroken.

"Thanks," Tuck shouted over the wave. "Thank you, Malink."

"You will come back." Malink said. It was not a question.

Tuck turned to look out to sea, then looked back to see the Shark People wading into the water after them. Behind them he saw a dark figure come out of the jungle.

There was no warning shot or demand to halt. Stripe came out onto the beach and opened up with the Uzi. Tuck pushed Sepie's head down under the edge of the gunwale just as a line of bullets stitched and splintered the wood. Kimi screamed and Tuck looked up to see a row of red geysers open in his back. He clung to one of the lines for a second, then fell into the sea.

Another scream, this one from Sarapul, the hideous screech of a raging lynx, and the old man went over the side. The gunfire stopped and Tuck risked popping his head up to look back to the beach. Stripe was slamming a new clip into the Uzi as he waded after the canoe. The Shark People had fled from the water and disappeared into the jungle or were cowering on the beach, unable to move.

With the sail loose, the canoe had swung around and was being carried by the tide toward the reef. They would miss the channel by only a few feet, but they would miss it and run aground on the reef. Tuck reached up to grab the steering oar just as Stripe let off another burst from the Uzi. At a hundred yards he was spraying a wide pattern, but Tuck heard a couple of bullets thunk into the side of the canoe.

The normally crystal water near the shore was clouded with the sand and silt thrown up by the Shark People's retreat, so Stripe did not see the dark shape moving through the water toward him. He wanted a shot. He set the Uzi to semiautomatic and unfolded the stock to take careful aim.

Tuck was standing now, leaning hard on the steering oar to bring the canoe around and through the channel. The outrigger scraped over the reef as the canoe approached broadside.

Stripe lined up the sights between Tuck's shoulder blades, held his breath, let it out, then squeezed the trigger.

Sarapul came out of the water like an angry marlin, spear-first. The metal point entered just under Stripe's chin and exited his skull at the crown, dragging brain and bone on its evil barb. As Stripe fell back, he emptied the clip into the sky.

The canoe slipped through the channel into the open ocean. Out on the horizon, a small cloud appeared and dropped a mercurial lightning bolt into the sea, followed a few seconds later by Kimi's thunder.

57

West with the Bat

The Sorcerer stood on the beach over the supine body of Yamata. The spear was still sticking out of the guard's skull like a gruesome note spindle waiting for a canceled receipt from the Reaper.

"How did this happen?" the Sorcerer asked.

Malink looked at his feet. The Sorcerer seemed more surprised than angry. A day had passed since Sarapul had killed Stripe, and Malink had waited in fear for the time when the Sorcerer would come looking for him. The other guards had torn the village apart looking for Tuck, and Malink had confessed that the pilot had left the island in an old canoe, but he had claimed ignorance of the whereabouts of the guard. Sarapul had been right. They should have pushed the body out to the edge of the reef for the sharks to eat. Actually, that had been Sarapul's second suggestion for the disposal of the body.

"It look like accident," Malink said. "Maybe he running and fall on his spear."

"I want the man who did this, Malink," the Sorcerer said.

"He is dead."

"The Filipino did this?"

Malink nodded. The other guards had found Kimi's body in the village, where the Shark People had been preparing it for burial.

"I don't think so. The Filipino took four bullets in the back. Whoever did this was very strong. Now you must tell me the truth or Vincent will be angry."

Malink was not afraid of Vincent's wrath. He only now realized that all the wrath his people had ever felt from Vincent had come by way of the Sorcerer and the Sky Priestess. He was afraid of the Sky Priestess.

"The American do this before he leave in the canoe. The guard shoot the girl-man and the American kill the guard."

"Why didn't you tell me about this before?"

"I am afraid Vincent will be angry."

"Where did they get a canoe? None of the Shark People know how to build a canoe."

"It was the girl-man. He know how. He build with Sarapul."

The Sorcerer balled his fists. "And Sarapul is gone too."

Malink nodded. "He sail away."

"Do you know where they were going?"

Malink shook his head. "No. Sarapul is banished. We no talk with him."

"Where's the guard's weapon?"

Malink shrugged.

The Sorcerer turned his back and began walking up the beach. "Have your people bury this man, Malink. Don't let the other guards see him. And be ready. The Sky Priestess will visit you soon."

Sarapul crawled out from some nearby ferns and stood at Malink's side, watching the Sorcerer walk away. "We should have eaten this guy," he said, kicking Yamata's body.

"This is very bad," Malink said.

"He killed my friend." Sarapul kicked the body again.

"The Sky Priestess will be very angry." Malink was, once again, feeling the weight of his position.

The old cannibal shrugged. "Can I have my spear back?"

Tuck knew that there was a way to use the hands of a watch in conjunction with the movement of the sun to determine direction, but since he wore a digital watch, it wouldn't have done him any good even if he knew the method, which he didn't. He guessed that Guam lay to the west, so he steered for the setting sun, spent the night guessing, and corrected his course to put the sun behind them at sunrise.

He did know how to sail. It was required knowledge for a kid growing up in a wealthy family near San Diego, but celestial navigation was a complete mystery. Sepie was no help at all. Even if she knew anything, she hadn't said a word since Kimi had been shot.

Tuck forced her to drink the water from a couple of green coconuts, but other than that, she had lain in the bow motionless for twenty-four hours.

He was now looking at his second sunset at sea. He corrected his course and realized that they must have been traveling north most of the day. How far, he couldn't guess. He steered southwest until the sun lay on the water like a glowing platter, hoping to correct some of the damage.

He really wished that Sepie would come around. He needed some sleep, and he needed some relief from his own thoughts. Thoughts of the Sky Priestess, of the Sorcerer, and of his dead friend Kimi. Despite the navigator's surly manner, he had been a good kid. Tuck, who had been brought up in relative luxury, couldn't imagine having endured the life that Kimi had lived. And the navigator had never given up. He had lived and died with courage. And he would still be alive if he hadn't met Tucker Case.

"Fuck!" Tuck said to no one. He wiped his eyes on his sleeve and squinted at the gunmetal waves.

There was a flapping noise up by the mast and Tuck adjusted the steering oar to catch the wind. The sail filled again, but the flapping continued for a second before it stopped.

Roberto caught the shroud line that was secured to the outrigger and did an upside-down swinging landing that left him looking to the back of the canoe.

Tuck couldn't have been happier if it had been an angel hanging from his shroud line.

"Roberto?"

"Yes," the bat said. He was speaking in his own voice, not Vincent's. The accent Filipino, not Manhattan.

Tuck almost burst out laughing. His mood swings were so rapid and wide now that he was afraid his sanity might be falling through the chasm. "I didn't recognize you without your glasses."

"I no like the light," Roberto said.

Tuck looked to Sepie, still lying in the bow. "Look, Sepie, it's Roberto." The girl did not stir.

"You are very sad about Kimi," Roberto said.

"Yes," Tuck said, "I am sad."

"He tell you he was great navigator and you no believe him."

Tuck looked away. Something about bats increases shame by a factor of ten.

"You are going the wrong way," the bat said. "Go that way."

He pointed with a wing claw. The wind caught his wing and nearly spun him off the shroud line. He braced himself with the other wing claw and pointed again. "I mean that way."

"You're shitting me," Tuck said.

"That way."

"That's north. I'm going to Guam. West."

"That's west. I am born on Guam."

"You're a bat."

"You ever see a lost bat?"

"No, but I've never seen a talking bat either."

"See?" Roberto said, as if he had made his point. "That way."

After all the evidence is in—after you've run all the facts by everything you know—and you're still lost, you have to do some things on faith. Tuck steered in the direction Roberto was pointing.

A few minutes later he looked up to see Vincent sitting on the pile of coconuts in the center of the canoe. "Good call, listening to the bat," Vincent said. "I just wanted you to know that the Shark People are going to build some ladders."

"Well, that's a useful bit of information," Tuck said.

"It will be," Vincent said. Then he disappeared.

58

Malink's Song

"They're flying the new pilot in tomorrow," said Sebastian Curtis. "I told them that Tucker wouldn't fly, so he had to be eliminated. They weren't happy about losing the heart and lungs."

Beth Curtis sat at her vanity, putting on her eye makeup for the appearance of the Sky Priestess. The red scarf was draped over the back of the chair. "Did you check the database? Maybe we can send another set of organs back with them. I can pick the chosen tonight and keep them in the clinic until tomorrow morning."

"The customer already died," Curtis said.

"Well, I guess he really was sick, then." She laughed, a girlish laugh full of music.

Sebastian loved her laugh. He smiled over her shoulder into the mirror. "I'm glad you're not concerned about Tucker Case. I understand, Beth. Really. I was just jealous."

"Tucker who? Oh, you mean Tucker dead-at-sea Case? 'Bastian, dear, I did what I did for us. I thought it would keep him under control. Write it off as one of life's little missteps. Besides, if he's not dead now, he will be in a day or so."

"He made it here on the open ocean. Through a typhoon."

"And with the navigator. Remember, I've seen him fly. He's dead. That old cannibal is probably munching on his bones right now." She checked her lipstick and winked at him in the mirror. "Showtime, darling."

➤

Malink trudged through the jungle, his shoulders aching from the basket of food he was carrying. Each day he had been taking food to Sarapul's hiding place. It was not that he didn't trust his people, but he did not want to burden any of them with such a weighty secret. The last of them to see the cannibal saw him covered with blood, gasping in the sand. Malink had told them that Sarapul was dead and that Malink had given his body to the sharks. A chief had to carry many secrets, and sometimes he had to lie to his people to spare them pain.

After the third day, Malink was ready to let the cannibal go back to his house on the far side of the island. The guards were no longer searching, and the Sorcerer had stopped asking questions. Perhaps things would go back to the way they were. But maybe that wasn't right either. Malink didn't want to, but he believed the pilot. The Sky Priestess and the Sorcerer were going to hurt his people. He was too old for this. He was too old to fight. And how do you fight machine guns with spears and machetes?

He paused by a giant mahogany tree and put the basket down while he caught his breath. He saw smoke drifting in streams over the ferns and looked in the direction it was coming from. Someone was there, obscured by a tall stand of taro leaves as big as elephant ears.

There was a rustling there. Malink crouched.

"You're not scared, are you, squirt?"

Malink recognized the voice from his childhood and he wasn't scared. But he knew he didn't have to say so. "I am not a squirt. I am old man now."

Vincent swaggered out of the taro. His flight suit and bomber jacket looked exactly as Malink remembered. "You're always gonna be a squirt, kid. You still got that lighter I gave you?"

Malink nodded.

"That was my lucky Zippo, kid. I shoulda hung on to it. Fuck it. Spilt milk." Vincent waved his cigarette in dismissal. "Look, I need you to build some ladders. You know what a ladder is, right?"

"Yes," Malink said.

"Of course you do, smart kid like you. So I am needing you to build, oh, say six ladders, thirty feet long, strong and light. Use bamboo. Are you getting this, kid?"

Malink nodded. He was grinning from ear to ear. Vincent was speaking to him again.

"You're talkin' my ear off, kid. So, anyway, I need you to build these ladders, see, as I am having big plans for you and the Shark People. Large plans, kid. Hugely large. I'm talking about substantial fuckin' plans I am having. Okay?"

Malink nodded.

"Good, build the ladders and stand by for further orders." The flyer began to back away into the taro patch.

"You said you would come back," Malink said. "You said you would come back and bring cargo."

"You don't look like you been shorted on the feedbag, kid. You got your cargo in spades."

"You said you would come back."

Vincent threw up his hands. "So what the fuck's this? Western Union? Don't go screwy on me, kid. I need you." The pilot started to fade, going as translucent as his cigarette smoke.

Malink stepped forward. "The Sky Priestess will tell us orders?"

"The Sky Priestess took a powder fifty years ago, kid. This dame doing the bump and grind on my runway is paste."

"Paste?"

"She's a fake, squirt. A boneable feast to be sure, but she's running a game on you."

"She is not Sky Priestess?"

"No, but don't piss her off." With that the pilot faded to nothing.

Malink leaned back against the mahogany tree and looked up through the canopy to the sky. His skin tingled and his breath was coming easy and deep. The ache in his knees was gone. He was light and strong and full, and every birdcall or rustle of leaves or distant crash of a wave seemed part of a great and wonderful song.

~~~~~~

59

Call in the Cavalry

They had missed Guam and Saipan (passing at night) and all the Northern Mariana Islands (drifting in fog) and Johnston Island and all ships at sea (no reason, they just missed). The sunscreen had run out on the seventh day. The drinking coconuts ran out on the fourteenth.

They still had some shark meat that had been smoked and dried, but Tuck couldn't choke down a bite of it without water. They had had nothing to drink for a full day.

They were at sea for three days before Sepie came out of her catatonia, and after a day of sobbing, she started to talk.

"I miss him," she said. "He listen to me. He like me even when I am being mean."

"Me too. I treated him badly sometimes too. He was a good guy. A good friend."

"He love you very much," Sepie said. She was crying again.

Tuck looked down, shielding his face so she couldn't see his eyes. "I'm sorry, Sepie. I know you loved him. I didn't mean to put him in danger. I didn't mean to put *you* in danger."

She crawled to his end of the canoe and into his arms. He held her there for a long time, rocking her until she stopped crying. He said, "You'll be okay."

"Kimi say he would sail me to America someday. You will take me?"

"Sure. You'll like it there."

"Tell me," she said.

She grilled Tuck about all things American, making him explain everything from television to tampons. Tuck learned about men, about how simple they were, about how easily they could be manipulated, about how good they could make a woman feel when they were nice, and how much they could hurt a woman by dying. Telling the things that they knew made them each feel smart, and sharing the duties of sailing the boat made them feel safe. It was easier to live in the little world inside the canoe rather than face the vast emptiness of the open ocean. Sepie took to curling into Tuck's chest and sleeping while he steered. Twice Tuck fell asleep in her arms and no one steered the boat for hours. Tuck didn't let it bother him. He had accepted that they were going to die. It seemed so easy now that he wondered why he'd made such an effort to escape it on the island.

Roberto hadn't spoken since the first night. He hung from the lines and pointed with a wing claw when Tuck called to him. When Tuck was still reckoning, he reckoned that they were traveling at an average speed of five knots. At five knots, twenty-four hours a day, for fourteen days, he reckoned that they had traveled well over two thousand miles. Tuck reckoned that they were now sailing though downtown Sacramento. His reckoning wasn't any better than his navigation.

On the fifteenth day Roberto took flight and Tuck watched him until he was nothing but a dot on the horizon, then nothing at all. Tuck didn't blame him. He accepted his own death, but he didn't want to watch Sepie go before him. At sunset he tied off the steering oar, took Sepie in his arms, and lay down in the bottom of the boat to wait.

Sometime later—he couldn't tell how long, but it was still dark—he woke with a parched scream when a tube of mascara dropped out of the sky and hit him in the chest. Sepie sat up and snatched the tube from the bottom of the boat.

"To make you pretty," she said. Her voice cracked on "pretty."

Tuck was too disoriented to recognize what she was holding. He took it from her and squinted at it. "It's mascara."

"Roberto," Sepie said.

Tuck looked around in the sky, but didn't see the bat. It was beginning to get light. "You brought us mascara? We're dying of thirst and you brought us mascara?"

"Kimi teach him," Sepie said.

Tuck didn't think he had the energy left for outrage, but it was coming nonetheless. "You . . ."

Sepie put a finger to his lips. "Listen."

Tuck listened. He heard nothing. "What?"

"Surf."

Tuck listened. He heard it. He also heard something else, a rhythmic stirring in the water much closer to the canoe. He looked in the direction of the noise and saw something moving over the water toward them.

"Aloha!" came out of the dark, followed by a middle-aged white man in an ocean kayak. "I guess I'm not the only one who likes to get out early," he said.

In their first hour at the Waikiki Beach Hyatt Regency, Sepie flushed the toilet seventy-eight times and consumed two hundred and forty dollars' worth of product from the minibar (five Pepsis and a box of Raisinets).

"You poop in here and it just goes away?"

"Yes."

"In this big bowl?" She pointed.

"Yes."

"You poop?"

"Yes."

"And you push this?"

"Yes."

"And it goes away?"

"That's right."

"Where?"

"To the next room." Plumbing. They hadn't talked about plumbing.

"And they push this and it goes away?"

"Look, Sepie, there's a TV in here. You push this and it changes the picture."

Tuck couldn't be sure because they'd never had sex and because she'd told him about how she could fool a man, but he thought she might have come right then.

He made her promise not to leave the room and left her there flushing and clicking while he went to the police.

The desk sergeant at the Honolulu police department listened patiently and politely and with appropriate concern right up until Tuck said, "I know I look a little ratty, but I've been at sea in an open boat for two weeks." At which point the sergeant held up his hand signifying it was his turn to talk.

"You've been at sea for two weeks?"

"Yes. I escaped by boat."

"So how long ago did these alleged murders happen?"

"I don't know exactly. One about a month ago, one longer."

"And you're just getting around to reporting them now?"

"I told you. I was trapped on Alualu. I escaped in a sailing canoe."

"Then," the sergeant said, "Alualu is not a street in Honolulu."

"No. It's an island in Micronesia."

"I can't help you, sir. That's out of our jurisdiction."

"Well, who can help me?"

"Try the FBI."

So Tuck, on the cab ride to the FBI offices, changed his strategy. He'd wait until he got past the front line of defense before spilling his guts. The receptionist was a petite Asian woman of forty who spoke English so precisely that Tuck knew it had to be her second language.

"I'm sure I can help you if you will just tell me what it is that you'd like to report."

"I can't. I have to talk to an agent. I won't be comfortable unless I talk to a real agent."

She looked offended and her speech became even crisper. "Perhaps you can tell me the nature of the crime."

Tuck thought for a moment. What did the FBI always handle on television? Al Capone, Klansmen, bank robberies, and . . . "Kidnapping," he said. "There's been a kidnapping."

"And who has been kidnapped? Have you filed a missing persons report with the local police?"

Tuck shook his head and stood his ground. "I'll tell an agent."

The receptionist picked up the phone and punched a number. She turned away from him and covered her mouth with her hand as she spoke into the mouthpiece. She hung up and said, "There's an agent on his way."

"Thanks," Tuck said.

A few minutes later a door opened and a dark-haired guy who looked like a mobile mannequin from a Brooks Brothers window display entered the reception room and extended his hand to Tuck. "Mr. Case, I'm Special Agent Tom Myers. Would you step into my office, please?"

Tuck shook his hand and followed him though the door and down a hallway of identical ten-by-twelve offices with identical metal desks that displayed identical photos of identical families in identical dime-store frames. Myers motioned for Tuck to sit and took the seat behind the desk.

"Now, Rose tells me that you want to report a kidnapping?" Special Agent Myers unbuttoned the top button of his shirt.

"You allowed to do that?" Tuck asked.

"Casual Fridays," the special agent said.

"Oh," Tuck said. "Yes. Kidnapping, multiple murder, and the theft and sale of human organs for transplant."

Myers showed no reaction. "Go on."

And Tuck did. He began with the offer of the job on Alualu and ended with his arrival in Hawaii, leaving out the crash of Mary Jean's jet, the subsequent loss of his pilot's license and pending criminal charges, anything to do with cargo cults, cannibals, transvestites, ghost pilots, talking bats, and genital injuries. As he wrapped up, he thought the edited version sounded pretty credible.

Special Agent Myers had not changed position or expression once in the half hour that Tuck had talked. Tuck thought he saw him blink once, though. Special Agent Myers leaned back in his chair (casual Fridays) and templed his fingers. "Let me ask you something," he said.

"Sure," Tuck said.

"Are you the Tucker Case that got drunk and crashed the pink jet in Seattle a few months ago?"

Tuck could have slapped him. "Yes, but that doesn't have anything to do with this."

"I think it does, Mr. Case. I think it affects the credibility of what is already an incredible story. I think you should leave my office and go about the business of putting your life in order."

"I'm telling you the truth," Tuck said. He was fighting panic. He worked to stay calm. "Why would I make up a story like that? As you pointed out, I've got enough on my plate just rebuilding my life. I'm not so stupid that I'd add charges for filing a false crime report to all the others. If you have to take me into custody, do it. But do something about what's going on out on that island or a lot more people are going to die."

"Even if I believed your story, what would you like me to do?"

And there Tuck lost it. " 'Special agent.' Does that mean that you had to take the little bus to the academy?"

"I was at the top of my class." A rise.

"Then act like it."

"What do you want, Mr. Case?"

Tuck jumped up and leaned over the desk. Special Agent Myers rolled back in his chair.

"I want you to stop them. I want covert action and deadly technology. I want Navy SEALS and snipers and spies and laser-guided smart stealth gizmos out the ying-yang. I want surgical strikes and satellite views and a steaming shitload of every sort of Tom Clancy geegaw you got. I want fucking Jack Ryan, James Bond, and a half-dozen Van Damme motherfuckers who can jump through their own asses and rip your heart out while it's still beating. I want action, Special Agent Myers. This is evil shit."

"Sit down, Mr. Case."

Tuck sat down. His energy was gone. "Look, I'm giving myself up. Arrest me, throw me in jail, beat me with a rubber hose, do whatever you want to do, but stop what's going on out there."

Special Agent Myers smiled. "I don't believe a word you've told me, but even if I did, even if you had evidence of what you're claiming, I still couldn't do anything. The FBI can only act on domestic matters."

"Then tell someone who handles international matters."

"The CIA only handles matters that affect national security, and frankly, I wouldn't embarrass myself by calling them."

"Fuck it, then. Take me away." Tuck held out his arms to receive handcuffs.

"Go back to your hotel and get some rest, Mr. Case. There are no outstanding warrants for your arrest."

"There aren't?" Tuck felt as if he'd been gut-punched.

"I checked the computer before I brought you in here." Myers stood. "I'll show you out."

After another cab ride and another truncated telling of his story, Tuck was also shown out of the Japanese embassy. He found a pay phone and soon he had been hung up on by both the American Medical Association and the Council of Methodist Missionaries. He found Sepie curled up on the king-size bed, the television still blaring in the bathroom, three minibottles of vodka empty on the floor. Tuck considered raiding the minibar himself, but when he opened it, he opted for a grapefruit juice instead of gin. Getting hammered wasn't going to take the edge off this time, and at this rate, the money he'd left on deposit at the desk in lieu of a credit card—the money that Sarapul had found in Tuck's pack—would run out in two days.

He sat down on the bed and stroked Sepie's hair. She had put on mascara while he was out and had made a mess of it. Funny, she'd walked into the hotel wearing one of Tuck's shirts—the first time she'd worn a top in her life—looking very much the little girl and now she had on makeup and was passed out drunk. Tuck had a feeling that coming to America was not going to be easy on either of them. He kissed her on the forehead and she moaned and rolled over. "Perfume tomorrow," she said. "You get me some, okay?"

"Okay," Tuck said. "A woman who smells good is a woman who feels good." The phrase rattled off the walls of his brain. He snatched up the phone and punched up information. When the operator came on, he said, "Houston, area code 713 . . ."

60

Meanwhile, Back at the Ranch

Mary Jean sat behind a desk fashioned entirely of rose quartz veined with fool's gold and stared out the window at the Houston skyline. A brown haze had risen to the level of her fiftieth-floor office as the exhaust of a million cars huddled against the stratosphere and curled around the city like a huge rusty cat looking for a place to nap. It just made her mad as a cowpoke wearing bob-wire pants, but not mad enough, of course, to sell her shares of GM and Exxon. Blue chips was blue chips, after all, and the great state of Texas ran on oil.

The intercom beeped and Mary Jean keyed her speakerphone, not because she needed her hands free to work, but because the phone receiver either got caught in her hairdo or her clip-ons rattled against it making all sorts of distracting racket. There'd been a time, before Prozac, when she'd thought for six months that the FBI was tapping her phone line, only to find out it was a pair of twenty-carat ruby cluster earrings banging against the earpiece.

"Yes, Melanie."

"Tucker Case on the phone, Mary Jean. He's been calling all day. I've tried to put him off, but he says that people are going to die if you don't talk to him."

"Does he sound drunk?"

"No, Ma'am. He sounds serious."

Mary Jean took a deep breath and looked up at the Monet hanging on the far wall. Twenty million dollars, depreciated as office furnishings, appreciated to twice its value and donated to a museum as a donation write-off at full value, with no capital gains, and there it would hang until the day of her death when it would go to the museum. And it also matched the couch.

"Put him through," she said.

"Mary Jean, it's Tucker."

"I was just thinking of you. How are you, sweetie?"

"Mary Jean, I'm stone sober and I need you to listen."

"Go on, Tucker. I got more ears than a cornfield in June."

"First, I know that there were never any criminal charges filed, and I don't blame you for trying to get me out of the way. But I could really use some help."

Mary Jean blanched. "Can you hold one second, darlin? Thanks." She pushed the hold button and then the intercom. "Melanie, dear, would you mind bringing me a couple of number five Valiums and a little glass of juice? Thank you." She clicked back to Tuck. "Go on, honey."

And Tuck did, for fifteen minutes, and when he finished, Mary Jean said, "Well, that's just not right. That's just terrible."

"Yes, it is, Mary Jean."

"We just can't have that," she said. "You give Melanie your number there. I'll see what I can do."

"Mary Jean, I really appreciate this. If I could go to anyone else, I would."

"And hurt my feelings? No, you wouldn't. Tucker Case, I've been selling the power to change yourself for forty years. Now, if I don't believe in the power of redemption, then I'm guilty of false advertising, aren't I? You sit tight, now. Bye."

She clicked the intercom. "Melanie, get me Jake Skye on the line, please. Thank you, dear."

~~~~~~

61

Roundhouse Aloha

Tuck stood at the arrival gate amid a group of Hawaiian college students wearing grass skirts and sarongs and festooned with leis they were draping on tourists as they came out of the tunnel from the 747. Tuck spotted Jake Skye well before he came out of the tunnel. He was a head taller than most of the tourists and one of the few who had a tan. Tuck waved to him and Jake tossed his head to show he'd seen him. He came out grinning with his hand extended.

Tuck smiled and hit Jake with a roundhouse to the jaw that knocked him back into a group of pseudo hula girls. Jake apologized to the girls and rubbed his jaw as he turned to Tuck.

"We done?"

"I guess so," Tucker said. He knew that Jake would never apologize for selling him out.

Jake fell in beside Tuck and they walked through the terminal. "I didn't see that coming. You've changed, buddy."

"I guess so," said Tuck. "Thanks for coming."

"I'm just here to take you home." Jake pulled two airline ticket folders out of his shirt pocket. "Mary Jean says you can bring your new girlfriend."

"I'm not going home, Jake."

"You're not?"

"No. I need your help, but I'm not going back to Houston."

"There's a stop in San Francisco. You can get off there."

"No. I've got some things I need to do."

"Buy me a drink." Jake turned and walked into an open cocktail lounge where a twenty-foot waterfall fell over black lava rock among a forest of bromeliads and orchids. "Cool airport," Jake said, pulling a stool up to the bar. "You ever think about living in the tropics?"

Tuck whipped around on his stool and Jake held up his hands in surrender.

"Just kidding. Okay, what's the story?"

This time Tuck told the story leaving out none of the details, and to his credit, Jake did not call him crazy at the end. "So what do you think you can do?"

"Well, first, I thought you could hack the doctor's computer and erase the database. It might slow up the process if he has to do all the tissue types again."

Jake was shaking his head, "Can't do it, buddy. Even if I wanted to."

"Why not? I've got the password."

Jake drained off the last of his third Mai Tai. "He's on a satellite uplink net. The connection only goes two ways if he wants it to. I won't be able to get in. Besides, it's not in the mission parameters. I'm supposed to come here, get you, and take you home. Period."

Tuck dug a slip of paper from his back pocket and unfolded it. "I've got these. Maybe they can help."

Jake was still shaking his head, but he stopped when he saw the numbers written on the paper. "Where did you get those numbers?"

"They were on the bottom of a desk drawer in Curtis's clinic."

"They're not computer codes, Tuck. You see those letters at the end? BSI? You know what that is?"

Tuck shook his head.

"Banc Suisse Italiano. Those are Swiss bank account numbers." Jake tried to snatch the paper and Tuck pulled it out of his reach.

"You willing to expand the mission parameters?" Tuck said.

Jake was staring at the paper in Tuck's hand. "How much?"

"Half."

Jake scratched his three-day growth of beard. "And they were getting how much per kidney?"

"Half a mil."

Jake cringed, then relaxed and put his hand on Tuck's shoulder. "What did you have in mind, partner?"

"I want to get the Shark People off the island."

"How many? Three hundred and change? Hire a ship."

"I want to go sooner. I want to fly them off."

Jake smiled. The wheels were working now. "It's going to take a big plane: 747 or L-1011. That island got enough runway for something that size?''

"Can we get something that size?''

"Not legally," Jake said.

"I'm not worried about legally. I'm worried about logistically.''

Jake stood up. "I'm not flying it. I get you a plane, I get half. Deal?''

"I'll give you one of the account numbers as soon as we get the plane. You take your chances whether there's money in it or not. If I don't make it, and the money's in my account, you're screwed.''

Jake considered it, then nodded. "I can live with that. Let's go watch the big planes take off.''

Tuck was amazed at the way Jake's mind worked. The second he'd accepted that they were going to steal a 747, it became a problem, and when it came to solving problems, Jake was the best. They stood on an open walkway that overlooked the tarmac, watching the 747s taxiing into the terminal.

"The best thing," Jake said, "about stealing a 747 is that no one assumes that anyone is crazy enough to try it.''

"I thought people tried to steal them all the time. It's a league sport in the Middle East, isn't it?''

"They hijack, they don't steal. With hijacking, you have to take a pilot with you.'' Jake pointed to a row of planes docked at the terminal by rolling walkways. "These guys? Out of the question,'' he said.

"Why?''

"Because they've just come in and they're low on fuel or they're being fueled to take off again, and most of the time, if you can get in them, there's a crew on board.'' He pointed to some jets parked near hangars at the far side of the airfield. "Those are our babies. They've got fuel, but they're waiting for a crew and passengers. After midnight nothing goes out of this airport except FedEx. The advantage of a vacation destination. Nobody wants to fly in or out at night.''

The planes were a good half a mile away. "That's a long way to go across an airfield without the tower seeing us and calling security. And we have to drive a ramp over to it to get inside.''

"No, we don't. There's an emergency escape hatch for the pilots in the roof over the cockpit."

"That's four stories up. How are you going to get up to it?"

"Down to it," Jake said.

"Down?"

"The problem is how to get the hatch unlatched. They only open from the inside."

"I'm still a little unclear on the 'down' part of the plan," Tuck said. At some point he was going to be on top of a 747 and heights made him nervous.

"Let me worry about that," Jake said. Then he snapped his fingers as if conjuring the answer to his problem out of thin air. "I've got the answer right here in front of me. What was I thinking? I'm working with the master."

Tuck looked around, thinking that Jake was talking about someone else. "Are you talking about me? I don't know how to do anything."

"But you're wrong, Tuck, you're wrong. For this part of the plan we need the cooperation of a flight attendant. Come on, let's get my bag. I've got an extra change of clothes you can wear."

"What's wrong with these clothes?" Tuck asked. He was still wearing the oversized and now distressed hand-me-downs of Sebastian Curtis.

"Like you have to ask."

Jake spent an hour studying flight schedules and talking to counter people at the different airlines. Tuck took the opportunity to call the hotel to check on Sepie. She answered on the second ring. "Hello. How much is washer-dryer combination?"

"What?"

"Maytag washer-dryer combination with minibasket and wrinkle guard. How much?"

"I don't know. Maybe a grand. Are you okay?"

She'd put the phone down and he heard her shouting at the TV, "Is a grand! Is a grand! You fuckin' mook! Oh, no." She picked up the phone again. "You wrong. Is eleven nine nine suggested retail. You lose."

"You're watching 'The Price Is Right'?"

"They give you things if you know how much. Is very hard."

"Do you need anything?" Tuck asked. "I can call room service from here and have them bring you some food."

"Perfume and lipstick," Sepie said.

"That'll have to wait. I'll be back soon, okay?"

"Okay. Tuck?"

"What, Sepie?"

"What is washer-dryer combination?"

"I'll explain later. I have to go now."

She hung up on him. Evidently, her fascination with plumbing and television didn't extend to the telephone. He found Jake talking to a girl at the United counter who was obviously taken with the grungy pilot's charm. He saw Tuck and said good-bye.

"I've found our plane and the crew assignments. We have a ten-minute window to get to Gate 38 so you can work your magic."

The plan was for Tuck to spot a flight attendant coming off the plane, get to know her, and convince her to go back into the jet and throw the latch on the emergency hatch before the plane was cleaned and moved away from the terminal. They waited at the tunnel into Gate 38. The passengers had long since deplaned, as had the pilots.

"Remember, you want to go ugly," Jake said.

"I know," Tuck said. He'd changed into Jake's clothes, which fit him, at least, even if he looked like a guitar player for a Seattle grunge band.

"And old if you can get it."

"I know," Tuck said.

"You want a woman who looks like she couldn't get laid in a men's colony."

"I know," Tuck said. "Would you back off? I haven't done this in a while."

"Like riding a bicycle, buddy."

The first flight attendant out of the tunnel was a pretty blond woman, about twenty-five. "Pass," Jake said.

The next was a man, and the next a tall black woman who could have been a runway model.

"They're killing us here," Jake said. "How would you feel about going for the guy? He's our best chance so far."

"Fuck off, Jake."

"Just an idea."

They waited for five more minutes before a tired-looking woman in her fifties came down the tunnel pulling her flight bag behind her.

"Go to it, stud," Jake said. He gave Tucker a little shove.

Tuck shoved back without taking his eyes off the woman. "I can't do this, Jake."

"What?" Jake Skye grabbed Tuck's wrist and pretended to be taking his pulse.

Tuck pulled away from him. "I can't do this."

"Don't pull this shit on me, buddy. She's getting away. This is what you do."

"Not anymore, I don't."

"Well, I sure as hell do." Jake pulled off the flannel shirt he was wearing open over his black T-shirt and threw it to Tuck. "Go back to your hotel and wait for me to call. What room are you in?"

"Twelve-thirty."

Jake pushed the T-shirt sleeves up just enough for his biceps to show and took off down the concourse after the middle-aged flight attendant.

Tuck went outside and found the shuttle to the Hyatt Regency. During the ride back to the hotel, he realized that he had no idea how to explain a washer-dryer combination to someone who had never worn shoes or a shirt until two days ago. He decided to go with magic.

~~~~~~

62

Like Clockwork Spies

Malink found the old cannibal in a small clearing in the jungle, urinating on a young banana tree. "I brought you food." Malink dropped the basket and sat down under a tree. Sarapul seemed to be taking a long time at his task.

"Sometimes it's hard," Malink said.

"Sometimes I can't go at all," Sarapul said. "It hurts." He shuddered and turned around with a grin, smoothing down his *thu*. "But not today." He sat down next to Malink and reached into the basket for a hunk of fish.

"I heard the music last night," Sarapul said. "The white bitch comes more often now." He offered Malink a piece of fish and the chief took it.

"There are three chosen in only ten days. I think they won't come back sometimes. Vincent says that she is not the Sky Priestess. The pilot said she will kill us."

"Then we must fight."

"Knives against guns? You remember the war."

"I remember. Come." He got up and led Malink through the underbrush to a hollow log. He reached in and pulled out a long bundle wrapped in oiled sharkskin. "A man must take the strength of his enemies. If he cannot eat him and take his strength, he must take his weapon."

Sarapul unwrapped the bundle to reveal a World War II vintage Japanese bolt-action rifle. He had obviously been visiting this spot because the rifle was covered with a thin coat of fish oil and gleamed like new. "I cut off his head and took his gun."

Malink remembered the wrath of the Japanese on his people

after the soldier disappeared. "You did that? You were the one?"

"It was a long time ago," Sarapul said. He reached into the bundle again and pulled out three shining cartridges. "But I saved these."

"They have machine guns," Malink said.

"She doesn't."

The call came a little after midnight. Tuck had slept since he got to the hotel, stuffing toilet paper in his ears to block out the noise of the television and Sepie talking back to it.

"Take a cab to general aviation at the airport," Jake said. "The hangar you want says Island Adventures on the side. I'll be waiting."

Tuck climbed out of bed and turned off the television.

"Hey," Sepie said. She was sitting cross-legged on the floor about a foot from the screen. Tuck crouched and took her face in his hands. "Tomorrow at six you take the tickets and go downstairs. Tell the man at the desk you want to go to the airport. The bus will take you."

"I know this," she said.

"Just listen. A tall man with long hair will be there."

"Right. Jake," Sepie said. "I know this."

"If he's not there, go to one of the men in the blue hats and tell him you need help getting on your plane. He'll help you. When you get to Houston, go into the airport and call this number. Tell the woman who answers that I told you to call. She'll help you."

"And you will come and get me soon, right?"

"I'll try."

"What about Roberto?"

They hadn't seen the fruit bat since the mascara bombing. "Roberto will be fine. He'll live here, but I have to go." He kissed her on the forehead and before he could pull away she wrapped her arms around his neck and kissed him on the lips so hard he thought he might have cut his lip.

"You come get me."

"I will."

He stood and went out the door. A few seconds later he heard Sepie call to him from down the hall. "Hey!"

Tuck turned.

"How come you don't try to sex me?"

"I will."

"Okay," she said, and she went back into the room.

Jake was waiting for him at the Island Adventures hangar. A Hughes 500 helicopter with its doors removed sat on a pad by the hangar. "I rented it for an hour. I fuck it up and we owe Mary Jean five grand for the deposit."

Tuck looked at the helicopter sitting on the pad like a huge black dragonfly and he began to get a very bad feeling. "You don't want me to do what I think you want me to do, do you?"

"I'll put the skid right over the hatch. You just step out of one aircraft onto another. No problem. It can't be half as bad as what I had to do to get the hatch left open."

Tuck began to protest, but Jake was already walking to the helicopter. Tuck climbed into the helicopter and slipped on the headset. Jake threw the switches and the turbine began to whine. In a few seconds the blades slowly began to rotate.

Tuck keyed the intercom mike on his headset so Jake could hear him over the blades. "You'll never get past the tower."

"I've done it before," Jake said. "I had to repo a Jet Ranger for a guy once."

"They'll never clear you."

"There's no traffic. Besides, you think they're going to clear you? It's Captain Midnight's rock 'n' roll express from here on out, big guy."

Jake pulled the collective lever by the side of his seat and the helicopter lifted into the air. Within seconds, Tuck heard the tower jabbering over the radio, warning the Hughes 500 to wait for clearance. Jake brought the helicopter up just high enough to clear the top of the hangar and flew in a low wide circle around the airport, then began his own jabber.

"Honolulu Tower, this is Helicopter One, approaching from the west on Runway Two. I have a problem with my tail rotor. Requesting emergency landing."

The tower came back: "Helicopter One, didn't you just take off without clearance?"

"Negative, Tower. I'm in from Maui. Request emergency clearance."

Of course, Tuck thought. Jake flew the circle below the radar and without the running lights. They have no idea whether this is the same helicopter that just took off.

Jake sent the helicopter into a horizontal spin that moved it closer to the planes by the hangars with every rotation, just as it moved Tuck closer to throwing up. Jake stopped the spin for a second and nodded toward a United 747. "That's your baby. Get out of your harness and get ready. They won't know you're there. Get inside and wait two hours before you start your taxi. I don't want them to connect the helicopter with the jet. By the way, how're you going to get your natives on board?"

"They've got ladders," Tuck said. "I hope." Tuck hung his headset behind the seat and unsnapped his harness just as Jake resumed his spin. Tuck grabbed on to the seat to keep from being thrown out the open door. What looked like an out-of-control aircraft was, in fact, a pretty elementary move called a pedal turn. Tuck found no comfort in that knowledge as he watched the tarmac spin below.

Jake pulled the helicopter up just in time to miss the tail of the 747, then leveled it off and crept forward along the length of the huge aircraft. The tail would obscure the view from the tower. "You ready?" he shouted.

Tuck shook his head violently. He could see the line of the hatch he was supposed to go through. He stepped out on the skid. Jake brought the helicopter down and the skid touched the top of the jet. "Now!"

Tuck stepped off onto the plane and ducked instinctively below the blades. He looked back at Jake, shrugged, and shouted, "That was easy."

"I told you," Jake shouted. He pulled the helicopter into the sky and started his spin toward the Island Adventures pad.

Tuck got on his knees, dug his fingers into the seal around the hatch, and pulled it open. He jumped into the dark plane, sealed the hatch behind him, then sat in the pilot's seat and began to study the controls. He clicked on the nav computer and punched in the longitude and latitude for Alualu, which he knew by heart, then pulled a piece of paper from his pocket and put in the coordinates for his second destination. He put on a headset and turned on the radios. The frequency was already set for the Honolulu tower. Jake was receiving the official FAA ass-chewing of the century, but there wasn't a word about anyone dropping to the top of a United jet. He had just taken off the headset to settle down for the wait when he heard a scratching sound outside the escape hatch. He opened it and Roberto plopped inside.

63

No Frills

The Sky Priestess was drunk. She and the Sorcerer had made two million dollars in the last ten days and she couldn't even buy a pair of shoes. The new pilot, Nomura, was a heavily tattooed, taciturn prick who spoke marginal English and looked at her like he'd rape her in a second, not for the pleasure of the violence, but to put her in her place. Since his arrival, even the ninjas had started to get cocky, joking in Japanese and laughing raucously when her back was turned. Even the Shark People seemed to be losing their fear of her. The last time she had appeared to them the children were left in the village. So the Sky Priestess was watching television in a torn T-shirt and some sweatpants and she was drunk.

The intercom beeped and she let it. If it hadn't run on batteries, she would have unplugged it. Instead, she threw it through the french doors, where it beeped the beach for two more minutes, then stopped. The next time she saw it Sebastian was standing in the door holding it like a prosecutor exhibiting a murder weapon to the jury.

"I suppose you think this is funny."

"Not particularly. Now if it had hit you in the head, that would be funny."

"We have an order, Beth. A kidney."

"Oh, good. I'm in great shape to assist a surgery. Let's do both kidneys. Give the buyer a bonus. What do you say?" She sloshed her tumbler of vodka.

Sebastian picked up the empty Absolut bottle from the end table. "This isn't going to work, Beth. You can't appear as the Sky Priestess like that." He seemed more afraid than angry.

"You are absolutely correct, 'Bastian. The goddess has taken the night off."

Sebastian paced back and forth in front of her, rubbing his chin. "We could stall. We could put you on some oxygen and amphetamines and you could be ready in an hour."

She laughed. "And ruin this buzz? I don't think so. Tell them to find another source for this one."

He shook his head. "I don't think I can do that. Nomura's been on the phone with them. He told them we could deliver in six hours."

She hissed. "Nomura's a fucking grunt. He does what we say. This is our operation."

"I'm not so sure, Beth. I really don't want to tell him no. Please take a shower and make some coffee. I'll be back in a minute with an oxygen cylinder."

"No, 'Bastian," she whined. "I don't want to spend six hours in a plane with that asshole."

"You won't have to, Beth. They've requested that we send him alone this time."

She sat up. "Alone? Who's going to watch him?" Suddenly she felt very sober.

"No one needs to watch him, Beth. He works for them, remember? You were right. We shouldn't have gotten a pilot from them."

An hour and forty minutes after he dropped through the hatch, Tuck started the procedure to power up the 747. He'd never actually flown anything this big—or anything nearly this big—but he had done twenty hours in a simulator in Dallas and only crashed twice. All planes fly the same, he told himself and he started the first engine. Once it had spooled up, he had the power to start the other three. He put on the headset and looked out the side window to make sure he had room to turn the plane and taxi it to the runway. As soon as it started moving, the tower began to chatter, trying first to get him to identify himself, then to stop. Roberto, who was hanging from the straps on the flight officer's seat beside Tuck, barked twice and let loose a high-pitched squeal.

"You're cookin' with gas, buddy," came over the radio. Jake was close enough to see the big jet.

"Where are you, Jake?"

"Out of the way, buddy, but thanks for using my name on the radio. Just thought you ought to know that you're going to need fifty-one hundred feet of runway to get that thing off the ground at your destination—and that's with full flaps, so save your fuel now. You'd better tell them what you're doing unless you've got collision insurance on that thing."

Tuck keyed the mike button on the steering yoke. "Honolulu Tower, this is United Flight One requesting immediate clearance for emergency takeoff on Runway Two."

"There's no such thing as an emergency takeoff," the controller said. Tuck could tell he was close to losing it.

"Well, Tower, I'm taking off on Two, and if you've got anything headed that way, I'd say you've got an emergency on your hands, wouldn't you?"

The tower guy was almost screaming now. "Negative on the clearance! Clearance denied, United jet. Return to the terminal. We have no flight plan for a United Flight One."

"Tower, United Flight One requesting you chill and be a professional about this. Clear to ten thousand. I am starting my takeoff."

"Negative, negative. Identify yourself . . ."

"This is Captain Roberto T. Fruitbat signing off, Honolulu Tower." Tuck clicked off the radio, pushed the throttles up, and watched the jet exhaust pressure gauges. When they got to 80 percent of maximum thrust, he released the ground brakes and one hundred and seventy thousand pounds of aircraft rolled down the runway and swept into the sky.

At ten thousand feet he began his turn toward Alualu.

The fighters joined him a hundred miles north of Guam. Evidently, they had found out that United did not employ a Captain Fruitbat. One of the F-18 fighters came in close and Tuck waved to him. The pilot signaled for Tuck to put on his headset. Why not?

Tuck assumed they would be broadcasting across a number of frequencies. "Yo, good morning, gents," Tuck said.

"United 747, change your course and land at Guam Airport or we will force you down."

Tuck looked out the window at the sidewinder air to air missiles hanging menacingly under the wings of the fighter. "And how, exactly, do you propose to do that, gentlemen?"

"Repeat, change your course and land in Guam immediately or we will force you down."

"That would be fine," Tuck said. "Go ahead, force me and my hundred and fifteen passengers down." Tuck let off the mike button and turned to Roberto. "Okay, you go in the back and pretend to be a hundred and fifteen people."

As Tuck had calculated, the fighters backed off while they waited for instructions. They were not about to shoot down an American passenger jet without very specific orders, whether it was stolen or not. He believed his biggest advantage was that the FAA and United would insist that no one could steal a 747. That sort of thing just didn't happen. Nice of them to give him an escort, though. He punched some buttons and the nav computer told him he was only half an hour from Alualu. He started his descent.

He checked the position of the fighters and hit the mike button. "This is the UFO calling the F-18s."

"Go ahead, United."

"Are you guys both listening?"

"Go ahead."

Tuck affected a singsong teasing tone: "Neener, neener, neener, you can't get me." Then he locked the microphone in the on position and began singing an off-key version of "Fly Me to the Moon."

Malink, I hope you built those ladders, he thought.

Malink had been awakened early by the Sorcerer's jet taking off and he was on his way to the beach for his morning bowel movement when Vincent appeared to him.

"Morning, squirt," the flyer said.

Malink stopped on the path and fought to catch his breath. "Vincent. I build the ladders."

"You did good, kid. Now get everyone together—and I mean everyone—and tell them to go to the airstrip. Take the ladders. I'm sending a plane for you."

Malink shook his head. "You send cargo?"

Vincent laughed. "No, kid, I'm taking the Shark People to the cargo. You'll need the ladders to get on the plane. Don't be afraid. Just get everyone."

"The Sky Priestess has three who have been chosen. One has just come back to the village."

Vincent looked at his feet. "I'm sorry, kid. You'll have to leave them. Go now. You don't have very long. I'll see you again." And he disappeared.

64

Deliverance

Beth and Sebastian Curtis were cleaning the operating room and sterilizing instruments when they first heard the jet.

"That sounds low," Sebastian said casually.

Then the fighters, running ahead of the 747, passed over the island.

"What in the hell was that?" Beth said. She dropped a pan of instruments and headed for the door.

"Probably just military exercises, Beth," Sebastian called after her. "It's nothing to be concerned about." He was glad to have help cleaning up and didn't want to lose it. Usually, at this point, she was on the plane heading for Japan.

" 'Bastian, come here!" she called. "Something's up!"

Sebastian shoved the last of the surgical draperies into a canvas bag and hurried outside. The sound of jet engines seemed to be everywhere.

Outside he found Beth staring at some coconut palms. The guards were standing outside their quarters, looking in the same direction. "Look." Beth pointed to the north.

"What? I don't see . . ." Then he saw movement behind the palms and a 747 coming toward the island at entirely too low an angle.

"It's landing," Beth said.

Sebastian's gaze was caught by more movement in his peripheral vision. He looked across the runway. The Shark People were coming out of the jungle. All of the Shark People.

➤

From the 747 the airstrip looked smaller than he had remembered. To conserve runway Tuck wanted to touch down as close to the near end as possible. He pulled full flaps and checked his descent rate. The Shark People were moving toward the plane in a wave. Some of the men carried long ladders.

As all sixteen tires hit the runway, Tuck slammed the levers that reversed the engines and they screamed in protest. Immediately, he hit the ground brakes and watched the brake temperature gauge zoom into the red as the jet screamed toward the ocean at the far end of the runway at a hundred and fifty miles per hour.

"Did you see the ladders?" Roberto said, but this time it was Vincent's voice coming from the bat. "Ya fuckin' mook, I told you they were makin' ladders."

"You must come," Malink said. He crouched at the edge of the jungle where the old cannibal was hiding. "Vincent said all of our people must go."

Sarapul watched as the huge jet slowly turned at the end of the runway. "No. I am too old. This is my home. They don't want me where you are going."

"We don't know where we are going."

"Your people didn't want me here. Would they want me in this new place? I will stay."

Malink looked to the runway. "I have to go now."

Sarapul waved him off with a bony hand. "Go. You go." He turned and walked into the jungle.

Malink ran into the open and began shouting orders to the men with the ladders. The Shark People poured onto the runway and surrounded the jet like termites serving their swollen queen.

Beth Curtis saw the first of the doors on the 747 open and immediately recognized Tuck. A tall ladder was thrown against the plane and the Shark People started climbing.

"He's taking them away!" she screamed.

Sebastian Curtis stood stupefied.

Beth shouted to the guards, "Stop them, you idiots!"

The guards had been spellbound by the landing of the jet as well, but her harpylike scream brought them to action. They were in and out of their quarters in seconds, running toward the airstrip with their Uzis. Beth Curtis ran behind them, screeching like a tortured siren.

All six doors of the 747 were open now, and the Shark People were streaming up the ladders, mothers carrying children, the strongest men helping the old.

The other guards piled up behind Mato while he unlocked the gate. He fumbled with the key, then finally sent it home and pulled the chain from around the bars.

Beth Curtis hit the chain-link and curled her fingers though it like claws as she watched her fortune piling into the plane. "Shoot!" she screamed. "Shoot that son of a bitch!"

The guards had no idea who she meant, but they understood the command to shoot. The first one through the gate pulled up and pointed his Uzi at the crowd of natives waiting to get up the ladder. There was a fat one who seemed to be giving orders. He aimed for the center of his back.

A bullet took the guard high in the chest, knocking him back off his feet. His Uzi clattered on the runway. The other guards pulled up, looking for the source of the shot..

"Kill them all, you fucking cowards!" Beth Curtis yelled. "Shoot!"

The guards crouched to make themselves into smaller targets as they scanned the edge of the jungle for movement.

There was a roar and the guards looked up to see two fighter jets coming in low over the runway. Their decision was made. They ran for the cover of the compound as Beth Curtis screamed at their backs.

She ran out to the dead guard, picked up his Uzi, and pointed it at the 747. A gunshot came from the jungle and a bullet ricocheted off the concrete next to her. She turned the Uzi toward the trees and pulled the trigger. It roared for three seconds, the recoil pulling her sideways as the bullets chopped a pattern in the vegetation like a remote-control Cuisinart. She brought the gun back around on the plane and pulled the trigger, but the clip was empty.

She threw the gun to the ground and stood shaking as the last of the ladders was thrown away from the plane and the doors were pulled shut.

65

Down to the Promised Land

Malink joined Tuck on the flight deck and tried to work the flight officer's harness around his belly as Tuck released the ground brakes and the jet started rolling. The two fighters did another pass overhead, one of the pilots warning Tuck not to attempt to take off.

"You forced me down," Tuck said into the headset mike. "What more do you guys want?"

He rammed the throttles to maximum. They either had enough runway or they didn't. What was certain was that he wouldn't know in time to stop. They were going into the ocean or into the sky and that was that.

The flaps were down for maximum lift, which would use three times as much fuel as a regular takeoff, but that was a problem to deal with once they were in the air. He looked at the ocean ahead, then at the airspeed indicator, then at the ocean ahead—back and forth, waiting, waiting, waiting for the airspeed indicator to reach the point where the plane would lift. He was twenty knots short of takeoff speed when the end of the runway disappeared from view and he started his pull up.

The rear wheels of the great plane grazed the water as it lifted into the air. Tuck heard what he hoped was a cheer coming from the back of the plane, but there was a distinct possibility that he was hearing collective screams of terror. He had just lifted off with three hundred and thirty-two people who had never flown before. Tuck thought of Sepie, who would have started her first plane ride two hours ago.

"Where are we going?" Malink asked.

He was trying to compose himself, but when Tuck looked at him, he saw that the old chief's eyes were as wide as saucers.

"A place called Costa Rica," Tuck said. "You ever heard of it?"

Malink shook his head. "Vincent tells you to take us there."

"No, it was my idea, actually."

"There is plenty cargo on Costa Rica?"

"Couldn't say, Malink, but the climate is nice and there's no extradition."

"That is good?" Malink said, as if he had the slightest idea what extradition was.

Tuck admired the old chief. He was here because his god told him to be here. He had just made a decision that would change the history of an entire population, and he had done it on faith.

Tuck set the autopilot and crawled out of the pilot's seat. "I'm going back to make sure everyone is strapped in. Don't touch anything."

Malink's eyes went wide again. "Who is flying the plane?"

Tuck winked. "I think you know." He turned and headed down the steps to check on his passengers.

Pushed to his limit and no little bit frightened, Sebastian Curtis sneaked up on his wife, who was in full tantrum, and injected her in the thigh with a syringe full of Valium. She turned and gave him a good shot to the jaw before she started to calm down. He caught her by the shoulders and backed her into the office chair in front of the computer.

"Don't worry," he said, "Nomura is on his way back with the Lear. We'll be long gone before anyone can get here."

"How did he do it?" Beth's voice was weak now, trailing off at the end.

"I don't know. I'm surprised he's even alive. We'll be fine. We have plenty of money. Not as much as we'd hoped, but if we're careful..."

"He turned them against me," she said. "My people..." She didn't finish.

Sebastian stroked her hair. The clinic door opened and Mato came inside carrying his Uzi. "Phone," he said.

"No," Sebastian said. "I've already called Japan. The Lear is on its way. Now give us some privacy."

Mato threw the bolt on the Uzi and said something in Japanese. Sebastian didn't move. Mato dug the barrel of the gun into the doctor's ribs. "Phone," he said.

Sebastian picked up the receiver that was connected to the satellite and handed it over.

"Out," Mato said.

Sebastian helped Beth to her feet. "Come on. We have to do as he says."

Beth let him lift her to her feet, then she pointed a finger at Mato. "You can kiss your Christmas bonus good-bye, ninja boy. That's it."

Sebastian dragged her through the door and helped her across the compound to her bungalow. Inside he lay her on the bed. Getting her out of the surgical greens was like trying to undress a rag doll. She babbled incoherently the whole time, but did not fight him. When he turned to leave the room, two of the guards were standing in the doorway grinning. One of them motioned for him to leave the room. The other stared hungrily at Beth.

"No," Sebastian said. He stepped into the doorway and pushed aside the barrels of their weapons. They stepped back in unison and raised the Uzis. Sebastian stepped toward them. They took another step back. He was a full foot taller than either of them.

"Get out," he said and he took another step. They stepped back. "Out. Get out. Or do you want to lose all your fingers?" He'd found the magic words. The people they worked for were notorious for taking the finger joints of those who disobeyed. The guards looked at each other, then backed out the door that led into the compound. One of them hurled a curse in Japanese as he went. Behind them Sebastian saw Mato coming out of the clinic. He marched right for Beth's bungalow, almost stomping the ground as he walked, his jaw clenched and his weapon held before him. Sebastian closed the door, locked it, and ran to the bedroom.

"Come on, Beth. Get up. We've got to get out of here." She was still conscious, but had no coordination. He picked her up and threw her over his shoulder in a fireman's carry, then went out the french doors onto the lanai and down the steps to the beach.

The warm water seemed to revive her somewhat and he managed to get her to kick as together they made the swim around the minefield.

The fighters veered off after an hour and the 747 was picked up by a B-52 that stayed on them until they were in fighter range of the Americas, where they were joined by two F-16s. Out of Panama, Tuck guessed. What exactly did they think they were going to accomplish? A 747 wasn't the kind of plane you ditch in the jungle and make your escape. In fact, Tuck didn't think that any plane was that kind of plane. He certainly wasn't going to ditch in the jungle or in the water for that matter. Despite his misgivings, they were going to make it to Costa Rica with plenty of fuel. They were well below the plane's passenger capacity and they carried almost no baggage and no commissary supplies. The only worry he had now was what would happen to him when they got on the ground. It was true, Costa Rica had no extradition treaty with the United States, but what he had done was an act of international terrorism. He might have done better to head back to Hawaii and take his chances with the FBI rather than risk rotting away in a Central American jail. Still, something told him that this was where he should be going. He didn't know why, really, he had picked Costa Rica, any more than he knew why he had stolen a plane and gone back to Alualu in the first place.

As he started his descent for Palmar Airport on the coast, the B-52 veered off to the north and was soon out of sight. Tuck had turned the radio off hours ago, tired of hearing the same threats and commands from the military pilots. As much as he hated the idea of giving the authorities a warning, however, he turned on the radio to advise the tower at Palmar that he was coming in. A midair collision might be even worse than a Costa Rican jail. Especially with three hundred and thirty-two lives riding his soul to hell.

He called to the tower, then took off the headset and sat back and relaxed, convinced that for once in his life he had done the right thing. Somehow he would see to it that Sepie got half the money from the Swiss bank accounts. He envisioned her in a big house with one bedroom and seventy-two bathrooms with a television in every one. She'd be fine.

Malink, who had gone to the back to reassure his people, came up the steps and climbed into the flight officer's chair. "We are going down?" he said.

"You'll like it," Tuck said. "The weather here is the same as Alualu. There are beaches and jungles just like home."

They could see the coast now, extending into the distance to the north and south, the rainforest running from beaches to mountains. "This island much bigger than Alualu."

"It's not an island." Tuck realized that Malink had never walked more than a mile without having to turn. "Your people will be fine."

"Are there sharks here?"

"A lot of sharks," Tuck said.

Malink nodded "My people will be fine." He was quiet for a minute, then said, "Will you come with us?"

"I don't think so, Chief. I'm going to be in a lot of trouble when we land."

"But didn't Vincent tell you to do this?"

"Sort of. Why?"

Malink sat back with a self-satisfied smile. "You'll be fine."

An alarm went off in the cockpit and Tuck scanned the instruments to see what had gone wrong. The red air collision warning lights were flashing. Tuck scanned the sky for another plane, then, seeing nothing, put on the headset to see if the Palmar tower could tell him what was going on.

Before he could key the mike someone said, "Darlin', I'll be whitewashed if stink don't follow you like a manure wagon in summer." A familiar, melodic Texas drawl, probably the sweetest sound he had ever heard.

"Mary Jean," Tuck said. "Where are you?"

"Out your window at eleven o'clock."

Tuck looked up and saw a brand-new pink Gulfstream running parallel to them.

"If you'd a been wearing your headset, you would have known I was here fifteen minutes ago."

"What *are* you doing here?"

"Jake called me from Hawaii and told me what you was doing. We cooked up a little plan. I'm gonna get your tail out of the fire one last time, Tucker Case, but you owe me."

"Boy, have I heard that before."

"Do you remember the corporate address in Houston? The number?"

"Sure."

"Well, you dial that up as a frequency and I'll give you the skinny. It's unladylike to broadcast your personal matters over the same frequency the tower's using."

They were lying in the jungle near the runway when the Learjet landed. Sebastian left Beth sleeping under some banana leaves and crawled to where he could see. The jet taxied to the gate and stopped with the engines still running. The guards came out of different buildings and converged on the plane. They'd stacked duffel bags near the gate.

"What's going on?" Beth crawled up behind him. The effects of the Valium were obviously wearing off.

"I think they're leaving."

"Not without us, they're not. I am the Sky Priestess and I won't allow it." She started to get up and Sebastian pulled her back down.

"They were coming to kill us, Beth. You were out."

"Right. If you ever drug me again—"

"You're insane," he said.

She reared back to slap him and he caught her hand. "Keep it up, Beth. I'm telling you that if they find us, they'll kill us. Do you understand that?"

"They're grunts. I won't . . ."

Suddenly there was a huge explosion from across the runway and they turned to see a mushroom of fire rising from where the clinic used to be.

The guards had loaded onto the jet and Nomura was taxiing to the end of the runway.

The guards' quarters went off next, then the hangar, the barrels of jet fuel throwing a column of flame five hundred feet in the air.

"Where did they get explosives?" Beth said. "Did you know they had explosives?"

"They're destroying the evidence," Sebastian said. "Orders from Japan, I'm sure."

The Learjet started its run for takeoff as Sebastian's bungalow went off like a fragmentation grenade, followed by Tuck's old quarters and Beth's bungalow. Fire rained down across the island.

"My shoes! All of my shoes were in there. You bastards." Beth pulled away from Sebastian and ran out on the runway just as the Learjet passed.

"You rotten bastards!"

The Sky Priestess stood in the middle of the runway and screamed herself mute as the Lear disappeared into the clouds.

66

If They'd Only Had Her at the Alamo

Mary Jean brought the pink Gulfstream in right on the tail
of the 747. Tuck kept the speed over eighty in the taxi,
turning it away from the terminal, where police jeeps and a hundred
men in riot gear waited. He also noticed a half-dozen TV news trucks
there as well.

"Ladies and gentlemen, welcome to Costa Rica, the new home
of the Shark People. The temperature outside is 85 degrees and it's
clear that things are going to get ugly. I hope everybody's ready."

The police jeeps were speeding across the tarmac toward the two
jets. Mary Jean turned the Gulfstream so that it was facing back
toward the runway.

Tuck turned to Malink. "Where's Roberto?"

Malink pointed up. Roberto hung from the handle of the emergency hatch. There was a spring-loaded spool of steel cable attached
to the ceiling next to the hatch. "Mary Jean, you ready?"

"Sweetheart, we'd better git while the gitten's good. We stirred
a hornet's nest out here."

Tuck grabbed Roberto and stuffed him inside his shirt. "Stay,"
he said. Then he opened the hatch and looked back at Malink. "I
have to go now."

Malink took Tuck in his big arms and squeezed until the bat
screamed. "You will come back."

"If you say so, Chief." Tuck flipped the intercom switch and
picked up the headset. "Go!" he said and climbed up into the hatch.

The six doors on the 747 all sprung open at once and the yellow
emergency slides inflated and extended to the ground as if the jet
was a huge insect suddenly growing legs. The Shark People piled

down the emergency slides and Mary Jean spooled up the Gulf-stream for takeoff.

Tuck climbed onto the roof and reached back into the hatch for the loop of nylon webbing that attached to the spool of cable. The police jeeps were pulling up on the sides of the two jets; men with rifles stood in the back trying to figure out what they should be shooting at. The Shark People crowded in between the jets, making a human corridor. Tuck took a deep breath and leaped off the top of the jumbo jet. The spring-loaded coil of cable did exactly what Boeing had designed it to do: It lowered the pilot safely to the ground from four stories up. Once on the ground, Tuck ran under the cover of the Shark People and leaped into the open door of the Gulfstream. "Go!" he yelled.

The Shark People scrambled away and Mary Jean released the ground brakes. The jet shot forward. Tuck slammed the door and got to the cockpit just as a jeep swerved out of the jet's path and flipped over.

"Don't try to play chicken with me, snotnose," Mary Jean said grimly. "I knew James Dean his own self."

"Think they'll let you get this thing in the air?"

"I'd like to see 'em try to stop me."

The police jeeps seemed to part for the jet as it headed back to the runway. For all the guns there, no one seemed interested in firing a shot. Tuck looked back and saw the Shark People waving as Mary Jean made her takeoff run.

When they were airborne, she said, "Tucker Case, when you make a turnaround, boy, you don't do it half-twiddle, do you?"

Tuck laughed. "Did you really know James Dean?"

"Sounded good, didn't it?" She turned to him. Not surprisingly, her makeup was done perfectly to complement her outfit and the Gulfstream's headset. She let out a little yelp. "Tucker, there's a var-mint in your shirt."

"That's Roberto," Tuck said. "He no like the light."

"Darlin', if I had a face like that, I'd gravitate toward dim and unlit territories myself. Remind me to give your friend a sample of our new depilatory."

"What was that all about back there?" Tuck asked.

"Heroics, son. I told you on the phone, I believe in redemption and I thought it was time I practiced what I preached. Were they really selling those poor heathens' organs?"

"Beg your pardon, Mary Jean, I really do appreciate the rescue, but don't bullshit me. Any one of those cops could have shot out the tires of this plane and we'd still be on the ground."

She smiled, a knowing smile with a hint of mischief, the Mona Lisa in a big blond wig. "Media event, son. You'd be surprised how far a little palm grease goes in the Third World. Why, I couldn't buy the media coverage my company's going to get on this with a year's profits. And of course you're going to reimburse me for the bribes. Jake says you'll be able to. The tax boys frown on taking bribes as a deduction. Although we could take it as advertising expense. Never mind, you don't owe me nothing."

"So that's the only reason you did it, the media coverage?"

"I was shabby to you, Tucker. Not that you didn't deserve it, but I wasn't feeling so good about myself for doing it. I aways kinda looked at you like my wayward little lamb. Course, I'm from cattle folk."

Tuck smiled. "Whatever. Where are we going?"

"Little place of mine in the Cayman Islands. Jake's going to meet us there with your little friend."

67

The Cannibal Tree Revisited

The Sky Priestess awoke with a terrible pain in her head. She couldn't feel her arms or legs, and something was cutting her between her breasts. She and the Sorcerer had been living in the deserted village for two weeks. The last thing she could remember was the Sorcerer going into the dark for more firewood and hearing a *thud*. When he didn't answer her call, she had gone to look for him.

She opened her eyes and blinked to clear her vision. The world seemed to be spinning and for a second all she could see was a green blur that was the jungle. Then things popped into focus. She was slowly turning at the end of a coconut fiber rope, suspended six feet above the ground. The harness was digging in between her breasts and cutting off the circulation to her limbs. She lifted her head and saw an ancient native tending a long earthen oven that was spouting smoke from either end. The Sorcerer's clothes were piled nearby.

The old native looked up and ambled over to her on spindly legs. There were chicken feathers stuck in his hair and his eyes had a rheumy yellow cast to them.

He grinned at her with teeth that looked as if they had been filed to points, then reached up and pinched her cheek. "Yum," he said.

Epilogue

Due to the influence of Mary Jean Dobbins, who opened a manufacturing plant in the capital, and a large land purchase by an anonymous buyer, the Shark People were accepted as Costa Rican citizens and their land was set aside as a national reserve. Malink remained chief for many years, and when he became too old to carry the responsibility—since he had no sons—he appointed Abo his successor. Abo learned to preside over the ceremonies in honor of Vincent and led the prayers for his return, for they all believed that he would return, but as time passed and history grew to legend, they believed that this time Vincent would return in a pink jet and at his side would be the prophet Tuck—who had delivered them from the Sky Priestess—and the great navigator Kimi, without whom, it was said, the prophet Tuck couldn't find his ass with both hands.

Every morning before breakfast, Tucker Case walked his bat on the beaches of Little Cay. Actually, the bat flew on those mornings. Tuck usually flew in the afternoons. He owned a five-passenger Cessna that he tied down on the airstrip next to the small house where he and Sepie lived. With what was left of his half of the money from the Swiss bank accounts—after buying the house and the plane and ten thousand acres of Costa Rican coastal rainforest, which he gave to the Shark People—Tuck was able to buy Sepie a satellite dish and a thirty-two-inch Sony Trinitron, which was all she asked for besides his love, loyalty, and that the bat stay out of the house. Tuck gave her all she wanted, and in return asked her to love him, respect him, and to turn down "Wheel of Fortune" when he was doing his books.

He chartered his plane out to fishermen and scuba divers who wanted to island-hop and made enough money to keep them in food and Sepie in perfume, lipstick and Wonder Bras, the latter a new obsession she had picked up and more often than not the only item of clothing she ever wore.

One morning, just before sunrise, after they had been on Little Cay for a year, Tuck spotted a figure standing alone on the beach. He knew who it was before he was close enough to see him. He could feel it.

As he got closer, he looked at the sharp dark features, the flight suit shot with starch and free of wrinkles, and he said, "You look pretty good for a dead guy."

Vincent took a pack of cigarettes out of his jacket pocket, tapped one out, and lit it. "You did good, kid. I'd have to call it even."

"The least I could do," Tuck said. "But can I ask you a question?"

"Shoot," said Vincent.

"Why'd you do it?"

"I didn't do anything. I didn't move a thing, I didn't touch a thing, I didn't change a thing. Believers do everything."

"Come on," Tuck said. "I deserve a straight answer."

The flyer turned away for a moment and looked at the corona over the water where the sun was about to rise. "You're right, kid. You do. You remember that speech the dame gave you about losers doing good on islands because there's no competition?"

"Yes."

"Well, it ain't the case. Islands are like, you know, incubators. You got to start things and let em grow. Isolate 'em. That's why all your loony-toon cult guys have to get their people out in the boonies somewhere where no one can talk any sense into 'em. Just nod if you're gettin' any of this, kid. Good.

"Well, I had this bet with these guys I play cards with that my little cult could go big-time if I could get enough citizens. I told 'em, 'Two thousand years ago you guys were just running cults. Get me to the mainland and give me a thousand years and I'll give you a run for your money.' All the conditions were right. You need some pressure, I got the war. You need a promise, I got the promise I'll come back with cargo. I'm on easy street. Then this crazy dame and the doc come along and start selling me up the river and I'm thinking it's my chance to make the bigs. You've got to have some bad guys so your citizens can recognize who the good guys are, right? So I says to myself, 'Vincent, it is time you got yourself a Moses. Get a guy who can get your people out of trouble and give them some stories to build a reputation on.' "

"And that was me?" Tuck said.

"That was you."

"Why me? Why did you pick me?"

"You weren't busy."

"And that was it? I wasn't busy?"

"Face it, kid, you were flying with full flaps down. You know that saying? 'The devil makes work for idle hands.' "

"Yes."

"It's true, but only if he gets there first. He didn't even want you, so I showed."

"So are you going to screw up the rest of my life?"

"You ain't got it so bad. It ain't like you have to go into the desert for forty years. What are you worried about?"

"Yeah, I'm happy now, but are we finished?"

Vincent butted his cigarette in the sand. "That kind of depends on what you believe, doesn't it kid? He began to fade as he walked down the beach. "Don't do anything I wouldn't do."

Tuck watched as a sailing canoe materialized on the beach. Kimi was at the tiller and waved as Vincent climbed into the front of the canoe. Tuck waved back even as the canoe dissolved to mist, then he walked home to have breakfast with Sepie. He stopped at the door to wipe his feet and Roberto landed with a thud against the screen, digging his claws in to keep from slipping.

"Boy, I'm glad all that supernatural stuff is over," the bat said.

Afterword and Acknowledgments

My approach to research has always been: "Is this correct or should I be more vague?" A quick word search of one of my books reveals that I use the term "kinda-sorta" more than any living author. My readers, who are the kindest and most intelligent people in the world, understand this. They know that using my books as a reference source is tantamount to using glazed doughnuts as a building material. They know that these pages serve the masters of goofiness, not those of accuracy. So . . .

While some of the locations in *Island of the Sequined Love Nun* do exist, I have changed them for my convenience. There is no island of Alualu, nor do the Shark People exist as I have described them. There are no active cargo cults in Micronesia, nor are there any cannibals. The position of mispel did exist in Yapese culture but was abandoned almost a hundred years ago. A strict caste system still exists on Yap and the surrounding islands, and the treatment of Yapese women is portrayed as I saw it. My decision to make the "organ smugglers" Japanese was dictated by geography, not culture or race.

Most of the information on cargo cults comes, secondhand, from anthropological research done in the Melanesian Islands. I have found since finishing *Island of the Sequined Love Nun* that the "Cannibal-Spam Theory" was first postulated in Paul Theroux's book *The Happy Isles of Oceania*, and I must give a jealous nod to Mr. Theroux for that twisted bit of thinking. The information on Micronesian navigation and navigators comes from Stephen Thomas's wonderful book *The Last Navigator*. My depiction of the shark hunt comes from a story told to me by a high school teacher on Yap about the people of the island of Fais, and I have no idea whether it is accurate. The day-to-day life on Alualu, with the exceptions of the religious rites and outright silliness, comes from my experience on the high island of Mog Mog in the Ulithi Atoll, where I had the privilege of living with Chief Antonio Taithau and his family. Many thanks to Chief Antonio, his wife, Conception, and his daughters, Kathy and Pamela, who saw that I was fed and who pulled me out of the well that I fell in after too much *tuba* at the drinking circle. Also, thanks to Alonzo, my *Indiana Jones* kid, who followed me around and made sure I didn't get killed on the reef or eaten by sharks and who I forgive for letting me fall down the well. Many thanks also to Frank the teacher, Favo the elder, Hillary the boat pilot, and all the kids who climbed trees for my drinking coconuts.

I also owe a debt of gratitude to those people who helped me get to the outer islands: Mercy and all the Peace Corps Volunteers on Yap, Chief Ingnatho Hapthey and the Council of Tamil, and John Lingmar at the Bureau of Outer Island Affairs on Yap, who educated me about local customs, gave permission, and made arrangements. Also to the people of Pacific Missionary Air, who got me there and back and answered my questions on flying in the islands.

Thanks to the Americans I met on Truk: Ron Smith, who loaned me his diving knife, and Mark Kampf, who gave me his sunscreen, Neosporin, and duct tape, all of which saved my life. (Research Rule #1: Never go to an undeveloped island without duct tape and a big knife.)

Here in the States, thanks goes out to the following people:

Bobby Benson, who told me about Micronesia in the first place.

Gary Kravitz for voluminous information on aircraft and flying.

Mike Molnar for more pilot stuff as well as patient explanations of computer and communication technology.

Donna Ortiz, who gave me the phrase, "you're just a geek in a cool guy's body" (and I have no idea who she was talking about at the time).

Dr. Alan Peters for medical information.

Shelly Lowenkopf for supplying out-of-print books on cargo cults.

Jim Silke and Lynn Rathbun for drawings and maps.

Ian Corsan for advice on equipment and how to survive in the tropics.

Charlee Rodgers, Dee Dee Leichtfuss, Liz Ziemska, and Christina Harcar for careful readings and helpful suggestions.

Nick Ellison, my agent and friend, for helping to keep the wolf from the door while I wrote.

Rachel Klayman and Chris Condry, my editors at Avon Books, for their confidence and support.

And most of all, my thanks to novelist Jean Brody, who took the time from her own writing to do a line edit on *Love Nun*.

While all the above people helped in the research and writing of this book, none of them are responsible for the liberties I took with the information they gave me. When in doubt, assume that I made everything up.

—Christopher Moore
November 1996

STRAP YOURSELVES IN, LADIES AND GENTLEMEN,
IT'S CHRISTOPHER MOORE TIME!

YOU SUCK: A Love Story
ISBN 0-06-059029-7 (hardcover) • ISBN 0-06-122718-8 (unabridged CD)

C. Thomas Flood (better known as Tommy) has just awakened. He and the girl of his dreams, Jody, have just shared a physical intimacy unlike any Tommy has known before. He opens his eyes, sees Jody smiling down at him, opens his mouth, and says, "You bitch, you killed me. You suck!" For Jody is a vampire. And now Tommy's one, too. They're still a couple, but they've got some things to work through. Tommy has new powers to explore. Jody doesn't know how much she should teach him, and how much she should let him discover for himself.

A DIRTY JOB: A Novel
ISBN 0-06-059028-9 (paperback) • ISBN 0-06-087259-4 (unabridged CD)

Charlie Asher has survived in the gene pool by doggie-paddling in the shallow end. But Charlie's safe life is about to take a really weird detour when his daughter, Sophie, is born—minutes before his wife dies of a freak medical condition. As if being a widower and the single parent of a newborn aren't enough, soon people begin to drop dead around Charlie, and he discovers that his worst fears were molehills compared to the mountain of poo he's in.

THE STUPIDEST ANGEL: A Heartwarming Tale of Christmas Terror
ISBN 0-06-084235-0 (paperback) • ISBN 0-06-073874-X (unabridged CD)

Ah, Christmas—the hap-hap-happiest season of all! Except for Pine Cove Constable Theo Crowe, who's looking for the local evil developer who disappeared after playing Santa at the Caribou Lodge Christmas party. Meanwhile the town braces for the annual onslaught of holiday tourists and the storm of the century. Oh, and did we mention the tall blonde stranger with supernatural strength—a clueless angel sent to Earth on a mysterious mission—who arrives looking for "a child"? Yikes! Pass the eggnog.

FLUKE: Or, I Know Why the Winged Whale Sings
ISBN 0-06-056668-X (paperback) • ISBN 0-06-055679-X (unabridged cassette)

Every winter, whale researchers Nate Quinn and Clay Demolocus, partners in the Maui Whale Research Foundation, ply the warm Pacific waters, trying to solve an age-old mystery: Just why do humpback whales sing? Then one day a whale moons Nate, lifting its tail to display a cryptic scrawled message: Bite Me. But no one else saw a thing—not Clay, not fetching research assistant Amy, not even spliff-puffing white-boy Rastaman Kona (née Preston Applebaum). The weirdness only gets weirder when Nate gets a call telling him a whale has made contact—by phone.

LAMB: The Gospel According to Biff, Christ's Childhood Pal
ISBN 0-380-81381-5 (paperback)

The birth of Jesus has been well-chronicled, as have his glorious teachings, acts, and divine sacrifice after his thirtieth birthday. But no one knows about the early life of the Son of God—"the missing years"—except Biff. Ever since the day he came upon six-year-old Joshua of Nazareth resurrecting lizards in the village square, Levi bar Alphaeus, a.k.a. "Biff," had the distinction of being the Messiah's best bud. That's why the angel Raziel has resurrected Biff from the dust of Jerusalem and brought him to America to write a new gospel, one that tells the real, untold story.

THE LUST LIZARD OF MELANCHOLY COVE
ISBN 0-06-073545-7 (paperback)

The town psychiatrist has decided to switch everybody in Pine Cove, California from their normal antidepressants to placebos, so naturally—well, to be accurate, artificially—business is booming at the local blues bar. Trouble is, those lonely slide-guitar notes have also attracted a colossal sea-beast with a thing for explosive oil tanker trucks. Suddenly, morose Pine Cove turns libidinous and is hit by a mysterious crime wave, and a beleaguered constable has to fight off his own gonzo appetites to find out what's wrong and what, if anything, to do about it.

ISLAND OF THE SEQUINED LOVE NUN
ISBN 0-06-073544-9 (paperback)

A wonderfully crazed excursion into the demented heart of a tropical paradise—a world of cargo cults, cannibals, mad scientists, ninjas, and talking fruit bats. Our bumbling hero is Tucker Case, a hopeless geek trapped in a cool guy's body, who makes a living as a pilot for the Mary Jean Cosmetics Corporation. But when he demolishes his boss's pink plane, Tuck must make a run for his life.

BLOODSUCKING FIENDS: A Love Story
ISBN 0-06-073541-4 (paperback)

Jody never asked to become a vampire. But when she wakes up under an alley Dumpster with a badly burned arm, an aching neck, superhuman strength, and a thirst for blood, she realizes the decision has been made for her. An eternity of nocturnal prowlings is going to take some getting used to, and that's where Tommy fits in. Biding his time night-clerking and frozen turkey bowling in a San Francisco Safeway, Tommy's world is turned upside-down when a beautiful, undead redhead walks through the door and proceeds to rock Tommy's life—and afterlife—in ways he never imagined possible.

COYOTE BLUE
ISBN 0-06-073543-0 (paperback)

As a boy, he was Samson Hunts Alone—until a deadly misunderstanding with the law forced him to flee the Crow reservation at age fifteen. Now a successful Santa Barbara insurance salesman celebrating his thirty-fifth birthday and his hollow, invented life, Samuel Hunter is offered the dangerous gift of love in the exquisite form of Calliope Kincaid, and a curse in the unheralded appearance of an ancient Indian god.

PRACTICAL DEMONKEEPING
ISBN 0-06-073542-2 (paperback)

Moore's ingenious debut novel introduces the reader to one of the most memorably mismatched pairs in the annals of literature. The good-looking one is one-hundred-year-old ex-seminarian and "roads" scholar Travis O'Hearn. The green one is Catch, a demon with a nasty habit of eating most of the people he meets. Behind the fake Tudor façade of Pine Cove, California, Catch sees a four-star buffet. Travis, on the other hand, thinks he sees a way of ridding himself of his toothy traveling companion. The winos, neo-pagans, and deadbeat Lotharios of Pine Cove, meanwhile, have other ideas.